Praise for Taylor Anderson's
Destroyermen Novels

Maelstrom

"Anderson's trilogy of cross-time naval action, Destroyermen, maintains its high quality to the end of this thundering concluding volume. . . . The climactic battle is long, bloody, and suspenseful almost to the last. The ending here doesn't quash hopes that we may see Anderson's displaced World War II Destroyermen again." —*Booklist*

"The pace was fast and kept me wanting to read just a couple more pages. . . . The ensemble cast has a little something for everyone. From a heroic leader and a tortured enemy to power-crazed enemies and wisecracking crew. If you like a fun tale set in a well-developed world, pick up the Destroyermen series and kick back and enjoy." —*SFRevu*

"With its blending of historical fact, thrilling battle scenes, and science fiction, *Maelstrom* is a novel that anyone who loves reading both military and alternative history SF books will want to add to their libraries. The characters are complex, three-dimensional, and show growth over the course of the series, and Anderson . . . has done his research, and it shows." —*BookSpot entral*

"Experienced military SF readers will enjoy the attention to technical and historical detail." —*Publishers Weekly*

"Once again it is the incredible naval battle scenes that make for a great military science fiction thriller (and saga). The story line is action-packed from the onset, but it is the war at sea especially that is fun to follow. Taylor Anderson uniquely combines the big-picture battles with an in-depth look at how the crew and others psychologically cope with maiming and death of friends and bunkmates knowing they can be next. . . . *Maelstrom* is an excellent military sci-fi." —*Genre Go Round Reviews*

continued . . .

Crusade

"Even better than the excellent *Into the Storm*.... What will happen in the forthcoming *Maelstrom* is anybody's guess, though there will surely be more ... intelligent action, more skillful handling of a very large cast, and an obstinately maintained refusal to slow the pace."
—*Booklist* (starred review)

"Anderson throws in tense land battles against overwhelming odds, a massive typhoon, and a phenomenal aerial duel, but despite the pyrotechnics, at heart this novel is about how honor and ideals can bend or break under the stressful, life-and-death conditions of total war."
—*Publishers Weekly*

"*Crusade* continues an entertaining story arc and exploration of war, honor, and evolution in a world similar to our own. Taylor Anderson is emerging, with two novels in quick succession only months apart, as a solid and imaginative storyteller. Whether or not Anderson's story concludes in the next volume, I'll happily ride along on the USS *Walker*."
—SFFWorld

"Descriptions and action-packed battle scenes add depth to a fast-paced plot. The two nonhuman races are well thought out, and there're enough twists to keep the pages turning."
—*Romantic Times*

"Taylor Anderson and his patched-up four-stackers have steamed to the forefront of alternative history. All aboard for a cracking great read!"
—E. E. Knight, author of *Dragon Rule*

Also in the Destroyermen Series

Into the Storm
Crusade
Distant Thunders

DESTROYERMEN
MAELSTROM

TAYLOR ANDERSON

A ROC BOOK

ROC
Published by New American Library, a division of
Penguin Group (USA) Inc., 375 Hudson Street,
New York, New York 10014, USA
Penguin Group (Canada), 90 Eglinton Avenue East, Suite 700, Toronto,
Ontario M4P 2Y3, Canada (a division of Pearson Penguin Canada Inc.)
Penguin Books Ltd., 80 Strand, London WC2R 0RL, England
Penguin Ireland, 25 St. Stephen's Green, Dublin 2,
Ireland (a division of Penguin Books Ltd.)
Penguin Group (Australia), 250 Camberwell Road, Camberwell, Victoria 3124,
Australia (a division of Pearson Australia Group Pty. Ltd.)
Penguin Books India Pvt. Ltd., 11 Community Centre, Panchsheel Park,
New Delhi - 110 017, India
Penguin Group (NZ), 67 Apollo Drive, Rosedale, North Shore 0632,
New Zealand (a division of Pearson New Zealand Ltd.)
Penguin Books (South Africa) (Pty.) Ltd., 24 Sturdee Avenue,
Rosebank, Johannesburg 2196, South Africa

Penguin Books Ltd., Registered Offices:
80 Strand, London WC2R 0RL, England

Published by Roc, an imprint of New American Library, a division of Penguin
Group (USA) Inc. Previously published in a Roc hardcover edition.

First Roc Mass Market Printing, April 2010
10 9 8 7 6 5 4 3 2 1

ROC REGISTERED TRADEMARK — MARCA REGISTRADA

Printed in the United States of America

ACKNOWLEDGMENTS

I must thank my parents again. They are, after all, my first and sometimes strictest critics. My wife, Christine, continues to endure ill-tempered remarks such as "I couldn't possibly care less what the cat did. When the door is shut, I'm *trying* to write." Thanks to my dear friends at Books and Crannies and all the helpful people I've met at maritime museums all over the country, who have bent over backward to help in every way they could without the least complaint or desire for recognition. My deepest appreciation (and apologies) to Darla and Ryan Goodrich, who never fail to remind me that I've left them out in the past. Nowhere is there a better resource for examples of acerbic wit. Sheila Cox continues to lead me through the labyrinth of online literacy—a most difficult chore, I assure you. Thanks again to Ginjer Buchanan, the most patient and gracious editor in the business, and of course, my friend and agent, Russell Galen, who continues to amaze me with his unwavering, steadfast support and encouragement. I think I've thanked the rest of my "crew" before, and if I've left anyone out, you have my most abject apologies. Trust me, you are appreciated.

Finally, I have, in general, acknowledged the sacrifices of the Asiatic Fleet before, but Alan Levine recently reminded me that it's high time I recognized the sad ordeal of a few ships and crews in particular. Unlike *Walker* and *Mahan*, USS *Pope* was actually there at the end when *Exeter* and *Encounter* met their fates. *Pope* was destroyed as well, but the torment her survivors suffered at the hands of her Japanese "rescuers" must never be forgotten. Nobody really knew what happened to USS *Edsall* until after the war, when grainy pictures of Japanese capital ships using her for target practice came to light. Apparently, a couple of her crew were "rescued," but they didn't survive internment. A similar fate likely befell USS *Pillsbury* and the gunboats USS *Asheville* and HMAS *Yarra*, but we will likely never know for sure. God bless and keep them.

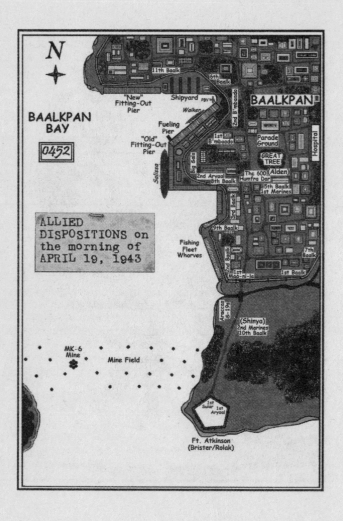

PROLOGUE

*T*here was a new rumbling sound below, but it went unnoticed by the eight-year-old girl swaying in the sailcloth hammock. Her slumber was already filled with the incessant rumbling and groaning of the working hull, and the endless, hissing blows of the pounding sea. Then came another rumble, and another, each more insistent than the last. Still, she didn't stir from her dream. In it she'd been swallowed by a leviathan, just as she'd dreaded since before the strange voyage ever began. Every night, as soon as the lids closed over her large, jade-colored eyes, the same terrible dream came again. She was in the very bowels of a leviathan, and the rumbling, hissing roar was the sound of its belly digesting the ship. The voices came—there were always voices—excited, urgent voices in a tone entirely appropriate. Of course there would be dreadful voices in a dreadful dream. She knew what would happen next. . . .

She was facedown on the thundering deck, and only her tangled bedding protected her delicate nose from the fall. Her eyes flew open, but she could barely see. The only light in the stateroom came from the meager glow of a gimbaled lantern on the far bulkhead. Slowly emerging from the dark nightmare of a moment before, she began to understand she'd entered another. The deck felt wrong, its motion contradicting what she'd come to perceive as normal. She still heard the voices, and although the words were muffled, they were louder and shrill with alarm. One word she clearly understood sent a spasm of primal terror through her heart: "Leviathan!"

The rumbling groan intensified, and the deck heeled sharply beneath her. She had the impression the ship was rising up, much of the noise coming from the mighty timbers of its very bones, stressed beyond endurance. With a screech of agony and a splintering crash, the stress fell away like a broken spring, and she tumbled against the aft bulkhead that had suddenly become the floor. With a sickening, wallowing lurch, the stateroom righted itself, but then quickly tilted toward the bow. She hugged her knees to her chest and sobbed.

The door crashed open and her heart leaped with relief to see the wispy form of her tutor, Master Kearley, stumble into the room.

"My lady!" he cried, over the rising pandemonium in the passageway.

"Master Kearley! Oh, Master Kearley!"

"There you are, child," he exclaimed in a more normal tone. He even paused to straighten the lapels of his frock coat. "Come along quickly—no, do not hesitate to dress! A simple shawl will do."

She was accustomed to following his orders, and she did so now without thought, snatching her shawl from the hook by the door and draping it around her shoulders.

"And your bonnet too, I suppose," he instructed. Obediently, she took the bonnet from its place beside the shawl and pulled it down over her long, golden locks.

"What has happened?" she asked tremulously.

"Come," he said. "I will tell you what I know as we go, but we must hurry."

The darkened passageway swirled with kaleidoscopic scenes of shadowy panic. Shrieks of terror rent the air, and bustling shapes surged aft against the increasing cant of the deck. An indignant roar rose above the turmoil, and the girl thought she recognized the voice of Director Hanes. Even his exalted status couldn't protect him from the animalistic instinct of the throng. The metallic *sheeng!* of a sword leaving its scabbard quickly silenced the dignitary.

"Hurry!" Kearley prompted as they wove, hand in hand, toward a companionway. "We have struck a leviathan—or it has struck us. It makes no difference. The ship will quickly founder. Her back is broken." The girl sobbed again, and her terror threatened to overcome her. The nightmare was true after all.

"Make way, there!" Kearley shouted at the broad back of a man blocking the ladder. "Are you unmanned? Don't you know who this is?"

The big, dark-skinned man whirled and made a fist, preparing to strike the frail scholar. His eyes were wide and white with fear, his huge, disheveled black mustache almost covering his entire mouth. Before he released the panicked blow, however, he recognized the small form below him.

"Yer pardon, young miss!" he almost squealed with contrition. "Clap onto me back, and I'll plow us a road!"

Kearley grabbed a handful of belt with one hand and took the girl's wrist with the other. Together they fought their way up the choked companionway to the tilting quarterdeck. Once there, to the girl's surprise, the big man stooped and swept her off her feet.

"We must put her in a boat this instant!" he cried. His voice had returned to what was surely a more normal growl.

"My thanks, good sir," Kearley replied. "I appreciate your assistance." The man spared him an incredulous glance. Now that he recognized the girl, there was no question he would die to save her.

The girl was oblivious to the exchange. Around her in the darkness, there was no longer any doubt: her terrible dream had come to life. Helpless canvas flailed and snapped, and the once fascinating scientific intricacy of the rigging was a hopeless mare's nest of tangled lines. A constant, deadly hail of blocks and debris fell from above. Beyond her immediate surroundings, she dimly saw the bow, twisting and bent, jackknifing ever upward until the bowsprit pointed at the sky. The fragile paddle wheels on either side, amidships, resembled twisted flowers shorn of their petals. Steam and smoke jetted from the funnel. In the center of this catastrophe, the deadly sea coursed into the ship.

Then, past the bow, coal dark against the starry horizon, she saw a monstrous form. It was clearly the great leviathan that destroyed the ship—possibly entirely by accident. It may have simply risen from the depths, unknowing and unconcerned, to inhale a cavernous lungful of air. Perhaps only then did it discover the water bug on its back. No matter, it noticed it now. Even as the girl watched with unspeakable dread, the island-size creature completed its leisurely turn and came back to inspect the wounded morsel in its wake. The big man saw it too.

"Into a boat!" he bellowed, carrying her to the larboard rail, where a dozen men frantically tore at the quarter-boat tackle. "Make way, damn ye! Can ye not see who I bear?" A wide-eyed young officer motioned them through the gathering throng that regarded the boat with frantic, greedy eyes.

"Are you a sailor?" the officer demanded of the big man. "You're not one of the crew."

"I was a sailor once," he admitted. "And a soldier. I'm a shipwright now, bound for the yard at the company factory."

The officer considered. "Right. Take her aboard under your protection. As soon as you launch, you must hold the boat close so we may put more people aboard." He cast an appraising glance. "You do look strong enough."

Before the girl could form a protest, she was hoisted over the rail by the man's powerful arms and deposited into the boat. Quick as a goat, he followed her and turned to accept the bundles hastily passed to him. A sailor jumped aboard too, encumbered by a double armful of muskets, which he quickly stowed.

The girl found her voice. "Master Kearley!" she wailed. "Master Kearley, you must come too!"

"I will, my dear," came a muted cry beyond the desperate mass.

"Lower away!"

The boat dropped swiftly to the water, and struck with a resounding smack.

"Fend off, you lubbers!" came the cry from above. "Hold her steady, now! I'll send them down two at a time on the falls!" The big man looped a rope around his powerful forearm and pulled with all his might, while the seaman pushed against the hull with an oar.

"Let 'em come!"

The girl gave voice to such a sudden, piercing, gut-wrenching shriek of terror that for an instant, in spite of their own fear, everyone froze to look. A massive cavern had opened before them, wide enough to swallow half the ship. Amid a chorus of muted screams it clamped down on the settling bow with a thunderous, rending crash. The main-mast toppled forward and fell against the darkened mass. More screams came when the mizzenmast also thundered down upon the horrified humanity on the quarterdeck.

"Master Kearley!"

With a terrible grinding, crunching sound, the titanic jaws gaped open, then closed once more on the pulverized forward section of the ship. Far in the distance, a monumental, explosive splash of mighty flukes crashed down, and with a convulsive jerk the entire ship lurched bodily away from where the tiny boat bobbed in the choppy sea.

"Master Kearley!" shrieked the girl with a desolate, perfect anguish, while the rest of the ship was shattered by the impossible strength of the beast. The boiler burst with a thunderclap roar and a swirling, scalding gout of steam. Further enraged by the discomfort this might have caused, the leviathan redoubled its attack. Terrible screams and splintering timbers filled the night, but soon all that remained was the surging sound of the agitated sea.

The seaman who brought the muskets had gone over the side, so there was no hope for him. The girl collapsed into the bottom of the boat and wept with disconsolate abandon. For a while the big man could do nothing except stare into the empty, endless night. Occasionally, his gaze fell upon the ragged, pulsing stump of his left arm. The rest of it had been snatched away so suddenly, and with such force, all he remembered feeling was a tug and a pop. Now his life was coursing into the sea, and he already felt the loss. Shaking himself, he snatched his belt from his waist and wound it tightly around the stump. Shortly the cascade reduced to a trickle, but, light-headed, he sat heavily in the boat and looked down at the sobbing girl.

"Little miss," he croaked, and the girl slowly raised her sodden eyes. "Yer Ladyship . . . I truly hate to impose, but if ye could see clear to bind me a bit better, I might be of more use to ye."

Seeing his terrible wound, the girl recoiled for an instant, but then scrambled lightly across the seats to his side.

"I will do what I may," she assured him bravely through her tears, "but I'm no surgeon."

"That's a fact," he agreed with a wan smile, "but I've no doubt ye could be if ye wished." As gently as she could, the girl tightened the tourniquet, then rummaged for something to use as a bandage. She finally settled for the sleeve on his other arm.

"They will search for us, won't they?" she asked while she worked.

"Of course, lass."

"Will they find us?"

The big man's smile faded completely, and he gazed out at the dark, endless swells. They'd lost contact with their consorts some nights back, but that happened all the time. The other two ships wouldn't grow concerned until several days after they reached the factory dock and the doomed ship and her important cargo still had not arrived. They'd traveled only half the distance to their destination, so it would be weeks before they were considered overdue. Months before the news reached home and a search was mounted. The wind and current would drive them quickly westward, far beyond the lanes traveled by men.

He blinked, then looked down into the huge, trusting eyes that seemed to pierce his callous soul.

"Of course they will, Your Highness."

CHAPTER

1

*T*he Great Hall was a raucous Babel when the council met shortly after dark. Nakja-Mur, U-Amaki ay Baalkpan, took his place on the platform encircling the trunk of the Sacred Tree, resuming his position as host. The Great Hall was nearly as crowded as the first time Lieutenant Commander Matthew Reddy, USNR, entered it. Then, there'd been a party atmosphere, and it was open to any who wished to come. Now, the mood was anything but festive, and only High Chiefs and the newly created "officers" were present. Matt was still surprised how many there were. He rubbed at the sticky, burning sweat film that he couldn't seem to keep out of his green eyes, and tried to banish the exhaustion. Ever since his battered, overloaded, leaking ship crept back into Baalkpan Bay three days ago, he'd been overseeing emergency repairs day and night. He'd changed into his least soiled uniform, but realized with chagrin he'd neglected to shave when he felt the stubble on his face. *Damn. It's always the details that get you*, he thought, and tired as he was, he didn't have the luxury of neglecting any.

He stifled a sneeze. Sometimes the musty, downy fur of so many "People" in one place could be hard to take. Courtney Bradford had coined the term "Lemurians" for their friends, based on their resemblance to Madagascar lemurs. They had, in fact, learned the People (they called themselves Mi-Anaaka) were almost certainly descended from the giant lemurs of that place, although they looked more feline. Most of his human destroyermen just called them

'Cats now, although a few still clung to the original monkey-cats, or cat-monkeys, depending on whether they were from the deck division (apes) or the engineering spaces (snipes). The Lemurians had become firm allies, and many were official inductees into the United States Navy. Like all Navy terms however—even slang—uniformity was important, so simply 'Cats had gradually prevailed. There were still 'Cat-apes, and 'Cat-snipes, but that had nothing to do with race. It was occupational.

He nodded a greeting when he saw Queen Protector Safir Maraan of B'mbaado, looking, as always, amazingly fresh and vigorous in her black cloak and silver breastplate. She nodded deeply and respectfully in return. She and Lord Rolak of Aryaal stood together, encircled by their respective staffs. The scarred old Aryaalan warrior didn't look as fresh as his former enemy. Not only was the "Orphan Queen" a third his age, but he'd been much harder-pressed to organize his displaced people. He'd started with no staff at all, to speak of, and because of the bitter division that had existed in his city at the end, he'd been forced to assemble one with care. Contention, under the circumstances, couldn't be permitted.

Chack-Sab-At, with his brindled fur, still wearing his red kilt, white T-shirt, and platterlike "doughboy" helmet, didn't seem to know where to stand. He was present as the commander of the Second Marines, but since *Walker* was his home, he wound up standing close to Matt, along with his lieutenants. Most of *Walker*'s and *Mahan*'s officers were there, except Nurse Lieutenant Sandra Tucker, who was at the hospital tending to the wounded and shell-shocked survivors they'd brought home. Also absent were Lieutenant "Spanky" McFarlane and Acting Lieutenant Frankie Steele, who'd been left in charge of the ships. A grim-faced Ben Mallory, head and shoulder swaddled with bandages, stood unsteadily next to Matt with Sergeant Pete Alden, and Lieutenant Tamatsu Shinya, late of the Japanese Imperial Navy. Keje-Fris-Ar, Geran-Eras, and the recently arrived Ramic-Sa-Ar, all High Chiefs of the remaining sea-going Homes—stupendous wooden sailing vessels roughly the size of an aircraft carrier—made up the rest of the naval contingent.

Fristar, and most of the other Homes collected in Baalkpan Bay, had left earlier that afternoon. Their departure came as no surprise. Their warriors would have been welcome, but only *Fristar* was armed. Everyone knew from the start where her high chief, Anai-Sa, stood. Now they were gone, on course for Manila. At least they carried the seeds of the various cultures that remained.

Nakja-Mur struck the pipelike gong suspended above the platform, calling everyone to attention with a harsh, resonant sound. Baalkpan's High Chief wore his traditional robes, and his fine, silver-shot black fur was elegantly groomed. His long tail swished behind him with dignified expectation. He was still about the fattest Lemurian Matt had seen, but he wasn't all flab. The blow he gave the pipe would have severed an enemy's head, had he held a sword instead of a striker. The sound reverberated for several moments with a bone-rattling vibration. With Adar's assistance, Nakja-Mur's aged sky priest, Naga, mounted the dais to stand beside him. It was the first time Matt had seen him since his return, and the priest appeared to have aged a dozen years. Slowly the hall grew quiet and Nakja-Mur spoke:

"The Allied Expeditionary Force has returned to us," he said in a proud, positive voice.

The mission of the Allied Expeditionary Force had been to raise the siege of Aryaal, or Surabaya, Java, as the Americans remembered it, and expel the Grik—the Lemurians' "Ancient Enemy"—beyond the Malay Barrier. The Grik were a seemingly numberless race of furry/feathery, reptilian bipeds, whose expansionist imperative seemed matched only by their merciless ferocity. Apparently centered in eastern Africa, their empire now spanned the coast of the Indian, or "Western," Ocean all the way to Ceylon and Singapore—and now Java too. Separated from the Lemurians by the vast, hostile sea for ages, they'd developed their seagoing technology to the point they could threaten their old "prey" again at last.

The campaign met success at first, before the unforeseen full might of the Grik swept down, accompanied by the mighty Japanese battle cruiser, *Amagi*. In one fell swoop, the fortunes of war had changed entirely, and contentious Aryaal had been evacuated. Also evacuated, albeit less thoroughly due to the constraints of time, were the people of Aryaal's hereditary enemy on the island of B'mbaado (Madura). The people there, led by their charismatic Orphan Queen, Safir Maraan, had been aiding Aryaal against their mutual enemy, despite their animosity, when the AEF arrived. B'mbaado had actually officially joined the alliance. But with the enemy bearing down, as many people as possible from both cities were stuffed into every available boat, as well as the four allied (cannon-armed) seagoing Homes that constituted Captain Reddy's "battle line." What ensued was an exodus unlike any since that first one had occurred countless ages ago, when all the People were driven from "paradise" by the same ravening enemy. Matt knew the Lemurian "Scrolls" gave few details about what transpired back then; the tale had been passed down by word of mouth for millennia before being written, but he imagined the trauma must have been very much the same.

"They achieved great victories against the Grik and were not defeated," Nakja-Mur continued, "but through their success, they discovered the Ancient Enemy has numbers beyond what we ever imagined. Wisely, they returned to bolster our defenses here, so together we will have the forces to destroy that terrible threat." He paused and stared out at the expectant faces. "They bring also new, veteran allies—warriors who have faced the Grik in battle, and come to our aid as we once went to theirs. Together we will field the largest army in the history of our race! There will be no defeat like that which drove us from our ancestral home!"

There were a few scattered cheers, and Matt had to admit Nakja-Mur was becoming a skilled orator. It was also clear he'd decided to concentrate on the positive—even to the point of glossing over a few blatant facts, like the tragedy that made those forces available. He supposed there was no harm in that. Everyone knew the story already, and those who remained were committed to the fight. They had no choice. All the mighty seagoing Homes that meant to leave were already gone, either fled or acting as giant freighters for goods and raw materials from the Fil-pin lands. Once again he was struck by the similarity of their current situation to that the Americans had faced nearly a year before, when the Japanese swept the Asiatic Fleet from the Philippines and Dutch East Indies. The irony was, this time the Philippines were the distant haven, instead of the first place they got kicked out of.

Nakja-Mur continued: "Safir Maraan, Queen Protector of the island of B'mbaado, has come with her personal guard of six hundred warriors, as well as the majority of her entire defense force of almost two thousand seasoned warriors!" Nakja-Mur didn't mention that over a thousand of B'mbaado's best troops had been lost with *Neracca*. *Neracca* was the final Home to evacuate, and was intercepted by the enemy. Reddy's old Asiatic Fleet "four-stacker" destroyer, USS *Walker* (DD-163), was escorting her to safety, and even tried to *tow* the much larger Home from the enemy's clutches, all to no avail. *Amagi*, slowed by damage she received once before at the hands of the Americans, was still unimaginably powerful. She cruelly smote *Neracca* from what seemed to the Lemurians an impossible distance with her massive ten-inch guns. *Walker* saved as many as she could, becoming dangerously unstable with close to a thousand aboard, but in the end, the uncounted thousands remaining on *Neracca* were doomed.

Tassat-Ay-Arracca, her High Chief, sent his daughter, Tassana, in the final gri-kakka boat to cut the cable herself. Matt could only imagine the weight of grief bearing upon the child's heart. In a fit of rage, or perhaps genius, he used the darkness, and the glare of the burning Home, to maneuver his damaged, overloaded ship into a position to fire his last remaining, fully functional torpedoes at the mighty ship. One exploded, damaging *Amagi* even further. Not enough to sink her, unfortunately, but enough to cause the Grik to postpone their final attack and turn their armada back to Aryaal. They must have decided, uncharacteristically, that they needed *Amagi* to ensure their success against what the Tree Prey had become (and the friends they'd made) since their last, ancient meeting. It was the only thing that gave Baalkpan this precious time they now had.

"Lord Muln-Rolak, Protector of Aryaal, has joined us with a trained force almost as large. Together with the majority of the civilian populations of both great cities upon which we can draw a levy, we stand prepared to face the enemy with over sixteen thousands able to bear arms!" There was a larger cheer, even though everyone must have realized how small that force was, compared to what was coming.

Nakja-Mur motioned Matt to join him.

First the sugar, now the salt, Matt thought, stepping up onto the platform.

"Cap-i-taan Reddy was acclaimed commander of the Allied Expeditionary Force, and he is the architect of its victories. The AEF has ended now, and with it the mandate of command. I propose he now be acclaimed Supreme Commander of the Allied defense of Baalkpan!" There were hoots and cheers, and the floor of the hall thundered with stamping feet. Matt just stood and watched until the tumult died away. "Then by acclamation, it is done! Cap-i-taan Reddy will assume command of all forces gathered here. Let all swear to follow his instructions in the coming fight. Swear on the honor of your clans! Swear now or leave!" Nakja-Mur turned to him then, and over the sound of the vigorous affirmations, he spoke in Matt's ear: "It is done. I've given them reason to hope, I think. I imagine you'll temper that with a large measure of despair. Taken together, perhaps a realistic expectation will emerge."

"I'll try to keep it upbeat, but I won't lie to them, my lord," Matt answered him. "These are our officers. We'll have a chance only if they know exactly what we face." He turned to the crowd and cleared his throat. Beginning with a summation of the previous campaign, he recounted how his ship had led the newly cannon-armed Homes against the invasion fleet that invested Aryaal. He told of the great victory in the bay, and how they landed and fought a desperate battle against the besieging force—a battle they won only by the skin of their teeth, prolific use of *Walker*'s modern weapons, and the timely assistance of Queen Ma-raan and Lord Rolak. He didn't dwell on the treachery of Rolak's king that cost them many lives, and nearly the battle. King Rasik-Alcas was surely dead by now. He told how they found *Walker*'s long-lost sister, USS *Mahan* (DD-102), and the pitifully few members of her crew who'd survived their own terrible ordeal. He spoke of things they'd learned about the enemy—still far too little—but also about how they'd defeated them. The Grik were terrifying warriors, but they fought without discipline—or even much thought. They'd beaten them, and they could do it again.

Then he talked about *Revenge*. She was a Grik "India-man" they'd captured and armed, and Matt had sent her to harass the enemy and scout the AEF's next objective, Singapore, the most tenuous Grik outpost. Ensign Rick Tolson had been captain of *Revenge*, and Matt had finally read his log. The narrative was inspirational. It also wrenched his soul. *Revenge* had been badly damaged in a storm, and was left to face the full brunt of a new, massive Grik fleet all alone. Mallory took up the narrative, and briefly described what he, Ed Palmer, and Jis-Tikkar saw from the airborne perspective of the PBY flying boat, and he haltingly, hauntingly recounted the sacrifice *Revenge*'s people made to destroy as many of the enemy as they could, and prevent the capture of their ship. Matt thought the example was good for all to hear. It was the story of a gallant struggle against impossible odds, something they were all likely to face before long.

Matt then described, as clearly as he could, the force that destroyed *Revenge*; the force coming there. The hall grew silent, and for the first time, probably—for the Baalkpans, at least—it began to sink in. He spoke of the courage it took for the B'mbaadans and Aryaalans to sacrifice their homes, hoping that by defending Baalkpan, they might someday see their own homes again. He described the desperate evacuation and the bravery of Tassat-ay-Arracca, who'd saved so many in the face of certain destruction, and of Tassana, his daughter, and her own personal horror.

And when he had everyone's undivided attention, he talked about *Amagi*. At 46,000 tons of iron, and over 800 feet long, she was much heavier and almost as big as the improbably huge wooden seagoing Homes of the People. Most present still hadn't seen the Japanese battle cruiser, although some survivors of *Nerracca* had. At least, they'd seen what she could do with her terrifying guns. Tassana stood beside her grandfather, Ramic-Sa-Ar, her eyes red and haunted, while Matt described the ship. Chack had seen it. He'd had a good long look from *Walker*'s crow's nest, and often, when Matt stopped for a moment, he continued quietly in his own language, speaking of what he saw. Finally, Matt described *Walker*'s vengeful torpedo attack and the damage he thought it inflicted. To those listening it was a stirring commentary, but that wasn't Matt's only intent. He massaged his brow with his fingers and glanced at Nakja-Mur. The High Chief knew what he was going to say to the hushed assembly.

"She's still out there," he said at last, and took a long, deep breath. So did everyone else. "Mr. Mallory confirmed by direct observation that she's still afloat and underway"—he managed a predatory grin—"but not very fast. We were right about the damage to her boilers. It looks like she's making only about four knots. The Grik are clustered around her, probably to prevent another torpedo attack, and she and the rest of the enemy fleet have turned back for Aryaal. Her damage is severe, and remember, she was already badly damaged after the last time she met up with us. After that fish we stuck in her the other night, I'm frankly amazed she didn't just roll over and sink. Maybe she still will," he added hopefully, "but we can't count on it. I think we can count on a little time, however, and maybe we evened the odds a little. A few enemy scouts were reported nosing around the mouth of the bay this morning, but Fort Atkinson's guns drove them off. My ship is still in pretty rough shape, but tomorrow we'll sortie and see if we can tow in some of the Grik ships we damaged in the strait. As you know, a couple have already arrived, captured by local crews. I understand the fighting against the survivors was fierce...."

"So *Amagi* and the main force have retired?" Keje asked for emphasis, speaking for the first time.

"As of Mr. Mallory's last observations before the PBY got jumped by one of *Amagi*'s spotting planes. I'm sure you all appreciate how lucky we are that plane and most of her people made it back? As for *Amagi*." He shrugged. "Maybe her other boilers will choke and that'll be the end of her. We could sure use one of those Strakkas right about now," he added, referring to an intense, typhoonlike storm spawned by the slightly different climate on this very different Earth. There were murmurs of agreement, mostly from the destroyermen. "In any event, Mr. Alden and Mr. Letts have improved considerably on the defense designs I left behind. They came up with stuff I never even thought of, and then the people of this city, working themselves to death, managed to finish the job. I'm impressed. Pete explained the differences and I had a good look at them this afternoon." He looked as many of them in the eye as he could. "They're *good* defenses, and they ought to hold against a very determined assault. That's good, because that's the only kind I've seen the Grik make." He paused, measuring the mood in the hall.

"Eventually, they'll come. *Amagi* will be repaired or not, but I expect if she can be, they'll try to wait for her. That may give us months to prepare, or it may not. They strike me as pretty notional, strategically. They might just get sick of waiting. Regardless, like I said, eventually they'll come, and we have to continue to prepare as if the attack will come next week ... or tomorrow." The mood was decidedly somber. "Without *Amagi*, I think we can hold. We've already seen that their ships are extremely vulnerable to gunfire, particularly the high-explosive shells from *Walker*'s four-inch guns and the big thirty-two-pounders—both on the Homes and emplaced here. That's good, and I've no doubt we'll thrash the lizards if they come into the bay. The landward defenses look good too, and they'll be in for a hell of a surprise if they try them. The problem is, as with any static defense, we don't have any depth. If they break through anywhere, we're done. The wall has to hold. The lizards outnumber us ten to one already. With the extra time they now have too, I expect those odds to grow even worse. They may try to force some strategic point, and keep piling in until the defenders are exhausted. That means we have to keep plenty of reserves, and we can't commit them too soon.

"We can do this, but it's going to take unflinching discipline"—he let that sink in—"and it's also going to take more troops."

"But ..." Keje spread his hands, palm up. "Where will we find them?"

"The Fil-pin lands," Matt said simply. "Manila. It's our only hope."

The Fil-pin lands and some other Homes not yet on the front lines of the war recognized the threat posed by the Grik and gladly sent almost everything asked of them. They knew the consequences if Baalkpan should fall, but for the most part they jealously reserved the one commodity Baalkpan needed most: warriors to match the countless hordes of the enemy. Token forces had been sent; Nakja-

Mur suspected that was mainly so they might learn the new ways of war taught by the Americans, but with the exception of the Sularans across the strait, their combined numbers would not make up a single regiment of Alden's "Marines."

"I know they've refused to send significant forces in the past," Matt continued, "but if we go and talk to them, tell them, *show* them what the stakes are, maybe they'll change their minds. Besides," he added with a strange expression, "we might find more friends than the Manilos. I've been thinking about those reports of an 'iron fish' in the Fil-pin Sea. If it's what I think it is, and if we can find it, *Amagi* might be in for a very big surprise if she ever comes here."

"But who will go?" asked Adar. "It is a journey of months." Matt turned to him.

"You'll go; so will I. So will *Walker*. After a few weeks in the yard she can get there, meet the Manilos, look around for the iron fish, and still be back in plenty of time. We'll establish another wellhead on Tarakan Island too. Bradford says it's a good choice, and we need a fallback fuel reserve."

"What if the Grik do not wait?" insisted Nakja-Mur.

"We'll stay in touch through the radio in the plane." Matt looked at Mallory. "If Ben somehow manages to get it airworthy again, he won't fly until and unless Lieutenant Riggs and Radioman Clancy's experiments with other types of receivers are successful. Understood?"

Mallory nodded reluctantly. "Understood, Captain."

"There," Matt said. "*Amagi can't* come before we get back, and if the Grik try to send their main force, you should be able to hold for a time, and we'll be less than a week away. This is what I propose to do...."

After the council adjourned, Matt and his former executive officer, Jim Ellis—now *Mahan*'s captain—were joined by Sandra Tucker, and together they strolled slowly along the pier. Ellis, burly, once ebullient, still showed the effects of his ordeal aboard *Mahan*. His limp, caused when he was shot by Kaufman—an Air Corps captain who'd taken over his ship after they came through the Squall—was better, but he was still haunted by what he felt was his less than stellar performance as *Mahan*'s commanding officer. Most of the already shorthanded old destroyer's remaining crew had died while she was nominally in his charge. Matt knew it wasn't his fault, but Jim didn't see it that way. Nor could he and the rest of *Mahan*'s survivors dispel the sense of dishonor that seemed to have settled upon their ship, due to Kaufman's actions and their own inability to prevent them.

Sandra Tucker was as petite as Ellis was physically imposing. The top of her head, long, sandy-brown hair coiled in a bun, reached only to Matt's shoulder, but her seemingly delicate frame concealed a strength of will and character that had been tested over and over again on the grisly battlefields of her operating tables. She'd faced wounds of a type and scope few Americans ever had, since the primary weapons of this war were designed to hack, stab, and slash. The unwarlike Lemurians had never seen anything like it before either, and she and Nurse Theimer had created, from scratch, a professional, efficient Hospital Corps. The 'Cats possessed a powerful analgesic, antiseptic paste, a by-product of the fermented "polta" fruit, so wounds were less likely to fester and fewer wounded were lost to disease. But battlefield medicine—the wholesale treatment of terrible wounds—was something the 'Cats had known nothing about. Sandra was just as tired as Matt. Many in her hospital now were younglings who'd survived the loss of *Nerracca*. The ship had been shelled into a sinking inferno, and a lot of the injuries she now faced were terrible burns on tiny, whimpering bodies.

The sky was clear, and in spite of the glow from the city and the pier, the stars stood out brightly overhead. In a way it was much like that night, so long ago now, when Matt and Sandra so tentatively discovered how they felt toward each other. On that occasion they'd been serenaded by drunken men singing an off-color song as they were transported back to the ship. Tonight the background music consisted of crackly, indistinct, upbeat tunes, from the dead gunner's mate "Mack" Marvaney's phonograph, playing over the ship's open comm. The music was accompanied by loud, hoarse voices and clanging metal, as the men continued working under the glare of the searchlights.

The main difference between that night and this, however, was that back then, they still had no real idea what they faced. They'd had a few minor successes against the Grik, and their concerns about fuel had been put to rest. In some ways it was a hopeful time. Matt had chafed at their ignorance regarding the enemy, but compared to now, that ignorance had indeed been bliss. Now they knew what they faced, and the mood was more somber. Back then, things seemed to be looking up. Tonight, hope and optimism were in considerably shorter supply.

They stopped at the end of the pier, a hundred yards aft of *Walker*. In the gloom, weirdly illuminated by the ambient light, the PBY was beached near its own short pier to keep it from sinking. The plane appeared to sag with exhaustion, its wings drooping low. The only things keeping them horizontal to the fuselage seemed to be the wingtip floats on either side, supported by blocks and makeshift braces. Matt remembered something else that had changed: he'd been committed to protecting and husbanding the irreplaceable Catalina. Since then, he'd nearly used it up, as his idealistic intentions gave way to the demands of reality. It was just as well, because if they'd kept to his original plan of, basically, not letting it fly out of sight, they'd all be dead right now. They'd have never known about the approach of *Amagi* and the Grik ships that accompanied her. He still felt a deep regret.

Few of the plane's injuries were visible in the shadows, but he could see them still by memory. Bullet holes and shattered Plexiglas, shredded control surfaces, the fire-blackened cowling, the terrible, violently amputated port wingtip . . . all added to the already generally dilapidated appearance of faded blue, brine-streaked paint. He didn't seriously expect her to ever fly again, in spite of Lieutenant Mallory's assurances. Even if Ben was right, the plane couldn't have many hours left to give them, and when it was gone, there'd never be another. Of course, the same could be said for *Walker* and *Mahan*, and the destroyermen that kept them alive. He was using them up too.

Matt finally broke the silence that had descended upon them. "So, Jim," he said, "what do you think of the plan? You didn't say a lot during the meeting."

Jim didn't answer at once. Instead, he stared back at the two destroyers tied to the dock. *Mahan* lay just ahead of *Walker*, lights burning aboard her as well. Even before the war they left behind, on another Earth, both ships had been antiques, commissioned in 1918 and 1919, respectively. Since then, they'd spent much of their lives toiling in neglect with the U.S. Asiatic Fleet. When the Japanese ravaged the Pacific Fleet at Pearl Harbor and ran wild during the early months of the war, all that stood in their way were obsolete relics like the ones he was looking at. Their sleek hulls and rakish, primitive appearance little resembled their more modern counterparts, and in comparison they were sadly underarmed. A meager four 4-inch guns and a single 3-inch gun constituted their "main battery," and a few machine guns mounted on the rails were all they ever had against aircraft. Their main offensive capability had always been their speed, and twelve 21-inch torpedo tubes. Now, both ships' speed had been reduced by battle damage and mechanical failure. *Mahan* had only one propeller, for example. Her other one had gone to replace one lost by *Walker*. They also had but a single—hopefully—operational torpedo between them; an obsolete MK-10 they'd scavenged from a warehouse of condemned equipment before evacuating Surabaya. During their "old" war. They'd originally fled that place with another American "four-stacker," *Pope*, and the British cruiser *Exeter*, and destroyer *Encounter*. All three other ships were destroyed by the Japanese, leaving only *Walker* and *Mahan* to face *Amagi*—and the Squall that swept them all here.

Any realistic assessment of the two destroyers would have left them condemned to the breaker, or at least several months in a dry dock after what they'd endured, but they had no such luxury. Therefore, with monumental ingenuity, jury-rigged parts, and the tireless efforts of their human/Lemurian crews, the ships were being prepared for yet another last-ditch defense.

"I don't like staying behind," Jim confessed, "and I don't think you should go. The stability of the alliance depends on you too much."

"Maybe once," Matt admitted grudgingly, "but I think we're largely past that now. Everyone knows what's at stake. Mr. Letts will be chief of staff in my absence—he's developed a genius for diplomacy, it seems. If anybody can keep everyone on the same page, it'll be him and Nakja-Mur. You'll control all naval forces. I still hope to get Keje to leave *Big Sal* as a floating battery and go with me, since he's been to Manila before. Pete'll have overall command of land forces. I'd like to take him with me too, but with Lieutenant Shinya's issues still unresolved . . ." He sighed. "Besides, *Walker*'s the fastest, so she's the one to go. She's my ship; therefore, I go with her. *Mahan*'s your ship, and she needs you here."

"But I'll just be sitting around," Jim protested. As far as they knew, the enemy believed they had only one destroyer left. *Mahan* would be fitted with a new dummy smokestack, to replace the one she'd lost, and painted with *Walker*'s number so any spies wouldn't suspect Baalkpan's weakened condition, or that *Walker* had gone away. Mostly, the enemy must never suspect there were, in fact, two American destroyers. Unless they got reinforcements, it was the only ace they held. Matt had given orders that *Mahan* should steam about and be seen, but never risk herself or venture far from the mouth of the bay.

"Besides, you won't be just 'sitting around,'" he argued. "The captured ships'll need refitting, and there's the new construction to consider. I expect you to use them to try to get as many of Queen Maraan's people off B'mbaado as possible. I promised her as much, and besides, we'll need them. If Haakar-Faask, her general she left behind to lead them, is as good as he seemed, we'll badly need him as well."

Jim grunted. "All right, Skipper, if you say so. I still don't like it."

"Well," said Sandra, somewhat haughtily, "now that that's settled, I guess I deserve some explanation why you're leaving *me* behind, Captain Reddy!"

Matt groaned. "We've been over this before. Karen did a good job while we were away, and now we've got our other two nurses, Pam Cross and Kathy McCoy, back. But there aren't going to be any battles where we're going. You need to continue your work here. We have Pharmacist's Mate Jamie Miller, and you know he's turned into a fine surgeon in his own right. He's certainly had enough practice! Besides, there's still that other . . . issue to consider."

He was referring to the increasingly acute "dame famine." As far as the human—and rambunctiously male—destroyermen were concerned, there were only four human females in existence. One, Karen Theimer, was clearly attached to Alan Letts, and Matt expected Letts to approach him on the subject before much longer. This was the source of considerable stress. Rumor had it that a few men had actually formed ... romantic relationships with the local females. One such relationship, between the irrepressible (acting) chief gunner's mate Dennis Silva and Chack's sister, Risa-Sab-At, was apparently more than rumor. Silva and Risa had done everything in their power to make it *seem* more than rumor, at any rate. Chack had been livid, but recently, strangely, Matt had noticed a visible thaw between Silva and Chack. Perhaps they'd sorted out their differences without violence this time, or maybe Chack had finally decided Silva and Risa were just joking after all. Whatever. He'd rather not have the distraction of females on this trip if he didn't have to. Out of sight didn't always mean out of mind, but if there were no women aboard, there shouldn't be any fights over them. Matt remained convinced there must be other women somewhere on this Earth; there was too much evidence of previous human/Lemurian contact, and even human/Grik—witness the enemy ships built along the same lines as eighteenth-century British East Indiamen. But until they found them, they had to tread carefully. That was why he and Sandra never openly acknowledged their own mutual affection.

His thoughts were interrupted by the sound of approaching footsteps. In the dim light, Karen Theimer and Alan Letts were walking arm in arm. *Sooner than I thought*, Matt speculated resignedly.

"Good evening, Captain ... uh, Captains," Karen said as they exchanged salutes. "Good evening, Lieutenant Tucker."

"Good evening, Karen. Mr. Letts."

For several moments everyone just looked at one another. Alan seemed uneasy. He acted as if there were something he wanted to say, but couldn't find the words. Matt had a rough idea what they'd be, and he clasped his hands behind his back and leaned forward expectantly. Letts wasn't ordinarily the tongue-tied type, so this ought to be good. Suddenly the young supply officer jerked and gasped through clenched teeth. Matt glanced down in time to see Karen's right foot reappear next to her left.

"Uh . . . Captain Reddy, I, uh, have . . . I mean, I'd like to have a . . . ah, word, sir. I mean, if it's convenient." He glanced quickly at Karen, probably afraid she'd kick him again.

"Of course, Mr. Letts. We were just discussing the plan for our expedition and Baalkpan's defense. Perhaps you'd like to add something?"

"Uh, no, sir, not just now." His eyes flicked to Sandra and Jim. "Actually, sir, what I need to talk to you about falls more in the line of . . . well, a private . . ." He stopped, unable to continue.

Jim Ellis leaned forward wearing a menacing expression. "My God, Mr. Letts!" he exclaimed, shifting his gaze to the nurse. "Ensign Theimer, if this rogue has behaved indecently toward you, I'll see he's punished severely!" He motioned with his head toward the water of the bay, full of terrifying creatures their own world had never known. "And I mean *severely*!"

The whites of Letts's eyes became visible in the dark. "Oh, no, sir, Mr. Ellis! I assure—" Karen kicked him again, surprising him completely. He hopped quickly away from her, uttering a soft moan. In spite of her earlier confrontational mood, a giggle escaped Sandra's lips.

"Just spit it out, you big dope!" Karen commanded, rolling her eyes.

"Captain!" Alan squeaked. "We want to get m-m-married!" he finally managed.

Matt waited a moment, looking at the mismatched pair. Letts with his fair, peeling skin; Karen, dark-haired, lovely, slightly taller. He nodded. "I assume you've thought this through?"

"Yes, Captain, we have," Karen replied. "Ever since the AEF set out, and we remained here, we've worked closely together." She shrugged. "Somehow I fell in love with the guy." She looked at Sandra. "I know you're the head of my division, Lieutenant, and I should have spoken to you first, but we saw you walking out here together and . . ."

Sandra nodded. "Perfectly all right, Karen. I have to agree with Captain Reddy, though. Are you sure you've thought this through? You want to do this . . . now?"

Karen nodded sadly. "We wanted to wait until things

settled down, but with everything going on . . . well, there might not be a better time."

Sandra sighed. "I understand. Very well, I've no objection. Captain?"

Matt rubbed his chin. "You know, Mr. Letts, some resentment's likely to arise out of this—what with the dame famine becoming more and more, ah, acute? If you ladies'll pardon me, I'll be blunt. Our men have gone literally months without female companionship, when, before we left the Philippines, to do so more than a few days would have been . . . extraordinary. A lot of pressure's building up. If not for the unending combat against the enemy, the elements, or the deterioration of the ship to help them . . . vent that pressure, I'm not sure we could've kept them under control. It's my hope, God willing, that someday we'll explore this new world. If that occurs, it'll be my very first priority to discover whether other humans exist here." He paused thoughtfully. "It's my belief they do. But first we have to survive the coming battle, and maybe the whole damn war. That's a lot of 'ifs.'" He waved away their concerned expressions. "That being said, I don't object either, I guess. I just want you to be sure this is what you want to do. It might be . . . difficult."

Jim chuckled. "I'd say that qualifies as one of those British understatements, Skipper. I also think if I were in their shoes, I wouldn't give a damn right now." He frowned. "Whatever time we've got left, I say make the most of it. Captain?" Matt nodded.

Jim Ellis beamed at the couple. "So. You want a big, fancy church wedding? Or are you going to elope?" He laughed at their confused expressions. "Run along, children," he said. "I'm sure our illustrious supreme commander'll be happy to perform a suitable ceremony directly."

After they were gone, Jim let out a breath and turned to Matt and Sandra. "You know," he began conversationally, "everything I just told those kids about 'making the most of it' and 'living while you can' goes double for you two." Only the darkness hid Sandra's sudden, deep blush.

"What the hell are you talking about?" Matt sputtered.

Jim laughed out loud. "Oh, c'mon! You honestly think you've kept your little secret? Wow. Patty-fingers on the bridge wing, moon-eyes whenever you're around each other! Queen Maraan thinks you *are* married and asked me if you have a *child*!" Ellis laughed again at their stunned expressions. "Keje finally believes you aren't already 'mated' and thinks you're a couple of idiots. Self-sacrificing deprivation isn't the norm with 'Cats."

"Is it really that obvious?" Sandra asked in a small voice. "We've both tried so hard!"

"Who else knows?" asked Matt through clenched teeth.

"The Mice may not have figured it out," Jim drawled dryly, referring to the two enigmatic, almost belligerently insular firemen, and their female Lemurian protégé, "but I wouldn't bet money."

"Damn."

Jim held up his hands. "Hold on, Skipper. Before you think your little act was a waste of time and the men'll resent you—like you warned Letts—let me tell you something. I told you everybody knows you're nuts about each other, but they also know why you've been acting like you weren't. They appreciate it, Skipper! They know what it's cost you, because they know how it would feel to them. I do too. Your crew admires you immensely. They'd follow you into hell. They already have!" He shook his head. "*Mahan*'s the same way. Everyone sees the weight on your shoulders, both of you, and they know you've denied yourselves the one thing that might help lighten the load. And they know you've done it for them." He grinned. "Even if they still think you're a couple of dopes."

Matt was embarrassed. Not for how he felt, but because the men had seen through his deception. He felt as though he'd let them down. He looked at Sandra and saw tears gleaming on her cheeks, the lights of the city reflected in her shining eyes. "Would you excuse us for just a minute?" he asked in a husky voice.

"Sure, Skipper, I could swear somebody called me." Turning, Jim walked down the pier toward the ships.

Tentatively, Matt put his arms around Sandra and drew her close. For the first time he didn't notice any pain in his shoulder, wounded at Aryaal, at all. She began to shake, and he knew she was crying. "I'm so sorry," he said.

"Don't be," she scolded. "It was the right thing to do."

She raised her face until she was looking into his eyes. "It still is," she told him firmly.

"I know." Then he kissed her. It was a light, gentle kiss, and their lips barely touched. He didn't dare make more of it. Still, it was enough to send an electric shock clear to the soles of his shoes. Finally, wistfully, retreating from their embrace, they began walking back toward the glare and racket of the feverish repairs. "There," he said softly. "Maybe that'll tide me over a little longer."

"I guess we have a wedding to arrange." Sandra sighed, wishing it could be their own.

Nakja-Mur lounged on his favorite cushion on the broad western balcony of the Great Hall of the People, apparently taking his ease. He often did so on clear evenings, watching the Sun slowly descend from the sacred Heavens into the impassable jungle beyond the bay. Sometimes, when the light was right, and his mood and eyelids were adjusted just so, he imagined the mighty orb quenching itself in the very bay. Many of his people had often watched him thus, equally content, at the end of a day's honest labor, or the beginning of a night's. They took comfort from his comfort, as he did from theirs, because it represented stability, prosperity, and, above all, the promise that they could continue to live their comfortable lives without want, fear, or change. Those had been happy times. Times he'd thought would continue throughout his life and reign as Baalkpan's High Chief. They were the only sort of "times" he'd ever known, and he'd taken them for granted. But that was before the Amer-i-caans came, and change became the norm, a necessity. That was before the War.

The Amer-i-caans didn't *bring* the war, of course, although some had argued they did. Many of those were long gone, having fled to "safety" in the Fil-pin lands, or just generally eastward in their huge floating Homes. Most who now remained were committed to the fight: the fight that, long as the odds were, they wouldn't have had the slightest chance of winning if the Amer-i-caans hadn't come. The People of Baalkpan would probably have been slaughtered before they even suspected war was upon them.

But still, when he could, he continued to take his evenings

on the balcony of the huge wooden edifice encompassing the trunk of the mighty Galla tree. The tree was so massive, it continued to soar through the ceiling and high above before branching into a dense canopy that dwarfed the bulk of the Great Hall below, as well as every other structure in the city. He'd sit there and view the city: the tall pagodalike structures housing many families, just as those aboard the seafaring homes had traditionally done. Larger structures, with many levels, sheltered Baalkpan's various industries: ropewalks, chandleries, looms, block makers, coopers ... industries supporting Baalkpan's primarily maritime economy, and her trade with the seagoing Homes. They'd once been a source of employment, prosperity, and pride. Now greatly expanded, and with the new industries the Amer-i-caans had instituted or improved, they represented the only hope of salvation for Nakja-Mur's Home.

Before, he'd gazed upon the bay and the busy commerce of the city's fleet of coastal traders and fishers with a sense of satisfaction. Sometimes as many as a dozen enormous seagoing Homes might be moored or snugged up at the piers, disgorging barrels of gri-kakka oil in exchange for services, necessities, and even luxuries they craved from the increasingly prosperous, influential, and just as increasingly resented "land folk." Occasionally, swift, tall-masted feluccas dashed across his view, hurrying to ports across the dangerous strait, or returning with cargoes from distant land Homes. He marveled at the speed they achieved with their fore and aft rigs and sleek, radical hulls. Now the seagoing Homes were mostly gone; only the transient freighters and the three ships of the Allied "battle line" remained.

With the return of the AEF, and the Aryaalan and B'mbaadan warriors it had managed to save, the city's defenses were nearly tripled, but they needed more just to survive. Nakja-Mur was skeptical that more troops would be forthcoming from Manila, beyond the hundred or so volunteers they'd already sent, and he'd come to agree with the argument Cap-i-taan Reddy once made before the AEF set out in the first place: they could prevent defeat, for a time, with static defenses, but they could only *win* if they attacked. Attack, now, was out of the question, and Nakja-Mur constantly brooded over the implications of that.

The water of the bay glowed red beneath the lowering

Sun, and except for the absence of most of the Homes, the bustle of small craft seemed undiminished even as they toiled for a much greater imperative than personal profit. His heart lifted when he saw one of the Amer-i-caan destroyers—*Mahan*. His newly practiced eye could tell by her awkwardly repaired pilothouse, even if she now sported a new fourth funnel. The ship was steaming slowly toward the mouth of the bay on some errand to Fort Atkinson, he guessed, or testing some repair. She was resplendent in a new coat of light gray paint, and he still marveled at the effortless grace with which she moved in any wind, though he knew she could use only one of her "engines."

Despite the fact *Walker* had seen more action in this war, *Mahan* was the weakest, most badly damaged of the two Amer-i-caan ships that came to them through the Squall. He now understood that that damage was due to an earlier encounter with *Amagi*. As powerful and indestructible as she seemed to him—she was made of iron, after all—he had to remind himself that if *Amagi* one day came—perhaps entered this very bay—she could swat *Mahan* aside with little concern. Such a thing was so far beyond his experience as to seem unthinkable. But he hadn't been there; he hadn't seen. Those he knew and trusted who'd beheld *Amagi* assured him it was true, and somehow he managed to believe them. The thought churned his gut with dread.

A servant, a member of his expanded wartime "staff," pushed through the curtain behind him and stepped into view, waiting to be noticed. Nakja-Mur sighed. "Oh, I wish you wouldn't lurk behind me like that; I won't eat you!" His tone was gruffer than he intended, and if anything it made the young servant cringe back a step.

"He does not know you as I do, lord," came a voice from beyond the curtain. It parted, revealing the hooded form of Adar, High Sky Priest of *Salissa* Home. Adar was tall for one of the People. He wore a deep purple robe adorned with embroidered silver stars across the shoulders and chest. The hood bore stars as well. His silver eyes peered from a face covered with fine, slate-gray fur. He gestured at Nakja-Mur's stomach, which, though considerably shrunken from its prewar dimensions, was still quite respectable. Nakja-Mur chuckled.

"I only eat youngling servants for *breakfast* these days,

you know." He patted his belly and it rumbled on cue. "Though perhaps . . ."

"I will bring food instantly, my lord!" cried the servant, and he vanished from view.

Adar blinked amusement. "Do you suppose he will return?"

Now that the youngling was gone, Nakja-Mur sighed again. There was no need to keep up appearances for Adar. "Of course. Please be seated," he said, gesturing at a cushion nearby. "We have much to discuss."

Adar folded himself and perched rigidly on the firmer cushion Nakja-Mur knew he preferred. For a moment he just sat there, looking at the High Chief and waiting for him to speak. Nakja-Mur was casually dressed in a light, supple robe, and sat with a mug of nectar loosely balanced on his knee, but his increasingly silver-shot fur, and the absently troubled cant to his large, catlike ears, would have belied his relaxed pose to any who knew him well.

"The Amer-i-caans are planning a 'fallback' source of gish, to power their ships," he stated abruptly. "So no matter what they say, they recognize at least the possibility Baalkpan will fall." The strange Australian, Courtney Bradford, had been an upper-level engineering consultant for Royal Dutch Shell. That occupation allowed him to pursue his true passion: the study of the birds and animals of the Dutch East Indies. Also because of that occupation, however, stuffed in his briefcase when he evacuated Surabaya aboard *Walker* were maps showing practically every major oil deposit in the entire region. There'd been some skepticism that the same oil existed on "this" Earth that they'd found on their own, but after the success of their first well—exactly where he'd told them to drill—they were all believers now, even the Mice. Tasked by Captain Reddy to locate another source, he assured them they'd find oil in a variety of places. Most, for one reason or another, were rejected, but Tarakan Island seemed perfect. It was more than halfway up the coast of Borneo, bordered by the Celebes Sea. It was beyond anything the Grik maps showed they'd ever explored, and it was in a fallback position not only toward the Fil-pin lands, but one of Baalkpan's "daughter" colonies nearby.

The "colony" was a growing settlement right across the

little strait in a marshy, swampy hell called Sembaakpan. There they gathered small crustaceans called graw-fish by basketfuls at low tide. They were very tasty in their premetamorphic stage, and considered a delicacy because no one knew them to exist anywhere else. They had a short shelf-life too, and were some of the strangest creatures the destroyermen had yet encountered. They looked and acted like little horseshoe crabs till they shed their shells and swam—and ultimately flew—away. Anyway, at least there were friends nearby, but they'd never even come up with their own name for the tiny, forbidding, impenetrably blanketed island, so Tarakan it still was.

"A prudent decision," Adar said, "and one I heartily approve."

Nakja-Mur grunted, his eyes still upon the bay. "It smacks of planning for defeat."

"You are mistaken. They plan for victory; why else embark on this expedition to seek allies—and a new source of fuel? No." He blinked in positive denial. "They do not *plan* for defeat, but prudently prepare for the possibility. Even if we are defeated, I do not think Cap-i-taan Reddy can imagine such a thing might be the end of the fight. Another setback, perhaps, and a serious one, but not the end."

The High Chief gazed out upon his city, contemplating it as a ravaged shell in the hands of the Grik. "How can such a thing *not* be the end," he breathed, then changed his tone, suddenly urgent. "How soon can you leave?"

Almost two full faces of the Sun Brother had passed since the AEF returned. Repairs were taking longer than anticipated. Evidently each time they fixed one problem, some new issue was revealed.

"A ten-day. *Walker*'s repairs are almost complete, but it will take much of that time to dismantle the rig at the well site and transport it to the city. By then, *Mahan* will be completely ready to masquerade as her sister, and the three damaged Grik ships towed in from the strait will be repaired, armed, and ready for sea. With the flying boat still grounded—and likely to remain so, I fear—we cannot leave you blind. If their scouts sneak past, they will see everything seeming as before. With *Mahan* pretending to be *Walker*, they will never suspect the other ship is gone, or that there are, indeed, two Amer-i-caan destroyers. That's a secret we must keep at all costs. Within another ten-day after that, the first of your own warships that you so wisely commissioned in our absence will be ready for sea." He blinked. "I understand it is a great improvement over those of our enemies."

Nakja-Mur nodded enthusiastically, his depression momentarily forgotten. "Indeed! She is far more modern." He gestured toward the shipyard, where two sleek hulls still sat on the ways. A third was down at the new fitting-out pier, undergoing completion. Even now, the ship seethed with busy shapes silhouetted against the ruddy, reflected sunlight on the bay. "I have watched them erect every frame, place every plank. Cap-i-taan Reddy and the engineer, Brister, provided the basic design, but even they say we have built them better and stronger than their people ever constructed such ships! They call them 'frigates,' but they have yet to be named. As you know, a great deal of thought must go into such things."

For the first time, with human help, Lemurians had bent their formidable engineering skills toward constructing dedicated warships. Human and Lemurian technology and techniques comingled at every hand, and at least as far as the wooden shipyards were concerned, the Lemurians gave as much as they got. Their structural designs were amazingly efficient, as well as highly redundant—in exactly the sort of way to be prized in a warship. The humans made many suggestions for lines based on speed, and the Lemurians took them to heart, but they built the ships their way. The result was, hopefully, ships much faster—and stronger—than any sail-powered vessels the world had ever seen.

Adar nodded, looking where Nakja-Mur pointed. "Of course. They are very beautiful as well. A pity . . ."

The High Chief snorted. ". . . there will be only three? True. We will never have time to build more, no matter how long the Grik delay. With but fifty such ships, the Grik would never dare attack if it weren't for *Amagi*!"

"I meant that it's a pity they will be the last of their kind. The next ones will have auxiliary steam engines, I understand. As for the Grik . . . Oh, I think they would dare," Adar murmured. "They might lose, as you say, but they would still dare. They would have no choice." He blinked discontent. "And even if we had them, we haven't the crews."

"True, and that brings us back to our original discussion. I yearn for you to be on your way. First to gain us allies, of course, but also so you might more quickly return. I cannot help but fear the Grik will come while *Walker* is away." He waved off Adar's protest. "I know Cap-i-taan Reddy believes that unlikely, and without more troops to defend my city, her presence might make little difference. But to many people, she has become more than just a ship. After all she has done, and particularly after *Nerracca* ... her absence will be felt."

"I understand what you mean," agreed Adar.

"Do you? Do you indeed? For it is not just the ship people look to, but the people who will be with her: Cap-i-taan Reddy and his crew, Braad-furd, Chack-Sab-At, my dear cousin Keje-Fris-Ar, if he goes ... and you, of course. As you know, my own Sky Priest, old Naga, has become increasingly ... disassociated. He cannot accept what has come to pass."

Adar nodded sadly. Naga had been his teacher, as a youngling, and had set a high example. His ancient mind was full of the lore and history of the People, and his knowledge of heavenly paths and mysteries was without compare. He once could recite, from memory alone, every word of the Sacred Scrolls, and unerringly describe every coastline drawn upon them. Recently, however, all that priceless knowledge and wisdom was increasingly locked away, inaccessible even to himself in any coherent fashion. Even though Adar was Sky Priest to Keje-Fris-Ar and *Salissa* Home, the people of Baalkpan, and strangely—given their different dogma—Aryaal and B'mbaado, increasingly looked to him for spiritual and moral inspiration. Ever since he'd learned the true nature of the Grik, Adar's most consistent inspiration was to fully embrace what the Amer-i-caans called "Total War." Only by doing so did the People have any hope of survival.

"Perhaps," he whispered.

The promised food arrived, and both Adar and Nakja-Mur forced confident grins and stilled their twitching ears. Fortunately, their tails were confined by their postures and couldn't betray their agitation by swishing back and forth.

"Leave us," said Nakja-Mur congenially, when the servant placed the tray before them. The youngling quickly departed. "Speaking of what this war has cost our Naga, how is Cap-i-taan Reddy? I will never learn to understand their grotesque face moving and hand waving, but he does not seem the same."

"He is driven," Adar conceded. "After what happened to *Nerracca*, he hates the Grik just as passionately as I, and if anything, I believe he hates the Jaapaan-ese even more." He cocked his ears. "Tragic as *Nerracca*'s loss certainly was, it is stunning how it has strengthened the alliance."

"True, but he seems distracted as well."

"There is tension," Adar confessed. "He is reluctant to mate with their healer, although their attraction is plain to all. I believe it has to do with the scarcity of females available to the rest of his people."

"Absurd."

"Perhaps. But there is also the issue of his secondary commander of land forces, Lew-ten-aant Shin-yaa."

"Shin-yaa is a 'Jaap,' I believe they call them, is he not?"

"Indeed. An enemy, yet they trust him; rely heavily upon him, in fact. Shin-yaa is of the same race, or clan, controlling *Amagi*, and he recognizes the evil she aids—represents—but he cannot believe all the beings aboard her have become evil as well. He is . . . conflicted, to say the least. It tortures him that his own people assist the Grik and did what they did to *Nerracca*. Yet, like us, the idea of fighting his own people tortures him just as much."

"But it is not the same! Hu-maans are much more warlike than we; they are more like the Aryaalans and B'mbaadans in that respect. . . . Oh."

"Precisely. To them, belonging to the same species does not keep them from killing others of different clans, or races within that species. And among the Jaap clan, the ties that bind them together seem even closer than those that bind the Amer-i-caans. The Amer-i-caans have much freer will to decide for themselves what is right and what is not. Among the Jaap clan, that decision is taken by a leader and imposed upon all others, regardless of what they might personally think."

"I see," murmured Nakja-Mur. "Do you think Shin-yaa can be trusted? Will he aid his clan against us?"

"I think not. I believe, even if he didn't know the right or wrong of it, his perception of what he calls his 'honor' would prevent it. Remember, before they ever came here, his clan and that of the Amer-i-caans were at war, but he has given his parole to Cap-i-taan Reddy, and rather than break it, he would resolve his personal conflict by ending his own life. More likely, in a confrontation between his people and ours, he will simply abstain. 'Sit it out,' as the Amer-i-caans would say."

"A pity. He is a fine leader, and the troops he leads—our own people—have no stake in his 'conflict.' I hope, for our sakes, as well as his own, he is able to resolve it in our favor."

Adar nodded. "Regardless, that is why he will accompany the expedition rather than remain behind."

"Probably best." Nakja-Mur changed the subject. "What is involved in dismantling and transporting the 'rig'?"

"Mostly time and labor. The 'rig' itself is not complex. If we had time, I'm sure it would be simpler to just build another. We will do that anyway, so we can sink more wells here, but we know this one works, and it is not needed at its present site. It would have to be moved in any case. The labor is something else; remember, there is a gri-gaantus maax-i-mus—a Gri-maax—in the area. The one that got their Tony Scott. I believe the Amer-i-caans call them 'super lizards.'"

"An appropriate term, if I translate correctly."

"Indeed. In any event, in order to convince a sufficient number of workers to go, we have to assemble an escort of almost equal numbers. Most inefficient, but necessary."

"Amazing!" gushed Courtney Bradford, removing his ridiculous hat and wiping sweat from his balding pate. (Acting) Chief Gunner's Mate Dennis Silva had to agree. Actually, the word that sprang to his mind was "prodigious," even though it was a word he'd never used before and had, in fact, only ever heard from the Australian engineer and self-proclaimed "naturalist." It was pretty "amazing" too, though.

"Biggest damn turd I ever saw," Silva agreed respectfully, slinging his BAR (Browning automatic rifle) on his powerful shoulder and crouching to view the thing in all its glory, "and I've seen my share of whoppers. Conjured up a few myself, but nothing to compare to *that*." The coiled heap of excrement wasn't exactly steaming, but it was fresh, and about the size of a grown man curled in a fetal position—which immediately set Dennis to thinking dark thoughts. He looked at the Australian and saw his eyes glisten with anticipation. He snorted. It was late January 1943 in the world they remembered, nearly a year since USS *Walker* passed through the Squall that brought them to this twisted, alien Earth. Personality-wise, Bradford had apparently changed least of any who'd survived. Outwardly, the change was complete. He'd finally given in to the inevitable and had allowed a salty, reddish blond beard to creep across his ruddy face. In fact, it struck the fine-furred 'Cats as hilarious that he now had more hair on his face than on the top of his head. In the heat and glaring sunlight of the latitude, that might've actually been dangerous, but Bradford had replaced his lost hat with a bizarre contraption most resembling a cartoon version of a Mexican sombrero. Of course, it looked ridiculous on his fair-skinned, somewhat rotund frame—a fact not lost on their friends.

Because of their large, catlike ears, Lemurians rarely wore any kind of hat. Some wore helmets into battle, but most had been fashioned with the ears in mind. Some, like Chack, insisted on wearing the round "doughboy" helmets of the Americans and managed to do so—uncomfortably—by wearing them at a jaunty angle that allowed one ear to stick out to the side and the other to protrude inside the crown. It worked, after a fashion, and the American helmets certainly provided more protection in battle than anything else the 'Cats had ever put on their heads. But Courtney didn't have even that excuse. He looked ridiculous and didn't care, and that was part of his charm. Or maybe he did care, and did it anyway. He and Captain Reddy had once discussed how important amusement was to morale, and sometimes, just by being himself, Courtney Bradford was very good for morale. Like now.

As entertaining as the eccentric Australian could be, he was also profoundly valuable—besides his knowledge of oil-bearing strata. He could be highly annoying, and the word "eccentric" wasn't really quite descriptive enough, but despite his amateur "naturalist" status, he was also the closest thing to a physical scientist they had. His specialty—if it could be said he had one—was comparative anatomy, and he'd provided many important insights into the flora and fauna they'd encountered. The Lemurians were always more than happy to tell them everything they could, but this information, of course, came from some of the very creatures he was intent on studying. In addition, he was the quintessential "Jack of all trades, master of none," but in his case, that was often a real asset. True, he didn't know everything about, well, anything, but he did know at least something about quite a lot, and that was more than anyone else could say.

Silva was darkly certain that when the captain found out he'd allowed Bradford to tag along, there'd be hell to pay, and with that realization came another: he cared. For Dennis's entire life, particularly since he joined the Navy, he'd always lived for the moment and damn the consequences. He was acting chief of the Ordnance Division, now that Campeti was *Walker*'s acting gunnery officer, but with his skill and experience he should have been one long ago. He just never cared before, and didn't want the responsibility. Now everyone was having new responsibilities thrust upon them whether they wanted them or not, and most had risen to the challenge. His old boss, Lieutenant Garrett, would soon have a command of his own. Alan Letts, once an undermotivated supply officer, had risen to the position of Captain Reddy's chief of staff. Bernie Sandison was still *Walker*'s torpedo officer (not that she much needed one), but he was also in charge of developing "special weapons." Sergeant Alden, formerly of the ill-fated USS *Houston*'s Marine contingent, was now "general of the armies." Chief Gray had been elevated to something else, still ill-defined. Maybe "super chief" described it best. Even the Mice had evolved beyond the simple firemen they still longed to be. He glanced at Bradford, who'd changed his appearance, perhaps, but remained essentially the same person. In all the ways that counted, Dennis suspected he himself may have changed more than anyone.

He hated the thought of letting the captain down, but felt a moral imperative to avenge the death of Tony Scott—someone he'd barely known before the Squall. He couldn't shake a sense of protectiveness toward all those who remained. He continued to act like the same Dennis Silva everyone expected to see: careless, fearless, irreverent, happy-go-lucky, perhaps even a touch psychotic. Outwardly, except for some new scars and a luxuriant blond beard, he remained the same. But now he did care, and that was a big change indeed.

"Smells like bear shit," observed the other gunner's mate, Paul Stites, nervously as he scanned the green, nightmarishly dense jungle bordering the pipeline cut. Dark haired, and as scrawny as Silva was powerful, he was Dennis's chief minion in mischief, and the closest thing to a human "best friend" he had left. He motioned at the enormous impressions all around them in the perpetually damp soil. "Bear shit from a giant turkey."

Stites, Bradford, and Dennis were the only humans along with the guard detail sent to dismantle the drilling rig called a "Fort Worth Spudder" they intended to transport to the new site. A respectable facsimile of a pump-jack had taken its place, and continued busily pumping oil to the expanded refinery near the pier. Stites, like the other humans, had smeared grease on his exposed skin to protect him from the dragonfly-size mosquitoes, but he was experimenting with used grease to see if it might prove more effective. Even though it was now streaked with sweat, he looked like he was in blackface.

The humans, however, along with a half dozen other 'Cats, had a different, unsanctioned agenda. Silva and Stites were there for revenge, pure and simple, and Bradford, curious as ever, upon learning their plans, had extorted an invitation.

"I don't know about where you're from, Stites," quipped Silva, "but turkeys in Alabama keep to a more manageable size." The tracks did look a little like a turkey's, except the impressions were more than a yard long.

"You don't suppose . . ." Stites mumbled, gesturing at the turd. Courtney looked up at him and saw his troubled expression.

"No, no. I shouldn't think so. It's been weeks since, well . . . Of course, I can't know for sure without more information about their metabolism. . . ."

"I was just wonderin' if we should . . . you know, bury it. Just in case it's . . . Tony. In case he's . . . in there."

Silva rolled his eyes. "That turd ain't Tony. Even if it is, I ain't buryin' it. We're all gonna be somethin's turd one of these days. We ain't got much time out here, and I'd rather spend it killin' the big bastard that ate him."

Before he was killed, Tony Scott had become Dennis Silva's friend. Dennis never had many friends, but those he had, he valued. Especially now. Scott had been *Walker's* coxswain before the Squall, and had remained in charge of the launch despite his growing, almost panicky terror of the water. He had reason to be afraid. Everywhere they'd been so far, the water seethed with deadly creatures, and he'd come to hate the sea he'd always loved. He was no coward, though. Despite his fear, during the battle to capture the Grik ship that became *Revenge* he'd jumped in the water to save Lieutenant Tucker. At the time, a storm was running and flasher fish were inactive then—but he didn't know that. Everyone knew what the act had cost him. He thought he'd been committing suicide. He'd been afraid of nothing but water, though, and once aboard the Grik ship he'd fought like a maniac.

The irony of his death was still painful. Despite evidence to the contrary, compared to the water he'd always felt as if the land were safe. In an unguarded, thoughtless moment, he'd left his ever-present Thompson in his boat when he went ashore to check the oil rig after a storm. When he never returned, there was little doubt what got him, and whether the turd was Tony or not, it was big.

They'd seen plenty of larger piles: the stupid, domesticated "brontosarries" the Lemurians used as beasts of burden created much more mass, but the droppings of the strictly herbivorous sauropods more closely resembled titanic cow-flops. The object they were studying so intently was clearly a giant, compacted turd, manufactured by an equally giant carnivore. A "super lizard," to be precise.

Bradford hated the term "super lizard," and insisted the creatures were unquestionably allosaurs, relatively unchanged from specimens in the fossil record. Also, unlike most other "dinosaurs" they'd seen throughout what should have been the Dutch East Indies, super lizards were not stunted in size. If anything, they were *bigger* than their prehistoric cousins. Fortunately, there weren't many of them, and they seemed highly territorial. When, rarely, one was killed, it was often quite a while before another took its place. They were ambush hunters that positioned themselves along game trails and the odd clearing. Bradford said they were built for speed, but they hunted lazy, Silva thought. That was probably how this one got Tony. Just snatched him up when he came ambling along the cut. Fresh anger surged within him, and he stood and brushed damp earth from his knee.

The voices of the work detail diminished as it slogged on toward the well, leaving them behind. Silva turned to a gap-toothed 'Cat with silver-streaked fur. He had no clan, and he was known simply as the Hunter. All 'Cats wore as little as they could get away with, but the Hunter wore nothing but a necklace and a quiver of large crossbow bolts. The massive crossbow he carried, and the super lizard claws clacking on the thong around his neck, seemed to establish his bona fides. "That not you friend," the Hunter said simply, referring to the spoor. "See thick black hairs? They from . . . I think you call 'rhino-pig'?"

"Rhino-pigs" were rhinoceros-size creatures, one of the few large mammals indigenous to this Borneo, and looked remarkably like massive razorbacks. They were extremely prolific and dangerous omnivores with thick, protective cases, and savage tusks protruding a foot or more from powerful jaws. They also sported a formidable horn on top of their heads. Regardless of the challenge, they were the Hunter's principal prey due to their succulent, fat-marbled flesh. Evidently, in spite of their horn, they were also the preferred prey of super lizards.

"How long?" Silva asked.

"Not long. He hear big group, loud walking. He go."

"Afraid of large groups?" Stites asked hopefully. The Hunter's grin spread.

"He no hungry enough for all. He waste good hunting place."

"Waste—"

Silva interrupted. "Where'd he go?"

The Hunter pointed toward a cramped trail disappearing into the jungle.

"You're kidding," Stites grumped. "I thought these things were big?"

Hefting his crossbow and setting off down the trail, the Hunter called back: "Trust me, he very big."

"Well . . . how many of these things have you killed, anyway?"

The Hunter paused briefly, and fingered his necklace. "Only one," he answered quietly.

"How come you know so much about 'em, then?" Stites's tone was skeptical.

The Hunter considered before making his reply. "With you magic weapons, maybe you not fear 'super lizard,' as you call him, but to slay even one with this"—he motioned with the crossbow—"I learn as much as I can about him. Also, even while I hunt other beasts, he always hunt me. I survive him long time, so maybe I learn much." He grinned hugely at Stites's expression. "Enough? We see."

"Then what brings you along?" Bradford inquired, visibly perplexed. "We cannot pay you."

The Hunter blinked pragmatically before turning back to the trail. "If he gone, this place be safer hunting for short time. Maybe long time. The Great Nakja-Mur reward me for meat I bring. . . ."

"Oh."

For the rest of the morning they crept carefully along, the Hunter in the lead, sometimes on all fours, tail twitching tensely behind him. Occasionally he paused, studying the ground disturbance in the dense carpet of decaying leaves and brush. Sometimes he motioned them to silence and listened, perfectly still, often for a considerable time. Silva grew certain that the 'Cat was using his nose as much as his ears. Ultimately, almost reluctantly it seemed, he'd move on. During one such respite, he gathered the eight others around him and spoke in a whisper that seemed almost a shout. Strangely, for once there were no raucous cries or any of the other sounds they'd grown accustomed to. Their quarry had passed recently indeed.

"We close," he hissed. "He pass this way soon ago. He know we come; he search for place to spring trap." The others, even Dennis, looked nervously around. "No, not here. He need more space. Maybe be clearing close ahead. He be there."

The jungle slowly came back to life, and even at their careful pace, the expected clearing soon appeared. It was much bigger than they'd expected, perhaps a hundred yards wide and longer than they could tell from where they stood. Blackened stumps, and new, fresh leaves testified to a recent lightning fire. They squinted for a moment in the dazzling sunlight, accustomed to the gloom of the trail, but the sun soon passed behind a cloud. The midafternoon showers—so common this time of year—awaited only the inevitable buildup. A dull, distant grumble of thunder echoed in the clearing. Silva unslung the BAR and raised it to the ready.

"No," pronounced the Hunter. "He not be so near opening. As I say, he want get us all. That need more room, I think. We go down main trail through burn. Where trail pass near jungle on either side, that where he strike."

"Are you suggesting he'll employ a *strategy*?" questioned Bradford, amazed.

"You ask, 'he plan this?' I let you judge. Super lizard is greatest hunter on all Borneo. He not stupid." He looked meaningfully at Silva's BAR. "I not stupid. You magic weapons kill him easy? Kill him fast?" Silva nodded confidently, although deep down, he was less sure than before.

"But I must see him alive!" Bradford insisted. "I must see him move! Really, I didn't come all this way solely to view a dead allosaur!" He turned to Silva. "I know you mean to kill this magnificent beast, and I understand your motive, but I insist you allow me to have as close a look as possible!"

The Hunter strode into the clearing with a strange chuckle. "You see alive, you see move, you see close. Hope you not see *too* close."

Tentatively, in single file, the others followed him. Silva walked behind the naked 'Cat, and Stites, armed with a Springfield, brought up the rear. All the others, including Bradford, carried one of the Krag-Jorgensens they'd discovered in crates in *Walker*'s armory. They were fine rifles, probably commissioned with the ship, but weren't quite as powerful as the .30-06s carried by the two gunner's mates. Their heavier bullets and slightly lower velocity might provide better penetration against something the size of a super lizard, however. None of the massive creatures had ever faced such formidably armed prey in all of history. That was the hope, at least, for all the comfort it gave them.

Two hundred yards into the opening, the Hunter paused.

"You see him, you shoot very fast?" he asked Silva. Truthfully, Dennis nodded. The BAR was a handful for most men, but he was less encumbered by it than Stites was with his '03. Certainly less than the shorter Lemurians were with their Krags. "Then stay here short time. I walk ahead. Tempt him with me."

"What you want me to do?"

"You know when time comes. Just no hesitate for Braadfurd, or I be 'turd' like your friend." Whistling a strange tune through his missing teeth, the Hunter stepped forward and continued walking, apparently unconcerned, as the trail neared the edge of the trees.

As he drew closer, even those behind thought they heard a new sound in the denseness around them. The cries of the lizard birds and grunting shrieks of the ground dwellers had largely returned. They even heard the distant bellowing squeal of a rhino-pig echo in the burn, but there was something else, indefinable—perhaps an anxious breath. The Hunter stopped about sixty yards ahead. He still whistled, but the tune had become monotonous. He appeared as casual as before, but his long tail swished rapidly, tensely, agitated. He was looking at the ground. For an instant his gaze swept across the jungle to his left; then he stooped and collected some stones. Abruptly shattering the natural quiet, he began a shrill, frightened barking sound, hopping to and fro. Whipping his arm forward like a sling, he flung his first stone into the trees. The only response was an indignant grunt, but the breathing came quicker, more defined. More barking and a second stone invited a deep, rasping inrush of air. Even before the third stone flew, the jungle erupted with a heavy, gurgling moan, and several substantial trees fell like grass blades.

Silva had been keenly staring at the jungle, BAR at his shoulder, but when the massive head rocketed from the darkness amid a cloud of leaves, branches, and fleeing lizard birds, he hesitated for an instant, despite his promise. The head appeared almost twice as high as he'd expected, and by the time he acquired the target, it was already descending, murderous jaws agape, toward the Hunter on the trail.

No one else fired either. Not even the other 'Cats had ever actually *seen* a super lizard before. Silva knew the

Mice had—perhaps this very one—and they'd both emptied their rifles into it before it simply stalked off. But nothing, certainly not their surly, monosyllabic description of the thing, could have prepared them for what they saw. Bradford only gasped in astonishment. Two great, rapid strides brought the thing completely in view, and it had to be fifty feet from nose to tail. Unlike many other creatures they'd seen, including the Grik, no fur or feathers of any kind adorned its hide. The skin was coarse, wrinkled like an elephant's, but blotched and streaked with a wild variety of dull colors. Even fully exposed, it was almost perfectly camouflaged against the dense jungle beyond. Only the sun, peeking from behind the clouds at a providential moment, showed them more than a rippling blur as it stooped to seize the Hunter with six-foot jaws lined with improbably long, sickle-shaped teeth.

Fortunately, with the agility of the cat he so closely resembled, the Hunter somersaulted out of the way, but he hit the ground hard and it was clear another step would pin him beneath the creature's terrible claws.

"Great God a'mighty!" Silva chirped, squeezing the trigger. A mighty *BAM-BAM-BAM-BAM* filled the clearing. Possibly, in his haste and surprise, the first few shots went wild. But Dennis was an excellent shot, and the familiar recoil of the heavy weapon pounding his shoulder steadied him. His training and experience took over. In a businesslike fashion, he confidently emptied his first magazine into the beast. Even before he snatched another to replace it, other shots sounded.

Silva didn't know how he expected the monster to react to the fusillade; a stately collapse would have been nice. Even a dramatic tumble and a long, flailing, writhing death would have been fine with him. What he didn't expect it to do, after absorbing most of a magazine from his BAR and numerous shots from his companions, was turn in their direction. The Hunter forgotten, it produced an ear-numbing roar and charged, its long-legged pace making it shockingly swift.

"Shit!"

Magazine in place, Silva racked the bolt and hosed the creature as it came. He knew he was hitting it, but the bullets appeared to have no effect. Way too soon, he burned through all twenty rounds and the bolt locked back. He turned to run, while groping at another magazine pouch, and saw that everyone else except Courtney Bradford had already fled. Even Stites. Bradford still stood, rifle hanging slack and apparently unfired, gaping at the charging beast.

"C'mon, you crazy son of a bitch!" Silva screamed. He tugged at the Australian's arm, and the two of them ran for their lives. They raced across the clearing, back to the trail through the jungle, gasping in the sodden air and at the unexpected, unaccustomed exertion. Silva reasoned that his shots must have had some effect or the super lizard would have caught them already, but even the confined space of the trail provided little impediment. The creature only lowered its head and surged after them, crashing through the brush and shattering trees. They gained a little, though, and Dennis managed to insert another clip and blast at the thing's head periodically as it came for them, gnashing and snapping through the undergrowth like some insanely huge crocodile.

"This close enough for you, Courtney?" Silva rasped.

They could see only a short distance ahead, but after only a few minutes of running as fast as they could, the trail that earlier took them over an hour to cautiously follow widened as they neared the pipeline cut. Bradford was spent, gasping, coughing, staggering as Silva pushed him along. He couldn't go much farther, and Dennis couldn't leave him. If the goofy naturalist got himself killed on this trip, Silva knew he might as well hang himself. After all the fighting, there weren't many destroyermen left. He was more than average valuable, but compared to Bradford . . . He emptied his gun at the ravening jaws yet again.

They burst into the cut, and Silva was surprised to see a skirmish line of riflemen. Stites had somehow managed to stop the fleeing 'Cats, and he'd gathered the rest of the returning guards. Now a dozen armed 'Cats waited with the other man. Bradford collapsed when he saw them, and Silva managed to drag him aside before inserting another clip—his last—into the BAR.

"I thought you were dead!" Stites shouted.

"I thought you were yellow!" Silva growled in reply.

Just then, shaking shattered brush from his back and roaring with a mindless, deafening frenzy, the super lizard appeared.

It was hurt after all. One eye had been churned to goo and dangled loosely from a shattered socket. A long, three-fingered "arm" seemed useless, and even some teeth were splintered or gone. Blood streamed from dozens of wounds, but it was still on its feet when it saw the new prey arrayed before it. He lunged forward once again.

"Open fire!" Silva yelled breathlessly.

A ragged volley erupted, sounding dully anemic in the humid air. For the first time the great lizard screeched in pain and staggered under the simultaneous impact of more than a dozen high-velocity projectiles. Silva continued firing short, three-shot bursts, while the others worked their bolts. Focusing on Dennis as a continued source of noise and irritation, the creature roared and swerved drunkenly toward him. Silva retreated, but didn't run—even though less than three full strides would see him devoured. The other side of the cut was at his back, and he had nowhere to go. Besides, this monster was Tony's killer. He was finished running. He'd kill it or die trying. He continued firing, but with much more care, aiming at the roof of its open mouth. Its brain must be in there somewhere. A single pace away, the super lizard stopped and shook its head, apparently disoriented. Great gobbets of congealing blood rained all around.

"Just *die*, you son of a *goat*!" Silva bellowed, and emptied his rifle down its throat. The bolt locked open with an audible *clack!* Out of ammunition, he simply pitched the rifle aside and drew the long cutlass, pattern of 1918, from his belt.

"C'mon," he breathed, planting his feet a little farther apart and raising the point of the cutlass. Vaguely noticing him once more, the massive beast took a tentative step in his direction.

"Fire!" came Stites's excited cry, and another volley, more carefully aimed than the first, slammed into the massive head.

For an instant nothing happened, and the air in the cut was filled with a gray, wispy cloud from the "smokeless" powder cartridges. Then, ever so slowly, but with increasing speed, Silva got his "stately collapse." It almost fell on top of him. The earth shuddered as the monster toppled lifelessly to the ground amid the sharp crackle of its own breaking bones. The riddled head struck less than six feet from where Dennis stood, and he was festooned with a splatter of gore and snot.

Silva almost fell to his knees, but somehow managed to keep his feet. Angrily slamming the cutlass back in its scabbard—to hide his shaking hands—he whirled and faced a grinning Paul Stites, as the gunner's mate rushed to him.

"What the hell'd you do that for?" he yelled, his voice filled with indignant wrath. "Goddamn it, I was just gettin' to the good part! What's the matter with you?" Yanking his cutlass back out, he stomped over to the head until he stared down at its remaining, unblinking eye. The thing seemed dead, but its abdomen still heaved weakly, and bloody bubbles oozed from its nostrils. He touched the eye with the sharp tip of his blade, pushing until the orb popped and a viscous fluid welled forth. The creature didn't stir.

"That's for chasin' us all over kingdom come and scarin' these poor cat-monkeys half to death," he said. Then he drove the blade deeper, feeling with the point. Finally he shoved it in almost to the hilt, and the ragged breathing abruptly stopped.

"That's for Tony Scott," he muttered darkly. "That's for killin' my friend."

"Wish we had a camera," Stites said languidly, slowly exhaling a blue cloud of smoke.

"Who cares about cameras; just gimme a damn bullet, will ya?" Silva pleaded. He and Stites were lounging on top of the dead monster, sharing a carefully hoarded cigarette, while Bradford—quite recovered—scampered around the beast, pacing its length and talking excitedly with the Hunter, who'd appeared in the cut soon after the shooting died away.

"Why?"

"Because I want one, damn it!" He sighed. "Look, shithead, I shot myself dry, see? I'm *totally out of ammo*! Right now that gives me the creeps like I never had before. So just shut up and give me a bullet, before I beat you to death!"

Stites smirked and opened his bolt, then stared into his own magazine well in horror. Frantically slapping his pockets with increased panic brought no satisfaction. "Jeez, Dennis! I'm empty too!"

Silva was grimly quiet a moment, considering the long trek back to the refinery and the boat. Suddenly he brightened. "Hey, Mr. Bradford!" Courtney paused his examination and looked inquiringly at him. He had every reason to be well disposed toward the big gunner's mate. After all, he'd gotten quite close to the monstrous creature and witnessed all sorts of movement before it was killed. Silva only hoped Bradford could protect him from the worst of his captain's wrath. "You got plenty of bullets left, right?"

Bradford sheepishly hefted the Krag. "Indeed. I'm certain I fired several times, there at the end, but somehow I still have as many rounds as I set out with. Strange."

"Musta had some extras an' thumbed 'em in without thinkin'. You got plenty of stuff to think about right now, though. Why don't you let me wag that heavy rifle back for you?"

Bradford grinned uncertainly. "Oh, thank you very much indeed . . . but I wouldn't want to be a bother. I can carry my own weight, you know! Still . . . the sling is bloody uncomfortable on my sore shoulder. . . ."

Silva tossed the empty BAR to a wide-eyed Stites and leaned down to accept the Krag. "No bother a'tall!"

CHAPTER
2

*U*nusually, despite the early hour, it was already raining by the time all the lines were singled up, and the special sea and anchor detail finished all topside preparations for getting underway. Matthew Reddy, captain of USS *Walker*, High Chief of the Amer-i-caan clan, and supreme commander (by acclamation) of all Allied Military Forces, stood in the pilothouse, binoculars around his neck, waiting for "Spanky" to report on the engines. Raindrops pummeled the slightly convex foredeck below him, and ran from the freshly painted steel to course down the side. Behind him the newly overhauled blower roared reassuringly, and he felt a sense of calm begin to edge out the anxiety he felt about the expedition. The routine procedures he knew so well had much to do with that: all the sounds and shouted commands, the twitter of the bosun's pipe. He was also encouraged just by the fact that they were finally getting underway. The expedition was his idea, and the mission they were on was crucial, but the time it had taken to prepare had cut deeply into the cushion he thought they had. He was glad to have his ship under him again, alive and straining for the open sea, but he was nervous about leaving all the same.

The bridge talker, Seaman Fred Reynolds, spoke: "Engineering reports ready to get underway."

"Very well. Cast off the stern lines." He nodded at Chief Quartermaster's Mate Norman Kutas at the helm. "Left full rudder. Port engine ahead one-third."

"Left full rudder, port ahead one-third, aye."

With a juddering vibration, dirty water boiled under the port propeller guard and the cramped, rounded-vee-shaped stern eased slowly away from the pier. Matt stepped into the rain on the port bridge wing and glanced aft. Immediately, water began soaking his hair beneath his battered hat. When the stern was far enough from the pier, he called back to the helmsman: "Rudder amidships. Cast off the bowlines." The orders were quickly relayed, and the human and Lemurian destroyermen on the fo'c'sle, already soaking wet, scampered to throw off the heavy ropes. "All astern, slow." He moved back into the pilothouse and quickly dried his face and the back of his head with a towel while he watched the proceedings. Quite a few people lined the dock in spite of the weather, watching the amazing ship depart. Many of their hopes rested with him and the successful completion of their task.

He noticed one person in particular standing with the furry, drenched Lemurians. Her small form already partially obscured by the deluge, he saw her sandy-brown hair hanging down in sodden strands. She raised a tentative hand. *We'll be back soon*, he silently mouthed, knowing she couldn't see, and he waved back at all the spectators, but one most of all. "We'll be back soon," he repeated aloud.

"Sir?" asked Reynolds.

"Nothing. Right standard rudder, all ahead one-third."

"Right standard rudder, all ahead one-third," Kutas replied. "Recommend course two seven five."

"Make it so. Reynolds, get the sea and anchor detail out of the rain and pass the word for the bosun and exec to join me on the bridge. Spanky too."

"Aye, aye, Captain."

To Sandra Tucker, standing on the old fitting-out pier, the new, light gray paint covering the battered old destroyer couldn't hide her many defects, but it did quickly blend with the driving rain. She felt a lump the size of her fist tighten in her chest as the ship grew ever more wraithlike and ethereal, and she wondered if she'd ever see it again. If she'd ever see Matthew Reddy again. She said a quick, fervent prayer for the ship and all those aboard her—and one in particular. With a sigh, she turned and melted into the throng and made her way through the dripping, awning-covered bazaar, back to her own duties at the hospital.

Lieutenant Larry Dowden, *Walker*'s executive officer, reached the bridge first, water running from the brim of his hat. Dowden was of average height and spare, but the young towheaded officer from Tennessee had stepped into his new job with energy and professionalism. He'd been a good choice to replace Lieutenant Ellis, Matt reflected once again, tossing him the towel. Soon afterward, Chief Bosun's Mate Fitzhugh Gray clomped up the metal ladder and joined them.

"Mornin', Skipper." He didn't salute because technically, as soon as he stepped out of the rain, he was no longer "outdoors."

Gray was a bear of a man, close to sixty, who'd gone a little to seed on the China Station before the war, but had since trimmed back down and muscled up considerably. He, at least, had thrived on all the activity and adventure they'd experienced since the Squall. He'd always demonstrated a clear—indeed, profound—understanding of the practical; that had perhaps been the very definition of his duty as *Walker*'s senior noncommissioned officer. Unlike many in the Navy who had the rank without the skill, Gray had the skill in sufficient measure to apply it beyond the insular world of *Walker*'s deck. As Spanky could, when it came to anything mechanical, Gray brought absolute moral authority to any discussion regarding what people were capable of, and his uncannily accurate assessments now included Lemurians as well.

"Mornin', Boats."

"I ran into Juan on the way up here and he said he'd be along directly," Gray said, referring to Juan Marcos, the Filipino mess attendant who had, for all intents and purposes, become Matt's personal steward. It was never discussed, and it certainly wasn't official, but that was how it wound up. Juan had seen to that. "He's bringin' coffee," Gray added ominously, but with an entirely innocent expression—quite an accomplishment for him. Matt grimaced. Juan wasn't good with coffee, never had been. Somehow he couldn't destroy the stuff that passed for coffee here as thoroughly as he had the "real" stuff, but it still wasn't exactly good.

"Maybe . . ."

Juan appeared, beaming, as wet as they. He carried a tray loaded with cups and a silver tureen. A towel was draped over his skinny brown arm.

"Good morning, Cap-tan! You slept well again, I trust? I am so pleased! Here is your coffee!"

"Uh, thanks, Juan." Matt took a cup and glanced at Gray. "Pour some for Chief Gray too."

"Oh, no, Skipper, I've had plenty already. . . ."

Matt arched an eyebrow. "Nonsense, Boats, I insist. Since you were so diligent in letting Juan know I was ready for my coffee, it's only right you should have some too." He turned to Dowden. "How 'bout you, Larry? No? Well, perhaps later."

Juan happily filled two cups, then set the tray on the edge of the chart table. "When that is gone, I will bring more."

"Thanks, Juan. You're too good to me." The Filipino smiled even more broadly, bowed, and turned away.

"Little booger should've been in the hotel business," Gray said, peering into his cup doubtfully after Juan disappeared. "There'd be few complaints as long as they kept him away from the coffee."

Matt sighed. "Yeah, but ever since my 'promotion' to supreme allied commander he's been treating me like MacArthur. It's weird and kind of . . . embarrassing." He was uncomfortable with his new title, and all the stuff that apparently went with it—in Juan's estimation, at least. But it was his job whether he liked it or not, and the people who'd given it to him deserved his very best regardless of how he felt. He briefly wondered what Admiral Tommy Hart would say if he could see him now—let alone General MacArthur.

Gray nodded. "Kinda hard to go through everything we have without makin' that comparison—all the runnin' around fightin' and such, with you right in the middle of it, and so much dependin' on every word you say." Matt started to chuckle. "Misery and strife shared by all, sword fights, for God's sake! Wounds, sudden death at any moment, *everything* wants to eat us . . ." Matt was laughing out loud. He held up a hand for the bosun to stop, but Gray continued: "Yeah, I can see how it'd be hard not to compare you to that Army idiot who let all our air cover get hammered on the ground and never even saw a Jap. The excitement and adventure. Honors and glory! It's everything *I* joined the Navy for in the first place."

"Okay, Boats, I give up," Matt said at last, still smiling at the older man. Gray never made any secret of his opinion regarding MacArthur's strategies. "I guess everyone's earned a little rest. Maybe this trip will provide one."

"Rest, is it?" Gray growled with a matching grin. "Don't say that, Skipper. I feel better than I have in years." His face became thoughtful. "You know, all that time on the China Station and in the Philippines, I was just goin' through the motions. Drinkin' San Miguel, fightin' in bars, gettin' fat. I did my job, but there wasn't any real point to it, I could see. I love the old *Walker*, sir; she's my home. But no matter how hard we tried to keep her ready to fight, nothing could've made her ready for the Japs. She was too old and worn-out. Just like me." He sighed. "Then the Japs ran us out of the Philippines. Beat us up and chased us out of the Java Sea, too. Beggin' your pardon, Skipper, but none of us were much good for anything but runnin' back then. You were right. Even if the Japs hadn't got us, *Walker* would've spent the war towin' targets . . . or bein' one, and most of her crew wouldn't have been good for much else either. After that last big fight with *Amagi*, when we got sucked up by the Squall, none of that mattered anymore."

A stormy frown creased Gray's face. "I hate the Japs for what they done to us, and I hope wherever 'home' is, our boys are kickin' hell out of 'em. But we wouldn't have been helpin' much, even if we were alive. Back there, *Walker* wouldn't have made any difference." His frown shifted into an expression of determination. "In this world, in this fight against those damn Griks, she has made a difference, and so have all her people. With God's help, maybe she will again."

"God's, and Spanky McFarlane's," Matt agreed quietly, referring to *Walker*'s engineering officer, who still hadn't arrived. The diminutive engineer had performed miracles keeping the battered ship not only afloat, but seaworthy, and three of her four boilers were probably in better shape than they'd been in years. Their arrival in Baalkpan, and the necessities of the war they found themselves in, had sparked an industrial revolution of sorts. The Lemurians had already possessed impressive foundries for casting massive anchors and other fittings for the Homes, but the Americans had taught them to make cannon, shot, and other things they'd need. The machine shops on the two destroyers turned out parts for lathes even bigger than themselves, and soon milling machines, lathes, and other heavy tools were operating in huge "factories" near the shipyard. They were running out of certain other spare parts fast, though, mostly bearings and things that Lemurian industry wasn't yet up to helping them produce. They'd have to figure that out pretty quick.

Gray nodded. "Yes, sir. Please don't ever tell him I said so, but Spanky's been a wonder. Him and everybody else."

"What?" demanded McFarlane, suddenly joining them, dripping like the rest, and striking his distinctive pose: hands on his skinny hips.

"Nothin'," Gray grumped, recovering himself. "I was just wonderin' who's gonna restow that junk your snipes scattered all over my topsides." He was referring to the disassembled drilling rig.

"Your deck apes," Spanky replied cheerfully. "That's their job."

Walker steamed past *Aracca* Home, one of the enormous seagoing cities of the Lemurians. She was moving toward the mouth of the bay to relieve *Big Sal* as a floating battery—a task all the sea folk despised, but knew was necessary. Larger than the new *Essex*-class aircraft carriers Matt had seen under construction, *Aracca*, like all her kind, was built entirely of wood. Her hull was double ended, flat bottomed, and diagonally plank laminated to a thickness of six feet in some places. Matt was impressed by the sophisticated design, and knew the ship was incredibly tough. It had to be. Despite the stresses inherent to her momentous proportions (1,009 feet long, with a beam of almost 200 feet), *Aracca* had been built to last for centuries upon a sea that was much more hostile in many ways than the sea Matt had known before the Squall. *Not in all ways, perhaps*, he reflected grimly—remembering that Homes like *Aracca* were not proof against ten-inch naval rifles.

Despite the rain, he saw her people going about their morning chores: preparing fish from the morning catch for drying, once the rain eased, and tending the polta fruit gardens on the main deck that ranged along the bulwark completely around the ship. The main deck was a hundred feet above the sea, and three huge pagodalike structures that served as apartments for many of her people towered above it like skyscrapers. Encompassing the structures were three massive tripods soaring another two hundred and fifty feet above the deck. They supported the great sails, or "wings" that provided *Aracca*'s only means of propulsion—other than the hundred giant sweep-oars her people could use for maneuvering when necessary.

Matt was always amazed whenever he looked at *Aracca*—or any Lemurian Homes. Not only because of their size, but also because of the industrious ingenuity they represented. 'Cats may have been a little backward in some respects when the Americans first arrived, but they certainly weren't ignorant. He had *Walker*'s horn sounded in greeting, and he and the other officers went back out in the rain on the bridge wing and returned the friendly waves they received. Slowly the massive ship receded in the rain behind them.

"I'm already anxious to be back," Matt said aloud, ruefully.

"We're getting a late start," conceded Dowden. He glanced apologetically at Spanky. "No offense, I know you went as fast as you could. It's just ..."

"I know," Spanky growled. "By the original timetable, we should've been on our way home by now. But one thing led to another ... It sure would've been easier with a dry dock, especially to get at the damage below the waterline. She won't ever be 'right' until we can do that."

"Agreed," said the captain, "but that'll have to wait. New construction has priority, and there just aren't enough hands, or hours, or days. ..." He shook his head. "Nothing for it. You've done an amazing job, Spanky. All of you have. My question is, are the boilers in shape for more speed than we planned on, and if so, do we have the fuel? How much time can we shave off our trip?"

Spanky took off his hat and scratched his head. "We're steaming on two boilers now, numbers two and three. Our range used to be about twenty-five hundred miles at twenty knots. We can't do that well anymore. I can't guarantee we can even *make* twenty knots on two boilers. If we light off number four, it'll take half again as much fuel to gain just those few extra knots. Now, the new fuel bunker we installed where number one used to be ought to give us a safe margin, but it might not—and until we get the new site on Tarakan up and running, there won't be anyplace to top off." He shrugged. "If you're putting me on the spot, I'd say we can light number four, probably squeeze twenty-five, maybe twenty-eight knots out of her, and still get back okay, but you won't be able to do as much poking around looking for that 'iron fish' as you hoped. If we burn it now, you might wish we had it later."

Matt grimaced. "Well, let's wait till we reach open water and see what she'll give us. Maybe she'll make twenty. If she won't, though, I'm inclined to burn it now. I just can't shake the feeling we need to get back as soon as we can."

"But . . . we'd still get back before any reinforcements could arrive," said Dowden. "What real difference would it make?"

"Probably none. We'll be in radio contact, and should have plenty of warning if the Japs and the Grik get uppity. We can take it easy on the way back if we have to."

"What's really bothering you?" asked Gray. "Is it *Amagi*?"

Matt nodded. "I guess. Theoretically, we should still have months before she's seaworthy again. They don't have a dry dock either, and she's got a lot of underwater damage. But she shouldn't have been here in the first place." He paused, considering the absurdity of his remark, but they knew what he meant. "I just hate being blind. It's like the 'old' war all over again. Without the PBY, we don't really have any idea what the enemy's up to, or what they're capable of."

The rain began to slacken, and before them lay the mouth of the bay. In it loomed *Big Sal*, or *Salissa* Home.

"Signal from *Big Sal*," announced the talker, relaying a message from the Lemurian lookout in the crow's nest. All allied vessels had been fitted with some means of making a signal by flags or semaphore. "It says Keje-Fris-Ar would like to accompany us after all, if we wouldn't mind slowing down enough to take him aboard."

Matt chuckled with relief. He'd been hoping his Lemurian friend would change his mind and come along. "Tell him we can't slow down, but we'll pass as close as we can and he can jump."

"Sir?"

The others chuckled too.

"Never mind. Tell him 'of course' and 'welcome.'"

Sandra went straight to the area of the roofed but otherwise open-air hospital, partitioned from the rest by hanging curtains, or tapestries, woven in bright, cheerful colors. It was the area many considered the "psych ward." She knew Selass, Keje's daughter, was working there, and she wanted to see her. The two had become friends, and the once spoiled, self-centered, and standoffish Selass had changed dramatically over the last few months. She'd become a real asset at the hospital, and her efforts in the psych ward in particular were tireless. Part of that was because she felt genuine concern for the people there. Most Lemurians, with the exception of Aryaalans and B'mbaadans, had never really known war before. They were a peaceful people, ready to defend their homes and families, but utterly unaccustomed to the horrors they'd seen and been forced to endure. Many of her patients had terrible physical wounds, sustained in the recent fighting, and she had to help them learn to cope with that. Others had been just as seriously wounded in the mind. The worst of these was a small, dwindling group of "survivors" they'd rescued from the first Grik ship they'd captured, the one that became *Revenge* and was later destroyed in battle. That was when they realized just how terrible their enemy truly was when they discovered that, to the Grik, anyone not allied with them was nothing but prey to be devoured, and when prey was captured, they kept them as living provisions. The survivors they'd found chained in the Grik ship's hold not only understood this, but they'd seen many others, in some cases their very families, butchered alive and prepared for Grik cook pots. Selass's own mate, Saak-Fas, was one who'd seen it all.

He'd been knocked unconscious and carried aboard the one Grik ship that escaped destruction when *Walker* first came to the People's aid. No one knew what became of him at the time; it was assumed he was lost overboard with so many others, and devoured by the insatiable fish. Not so. Somehow he'd been captured and survived for months in first one hold, then another, and he'd seen . . . terrible things. He was quite mad when finally rescued. In the meantime, considering him dead, Selass finally realized she'd been wrong to take him to mate in the first place, and developed a real affection for Chack-Sab-At, who'd hopelessly wooed her before she made her choice. At the time, she hadn't thought much of the young wing runner, but since then, Chack had become a noted warrior and a true leader. When she made her feelings known to him, he'd promised to give an answer after the battle for the ship. Instead, he'd returned to her with her long-lost mate. It was a crushing, emotional scene, and Sandra felt terribly sorry for Selass. Since then, Chack seemed to have fallen for the exotically beautiful B'mbaadan queen, Safir Maraan, but Selass's feelings for him were undiminished. Added to that was the fact that her mate still lived and she could never leave him in his current state. It was a terrible hardship for Selass to bear: unrequited love for someone increasingly beyond her grasp, mixed with terrible guilt that she had those feelings while her legitimate mate still lived.

Even so, it might not have been so tragic, but Saak-Fas wouldn't even speak to her, no matter how hard she tried to elicit some response. He wouldn't speak to anyone. He was recovered, physically, from his ordeal, and almost feverish daily exercise had left him in better shape than he'd ever been. Sandra doubted he knew about his mate's inner turmoil, so that probably wasn't the reason for his behavior. When his old friends from *Big Sal* visited, he said nothing at all, and showed no interest in life aboard his old home. He cared nothing about reports of the war, and wouldn't even acknowledge the existence of others who'd been through the same ordeal as he. Worst of all, no matter what she said or did, when Selass spent time with him each day, he acted as though she weren't even there. The torment Selass felt was a palpable thing, and it wrenched Sandra to her core.

Sandra nodded and smiled at Pam Cross, who led a small procession of medical recruits through the fabric opening, showing them around. She knew Pam had issues of her own. It wasn't much of a secret anymore that she and Dennis Silva had a "thing," and she couldn't help but wonder how that worked. It was even less a secret that Silva and Chack's sister, Risa, had a "thing" of some sort going on as well, and as much as Sandra hoped it was a joke, with Silva there was no way of knowing. She shuddered and hoped Pam knew. She had to, didn't she? Pam's "thing" with Silva was proof, wasn't it? She shook her head and went to stand beside Selass, where the Lemurian female was watching Saak-Fas do an unending series of push-ups.

"Good morning, Selass," she said softly, the sorrow of the scene wrenching her anew.

For a moment Selass said nothing, but just sat cross-legged, watching the almost mechanical laboring of her mate. Finally, she sighed. "Good morning." Her face, as usual, betrayed no emotion, but her tone was ironic, desolate. "Have they left?" she asked, referring to *Walker*, and more specifically Chack and Matt. Chack was accompanying the mission as commander of a company of the First Marines. She was also well aware of Sandra's affection for Captain Reddy.

"Yes."

For a while, both were silent. The only sounds were Saak-Fas's heavy breathing, the rain on the dense canvas overhead, and the tormented moans of others in the segregated sections of the ward.

"He spoke," Selass said at last.

Sandra rushed to her side. "That's wonderful!" Perhaps some of Selass's misery might be relieved. "What did he say?"

"He did not speak to me." The ironic tone remained, but Selass's voice broke with emotion, and tears welled in her large, amber eyes. "He merely made an announcement, as if it mattered little to him whether anyone heard. As if I were . . . anybody."

For a breath, Sandra was speechless, appalled by Saak-Fas's apparent cruelty. "Well . . . what did he say?" she managed at last.

"He is leaving the ward. He is entirely well and strong, and ready to resume his missions."

"Missions?" Sandra was taken aback.

"Yes. While he was . . . in captivity . . . he swore an oath much like Adar's: if somehow he was spared, he would never rest until he destroyed as many Grik as he possibly could. No consideration would be allowed to compete with that goal: no distraction, no emotion, no thought. Not even

me. No other obligation binds him now, not even to his
Home. He has decided the best way to accomplish his mis-
sions is to join your Navy." She looked at Sandra. "To join
Mahan's crew."

"What if we don't release him? He's still clearly unwell.
His mental state—"

Selass interrupted her. "Release him?" She gestured at
their surroundings. "How could we prevent him from leaving? We cannot guard him; nor should we. We have too few
to do too much already. Besides, I think it would be wrong.
He knows what he is doing and why. It . . . hurts, but I believe I know why too."

Sandra stubbornly set her jaw. "Well, whatever *his* intentions are, I believe Lieutenant Ellis would have the final
say. Saak-Fas might sneak out of here, but he certainly can't
sneak aboard *Mahan* and remain there if I don't want him
to. I'll have a word with Jim. . . ."

Selass rose and faced her. Behind her, Saak-Fas continued his workout, heedless of their words. "Do not," she
pleaded. "He must go. I have lost him already to his oath
and what the Grik did to him. He exists only for revenge,
and if I ever cared for him at all, I cannot stand in his way.
He *will* perform his missions. At least this way it might be
of some help, have some meaning."

Sandra slowly nodded, and tears stung her own eyes.
"Very well. But you keep saying 'missions,' plural. What
other mission does he have, and why *Mahan*?"

Selass sighed and averted her gaze. "He wants *Mahan*
because, in the fight to come, he believes she will give him
his best opportunity to fulfill *all* his goals: to kill many of
our enemies . . . and to die."

The following morning was as great a contrast to the previous as was possible at their current latitude. The sky
was utterly cloudless, and for once there wasn't even the
usual morning haze. To starboard, the violet sea sparkled
with gentle whitecaps, stirred by a freshening breeze, and
to port, the Borneo coast loomed sharp and green, bordered by creamy blue shoals. Alongside, adolescent graw-
fish leaped and capered like dolphins, effortlessly keeping
pace with the ship, the sun causing their new wings to flash
with color. In the distance, near shore, bright lizard birds

swooped and circled above a churning school of flasher fish that had cornered their prey against the shallows. They'd learned it was only in the mornings and evenings that "flashies" congregated in shallow water in such horrifying numbers—of course, there were other things. . . . Occasionally the flying lizards tried to snatch some floating morsel. Often they were snatched themselves, by the voracious flashies below the surface.

Spanky McFarlane stifled a shudder at the sight. He hated flashies passionately, and wondered if the things were somehow smart enough to school together just to draw the fliers down. He wouldn't put it past them. They always seemed to figure out ways around every defense they'd used to put men in the water to perform repairs. They hadn't lost anyone during those efforts, luckily, but there'd been plenty of injuries, mostly caused by blows delivered by the flashies' bony heads. God, how he wanted a dry dock!

Reaching in his pocket, he removed a pouch and took a handful of yellowish brown leaves. Stuffing them in his mouth, he began to chew. For the first few minutes he grimaced at the initial foul taste, but once he got past the nasty, waxy coating on the leaves, a flavor like actual tobacco began to emerge. They'd decided the stuff really was tobacco, of a sort, and that had caused jubilation among the crew. It was clearly laced with enough nicotine to satisfy anyone, and was now almost universally used, even by some of the 'Cats, who'd never habitually imbibed. The only bad thing was, no matter what they tried, it simply couldn't be smoked. It probably had something to do with the coating, but whatever the cause, experimenters always became violently ill when they tried to light up. Maybe they'd solve the problem, maybe not, but chewing it was better than nothing.

Spanky stood between the vegetable locker and the empty number two torpedo mount on the port side of the number three funnel, listening to the sounds of the ship. Occasionally he took a few steps and listened some more. It was a habit he'd formed in his early days aboard *Walker*, and it had stuck: trying to discover problems or impending problems by simple sound and feel. It was harder now, because after all the damage, repairs, and jury rigs, nothing sounded "right" anymore, but he was constantly trying to learn which new sounds were okay and which weren't. He'd already stood over the number two boiler, and was working his way aft. After he "listened" to the engines from topside, he'd go below and do the same thing, working his way forward. He figured if anything was really wrong, he'd detect it topside first.

He saw Silva on top of the amidships deckhouse gun platform, drilling a mixed human/Lemurian crew on the number three four-inch-50 gun. The long barrel was trained out to sea, and its crew was going through the motions of loading it. Terrifying as they'd be to the trainees, Spanky thought Silva's bellowed epithets were just as inventive and amusing as usual. In fact, any casual observer wouldn't have noticed any change at all in the new (acting) chief gunner's mate—his recent run-in with the captain over the now epic "Super Lizard Safari" being ample proof he was the same old Silva.

Spanky knew better. He also knew that the public dressing-down Dennis got over the incident was a sham for the crew. The captain was just as glad as anyone that the monster that got Tony was dead, and the killing had been good for overall morale. Spanky also suspected the captain knew Silva—and Stites—had done it for that exact reason as much as any other, and not just as the usual stupid stunt it would once have been written off as. The proof was that, for once, Silva hadn't been reduced in grade for his "stunt." His only punishment at all, in fact, had been restriction to the ship for the duration of their mission. (Like he would really want to go anywhere.) Besides, the last thing they needed, even changed as he was, was Silva on the loose in Manila during diplomatic negotiations.

Apparently, the only thing Captain Reddy was really mad about was that they'd risked Courtney Bradford. Of course, there'd been an element of relief associated with that as well. Bradford had been driving them all nuts with his constant demands to study stuff. Now he had a fresh (albeit shot to pieces) super lizard skull to gawk at and display, and an entertaining, ever-expanding story of heroism and adventure to go along with it. Maybe now there'd be a short respite.

After "feeling" the aft engine room, Spanky moved to the rail and spit a long, yellowish stream in their wake.

After a final, wistful survey of the beautiful day he probably wouldn't see again, he dropped down the companionway into the engineering spaces below. The noise of the giant turbines quickly grew louder as he descended, and he was immediately faced with a shouted altercation between the new (acting) chief machinist's mate, Dean Laney, and one of the 'Cat Marines.

"What the hell's going on here?" he bellowed. Despite his diminutive frame and years of smoking, there was nothing wrong with his lungs. Laney, a slightly shorter, less depraved, but also less bold and imaginative "snipe" version of Silva, glared down at him through beaded sweat and bulging eyes. The Lemurian Marine came to attention and merely stood, staring straight ahead. He was short, like most 'Cats, but heavily muscled. Around his waist was the dark blue kilt that had evolved as the unofficial Marine uniform. Three thin red stripes around the hem made him a sergeant, and to gain that rank he had to be a veteran of savage fighting. That was the only kind of fighting there was in this terrible war. His apelike feet were shod with thick leather soles held on by crisscrossing straps wound up to his knees. In battle he'd wear bronze greaves, breastplate, and helmet, and carry a short stabbing sword, bow, and spear.

"This goddamn monkey wants some of my guys to go topside and help sort out their mess, like we ain't got enough to do down here!" Laney complained. He watched Spanky's brows knit together as he furiously chewed his quid. "Sir," he appended.

"I told you last night we'd have to help," Spanky growled. "Our guys left pieces of the rig scattered around the deck like tinker toys. Half the deck-apes aren't even Navy; they're Chack's Marines."

Technically, the Marines weren't Chack's; they were from the First Marine Regiment—some of whom were armed with the fortunate windfall of Krag rifles. They'd become as deadly with the things as their limited practice would allow, but most had seen little action in the war so far. Aboard ship, however, Chack had returned to his old duties as bosun's mate to the 'Cats, using the Marines as crew.

"But there's only so much even he can do," Spanky continued. "Hell, most of his Marines are Baalkpans—land folk. Can't even tie a knot. Even the ones from Homes might as well have spent their lives on battlewagons or flattops. They aren't used to the way the old gal rolls and pitches and they're pukin' their guts out." His tone softened slightly, and a trace of amusement crept into it. "I know you're just guarding your turf, and Chief Donaghey left mighty big shoes to fill in that regard, but you have to bend a little."

Laney looked unconvinced. "All right, Spanky. I hear you. But we're covered in shit down here. After all the repairs, this is like her sea trials all over again. Everything needs adjusting, and the feed-water pump on number three don't sound right. Gauges are all over the place, and we're makin' smoke!"

McFarlane nodded. "All but number two. When the new firemen are off duty, have them go watch the Mice for a while. Maybe they'll learn something."

Laney rolled his eyes. "Those kooks? Besides, they're some of the ones this monkey Marine wants. Says they built the rig in the first place, so they know what needs to go ashore first, and how it ought to be stowed."

Spanky's tone sharpened once again. "Yeah, they built the rig. They found the oil we're burning too, if you'll recall. And they're also kooks. But they're my kooks—and yours now, too—aside from being the best boilermen in the firerooms, so you'd better figure out how to handle them. We need those squirrelly little guys. Use them. They can't teach with words worth a damn, but the new guys, the 'Cats, can learn by example. *Make* 'em watch them." He turned to the Marine. "You can run along now. I'll send them up myself."

When the 'Cat was gone, Spanky turned back to Laney. "Listen," he said, "you're doing a good job, but you need to get along better with the apes—I don't care if they're human or 'Cats. The bosun's already casually referred to you as an asshole in my presence, and I'd take that as a powerful hint if I were you. You don't want him on your bad side." Laney gulped. There was no question about that. "The upper and lower deck rivalry exists for a purpose," Spanky continued. "It spurs productivity and even camaraderie in a way. Besides, it's fun. But don't take it too seriously or let it go too far. Never lose sight of the fact we're all on the same side." He paused. "And *don't* call 'em monkey Marines anymore. They don't like it, and neither do I. It'll just make you look bad in the eyes of the 'Cats in our own division. Don't forget some of them—the best ones—were Marines before they were snipes. Clear?"

"Clear," Laney grumbled.

"Good. Now see if you can sort out the feed water problem, and let me know what's up." He paused. "How many of our guys did he say Chack wants?"

"Half a dozen or so."

Spanky nodded. "Well, just keep working. I'll pick 'em out as I move forward."

With that, McFarlane eased past the sweating men and panting 'Cats and worked his way forward through the condensation-dripping maze of pipes and roaring machinery. The scene in the forward engine room was much the same, and after detailing a couple of guys topside to help Chack, he paused for a few words with the throttlemen. Continuing on, he cycled through the air lock to the aft fireroom. The firerooms had to operate in a pressurized environment to allow constant air and fuel flow so the fires would burn hot and steady. Once inside, he was greeted by yet more activity: men actually working on the feed-water pump, for example, as well as other things he thought were already fixed. He also noted a dramatic increase in temperature. It was probably a hundred and twenty degrees.

Sweat gushed in the hot, humid environment, and he wiped it from his face and flung it aside to join the slimy black slurry coating the plates beneath his feet. The stench was unbelievable. It was the usual combination of bilge-water, sweaty bodies, mildew, fuel oil, and smoke. Added to those was something more like wet dog than anything else he could think of. Ultimately, the sum was greater—and far more nauseating—than the parts. He didn't know how the 'Cats, with their more sensitive noses, could keep their breakfasts down. Number four was offline while repairs were underway, but the 'Cat burner batter on number three stood panting, ready to replace the plate if the fuel tender called for it. The 'Cat looked miserable, and Spanky honestly couldn't see how the furry little guys stood the heat. When they began accepting Lemurians into the Navy as full-fledged crew members, he'd never dreamed so many would strike for the engineering spaces. It was just too hot and confined. He'd been surprised when he was swamped with applications. 'Cats *loved* machinery, and regardless of the environment, they clambered to be close to the most complicated examples—like the engines and boilers. Some couldn't hack it. Even the ones that stayed, and apparently thrived, shed their fur like mad, and tiny, downy filaments drifted everywhere. Even though they tried to clean it every day, the slurry on the deck and catwalks was tangled with the longer stuff to the point that, from one end of the fireroom to the other, it looked like a clogged shower drain. Every time he entered the firerooms he sneezed, but the 'Cats that stayed were diligent and enthusiastic, and he couldn't have done without them. Maybe some didn't understand everything they were doing, but they didn't always have to, and they treated him like some sort of omniscient wizard.

He listened for a moment, as they expected him to, and occasionally touched a gauge or felt a pipe. It was only his normal routine, but it always left them wondering what mystical significance the act represented. He stifled a grin and nodded friendly greetings before sending a couple of the least occupied above. Passing through the next air lock, he entered the forward fireroom.

"Oh, good God!" he exclaimed, when, looking up, he was immediately greeted by a pair of large, naked, and entirely human-looking breasts (if you could get past the fine, soot gray fur covering them). "How many times do I have to tell you to wear some goddamn clothes? At least a shirt!"

"It too hot!" Tab-At (hence, Tabby to the other Mice) declared. Somehow, her slightly pidgin English also contained a hint of a drawl she'd picked up from the other "original" Mice.

"It's no hotter than usual. You just do that to aggravate me," Spanky complained, knowing it was true. When Tabby first came to the firerooms he'd thrown an absolute fit. To have females of any kind in his engineering spaces went against everything he stood for, from ancient tradition to his personal sense of propriety. He'd even tried to force the issue once by decreeing everyone under his command would perform their duties in full uniform, something never before required. It was a blatant attempt to get her to strike for a different, more comfortable division. All the Lemurian deck-apes, male or female, were required to wear only their kilts, after all. Tabby's allies rose to the challenge, even so far as providing her with trousers—with a hole cut in the seat for her tail—and he realized he was being mocked.

He finally relented for several reasons: First, he recognized that his stance was ridiculous, and even the captain had decreed—surely reluctantly—that full equality of the sexes would be enforced aboard the ship. It was the Lemurian way, and with at least half the crew filled out with 'Cats, they certainly couldn't antagonize their allies. Second, all the snipes suffered under the order, human as well as Lemurian. It *was* too hot for them to work efficiently under such regulations. Third, and perhaps most astonishing to him, Tabby made a damn good "fireman." She was small and agile enough to perform many tasks that were difficult for others; she could scamper through the bilges like, well, an ape. She was probably the best burner batter aboard, and she'd proven herself absolutely fearless. Sometimes she had a little trouble with rough weather—many 'Cats did—but otherwise she was perfectly competent. Finally, she was probably the only 'Cat in his division that fully understood what she was doing and didn't consider him some sort of mechanical mage. That came from her association with the irascible Mice, surely, but even though she'd virtually become one of them, she hadn't lost her sense of humor. She'd gotten his goat, and he respected that. She was supposed to be wearing a T-shirt, however.

He looked around the gloomy compartment, spotting a dingy shirt draped nearby, and knew she must have taken it off deliberately, just now, simply to "get his goat" again. The fur where it should have been was far too clean.

"Shirt. Now."

Grinning, she retrieved the shirt and languorously pulled it over her head.

He rolled his eyes. Spotting the other Mice, Gilbert Yager and Isak Rueben, beyond her, he growled exasperatedly. "Why do you let her do that?" he demanded. "Next time I'm putting her on report, swear to God!"

Frowning grimly, the two men looked at each other. "Do what?"

No single word or phrase was adequate to describe the

Mice. "Strange" came closest, but was still almost too specific. By their appearance, Isak and Gilbert might have been brothers. Both were intense, wiry little men with narrow faces and sharp, pointed noses that contributed much to the rodentlike impression they made. They were unfriendly and annoying to just about everyone they came in contact with. They never socialized, and back when there'd been one, they shunned the ship's baseball team. They were quintessential "snipes"—firemen, to be precise—but they took it further than that. Given a choice, they'd never leave the sweltering heat of their beloved firerooms and the boilers they worshiped there. They were painfully insular and just as apparently unimaginative, but Spanky had learned there was more to them than met the eye. Normally their skins were pasty with a belowdecks pallor they worked hard to maintain, but now their exposed skin still bore the angry red-brown tans they'd accumulated while operating the first oil rig outside of Baalkpan. A rig they designed based on a type they were intimately, if ruefully, familiar with, from their years in the oil fields before escaping that hated life and joining the Navy.

They treated Tab-At like a puppy, and she followed them around like one. Since Spanky knew she certainly wasn't, he suspected her association with them was, at least initially, an attempt to learn as much from them as she could. She'd worked with them on the previous rig and considered them enigmatic fonts of wisdom. When they spoke, if nobody understood what they were trying to say, it was because they were too stupid to understand the words. It never occurred to her that much of their irascibility was due to compensation for a profound shyness, and they spoke only monosyllabic words whenever they would serve. Presumably, she knew them better now, but instead of moving on with the knowledge she'd gleaned, she acted more and more like her mentors—except for the shyness. She obviously liked them, although he couldn't imagine why. Their reaction to his obvious question didn't seem feigned, and he couldn't decide whether it was ignorance on their part, or a mental effort to block her full, rounded breasts from their consciousness.

Gilbert peered at him through slitted lids and proceeded to perform another feat he and Isak were very good at: mentally tripping Spanky up with their disjointed stream-of-consciousness thought processes. "We're goin' to set up the spudder someplace else, ain't we?"

"Well . . . of course. That's part of the reason for this trip."

Gilbert looked at Isak significantly. "We know that, but you've come here to tell us *we're* gonna hafta do it!" he accused. "Leave our boilers and toil away onshore, just like last time!"

"Ain't fair!" Isak proclaimed. He held out his tanned, skinny arm like a bloody rag. "Just look at that, what the damn sun did to me! We joined the Navy to burn oil . . . not to keep diggin' it up!"

Spanky glanced at his battered wristwatch, an item he'd always taken for granted, but which was now precious beyond words. A few Lemurian artisans had experimented with large clocks, achieving mixed results. Right now everyone's priorities were elsewhere, and the best potential clock makers were consumed by the necessity of creating the more complicated armaments. If he didn't hurry, he'd be late for the meeting in the wardroom.

"Life isn't fair," he said, "but you do your best. My curse is, I have to put up with you. But right now you're the best oil men we've got, and if that means you keep working on your tans, that's what you'll do. For what it's worth, though, that's *not* what I came to tell you. Right now I want one of you to run topside and show those apes what parts of the rig have to come off first. They want to restow the stuff. There's not much point; we'll be there tomorrow, but just make sure they don't screw anything up. As to the other . . ." He scowled, contemplating. "I'd just as soon you didn't go either. We've got too many green firemen down here, and I need someone to show them what to do. Maybe I can get the captain to let me keep one of you, at least."

He expected an argument over that, something like, "Where one goes, we all go," but there was only silence and calculating expressions.

"Jeez. Well, carry on." With that he strode forward, past the other firemen in the compartment. He chose one more to accompany one of the Mice above and then paused at the huge copper fuel tank taking up most of the space once occupied by the number one boiler. He felt the cool metal and was relieved, as always, that the hellish temperatures didn't seem inclined to heat the fuel inside. All the sloshing around probably helped dissipate the warming effect. He didn't like the idea of all that fuel right here in the fireroom; if they ever had an accident . . . but there was nowhere else to put it, and it was his idea, after all. Oh, well. He patted the tank and went through the forward air lock.

"I swear, Tabby, how come ye're always waggin' yer boobs at the chief?" asked Gilbert after Spanky was gone. "You know it drives him nuts. Just havin' wimmin aboard at all is enough to cause him fits—and then you do that!"

"Yeah," agreed Isak, "ain't ever'body in the Navy as sensitive as us two."

"He needs to laugh," Tabby replied, "and he will, later."

The meeting in the wardroom was also a late breakfast, catered to perfection by Juan. The food was laid out, buffet style, on the wooden countertops on the port side of the compartment spanning the width of the ship. Juan and Ray Mertz, a mess attendant, stood ready with carafes of ice water and coffee. Those eating were seated at a long, green, linoleum-topped table that also served as an operating table when necessary. A bright light hung above it from an adjustable armature allowing it to be lowered over a patient. It was currently raised and stowed, but there was plenty of light, and even a slight breeze through the open portholes on each side. Much of the food looked familiar to the humans, even if the source wasn't. Mounds of scrambled eggs and strips of salty "bacon" tasting much like one would have expected them to—even if the eggs came from leathery, flying reptiles, and the bacon from . . . something else. Biscuits had been baked with the coarse-grained local flour, and pitchers of polta juice were provided for those who cared for it. There was no milk, although there was something that tasted a little like cream with which they could season their ersatz coffee if they chose. Lemurians were mammals, but considered it perverse for adults to drink milk. Understandable, since the only other creatures that might have provided it were decidedly undomesticated.

Juan had worked wonders to lay in the supplies and logistical support necessary to provide the simple, "normal" breakfast. Standard Lemurian morning fare was dry bread, fruit, and fish. It *had* been standard, at least, until Juan Marcos stepped up. Many Navy 'Cats had developed a liking for the powdered eggs and ketchup the American destroyer-men ate, but that was long gone now. The refrigerator was stocked with fresh eggs, though, and that would serve until they ran out. Alan Letts was working on several projects to desiccate food—eventually, for longer trips, they'd have to come up with something—but for now they'd laid in a supply of dried fish and fruit for when the fresh stuff ran out. Strangely, they did still have plenty of one type of food they'd stocked so long ago when *Walker* escaped Sura-baya: crates of Vienna sausages. The cook, Earl Lanier, still tried to infiltrate the slimy little things into meals on occa-sion, carefully camouflaged, but the men hated the "scum weenies" with a passion, and always ferreted them out. Even the 'Cats had finally grown to dislike them. Regard-less, the fat, irascible cook refused to get rid of them, calling them "survival rations."

After cordial greetings, the officers in the wardroom ate in silence, for the most part. It was the Lemurian way not to discuss matters of importance during a meal, and Matt thought the custom made sense. Instead of talking, he enjoyed his food and looked around the table at his companions. Seated to his left like some reddish brown, cat-faced bear was Keje-Fris-Ar, High Chief of *Salissa* Home—*Big Sal*, as the Americans called her. Matt was glad his friend Keje felt free to make the trip. Like the other Homes in the alliance, Keje's would take its turn guarding the mouth of the bay, but under the command of his cousin, Jarrik-Fas, she didn't really need him for that. Also, he'd finally decided to allow some of the "alterations" Letts and Lieutenant Brister had been harping on, so *Big Sal* would spend much of his absence at the fitting-out pier. Initially reluctant, Keje was now prepared to allow any modifica-tions whatsoever to his Home that would make her more formidable. He'd cast his lot, and that of his people, entirely for the cause of destroying the Grik forever. Matt was grate-ful not just for the sake of the alliance, but for his own. He'd grown extremely fond of the gruff, wise Lemurian, and had come to rely heavily on Keje's judgment and support.

Keje's sky priest, Adar, sat in the next seat. He was the only sky priest Matt knew well, and he'd been Keje's child-hood friend. With Naga's decline, he had, for all intents and purposes, become High Sky Priest of all the allied powers, so his presence on the expedition, while chancy, should help immensely with negotiations. In theory, even among the Maa-ni-los, every high chief of every Home, whether land-based or seagoing, was a head of state in his own right, and all enjoyed equal status according to custom. But Sky Priests were a little different. As High Sky Priest of the entire alliance, there was no question but that Adar was a little more "equal" than the others. He hadn't planned it that way, but that was the way it was, was the way it had to be. His position was fragile, but potentially very powerful. Right now that power was founded on trust. A well-founded trust, in Matt's opinion. It was Adar who'd have to convince the Maa-ni-los it was in their best interest to openly join the alliance, and if anyone could do that with heartfelt arguments, it was Adar. Time would tell.

If there was a potential weak link in the command staff chain represented on his ship, there was only one. Everyone at the breakfast table had been tested in a variety of ways and hadn't been found wanting, but seated to Matt's right, beyond Lieutenant Dowden, was Lieutenant (Brevet Major) Tamatsu Shinya: a fellow destroyerman, but one who'd served the Japanese Imperial Navy. The compact, dark-haired man had once been an anonymous enemy on a half-glimpsed ship in an impossibly far-off war. Unbelievable as it sometimes seemed even now—he was a Jap, for crying out loud!—Shinya had become a trusted and valuable friend. He'd found his calling as a commander of infantry, and had served with distinction in every battle since the Squall brought them together. He was highly regarded by his 'Cat infantry, and even the old Asiatic Fleet destroyermen had grown to grudgingly accept and respect him. Matt doubted he'd need his services on this trip, and he'd probably have been more use back "home" helping prepare defenses, but it was clear he had issues that needed sorting out. Perhaps the trip might help.

To Shinya's right was the captain of the Second Marines and also one of *Walker*'s bosun's mates when he was aboard: Chack-Sab-At. Of all the Lemurians Matt had come to know, Chack was possibly the most remarkable. He'd come aboard *Walker* right after she first met the 'Cats as a kind of full-immersion exchange student. He'd been a willing, happy addition to the crew, and as time went by Matt came to realize just how skilled an ambassador he'd been. He came among the Americans at a time when they'd just lost a lot of friends and were only beginning to grasp the fact that something terrible and extraordinary had happened to them. They were afraid, and a little shocky, and even with their relatively sophisticated weapons, they'd been vulnerable. They hadn't been vulnerable to the People of *Big Sal*—or the thousands of Grik they helped defend her from—but they were quite vulnerable to their fears. They were on a hair trigger, and none of the People wanted it to go off pointed at them. Matt now knew Keje chose Chack to send over partly because he had just, somewhat unexpectedly, proven himself a warrior of unusual skill, and Keje believed it took a warrior to evaluate warriors. But the main reason was that no other of his people combined the skill of a warrior—newfound as it was—with anything close to Chack's simple, inherent friendliness. He'd been the perfect choice.

Once aboard, Chack had been his normal, inquisitive, gregarious self, and if not all of *Walker*'s crew was smart enough to realize he was at least as smart as they were, nobody considered him any more dangerous or offensive than a pet monkey. The fact that the Americans had already formed something of a protective attachment toward his people, combined with Chack's engaging ministry and a mutual desire for allies in the face of the Grik threat, had resulted in what was probably the most seamless amalgamation of purpose two races had ever experienced. Let alone two entirely different species. Matt wasn't sure anyone else could have done it. *Walker*'s Asiatic Fleet sailors had been worldly, but also extremely insular. Much like Chack's sea folk or "People of the Homes," they'd seen much of the world as they knew it, but wherever they went, their "home" was still USS *Walker*. Even when they were in foreign ports, they went ashore with people they knew, to visit familiar haunts, and do familiar things—often with familiar results. (Chief among these were hangovers and "social" afflictions.)

Walker, and a fair percentage of her people, had been on the China Station so long that any change in the ordinary routine of life was potentially traumatic. The word that reached them in the wee hours of the Philippine morning of December 8, 1941, had been catastrophic. An endless procession of brutal changes proceeded to destroy the world as they knew it, when they were forced to evacuate the Philippines and participate in chaotic, ill-conceived battles against overwhelming forces. The pitiful remains of the outdated Asiatic Fleet withered under the Japanese onslaught like a candle under a blowtorch. Then, during the mad dash to escape the relentless enemy, the greatest change of all occurred: the Squall that swept them . . . here.

Chack had been a calming influence during the difficult time following their arrival, and everyone now knew he had far greater depths than he'd first displayed. Probably deeper than he'd known himself. Events since then had changed the young Lemurian, matured him beyond his years. He wasn't as gregarious as before, was less engaging and carefree than the Chack they'd first come to know. After all the battles and suffering they'd endured together since that first strange day, it was no wonder. Like all of them, he'd lingered in the hellish heat of the cauldron of battle a little longer than might have been wise, and emerged as something different. Harder, maybe. Similar, but not quite the same. Matt recognized the shift, just as he'd once seen it in himself. At the moment, however, any change was hard to see. Chack was grinning and blinking amusement at something Courtney Bradford had said.

Matt took a bite of the ersatz bacon and contemplated the strange Australian for a moment. Just as he'd been genuinely angry at Silva for taking the self-proclaimed "naturalist" super lizard hunting, he'd actually hesitated to bring Bradford on the mission because he was just too damned valuable to risk. Bradford would have none of it. He'd "suffered in silence" long enough, he claimed. How could Captain Reddy, if he possessed a conscience at all, continue to persecute him by refusing him yet another opportunity for discovery? He'd finally threatened to "feed himself to death" if left behind, and ultimately Matt relented. Not because he thought Bradford was actually willing (or able) to carry out his threat, but he knew Bradford would be an asset to the trip. Not only was he a fair diplomat, but he spoke fluent Latin—the liturgical language of the Sky Priests in which their Sacred Scrolls were transcribed. Also,

Matt had to admit he liked having someone around to bounce ideas off of who didn't look at everything almost solely from a military perspective. Sandra was the only other person who fit that description, and he couldn't have allowed her to come along. For lots of reasons.

He nodded at Spanky, coming in late and sitting down with a plate of food. The engineer was already sweaty and stained, and his slight tardiness wasn't even worth mentioning. There was bound to be a good reason. He missed the other officers who would normally have joined them, but those still alive had remained in Baalkpan to continue defensive preparations. That left space for a few new faces. Acting Lieutenant and Gunnery Officer Charles "Sonny" Campeti was there for the first time, replacing Lieutenants Greg Garrett and Pruit Barry, who'd have command of the first new construction frigates. Campeti looked a little nervous. He'd always dined with the other chiefs in their own, smaller version of the wardroom. He'd get used to it, Matt predicted. Chief Gray had.

The Bosun was the only noncommissioned officer to join them, but ever since the Squall, his presence had been fairly routine. Besides, he wasn't really just the chief bosun's mate anymore. He was something else, ill-defined, but damned important. Of necessity, promotions had rained down on many of the crew, but to what did you promote the Bosun? Only the most senior officers would dare give him an order, even though the most junior 'Cat ensign technically outranked him. "Promoting" him to ensign, or even lieutenant, would be almost like a demotion, practically speaking. So the Bosun remained the Bosun, but his real status was something akin to Spanky's or Dowden's: one of the captain's right-hand men.

As each officer finished his meal, Juan or Mertz swept the dishes away and refilled the coffee cups that remained. The 'Cats couldn't stand the stuff, but their cups were filled with more water or polta juice. There was still a little tea left, something Lemurians had become fiends for, but it was now reserved for special occasions. After Spanky wolfed down his meal (it was a very late breakfast for him, after all), Matt gently tapped his cup with his spoon to get everyone's attention.

"First," he said, "I have some good news. The morning

radio check was successful, and High Chief Nakja-Mur reports the christening of our first new construction frigate. Gentlemen, I give you USS *Donaghey*!" Palms slapped the table all around in satisfaction. Chief Donaghey had been a true hero, sacrificing his life to save his ship. "I've also been informed, although they haven't been launched yet, that the next two frigates will be named after Rick Tolson and Kas-Ra-Ar." The acclaim was even greater than before. Rick and Kas had commanded *Revenge* and had died defending her against overwhelming odds. Ultimately they'd destroyed their ship and all aboard to keep her (and her guns) from falling into enemy hands. Clearly the names were popular choices.

"It's a shame we missed *Donaghey*'s christening, but we should be back in time for the others. I understand *Donaghey* will sail within days, in an attempt to rescue more of Queen Maraan's people from B'mbaado." He glanced at Chack for some reaction, but there was none. Everyone knew he and the B'mbaadan queen were besotted with each other. They also knew that, regardless of risk, she'd accompany the expedition.

"Next, as you know, we should reach Tarakan Island tomorrow morning. The supply ship set out more than a week ago, so she should be waiting for us now. We have much to do there, obviously, but I don't want to linger longer than necessary. We're constrained by time and fuel, so hopefully we can off-load all the equipment and personnel in a single day and be on our way. We still have a long trip ahead of us." The others murmured agreement, and he turned his attention to Shinya. "Chief Gray will be in overall command of the operation. He'll have to coordinate the off-load with Spanky, but once we're gone, he'll be in charge. That being said, have you decided who will command the security force?"

Shinya was silent for a moment, looking at the Bosun. He knew Matt was giving him an out. Of all the crew, Gray had probably maintained his hatred of "Japs" more fiercely than anyone else. In that one respect he seemed almost irrational. Shinya didn't even think it was personal; the man had, after all, once saved his life. But Gray couldn't get over the fact that when they went through the Squall, three months after Pearl Harbor, his son was still listed as missing. The younger Gray had been aboard the USS *Oklahoma*, one of the battleships sunk in the attack. She'd capsized and settled, upside down, to the muddy bottom of the harbor, trapping countless souls aboard. Many had never even known who was attacking them. Even though Shinya hadn't been there, he knew Gray could never forgive him—for being a Jap.

"I will command the security force," he said at last, "if Mr. Gray has no objections." The Bosun only grunted. "Chack will command the Marines remaining aboard the ship."

Matt nodded thoughtfully, noting the tension between the two. It would probably actually be better to leave them both there, he decided, and let them sort things out. He didn't think either would let their animosities interfere with their duties. Besides, if things got out of hand, they were still close enough to Baalkpan for the Bosun to send Shinya home on a supply ship.

"Very well. Fifty Marines will land from the supply ship, and we'll leave twenty of ours behind. That should be more than sufficient to deal with any local menace. I'd highly recommend beginning defensive fortifications, however. Seventy Marines and about a hundred workers from the Sixth Baalkpan might seem a formidable force, but if only one Grik ship should come as far as Tarakan, you'll be outnumbered two to one—and we know the Grik usually operate in threes."

"Of course, Captain Reddy. Defenses will be my first priority."

"Mine too," the Bosun growled.

"Of course. Now, Mr. Bradford, I assume it will be no inconvenience for you to accompany the landing force? Bear in mind your primary duty will be to pinpoint an appropriate place to sink the first well and establish our refinery. Fascinating as I'm sure you'll find them, don't be distracted by every new bug and beetle you come across. I promise you'll have plenty of opportunities to play tourist later on. Just find them a place to drill; then get back aboard."

"I suppose I can delay my explorations for the sake of the war effort," replied Bradford with a rueful grin, "but really, I must protest. Plotting the best spot to drill should not be difficult at all. Tarakan was a veritable island oil well before the war. The Jappos snapped it up right quick, let me tell you!" He glanced at Shinya. "No offense personally, I'm sure! Anyway, the place looked like one great refinery sprouting from the very sea. You could poke a hole in it just about anywhere and find oil, I expect. It's disgraceful how little time you've included in your schedule for scientific discovery."

"Discover a magic twig that, when waved about, will erase the Grik from the world and I shall devote myself to carrying you to unknown shores for the rest of your life," Keje barked, and everyone, even Gray, laughed at that.

"Details, then," said Matt, smiling, and the discussion began in earnest.

A nother beautiful morning dawned over the Makassar Strait, and even before Matt could see much beyond the fo'c'sle, he heard a cry overhead from the crow's nest. Moments later the talker repeated the belated report of the lookout.

"Tarakan Island, sir, off the port bow."

Binoculars swung and Matt raised his own to his eyes. It was difficult to tell, but he thought he could discern a vague, bulky outline of black against the darkness. Slowly, as more light gathered around them, the shape became more distinct.

"Well, gentlemen, it seems we've arrived." He looked at Keje, standing beside him. "You've been this way before; does that look like the coastline in your Scrolls? It doesn't much resemble the Tarakan I remember." The last time *Walker* steamed past the island it was dark, but the only thing protruding from it then were brightly lit wells, tank batteries, refineries, and other works of men. The island before them had none of those things, and was blanketed by a dense, opaque jungle. Keje took the binoculars and studied the land.

"Certainly, but I have never been ashore there, so I can tell you nothing of what to expect. People live near, on the mainland, I am told. . . ." Matt knew that, but questioning them would probably be of little use; the graw-fish gatherers made their harvest in the shallow, swampy river at low tide. There were no graw-fish on the island; the water around it was too deep and the currents too turbulent.

"We'll just have to explore it," Matt replied. "That should make Courtney happy. Besides, as American territory, I suppose it's appropriate."

It had been decided, since the island was to be developed primarily for the American Navy, it should be considered an American possession. That would actually make political and administrative matters easier, since it would add no new High Chief to the budding alliance bureaucracy. It could simply be enfolded into what most considered the "Amer-i-caan Naa-vee Clan," which was already growing by leaps and bounds on this new Earth. Some in the alliance had protested the . . . unorthodox nature of this "clan," since it represented multiple ships, and now a land possession as well, but most realized the war required considerable adjustment to the way things had always been. A few, like Keje, and possibly Queen Maraan, were even beginning to envision the far more radical adjustment of combining the alliance into a unified nation. In any event, there were so many willing recruits for the American Navy, they didn't have the ships for them all. Nakja-Mur was trying to help. Just as Matt gave his first "prize" to Nakja-Mur (*Revenge*) so Baalkpan would have a physical presence in the expeditionary force, some of the prizes they'd captured after the escape from Aryaal had gone to the Americans. Even Nakja-Mur's beloved "new construction" ships were being placed under Matt's authority. The combined alliance would eventually have a navy of its own, but in the meantime, the Amer-i-caan Naa-vee was the "academy," the school where their own people learned their craft, as well as the necessary discipline to employ it.

An example of Matt's "prize" Navy became visible south of the island. It was the "supply" ship USS *Felts*, named for Gunner's Mate Tommy Felts, who died saving Captain Reddy's, Keje's, and Chief Gray's lives at the Battle of Aryaal. *Felts* was actually rated a ship-sloop in the new/old way they'd resurrected of defining such things, since she mounted only twenty guns, but despite her original owners she was a beautiful sight. She was on a tack taking her directly into the morning sun, and Matt shielded his eyes against the glare. The water was an almost painfully brilliant blue, and was still touched by the golden glory of the new day. At present it was still somewhat cool as well. It would soon warm up, and at some point there would almost certainly be rain. Even now, in the distance, a vigorous squall pounded an empty patch of sea. He contemplated it for a moment, as he always did, hopelessly unable to prevent himself from wondering what it had been about the Squall that brought them here that had, well ... brought them here. If they ever entered another with that strange green hue, would it take them back again? Home? He massaged his temples. Would he really want it to?

He shook his head and looked at *Felts*. The former Grik "Indiaman" was now a United States sloop. Her once bloodred hull was painted black, with the exception of the broad white band down her length highlighting the closed black-painted gunports piercing her side. One of Matt's decrees as supreme commander had been, with the exception of "spy" ships that would retain Grik colors, all allied warships (other than the two old destroyers) would be painted in the same scheme that adorned their final sailing cousins on that other Earth long ago. He was glad he'd made that choice. The total difference it made in their appearance went a long way toward divorcing the ships from the terrible creatures who built them, and it was easier to look at them, and live on them, and give them proud names, if their loathsome makers were not so closely associated with them anymore, even by color. And red, the color of blood, was easy to associate with the Grik. Now, in spite of who made her, *Felts* was a heartwarming sight, loping almost playfully along under close-reefed topsails so she wouldn't shoot ahead of the approaching destroyer. Matt could see her barge in the water, coming their way. "Ahead slow," he called to the helmsman. "We'll bring her in our lee as she closes."

The bosun's pipe twittered, and Carpenter's Mate—now Lieutenant (JG)—Sam Clark arrived on deck, followed by his Lemurian sailing master and second in command, Aarin-Bitaak. Clark was from *Mahan*, and had been given *Felts* because of an extensive sailing background. He was raised building boats in his father's shop. Matt, Keje, and Lieutenant Dowden returned his salute.

"Am I glad to see you guys!" Clark exclaimed, then winced and added, "Sirs!" Matt made no comment. He normally didn't discourage familiarity between his officers and himself, but in public, where they now were for all the crew to see, he expected proper behavior. It was as important to morale as it was to discipline. Clark was young and exuberant, and not quite used to being an officer yet. He'd understandably want an assignment like Rick Tolson had had: essentially, harassing the enemy any way he could. He wouldn't enjoy being a freighter, but that was part of the responsibility of command: doing what you were told whether you wanted to or not. Duty was the same for anyone in the Navy, but with command came the added responsibility of inspiring an equally disgruntled crew with the importance of the task. Exuberance must be leavened with introspection, and at least the appearance of calm confidence. Matt suspected Lieutenant Dowden or maybe even the Bosun might slip Clark a word or two before he left.

Clark continued: "We've been tacking back and forth for two days. We tried to anchor, but the tidal race around these islands is something fierce! We had a hard time getting everything ashore."

"I assume you managed?"

"Yes, sir. All baggage and supplies are ashore, and the Marines have established a defensible beachhead." He paused and shook his head. "I have to say, sir, getting the brontosarries ashore was a task I'd sooner not have to repeat." Matt could imagine. Brontosarries were pygmy versions of the dinosaurs they so closely resembled from the fossil record and were indigenous to most of the large regional landmasses. Bradford proposed that one of the reasons their charts were a little off, regarding various coastlines, was that this Earth might be experiencing an ice age of sorts, lowering the sea level. He believed whatever event caused evolution to take such a drastic diversion here was also at work on the planet. Therefore, the seas were not quite so deep as they should be. Perhaps, aeons ago, an even more severe ice age left many of the islands connected in some way. That would explain why brontosarries and other large creatures, clearly unfit for a long swim in such hazardous seas, might be as prolific as they were.

Regardless, the beasts they'd brought were domesticated and "trained"—if such a word could be used regarding a creature with roughly the intelligence of a cow—to provide

motive power for the drilling rig. The task of not only transporting them (small as they were, compared to their ancestors they were still twice the size of an Asian elephant) but
off-loading them and rafting them ashore must have been
harrowing, to say the least. Inexperienced as Clark was, it
spoke well of him that he'd accomplished it.

"Very well." Matt grinned wryly. "We'll try not to delay
you much longer"—the young lieutenant winced again—
"but I'll trouble you for your boats and crew to help us
unload as well."

"Aye, aye, Captain Reddy!"

Clark was right about the tide. When it came in, it did
so with a mounting fury, and when it ebbed, the drop was
equally dramatic. In between, the currents surged and
swirled so violently they were forced to moor the ship fore
and aft (with plenty of water under her keel) to begin off-
loading the large pieces of the rig. This took much longer
than Matt had been prepared for, but there was nothing for
it. Powered boats and launches (*Walker* had all of *Mahan*'s
for this trip, while new ones, using the salvaged engines of
the old, were built at Baalkpan to replace those that were
destroyed) plied back and forth from the beach carrying
supplies and personnel, as well as the smaller parts of the
rig. The heavier pieces were swayed out, causing the ship
to lean noticeably to port, and lowered onto barges and
rafts that were then either towed or heaved ashore by the
monstrous beasts of burden. The loud bellows of the Bosun
and the croaky shouts of the Mice made sure everything
was accomplished as quickly and efficiently as possible, and
by the afternoon watch, the transfer was finally complete.
Matt moved to stand next to Bradford, who leaned on the
bridge wing rail, intently studying the island through his
binoculars. He was clearly impatient to go ashore.

"Take the Mice, Silva, and a dozen Marines, and find a
suitable well site as quickly as you can. Shinya's going to
be tied up with the security situation, but I'm sending the
Bosun to chivvy you along, so don't go chasing lizards and
bugs, clear? Also, the Bosun'll be in charge after we leave,
so make sure you mention any *pertinent* observations you
make to him."

"Absolutely clear, Captain! I'll impart what wisdom I

may . . . and obey Mr. Gray's every whim. But are you certain I mustn't remain here to help? I'm sure there's much I could contribute."

"Absolutely positive. Remember, this is just our first stop. We'll be crossing deep water for the first time. Just imagine the strange creatures we may find on our *next* landfall. Besides, we might even see a 'mountain fish' and get to try our experimental defenses!"

"My God! Of course you're right, Captain. I'll certainly be of more use later on. I fear my current excitement must have addled my thoughts."

"Good. For now, though, prepare to go ashore"—he raised a warning finger—"but don't get sidetracked."

"I don't even know why I'm here, goddamn it!" Dennis Silva complained. "I'm still restricted to the ship!" He gestured at the impenetrable jungle around them. "This look like the ship to you, Bosun?"

Chief Gray shook his head, avoiding another branch Silva let spring back toward his face. "It damn sure don't look like Tarakan Island!" he gruffed. "We steamed right by it when we retreated from the Philippines. It had a lot of oil field equipment, some big sheds, and a few palm trees. . . . Hell, I wasn't expecting that, but I didn't expect to hack my way through steel wool neither!" The large group of men and Lemurians were creeping down a well-used game trail. It was, apparently, the only way to move on the densely forested island. To make matters worse, whatever made the trail couldn't have been taller than a cow, and although it was a minor inconvenience to the 'Cats, the constant crouching and hacking with their cutlasses was hell on the destroyermen.

"How much farther?" Gray asked.

Bradford had stopped to consult a compass. Landmarks were, obviously, out of the question. Sweat dripping from his forehead obscured the dial, and he wiped at it with his sweaty shirt and sighed.

"Can't be much farther now, I'm sure. Bloody island's only ten miles long, from tip to tip! We came ashore south-southwest, and the site I wanted was only about two miles inland. We should be there . . . well, now."

Silva looked around. "Why can't we just burn the bas-

tard off?" He was the tallest in the group and was suffering the most. At one point he'd grumblingly suggested they
name the place "Spanky Land" after *Walker*'s engineering
officer. He didn't say why. They'd been searching for three
hours, but the twists and turns the game trail took made it
impossible to go straight to the spot Bradford wanted.

"That big ape Silva might actually have a point," grumbled Gray. He kicked the mushy jungle floor. "If we could
even get this shit to burn, I'm for trying it. Wait for a day
when the wind is right . . ."

"Outrageous!" Bradford declared. "You're contemplating ecological . . . murder! It would be a crime against nature and humanity to raze this island. I've already glimpsed
many creatures I've never seen on the mainland! They
might exist nowhere else!"

Gray sighed. "If you'd let me finish . . . I wasn't talking
about burning off the whole damn place, just part of it. Besides, you can't tell me there's never been a lightning fire
here. If we do it—if we *can* do it—we'll be careful."

Somewhat mollified, Courtney considered. "Well, yes, that
might work. But you'd have to be very careful indeed."

Silva glanced back at the Bosun and rolled his eyes.
"There wasn't nothin' here on the 'old' Tarakan," he said.

"Well . . . of course not, but that's entirely different."

"How's that?"

"Because," Gray remarked cynically, "there was nothin'
left for him to ogle before. Now there is." His tone changed.
"I'm sorry, Mr. Bradford, but we'll do whatever we have to
to get oil outta this rock. If that means burning the whole
thing down, we will. We'll try to be careful, but the 'needs of
the service,' et cetera, not to mention the needs of our allies
and ourselves, must be met. Now, how much farther?"

Bradford sighed. "I suppose this is as good a place as any.
The captain was adamant that we be back aboard before
nightfall." He glanced absently at his watch, but couldn't
see the numbers through his sweat-streaked glasses. He
took them off and wiped them vainly on his sweat-soaked
shirt.

Suddenly there was a violent commotion to the side of
the trail, and something upright, about the size of a large
crocodile, lunged from its hiding place and snatched one
of the leading 'Cats by the arm. With a shriek of pain and

terror, the Lemurian was dragged into the impenetrable gloom.

"Shit!" Silva bolted forward, even as the others backed away in fright. Several were bowled over by his rush. Another scream marked the place the 'Cat disappeared, and he knelt and fired at a dim shape in the darkness. He fired again and again, on semiautomatic, and his efforts were rewarded by a different type of shriek, and muffled, panicky jabbering. On his hands and knees in the damp mulch, he scurried into the tunnel of brush.

"Well, don't just stand there, you useless sons of bitches!" roared the Bosun. He dashed forward, sweeping all the others, including the Mice and Courtney Bradford, along. More shots, muffled now, sounded from within the hole. Gray crouched at the opening as others fanned out behind him.

"Silva!" he shouted. "Silva, goddamn it! Where are you?"

A moment passed, and a final shot reached their ears. "Here!" came a breathless shout, sounding much deeper in the tunnel than they could credit. "I'm comin' out with the 'Cat, but some of you bastards need to come get my 'trophy.' He ain't much, but I want a better look at him!"

"Is your, ah, 'trophy' quite dead?" Bradford inquired anxiously.

"Yep. But this 'Cat ain't, so you'd better have some first aid ready."

Several moments later Silva's back appeared, and he dragged the moaning, bloodied Lemurian clear. He had him by the scruff of the neck and one arm. The other arm had been savagely mauled. Gray directed their two corpsmen to attend to the wounded 'Cat and then regarded Silva.

"What was it?"

"Not sure," Silva panted. The exertion and excitement had caught up with him. "It's dark in there." He gestured at the 'Cat he'd saved. "Lucky I didn't hit the little guy, but I had to shoot. It was draggin' him down another trail back in all that shit. I don't know, but it looked sort of like a midgety super lizard."

"The method of attack would seem consistent," Bradford agreed, with feeling, "but the size difference . . ."

They ceased speculating, knowing soon they'd see the

creature for themselves. Several Marines had already ducked into the brushy tunnel. Soon they heard panting, and an occasional chittering curse. Whatever they had was heavier than they would have thought after their fleeting glance.

"My word!" Bradford exclaimed, when they finally dragged the dead creature clear. Once everyone could see it, the Marines backed away and acted eager to cleanse themselves. They quickly stooped and grabbed handfuls of moldy mulch, rubbing it between their palms and fingers.

"Lawsy," muttered Isak Rueben, the first word any of the Mice had spoken since they came ashore. They had all, including Tabby, been too preoccupied with gloom over the prospect of at least one of them remaining on this miserable island. The creature before them, adding its blood to the damp soil, looked like nothing they'd seen before. Certainly there were similarities to several others, but taken as a whole, it was unique. Silva's comparison to a small super lizard wasn't without grounds; it had a long tail and coarse, crocodile-like skin, and its physique was similar, on a smaller scale. But its head was smaller in proportion to its body, and the tooth-bristling jaws were longer and slimmer. Its sightlessly glaring eyes were much bigger too, proportionately, and positioned closer to the top of its head—again like a croc—but it had long, powerful forearms with viciously clawed, grasping fingers. The arms were long enough for it to roam on all fours if it wished, but it could obviously use them for grasping or carrying prey. This last reminded them of the "aboriginal" Grik the destroyermen had encountered on Bali—the ones that got Mack Marvaney. Those creatures weighed about two hundred and fifty pounds. This one was closer to four hundred.

Thunder muttered indistinctly, and rain began pattering the canopy above. It would probably be a while before any made its way down to them.

"Raunchy-lookin' booger," Gilbert Yager agreed with his companion.

"Amazing!" Bradford said. "I walk in the very footsteps of Mr. Darwin himself, except here, every land is a Galapagos!" He gestured at Silva's "trophy," its two-foot purple tongue lolling from between its jaws. "Don't you see? This creature probably is the 'super lizard' of this island, filling the exact same ecological niche." He pointed at the diminutive trail. "Smaller island, smaller prey, smaller predators! We've already theorized the hostile sea must prevent dissemination of species on this Earth to a much greater degree than our own, and we find truly similar fauna only on lands that must—quite recently, geologically speaking—have somehow been in contact. But this . . ." He paused in happy contemplation. "This proves lands with no 'recent' physical contact with others might have evolved even more unimaginable species! Just think what creatures might dwell in America or Europe . . . or Australia!"

"Keje's been to Australia; the 'Cats have land Homes there. And yeah, he says they have some goofy-lookin' critters runnin' around," said the Bosun curiously, "so there might be somethin' to what you say. I never was a 'Darwin man' before, especially when it comes to monkeys and folks, but I've had to . . . adjust my thinkin' a little since we came here. How do you get all that just by lookin' at one dead lizard, though, and what difference does it make?"

"Yeah, and who cares?" grumped Isak.

"Look closely, gentlemen; that creature is clearly not an allosaurus gigantus," Brådford said, insisting on his own term for super lizards. "Believe me," he added with feeling, "I *know*!" There were a few chuckles. Even the wounded 'Cat managed a tight grin, while the corpsmen applied the antiseptic paste to his arm and began binding it up. He'd require much more care when they got him to the beach, but the paste was an analgesic as well as an antiseptic, so his pain was under control. "That being said," Bradford continued, "I believe its distant ancestors were. They arrived on this island aeons ago—my ice age theory again!—and when it was separated from the mainland by water, they had to adapt or die. Can you imagine an island this size supporting even one creature as big as the one we took on the pipeline cut near Baalkpan? Of course not. In fact, those that came here must have been smaller to begin with. Over time, they got even smaller, but also evolved other differences to make them more efficient predators within their limited domain. I shouldn't wonder if their metabolisms were slower as well. My point is, besides the scientific interest it inspires, we may not be stuck on a world ruled entirely by the descendants of dinosaurs! On other lands, with different or greater varieties of climates, entirely different creatures—perhaps even mammals—might have risen to the fore . . . and dare I say it? If Mr. Darwin's theories and your own religious teachings are both correct, Mr. Gray, perhaps we might one day find other humans not simply stranded here as we were, but who are indigenous to this world!"

"All that from one dead lizard?" Gray inquired again, with an arched brow and a skeptical tone.

"Well . . . of course, it's a stretch. But I feel quite reanimated by the possibility!"

Ever practical, Silva bit a chaw from a plug of local tobacco. He'd taken to compressing the stuff in the ship's hydraulic press. He kicked the "lizard" in question. "Well, nothin's gonna reanimate this booger!" He stooped to examine the bullet holes. "Took six shots to kill it," he said with the objective air of a professional, "but none of 'em was particularly well aimed. One good shot'll take down a Grik. I expect the same's true with this 'un." He looked at Gray. "They ain't nothin' your boys can't handle. They'll just need to be careful." He glanced toward the sky he couldn't see, then looked at Bradford. "We better reanimate our own asses and get back to the ship before the captain decides he's better off without us after all. If it was just me, I bet he'd already be long gone." He kicked the lizard again, spit on it, and turned back to Gray. "If you want to muck around out here awhile longer, that's fine, but I gotta get Mr. Brain back to the ship. He's gonna want to take his new lizard back to play with," he added resignedly, "so you better give me a detail to drag the damn thing. That just leaves one final question." An evil grin split Silva's face, and he looked at the Mice. "Which one of these squirrely snipes are you gonna keep? You only get one; Spanky's orders, and the captain said so too." He shook his head. "I'd leave all three, except maybe Tabby, and hope they get ate. Tabby's smart enough; we might still straighten her out."

Gray looked at the Mice, standing dejectedly, eyes lowered. "What do you want to do? Flip a coin?"

"There's three of us," Isak objected, "only two sides on a coin. 'Sides"—he glanced fleetingly at his comrades—"we ain't got a coin."

"Tabby's going back to the ship," Gray declared. "She

didn't start working with you two until you had the rig set up. Besides, if we have problems, I want one of you with real experience."

"Ain't fair," Isak almost moaned.

"Yah!" Gilbert agreed, spearing Tabby with a suspicious glare, as if she'd somehow cheated. "That cuts our chances in half!"

Gray rolled his eyes and fished in his pocket, producing a tarnished silver dollar. He looked at it with a strange expression. "Only thing I keep it for," he said softly. "Only thing it's good for anymore."

Parting company with *Felts*, *Walker* steamed east, northeast, then almost due north as the sun sank into the Borneo jungle, beyond Tarakan, off the port quarter. Gilbert Yager sat on the gun platform atop the aft deckhouse near the auxiliary conn. Tabby was beside him, sitting in a similar fashion: legs crossed and elbows on her knees. Both stared glumly at the silhouetted island in the middle distance. Gilbert hadn't seen many sunsets in the last few years; he was usually below when they occurred, and he was immune to any aesthetic appreciation of them in any case. The only significance they generally held for him was, after they took place, the firerooms gradually became a little cooler for a while. But this sunset was remarkable to Gilbert in several ways. It marked the close of a day that had seen a profound change in his everyday life, and change was always bad. For the first time, really, since he'd joined the Navy—since he could remember, in fact—Isak Rueben was not within earshot, and he felt an inexplicable . . . emptiness. He also became aware that he wasn't sure he really even liked Isak very much, and that caused him to spend a moment or two engaged in an extremely uncharacteristic activity: introspection.

He was comfortable around Isak—they were brothers, after all, although nobody aboard had any idea. They shared physical similarities, and that was not unremarked upon, but they had different last names, and apparently no one ever came to the obvious conclusion that they had different fathers. He relied on Isak in many ways; he was the "smart" one who prodded him to join the Navy to escape the oil fields in the first place. He was someone to talk to in a world with few such individuals, except maybe Tabby, now. But did he like him? How would their lives have differed if they'd taken separate paths? Had they held each other back by their self-imposed seclusion? Maybe they'd taken Tabby on only as an experiment to see if they could even make friends. If that was the case, all they seemed to have done to her was create a copy of themselves. She'd become almost as acerbic and insular as they were. Maybe he should use this sunset as a break, a dividing line between his old life and a new one, somehow different. He could take his isolation from his brother, brief as it was supposed to be, and see if he could change himself, make a friend, "get out more," as Spanky always suggested. He would try, he determined, without ever deciding whether he liked his brother or not. That realization would probably come when they saw each other again. Still, invigorating as his decision was, he couldn't help feeling a sense of deep foreboding as he stared at the last light of the setting sun. Something was bound to happen; it always did. Change was never good.

"Let's get sumpin' ta eat," he suggested, and Tabby nodded her head. He suddenly wondered what she'd been thinking. Were her thoughts similar to his? He hoped not. It was suddenly important that she, at least, like him. They climbed down the ladder to the main deck and worked their way forward past the covered holes where the numbers three and four torpedo mounts used to be, past the searchlight tower and the aft two funnels, until they stepped under the raised gun platform/roof over the amidships deckhouse and open-air galley.

A short line leaned on the stainless-steel counter under a window, waiting their turn to snatch a sandwich from a dwindling pile on a large tin platter. The group were mostly humans, since they generally preferred sandwiches to Earl Lanier's cooking. The 'Cats were the other way around; they liked his stews and other concoctions. That was understandable, since he made them from animals and vegetables they were familiar with. The way he cooked them and the seasonings he used were still novel, and they enjoyed that too. Most of the humans liked things they were used to, though, and even if the sandwiches tasted a little strange, they were still sandwiches. As they approached the window, they heard Lanier heaping abuse on those he was serving.

". . . wouldn't have to build so many goddamn sammiches if you bastards'd eat real food!"

"You ain't cooked real food since you was in the Navy!" retorted Paul Stites.

"Why don't you fry me up one of your fishes?" taunted another man. Lanier was known to fish over the side when the occasion permitted, because he was deeply devoted to fish—and he couldn't stand to eat the other stuff he cooked either. Some of his fishing exploits had become legendary, and a few of the creatures he'd brought from the depths had even provoked desperate gunfire.

"Be a cold day . . . here . . . before I waste one of my beauties on you ungrateful turds. You wanna eat fish? Catch 'em yourselves and cook 'em on the boiler burners!"

Tabby reached the platter next, behind the laughing destroyermen, and took a sandwich. Gilbert snagged another, then paused. Isak was the one who usually instigated conversation, but he thought he'd give it a try. He leaned in the window and saw Lanier's massive shape within, sitting on a creaky wooden chair, while Ray Mertz and a black-and-white 'Cat Earl called "Pepper" assembled another platter of sandwiches.

"Ah, how's repairs to the Coke machine goin', Earl?" Gilbert inquired, expecting a diatribe. He was surprised when Lanier's face brightened from its customary glower.

"Purty good." He gestured beyond the bulkhead Yager leaned on, and the fireman turned to look at a bench behind him upon which the treasured Coke machine had lain in state ever since it was killed in action against the Japanese. Lanier had clearly been working on it, and many of its internal parts were restored. There hadn't been any Cokes for months, even before it was destroyed, but the crew had taken perverse comfort from the fact that, no matter how bad things got, the Coke machine still worked. When splinters from a Japanese shell eviscerated it during their final torpedo attack on *Amagi*, after *Nerracca* was destroyed, the crew took its loss disproportionately hard.

"Compressor's back in, and most of the lines are patched. Won't be long before I try some ammonia in her. Cross your fingers!"

"Will do, Earl," Gilbert said fervently, and stepped away, still looking at the battered remnant of another world.

"It'd be a fine thing if it was workin' again," he almost whispered.

"Why?" asked Tabby around a mouthful of sandwich, her long whiskers festooned with crumbs. "You say ain't no Cokes. I never had me no Cokes. Why fix thing to keep something cold . . . there ain't none of?"

"We could use it to cool other stuff," Gilbert defended. "Besides . . ." He thought of comparing it to a pet, but Lemurians thought the very idea of keeping pets was silly—for good reason. There weren't many animals on this world that would make suitable—or survivable—pets. Much as they treasured their Homes, on land or sea, they didn't seem particularly sentimental over inanimate objects, either. They did take trophies, though. "Think of it like a necklace of Grik claws. When the Japs busted it, it was like the string on the necklace broke and you couldn't wear it no more. Fixin' the Coke machine is like fixin' the string." He knew it wasn't a very good comparison—"analogy" was a word he'd never encountered—but it seemed to suffice, and Tabby nodded apparent understanding.

"I see. You captured Coke machine from God-daam Jaaps?"

Gilbert closed his eyes and shook his head. He was about to correct her when he was interrupted.

"There you are, you little twerps!"

He looked up and saw Laney standing before him, hands on hips, a grossly oversize affectation of Spanky's authoritative pose.

"What do you think yer doin'? Both of you was supposed to be on watch!"

"We been ashore, Laney," Gilbert grated. "You know, with the *shore* party."

Laney's face clouded. "That don't cut no ice with me. I don't care if you been 'rasslin' sea monsters, you'll stand your watches when you're told! And that's 'Chief' Laney to you slacking malingerers!"

"We ain't lingerin'; we just got here. We's eatin' and movin' along. Earl didn't yell at us for lingerin'."

"Just . . . get your asses down to the aft fireroom, and get that goose-pull sorted out. Most of them 'Cats can't tell fuel oil from bilgewater. And check on that damn feed-water pump! It's still makin' screwy noises!"

"All right, Laney, quit yer fussin'. We'll be along." Gilbert sighed and began wolfing his sandwich down. Laney stood a moment, still cloudy, then moved away. Gilbert couldn't help but compare his tyrannical attitude to poor old Chief Donaghey's. Donaghey had been a professional who inspired proper behavior and diligence by example, as well as an inherent ability to lead. He didn't lord it over the snipes in his division, and he was usually as grimy as they were because he worked alongside them. He'd been in the Asiatic Fleet a lot longer than Laney too. Volunteered for it. Even had a Filipino wife . . . back there. Everyone knew his worth, even the captain, and when he was killed saving the ship from an improvised mine, Captain Reddy was prepared to risk the very alliance to avenge him.

Now they had Laney.

"Like I've said, change is always bad," he muttered.

Matt paced slowly between the starboard bridge wing and his chair, bolted to the right side of the forward pilothouse bulkhead. It was how he spent the majority of his time on the bridge, particularly over the last six days. He believed the smudge of land he'd seen off the starboard bow was the poignantly familiar Dumagasa Point, on the western peninsula of Mindanao; the sextant said it was, so did the scriggly lines on the Plexiglas over the chart, but it didn't look quite the same as he remembered it. Funny. He'd been to Surabaya—now Aryaal—and Balikpapan—now Baalkpan—and they bore no resemblance whatsoever to the places he'd known, but somehow the only slightly different promontory they'd passed filled him with a new sense of loss. Perhaps because they were entering what had once been considered *Walker*'s "home" waters.

Ahead lay the Philippines—which he'd never even liked. The place was too sudden and too big a change from his native Texas, where he'd returned after being discharged during a force reduction frenzy. Then, when the worldwide threat loomed ever larger, he'd been snatched back up by the Navy and immediately sent to the, to him, already alien land. The Philippines, at least the parts frequented by Navy ships, had been a den of iniquity paralleled only by those parts of China the Navy had even then been evacuating. The short, brown people jabbered in Tagalog, or a version of Spanish he could barely comprehend. The military situation was clearly unequal to the growing Japanese threat, and those in charge didn't seem to care, or tried to pretend the threat didn't exist. When hostilities commenced, the incompetent, almost slapstick response would have been hilarious if it hadn't been so tragic. The litany of mistakes that rendered the islands indefensible was without end, and was itself indefensible. It still made him sick to remember how the formidable airpower gathered there, which alone could have made such a huge difference, had been so criminally squandered.

He had to remind himself that many of the crew felt quite differently. To some, the Philippines had been paradise. The waterfront had been a place they could find anything their hearts desired, where they could slake any thirst or lust if they chose, or set themselves up almost like gentlemen on their comparatively munificent wages. Of course, quite a few knew the islands far better than he, and spent their time away from the waterfront, where the atmosphere of iniquity prevailed. In the suburbs or the country, they could find virtuous women and homes where they could settle down and forget the stress of their duty. He wondered how their approach might affect the men who'd loved it there, had expected to retire there and spend the rest of their lives with women they loved. Women who weren't there anymore.

During the last six days, counting the time they'd lingered at Tarakan, *Walker* had left her new "home waters" of the Makassar Strait, and entered the Celebes Sea. Their average speed was reduced, by necessity, from the almost twenty knots they were gratified to learn their ship could still make on two boilers, to less than ten, and finally to the excruciatingly slow pace of six knots. They'd picked their way through the tangled, hazardous islands off the northeast coast of Borneo, before tentatively beginning their island-hugging journey through what the Americans still called the Sulu Archipelago. They had finally, that morning, increased speed back to fifteen knots, but would likely have to slow again. The sea was shallower than it should be, and they couldn't entirely trust their old charts anymore. Six long, torturous days, and according to the landmarks, and Keje's and Dowden's calculations, they were only about halfway to their destination. He rubbed his face and wished Juan would hurry with the coffee he'd promised.

This tedious, circuitous route was intended to allow them to avoid the abyssal depths of the Celebes and Sulu seas—and the monstrous creatures that dwelt there. Among those they were trying to avoid was one so huge it actually posed a significant threat to ships as large as Lemurian Homes. "Mountain fish" they were called by some, or "island fish" by others. Whichever it was, it made no difference. The name was not idle exaggeration. Matt had never seen one, nor had anyone who'd been aboard *Walker* since the Squall. Jim Ellis and the crew of *Mahan* swore they'd been *chased* by one when that ship attempted to cross to Ceylon while under the deluded command of the now lost Air Corps captain named Kaufman. *Mahan* was badly damaged at the time, and could barely make fifteen knots. Ellis still insisted the fish nearly got them, and was convinced only the shoaling water discouraged it. Impossibly big *and* fast. The Lemurians were just as insistent that if the thing had indeed caught *Mahan*, if it was mature, it could certainly have seriously damaged or even destroyed the three-hundred-foot destroyer—iron hull or not.

They had a few "surprises" if they met a mountain fish on this trip, but Captain Reddy hoped they wouldn't be needed. Discovering whether they worked was important, particularly in the long term, but making it to Manila and securing an alliance was of first importance, and they couldn't risk damage to the ship before that was achieved. Bradford was disappointed, and Matt was anxious to complete their mission, but so far the daily radio transmissions left them reassured that the Grik remained quiescent, content to consolidate their hold on Aryaal and make repairs to the damaged Japanese battle cruiser. USS *Donaghey* had begun her maiden voyage—another trip to take more of Queen Maraan's people off B'mbaado—and maybe she'd have something to report in a week or so. In the meantime, there seemed no reason to rush, so they chose the safest, most conservative course that left them least exposed to the giant fish.

Fortunately, the things were pretty serious about avoiding shallow water, "shallow" being anything under three hundred feet or so. The Makassar Strait was considerably deeper than that, but the 'Cats believed the hundred-mile width of the strait was too confining for the monsters. Usually. They were known to haunt the deep water of the Celebes and Sulu seas, however. They cruised along with their mouths open wide, much like the blue whales Matt was familiar with that constantly ingested swarms of krill to sustain their tremendous bodies. Mountain fish were similar in principle, except the "krill" they consumed was anything else that swam in the sea, up to and including the huge plesiosaurs the Lemurians called "gri-kakka." Matt had seen gri-kakka as large as sperm whales.

For obvious reasons there weren't many mountain fish, and the estimated half dozen or so that could sustain themselves in a body of water the size of the Celebes Sea were highly territorial. They didn't migrate, as far as anyone could tell, which meant they must not have to eat all the time, because the majority of their prey did move from place to place. Regardless of the hopefully effective "surprises" *Walker* had in store for the immense creatures, Matt was perfectly content to leave them in peace as long as they extended the same courtesy to his ship.

Juan finally arrived with his coffee, and he took the cup with gratitude. Vile as the stuff was, it might help keep him awake. In spite of what Juan might think, he hadn't been sleeping well. There'd been no recurrence of the old dream that once eluded him so, not since *Nerracca*'s destruction, but it had been replaced by others, ones he remembered when they woke him. The difference, he now knew, between the old dream and the ones that plagued him now was significant. Before, he'd been tormented by a sense of loss and failure—guilt, almost, that they'd survived that long-ago flight from the Japanese juggernaut when their consorts, *Exeter*, *Encounter*, and *Pope*, were all rubbed out by the relentless enemy. That they could do nothing to help, not even slow to pick up survivors, haunted him still. But the destruction of *Nerracca* and the thousands aboard her put that previous loss in perspective. They'd rescued some survivors from *Nerracca*, but only a tithe, and the hopelessness of saving more and the risk of what little they'd done in the face of *Amagi*'s guns finally galvanized his subconscious agony with a burning hatred for their foes, old and new: the Grik, and the Japanese allied with them.

He dreamed of frantic orders and desperate attempts to save all they could, of bright, distant muzzle flashes and towering geysers of spume. Blood-streaked bodies and mangled flesh aboard his own ship, where some of the enemy's fury found its mark, a swirling typhoon of raging flames consuming the gallant Home as shells continued to fall—these were the dreams that tormented him now, but they didn't leave him weak; they goaded him to revenge. A revenge that would be complete only when the Grik were exterminated forever, and *Amagi* lay broken on the bottom of the sea.

His thoughts must have been evident on his face, because a familiar, gruff voice interrupted his reverie.

"It's an important mission," Keje said. He and Adar had approached unnoticed. They were both given the privileges of officers aboard his ship, and hadn't asked permission to come on the bridge.

"I know. And it's a good idea. We're going to need all the help we can get to beat the lizards once and for all. I hope we can stir some up." He smiled with little sincerity and lowered his voice so only his Lemurian friends could hear. He knew they were at least as passionate about their task as he. "I guess I'm just a little antsy."

"Antsy," tried Keje. "It means nervous, but not afraid, correct?"

"Sort of."

"Hmm. A new word to add to a new phrase I learned from Mr. Braad-furd today. He just said he came up here to speak to you about his new liz-aard." He wrinkled his nose. "What a stench! Must he dismember his toys so close to the galley? Mr. Laan-ier has threatened his life! In any event, he told us you did not even notice his presence, that you were in a 'brown study,' whatever that might be."

"Is it much like 'antsy'?" Adar asked.

Matt's smile turned genuine. "Maybe a little. I think 'brown study' is more like 'thinking disturbing thoughts.' Add 'antsy' to it, and I guess that's a pretty good description." He sipped his coffee and grimaced. It had grown cold.

"I am 'antsy' as well," Adar confessed. "Reports from home are reassuring, yet . . . perhaps too reassuring?"

Matt nodded. "The farther we get from home, the more

I think how unlike the Grik it is for them to just sit pat and goof around. Their warriors might be mindless killing machines, but there's a brain behind them, something that aims them and turns them loose. Those Hij. Just think of the logistics required to support a force their size, to equip it and build the ships to move it." He shook his head. "I just can't shake the feeling that they're up to something."

They finally knew a little about their enemy now, thanks to the charts, logbooks, and other papers they'd captured aboard their various prizes. They'd even taken a few of the enemy alive for a change, although no information had been forthcoming from them. They'd seemed insane, but with no comparisons they couldn't confirm that. Regardless, the prisoners all died within days of being placed in captivity, either from the wounds that let them be captured, or other unknown causes. But some information had been gleaned. They'd discovered before, to their horror, that a lot of Grik formal correspondence was printed in English. Whatever bizarre language they spoke, English seemed their official or liturgical written language, much as Latin served the 'Cats. For the Grik, however, English was a captured language they'd probably adopted of necessity to make sense of the information they'd captured with the East Indiaman so long ago. Matt felt a twinge when he thought about how those ancient British mariners must have been persuaded to reveal their secrets. Latin was given to the Lemurians willingly, from two other East Indiamen that decided to sail east instead of west, after all three came to this world the same way *Walker* had. They'd apparently used Latin so only approved information could be funneled to the 'Cats, and not just anybody aboard could communicate with them. Fortunately, the westbound ship had been stripped of her guns and powder.

In any event, they still didn't know what drove the Grik to such extremes of barbarity, but they'd learned a little about their social structure from the captured documents. For example, they now knew the average Grik warrior came from a class referred to as Uul, and they possessed primary characteristics strikingly similar to ants or bees. Some were bigger than others, some more skilled at fighting. Some even seemed to have some basic concept of self. All, however, were slavishly devoted to a ruling class called the Hij, who manipulated them and channeled and controlled their instinctual, apparently mindless ferocity. There were different strata of Hij as well. Some were rulers and officers; others were artisans and bureaucrats. Regardless of their position, they constituted what was, for all intents and purposes, an elite aristocracy collectively subject to an obscure godlike emperor figure. Nothing more about their society was known.

The Hij were physically identical to their subjects, but were clearly intelligent and self-aware to a degree frighteningly similar to humans and their allies. They didn't seem terribly imaginative, though, and so far that had proved their greatest weakness.

"We know they plan to attack us at Baalkpan. Isn't that enough?"

Matt looked at Keje and sighed. "I don't think so. I don't *feel* so." He watched the men and 'Cats working on the foredeck under the glowering gaze of Silva and Chack. Both stood side by side, hands on their hips, occasionally trading comments. Silva, in his stained khakis and battered hat, towered above the furry, muscular, brindled 'Cat in the red kilt and white T-shirt. For now, in his bosun's-mate persona, Chack had traded his usual helmet for a white cotton "Dixie cup" hat like most of the enlisted destroyermen wore. Silva, in exasperation, moved to show a group of 'Cats how to run a long shaft with a bristle brush down the muzzle of the number one gun. For a moment he was partially obscured by the patched and dented splinter shield, but then he stepped back, evidently watching his pupils perform the task. He shouted instructions that were swallowed by the wind before they reached the bridge, then nodded. A few moments later the big chief gunner's mate returned to where Chack was standing, Wiping his brow with a rag, he resumed their conversation.

It struck Matt again how harmoniously the two races worked together. Once, not long ago, some of his destroyermen might have objected to sharing their labor, berthing spaces, even the drinking fountain on the side of the huge, ridiculously exposed refrigerator on deck, with another human who just happened to be a different color. Now those same men worked companionably alongside "people" of an entirely different species. He was gratified there'd been so few instances of racism—none at all after the mysterious disappearance of a certain *Mahan* crew member, who'd reportedly been something of a problem—but he couldn't help being amused by the irony. He knew the camaraderie of his integrated crew would be tested, eventually, in the cauldron of combat, and he believed it would withstand the test; humans and Lemurians had fought well together so far. But the coming test seemed so far beyond their capacity. No matter how well they got along, or how well trained they were when the Grik—and *Amagi*!—finally came in force, they were just too few and *Walker* too frail. Strangely, though, he no longer dreaded the inevitable confrontation; he almost welcomed it . . . but he *was* antsy.

Nothing yet, Cap-i-taan," hailed the muted, yowly voice of the Lemurian lookout in the mizzen-top above. Lieutenant Greg Garrett, former gunnery officer of USS *Walker*, now captain of the brand-new sailing frigate USS *Donaghey*, could barely discern the speaker from the predawn gloom, but knew the lookout's eyesight was much better than his own. With watchers at all three mastheads, the little flotilla of refugee-laden barges would undoubtedly be seen as soon as it pushed off from shore. He paced the length of the darkened quarterdeck. The almost entirely Lemurian crew went about their duties professionally, quietly, leaving him room to pace and think. He paused for a moment by the smooth, polished rail and peered intently at the hazy shore. *Donaghey* was hove to, with nothing to do but wait, less than two miles from the treacherous breakers.

The ship was Garrett's first command, and he loved her for that, but he also loved her classic lines and intrinsic beauty. He was highly conscious of the singular honor of being named her first commander. Those given the "prize ships" could never quite get over who made them. The barbaric nature and practices of their previous owners, and the acts performed aboard them, tainted them forever, regardless of how well they were scrubbed. They'd been found adrift, mostly, damaged by *Walker*'s guns during her escape from Aryaal and the battle that cost them *Nerracca*. Boarding parties faced ferocious, if uncoordinated defenders, but some of the Grik "survivors" went into an apparently mindless panic Bradford called "Grik Rout," and simply leaped over the side. No one would ever know for certain how many defenders there'd actually been. Hundreds were slain in the brutal fighting aboard the several ships, but more met their fate in the sea, and the water around the ships had churned as the voracious "flashies" fed. Allied losses had been high, particularly when they fought to rescue any Lemurian "livestock" they found chained in the enemy holds. Just as when they first captured *Revenge*, the sights they saw in those dark, dank abattoirs prevented the ship's new owners from ever being able to love them.

No such stigma clung to USS *Donaghey*, and her people loved her unreservedly. She was larger than the prizes, with a more modern and extreme hull configuration that, combined with her more efficient sail plan, made her considerably faster than the enemy ships. She was a true frigate too, being armed with twenty-eight precious, gleaming guns.

Unfortunately, she was one of only three such ships likely ever to be built. She was considered a transition, a stopgap. Future variants would combine steam and sails and therefore sacrifice some of their purity and grace. But this was war, and one took every advantage one could when the consequence of defeat was extinction.

They'd bloodied the enemy at Aryaal and in the following actions, but if the charts they captured showing the extent of the enemy holdings were to be believed, the Grik could quickly replace their losses. They apparently bred like rabbits, and according to Bradford's theories, their young reached mature lethality in about five years. If the remaining Americans and their allies were to have any chance of survival—not to mention victory—they needed innovation. That was why there were so few humans in Garrett's crew. Combined, the surviving destroyermen from *Walker* and *Mahan* numbered just a little over a hundred and twenty. Forty were still aboard *Walker*, and twenty or so were on *Mahan*. The rest were involved in various projects and training regimens they'd need to build the army and navy they needed to survive. The skills and experience of every last destroyerman had become not only essential, but irreplaceable. Garrett found it ironic at times that the ragtag remnants of the Asiatic Fleet who'd wound up in this place—men once considered by some to be the dregs of the Navy—were now an indispensable, priceless resource. They were the core, the innovators, the trainers of the native force needed to see them through, and there were not nearly enough hands and minds for all the work.

Certainly great work had already been accomplished. They'd transformed the nomadic, insular, and, in some cases, fiercely isolationist Lemurians into seasoned, professional soldiers and sailors. But their ranks had been horribly thinned as well. Recruitment was constant, and hopefully Captain Reddy's diplomatic mission to the land that had been the Philippines would bear fruit. In the meantime, they had to make do with what they had, and there just weren't enough of them. Part of Greg's current assignment was to try to remedy that to some small degree.

When the Grik armada swept down from Singapore and forced the Allied Expeditionary Force to abandon the city of Aryaal, as well as the island of B'mbaado, Aryaal had been thoroughly evacuated, but there'd been little time. Hundreds, perhaps thousands had been left behind on the island, and its queen protector, Safir Maraan, had sworn to get them out. So had the Americans. Therefore, a series of stealthy nighttime missions had been undertaken to rescue as many B'mbaadans as they could from under the very snouts of the Grik. So far there'd been few incidents or encounters, and quite a few refugees had been carried away. The Grik were not yet as thick on the island as they might have been. The cream of a portion of their invasion force had been mauled by *Walker* on its way to Baalkpan. Only about half of their "Grand Swarm" had been diverted to Java, and when the rest were turned back, they became busy repairing *Amagi*, consolidating their gains, and rebuilding the walls and fortifications of the cities the retreating force had destroyed. That meant *Donaghey* "only" had to avoid around two hundred and fifty ships and a hundred and fifty or sixty thousand crazed, ravenous warriors. But again, so far it had been a snap. Over the last couple of months Jim Ellis had made several trips in command of one of the prize ships, and either the Grik were unaware the missions were taking place, or they just didn't care. Their ships seemed content to remain at anchor in Aryaal/B'mbaado Bay, and let the rescuers come and go at will. Perhaps they just didn't know there was still a sizable number of Lemurians clustered on the southeastern shores of B'mbaado. Greg Garrett felt relieved, but also strangely cheated. His new ship was more than a match for any Grik ships yet encountered, and he yearned to strike a blow.

Before the war began, the Grik had no concept of gunpowder, and their artillery was limited to a ballistic device that hurled clay pots full of incendiary substances. "Grik Fire," it was called. Garrett would have loved nothing more than to pound a few Grik ships into floating splinters and send a few hundred of their warriors to the ravenous, waiting jaws of the hungry fish. At the same time, he'd seen enough of war by now to know that once any battle was joined, there was no way to predict what would happen. Every encounter carried a measure of risk, and in this war, surrender wasn't an option. Much as he yearned to lash out against their loathsome enemies, he'd be content with the successful and uneventful completion of his mission.

He paced the quarterdeck again, conscious that he might appear nervous, but he couldn't help himself. In addition to his mission, he'd also been entrusted with the safety of the headstrong Queen Maraan, who'd personally gone ashore to gather her people, and Pete Alden, once a simple sergeant and now the commander of all allied land forces, who'd accompanied her. Safir Maraan could usually take care of herself. She was a charismatic leader and a skilled warrior in her own right, but those were the very qualities that made her too precious to risk. At least, as far as Garrett was concerned. Not to mention that he personally liked her quite a lot, and she was betrothed to his friend Chack-Sab-At. In spite of a clear understanding of her important role, Safir Maraan remained committed to an oath she'd sworn to personally rescue the people she'd left behind, no matter the cost. To her, no role could supersede that of queen protector of B'mbaado.

Pete Alden accompanied her for little good reason Greg could see, besides imposing a measure of vigilance and reason upon her. In military matters she'd acknowledged him as her superior, and he probably hoped he could prevent her from doing anything rash if the rescue met with difficulty. That was how he justified it, anyway. Garrett thought there might be more to it. In spite of being their land force commander, Pete had mostly been on the sidelines of the war so far. He'd participated in the boarding action that captured *Revenge*, but since then he'd been consumed by the necessity of improving Baalkpan's defenses. He'd missed the Battle of Aryaal, and Garrett sensed a supreme unwillingness on the Marine's part to send others into situations he hadn't shared. Going ashore in this instance probably had as much to do with that as anything else. Besides, this mission was their last, and Queen Maraan's great general, Haakar-Faask, would come off with the final refugees and warriors he'd managed to gather, and Pete probably wanted to greet him personally. In any event, there were far more precious eggs in a dangerously exposed basket this morning than Greg Garrett would have liked.

High clouds appeared as wispy pink tendrils in the eastern sky, and the shore party was considerably overdue. Daylight might reveal the solitary ship to searching eyes, and just because the Grik hadn't interfered with previous missions didn't mean that would remain the case.

"They should have returned by now," murmured Taak-Fas. The 'Cat was *Donaghey*'s sailing master, and Garrett's second in command. Garrett turned to look at the brown-and-tan-furred officer. As usual, the strikingly feline face bore no expression, but his voice betrayed growing anxiety.

Garrett replied with a quick nod. "She's pulled stunts like this before," he said with a sigh. "Jim—Lieutenant Ellis—said she did it twice when he brought her here. She won't leave anyone behind who's at the appointed rendezvous. I can't blame her, but this waiting sure is nerve-racking."

"Why can't the refugees just wait for us on the beach, and meet us when the shore party goes in for them?" The question came from Russ Chapelle, former Torpedoman First Class from *Mahan*, and now *Donaghey*'s gunnery officer, or master gunner. He'd stepped up to join the conversation.

Taak-Fas shook his head. "Grik scouts might see them while they wait for us. Also, since our ships look similar to the enemy's, even painted differently, it might be difficult to persuade some civilian refugees to come out if we didn't meet them at an inland rendezvous."

"On deck," came a sudden cry from above. "Three barges in the surf."

Russ grinned with relief. "Well. All that good worryin' wasted."

It was much lighter now. Garrett raised his binoculars and studied the three wide-beamed boats laboring through the breaking waves. They were packed to overflowing with Lemurians of every color. Most looked thin and haggard. *Understandable*, he mused grimly, *after all they've had to endure*. He focused the binoculars on a figure standing in the bow of the center barge, and could just make out the black-furred form of Queen Maraan, resplendent in her silver breastplate and helmet. Alden's distinctive, imposing form was beside her, as was a 'Cat wearing battered armor over a stained leather smock that stood almost as tall as the Marine. "It's about time," he grumped. "Have the boarding nets rigged, and prepare to bring them aboard. As soon as they have been, we'll make sail. Shape a course for Baalkpan." He paused and grinned at his subordinates. "We've been goofing around here long enough."

Just then, another cry came from the masthead.

"Sail! Two sails . . . Three!"

"Where away?" Garrett shouted. For a moment the lookout fumbled with the words. Most of *Donaghey*'s crew could speak at least a little English by now, but sometimes the nautical terms of the Americans were confusing. The ones pertaining exclusively to square-rigged ships were still awkward even for Greg. He'd had little sailing experience back home, and competent as he'd forced himself to become, most of his knowledge of sailing terms, practices, and commands came from an old book entitled *A Manual for Young Sea Officers in the Service of Her Majesty's Navy*. The book, like so many others they'd found of use, was a legacy of *Walker*'s long-dead surgeon, Doc Stevens, and his eclectic library. It was authored by a retired British admiral in the 1870s, during the transition to steam-powered warships that still used sails as well as engines.

"Port . . . ? Port bow."

Garrett redirected his binoculars and thought he saw something against the purple horizon, but wasn't sure. The lookout was certain, however, and he trusted the 'Cat. He glanced aloft at the floating pennant and turned until the wind blew directly in his face. "Not good," he said aloud to himself. "They have the wind in their favor."

"So what?" Chapelle shrugged. "What are they gonna do? If they get too close we'll blow the hell out of them."

Garrett spared him a glance. "If they get here before the boats do, they could stop us from loading the refugees. They might even attack the boats themselves."

Chapelle's eyebrows rose. "You want me to get ready for them?"

"By all means. Clear for action and sound general quarters."

A rapid, rhythmic gonging reverberated through the ship as the general alarm bell was struck. The tense mood of anticipation clutching the crew since before dawn was shattered by frenzied but purposeful activity. The decks were sanded, and overhead netting was rigged to protect against falling debris. Buckets with ropes attached were dropped over the side and hauled back aboard, filled with seawater. These were distributed around the deck and sent up to the tops to defend against enemy firebombs. Guns were loaded and run out, and soon the smell of smoldering slow match reached Garrett's nose. Marines lined the quarterdeck rail with their bows, and the few armed with Krag rifles scampered into the tops, prepared to pick off the enemy officers. *Donaghey*'s well-drilled crew prepared for battle very quickly, but by the time they were finished, the enemy was clear to see from deck, and the brightening sun shone upon the leaning pyramids of canvas.

Chapelle rejoined Garrett on the quarterdeck. "Taking their time," he observed, referring to the barges still laboring against the offshore swells. Dripping oars flashed in the morning sun, and Garrett glassed the figure with the flowing black cape and silver armor. She was staring in the direction of the approaching ships.

"They're coming as fast as they can," Garrett said.

Taak-Fas gauged the distance. "They will not reach us much before the enemy, if they do at all." He sounded worried.

"Yeah. This could get tricky," Garrett agreed. "If it looks like they aren't going to make it, we'll secure the boarding nets. I don't want to make a present of them for the Grik." He turned and saw the shocked expression on Chapelle's face. "No, we won't abandon them! We'll stand toward the enemy and destroy them, then come back for our people." Garrett shook his head and turned his back on his gunnery officer. The former *Mahan* torpedoman didn't know him very well, but it irked him that the man thought it even possible he might leave anyone at the "mercy" of the Grik. Let alone anyone as important as Queen Maraan and Pete Alden.

"Damn lizards are really flyin'," Chapelle muttered a few moments later. "They must know what we're up to. Afraid we're going to steal their 'rations,' I guess." He spit a yellowish stream of the local tobacco juice over the side.

Garrett nodded, but didn't take his eyes off the approaching ships. Something wasn't right. The Grik were notorious for their single-minded aggressiveness. The all-out frontal assault, regardless of losses, had seemed to be the only military tactic they knew before and during the Battle of Aryaal. Since then, however, whenever they encountered an Allied ship, they'd demonstrated an uncharacteristic caution and respect. Garrett suspected they were capable of learning from their mistakes, and believed the Hij commanders of the Grik fleet had figured out that tangling with artillery-armed allied ships without overwhelming numbers was pointless. Up till now his suspicions had been confirmed, but the three Grik vessels approaching from the northwest were really cracking on. They were coming on in the "same old way," and he couldn't help but wonder why.

He carefully studied the laboring boats. The oarsmen had redoubled their efforts when they saw the Grik, but their progress against the wind and current was excruciatingly slow. He yearned to move *Donaghey* closer in, but the shoals here were treacherous, and, deprived of engines, he'd already gained a healthy respect for a lee shore. Totally at the mercy of the wind, *Donaghey* might be driven aground. He refocused on the enemy. Chapelle was right: they were flying. With another last look at the boats, he lowered the binoculars to his chest.

"They're not going to make it," he stated flatly. "Secure the nets and signal Her ... Highness ... and Sergeant—I mean *General* Alden that we'll return to pick them up as soon as we've dealt with the enemy."

"Aye, sir," Taak-Fas replied with a frown. Unease over the brazen Grik advance was affecting him too, but it didn't show in his voice when he relayed Garrett's order at the top of his lungs. Chapelle spit again, and his lips formed an ironic grin, slightly distorted by the chaw in his cheek.

"I'm afraid we're gonna get our brand-new ship all scratched up, Skipper."

Safir Maraan, queen protector of the People of B'mbaado, representative to the Allied Council and general in what she liked to think of as the Allied Army of Liberation, watched with dread as the three Grik warships slanted swiftly down toward *Donaghey*. Quietly she urged the exhausted oarsmen to even greater effort. A few civilian refugees wailed with fright, but the sailors, warriors, and Marines at the oars made no complaint. They merely reached down and somehow grasped the final measure of their flagging reserve of strength. The gunwales creaked and timbers groaned as the panting Lemurians heaved against the disorganized swells.

"A signal from *Donaghey*," observed Haakar-Faask, captain of Safir's personal guard of six hundred, sometimes called the "Orphan Queen's Own," and general of the army of B'mbaado, who stood beside her in the front of the boat. He rolled his massive, muscled shoulders and regarded Pete with a steady gaze. "What does it say?"

Pete Alden scratched his bristly black beard and stared, his eyes shaded by his battered, faded fatigue cover. "They mean to engage the enemy and return for us."

Safir responded with a curt blink of her wide, silver-gray eyes. "I have learned the Amer-i-caan signals, Captain," she said, addressing Faask by his Guard rank, which in both their estimations was superior and more intimate than his other. "Allow the rowers to rest, but let us try to maintain our position."

"As you command, Queen Protector," Faask replied in a pious tone that made her snort.

"Now he obeys me," she said aside to Pete. "He was insubordinate enough on earlier missions, when I ordered him to come out to the ship."

Haakar-Faask had been her personal protector since the day she was born, and he often behaved more like a long-suffering elder brother, or even father, than she would have liked. Often. She loved him as she would have her father or brother if they'd lived, but sometimes his obsessive protectiveness could be infuriating. She'd left him behind—ordered him to stay—to gather and organize the people they'd been forced to abandon during the hurried evacuation of their homeland, and she'd been torn by anguish and missed him terribly. Compared to his former mighty self, he was weak and malnourished like the other refugees, but in spite of her efforts to protect him for a change, he'd immediately resumed his former role. She glanced at his still-powerful form and realized for the first time, with a quick stab of grief, that not only had he suffered from deprivation in the months since the evacuation, he was getting old.

"As I *command*," she said with a false, triumphant grin, stressing the word.

Haakar-Faask regarded her with an innocent stare. "I have seen the Amer-i-caans fight," he said. He'd been there when *Walker* savaged the first Grik invasion fleet that tried to conquer Aryaal. "But that new ship, it is not made of iron like the other." He glanced at Alden. "There is no question of valor, but one against three is questionable odds. Should we not return to shore? We might be forced to hide or disperse if the Grik are victorious. They will search for us."

"They will not be victorious, Captain," Safir replied before Pete had a chance. Her grin had become predatory. She watched while *Donaghey*'s sails filled, and she heeled sharply to starboard, slanting away from the waiting boats. To the unknowing eye, it looked as though the ship were abandoning them, leaving nothing between them and the Grik. Cries of alarm arose from the boats, and she understood her people's fear, even though she knew it was unfounded. She was no sailor, but she knew the ship would soon tack back across in front of the approaching enemy. Garrett was trying to force the battle farther away from the boats and the shore, where his ship would have better maneuverability and more water beneath her keel.

"Do not fear," she cried out as soothingly as she could. "They will not leave us."

Long moments passed while the Grik grew closer and *Donaghey* became more distant. Even to her it was a terrifying sight. Just as the first sense of doubt touched her soul however, she saw *Donaghey*'s aspect change, and she was filled with exhilaration when the tall ship came about and began a headlong rush toward the enemy. A cheer rose up.

"Now you will see something!" she promised.

The sun crept ever upward and the day grew hot as the four ships came together. From their current angle it looked like all were heading straight for her, but Safir could see the distance between the one and the three dwindling rapidly. *Donaghey* would soon "cross their tee," as she'd heard the maneuver called. She would destroy the Grik, and the refugees would remember the long morning they'd spent in the boats as a stirring adventure: an exciting, reaffirming proof that the hardships they'd endured hadn't been for nothing, and most of all, in spite of everything, victory might someday be achieved. She watched with growing inspiration as a large battle flag, the one with the stars, blue field, and curious red stripes, unfurled at *Donaghey*'s masthead and streamed to leeward. She'd heard Captain Reddy tell a tale about a battle on the world the Americans came from when a ship called *Exeter* defiantly flew a giant flag in the face of certain destruction. Matt had clearly been moved by the act, just as Safir Maraan was now. The flag of the Americans had become a powerful symbol to her: in some ways an even more powerful symbol than the nine trees and one gold star on the stainless field now representing the alliance facing the Grik. It was a symbol of hope and defiance in the face of overwhelming odds. Even despite their setbacks, it had become a symbol of victory.

She knew the flag meant much the same to *Donaghey*'s crew, though there were few human Americans aboard her. Her people were land folk; descendants of that great, prehistoric nautical exodus that had carried her race from their ancestral home and deposited them here. The Grik had been the ancient enemy from which her people fled. Rejecting a seafaring life, they estranged themselves from the majority of their species. They became isolationist, feudal. Warlike as they were, compared to sea folk they'd been vulnerable to the first major Grik incursion.

Among sea folk, each of their huge, island-size ships were nations unto themselves, and their leaders enjoyed coequal status as High Chiefs among their peers. With the coming of the war, and the Grik Grand Swarm, changes to this age-old system began to evolve. The alliance now included not only sea folk, but land folk as well, and a collective, coordinating leadership was required. Captain Reddy was supreme commander, but Nakja-Mur, High Chief of Baalkpan, had become the civic leader of the alliance by default, since his was the "nation" hosting the other chiefs:

Baalkpan was also the center of all their collective industry. Safir was beginning to see the advantages of the formation of a true, formal alliance. Not one of expedience only, but one evolving to unite all willing Lemurians beneath the Banner of the Trees into a strong political union such as the Amer-i-caans claimed to spring from.

The one gold star on the stainless banner represented the Americans. It was placed in the center not to show dominance, but to symbolize that they were the organizing force, the glue holding all together during these early, terrible, trying times. Also, unlike the golden trees surrounding it, the star now represented more than the single city-state personified by a single ship. Matt continued to insist the star didn't represent him and his surviving destroyermen, or even just his tiny but growing fleet; it represented the United States Navy in particular, and that vaguely understood nation his navy defended in general. He wanted it clear that, wherever it was, his "America" was part of this alliance. Every Lemurian joining an "American" crew became a member of the United States Navy, and swore to defend an even more vaguely understood Constitution. Captain Reddy insisted on that too. Therefore, wherever they came from, and for however long they served, any Lemurian who swore the oath became a "Navy man" and was considered by all to be an Amer-i-caan for as long as they kept that oath, and followed the Americans' strict rules.

Nothing like those rules—or "regulations," as they were called—had ever occurred to any Lemurian, anywhere. People did as their leaders specifically instructed them, of course, but otherwise they did as they pleased. Even in the more socially stratified lands of B'mbaado and Aryaal, behavior was not regulated by written rules or laws, but by decrees generally favoring those, like herself, who made them. She'd never imagined so many of her people would willingly submit to the level of discipline demanded by the Americans. To her surprise, as many of her people volunteered for the "Amer-i-caan Naa-vee" as did for the B'mbaadan infantry regiments forming in Baalkpan—even though those were now held to the same high disciplinary standards by General Alden. Most were turned away from the Navy because they just didn't have the ships, but it was something to consider. The American Navy had become a

tight, close-knit clan of elite professionals that watched out
for their own, no matter what they looked like. Safir wasn't
sure if that was a good thing or not, although she tended to
believe it was, and she suddenly wondered if it might not be
the strict regulations themselves that made the difference.
Not only did they enforce discipline; they also enforced the
rights of those subject to it. It was a concept she'd been
giving much thought. In any event, as far as she or anyone
else was now concerned, the streaming flag showed that
everyone aboard *Donaghey*—human or Lemurian—was
"Amer-i-caan."

The ships converged rapidly now, their hulls and towering canvas contrasting sharply against the dark, cerulean
sea. The American ship was bigger than the others, and
clearly faster. It was a stirringly beautiful scene, in a way,
that would soon be more beautiful still, when *Donaghey*
began her destructive work.

"Just a few moments more," she breathed.

"Son of a *bitch*!" shouted Chapelle when the side of the
nearest Grik ship disappeared behind a heavy cloud of
white smoke. He'd been reminding his gunners to aim for
the enemy's rigging when somebody pointed at the curious
squares spaced evenly along the sides of the enemy ships.
Squares just like *Donaghey*'s. Even as he stared, stunned,
the squares opened and the snouts of crude cannons poked
through. Too quickly for accuracy, a broadside—a *cannon*
broadside—erupted from the enemy ship.

The angle was terrible. The Grik commander must have
decided it was a matter of "use it or lose it" and given the
order to fire, even though few guns would bear. As it was,
not a single ball struck *Donaghey*, but the surprise caused
by the sudden realization that they'd lost their only material advantage over the enemy was almost as damaging as
an effective broadside would have been. As the distance
closed, and *Donaghey* prepared to cross the bow of the ship
that had just fired at them, all the gunners on the starboard
side merely stood, transfixed by what they'd seen. Chapelle
glanced at the quarterdeck and saw the shocked expression
even extended to the captain's face, and he knew there was
no time.

"What the *hell* are you doing?" he bellowed, in a voice

carrying the length of the ship. He ran forward, yelling as he went, "Starboard battery! At my command! Fire as they bear!" Reaching the foremost gun under the fo'c'sle on the starboard side, he elbowed the Lemurian gunner aside and peered through the gunport, sighting along the top of the barrel. A moment more and it would be pointing at the enemy ship. All thought of finesse, and firing at a specific point, was gone. They had to get this first broadside off as quickly as they could, as effectively as they could, and break the shock that had seized the ship. Stepping back, Chapelle looked at the 'Cat gunner.

"Get hold of yourself," he growled. "So they've got guns. So what? They don't know how to use them, do they?" The gunner jerked a nod. Chapelle glanced through the port again. "Fire!"

The refugees in the boats cheered lustily when the first blossoms of smoke appeared. Safir had told them what to expect, and they probably thought the stabbing flames and smoke were the result of *Donaghey*'s fire. But in the front of the barge where she, Alden, and Haakar-Faask stood, there was silence. The queen clutched her protector's arm, and her blood felt like ice.

"Holy shit." Pete gasped.

"Should we return to shore?" Faask asked her quietly.

"Not yet."

"No, not yet," Alden agreed grimly. "We need to see this."

One by one, *Donaghey*'s guns replied to the unexpected barrage, as Russ Chapelle raced down the line, exhorting the gun's crews to do their duty. With each resounding crash it seemed the effect of the enemy surprise lifted a little more. By the time he reached the last gun under the quarterdeck, he believed the crisis was past. All the crew were veterans of fierce fighting, and many, survivors of *Nerracca* or transferees from *Walker*, had even been on the receiving end of *Amagi*'s mighty salvos. The constant drill and discipline they'd learned also helped them recover, and soon they were firing with the same skill and dedication they showed during the daily exercises. Guardedly satisfied, Russ mopped his brow and left the gun divisions under the direction of the officer trainees, or midshipmen, commanding them and ascended to the quarterdeck. Garrett was standing near the wheel, glassing the results of their fire on the first Grik ship. Chapelle was hard-pressed to see through the smoke, but it looked like they'd done little damage. A few shot holes in her sails, maybe. He shook his head.

"Sorry about that, Skipper," he said, joining *Donaghey*'s commander.

"Nothing to be sorry about. It shook everybody up. Me too. My God . . . *Guns!*" He lowered his voice. "Thanks."

"What for?"

Garrett's lips formed a small smile; then he gestured at the enemy ships. They were about to cross the second ship's bow. The starboard battery of the first—they seemed to have only five or six guns to a side—fired another ineffectual broadside that did little more than churn the sea in their wake, but the gunports were open on the ship they approached.

"At least their gunnery isn't very good," Chapelle observed. Just then, a rolling broadside erupted from the next ship in line. Like the first, the angle was poor, but the range was much closer, and they felt an unmistakable shudder beneath their feet when a couple of shots struck home. A high-pitched, keening wail arose from forward.

"They're learning fast," said Garrett grimly. He turned to his second in command. "As soon as we rake the third ship, we'll come about and do it again. Make sure we keep our distance. If we foul one of them, the others will gang up on us and board"—he paused—"and their crews are a lot bigger than ours." He didn't need to remind them what would happen if they were overwhelmed. A quick death, at best. He glanced astern at the distant, bobbing barges. "We have to win this, and we have to do it quickly." He looked at Chapelle. "I want you to hammer those ships if you have to aim every gun yourself." Russ nodded and raced back down the ladder. Garrett watched him go and then shook his head at Taak-Fas. "A hell of a thing," he said in frustration.

The cheering in the boats had stopped when it became obvious that all the ships were using cannons—something their queen assured them only the alliance possessed. They watched in quiet awe as the single ship opposed the three, and nimbly maneuvered to cross their vulnerable bows again. The deep, throbbing boom of gunfire reached them from across the water, and white smoke gushed down-wind. A small cheer was raised when a Grik mast tottered forward, taking the top of the next one in line. The ship quickly slewed, beam-on to the wind, as the fallen mass of timber and sails dragged it around. As though a preplanned maneuver, the newly presented broadside thundered out and *Donaghey* visibly shivered from the impact. Splashes from debris and shot fell all around her, but she appeared little damaged, and punished her tormentor in response. For a long while, it seemed, while *Donaghey* gathered way, she lingered near the bow of the closest enemy ship, and a furious exchange of gunfire ensued. Two of the Grik were now firing at *Donaghey* while she concentrated all her ef-forts on the one helpless to respond. Even from the dis-tant, pitching boat, Safir saw that the enemy was beginning to hurt Garrett's ship, and she shrank from the thought of what he and his crew were enduring. The choking smoke, the noise, the flying splinters and metal that could tear their bodies apart. But she knew what he was doing. He was try-ing to destroy the enemy by concentrating all his fire on one at a time, and it was working. By now, the closest Grik was a battered wreck. Only her mainmast still stood, and flailing lines and fallen spars hopelessly snarled the yards. *Donaghey* edged past, beginning to play her guns upon the next in line.

Suddenly black smoke gushed from the derelict, and al-most immediately the people in the boats saw orange flames leaping from her forward gunports. They cheered. All three of the other ships—both Grik and alliance—immediately steered away from the one that was afire. The Grik in the center of the line was too eager to get at *Donaghey*, how-ever, and had closed the distance too much. When she tried to turn, her mizzen rigging fouled the shrouds of her burn-ing sister, and they collided and twisted together in a flam-ing embrace. White smoke vomited skyward, mixed with black, and clouds of burning canvas and ash drifted down-wind, some coming to rest on *Donaghey*, as she tried to gain some distance.

A brilliant flash of light followed by a tremendous thunderclap explosion tore across the wave tops at the drifting boats, now less than four miles away. Only the hands of her devoted protector prevented Queen Maraan from falling into the sea. When she regained her balance and looked again, at first all she saw was a monstrous fog bank of dirty smoke and thousands of splashes, large and small, covering an area of several square miles. A few even came uncomfortably close to the boats. As the smoke gradually dispersed, she finally caught sight of the two remaining ships.

Both had been horribly mauled by the massive explosion. *Donaghey*'s sails were a tattered, flailing mess, and her mizzenmast had fallen against the main, fouling its yards and creating a jumble of tangled rigging. She was listing to starboard, and her stern looked like a mountain fish had taken a bite out of it. The Grik still had all her masts, but her sails were shredded to the point of uselessness.

"We must return to shore," she said, her voice wooden.

"But . . ." Faask began to object, but Safir shook her head.

"Cap-i-taan Gaar-ett cannot concern himself with us now. He will be hard-pressed to save his ship. We are land folk, but I can tell which way the wind is blowing. If *Donaghey* is very fortunate, she will be carried around the point. Perhaps she can make repairs and return for us then. If she does not clear the point, she will be wrecked, and there is nothing we can do to stop that."

For a long moment she watched the stricken ships drifting downwind. Occasionally a puff of smoke heralded the report of a gun from one ship or the other as they continued to fire whenever they could. She thought she could even hear the shrieks of the wounded and shouted commands over the intervening distance, but that was probably just her imagination. Whatever happened to *Donaghey* now, she'd have to see to her own survival, just as Safir Maraan had to see to the survival of those who depended on her. If *Donaghey* couldn't return, she knew it would become far more difficult to rescue them. With the Grik guarding the approaches with cannons on their ships, no single ship would dare make the attempt.

Without the explosion that crippled her, she believed *Donaghey* could have defeated all three Grik vessels armed with cannons. The enemy had clearly not known how best to employ their new weapons. But they were learning, and with their limitless numbers, they were unlikely to be so amateurish and unprepared again. Next time there might be a dozen ships sent to do what three had done today.

Safir sent a prayer to the Sun that *Donaghey*—and her friend Garrett—could escape or defeat the remaining Grik ship, and quickly mend her wounds. Perhaps then she might return for them before the enemy did. The thought of Garrett sent a chill down her spine, because it reminded her of someone else. If *Donaghey* survived but couldn't come back, Safir would be stranded with the rest of the refugees the alliance may no longer have the power to rescue. What would Chack think? What would he *do*? Chack had accompanied Captain Reddy on the expedition to Manila, but with the magic of the Americans' radio, he'd know what happened as soon as *Donaghey* made port. With the sudden thought of her beloved, a shiver of sadness and fear crept deep into her bones.

"To the shore," she repeated in a voice she didn't recognize.

An hour after the explosion, the surviving Grik ship was worse off than she'd appeared at first. None of her masts had fallen, but all her sails were rags, and so far no replacements had been sent aloft. Her deck was like an anthill, stirred with a stick, choked with her surviving warriors. They seemed to have no direction, no guidance at all, and all they appeared able to manage was to rush about and roar with frustrated rage as the wind and current swept them ever closer to the breakers. At least *Donaghey* could still make steerageway, and she'd continued to claw away from the menacing shore until the two ships exchanged their relative positions. The cannonade never completely ceased, but it became sporadic and ineffective. Occasionally the Grik ship commenced a spirited fire, but as often as not the guns weren't even pointed in *Donaghey*'s direction. It was bizarre. The only explanation was perhaps her Hij officers had been killed, and no one remained to tell the Uul warriors what to do. Once it was clear they had little to fear from the enemy, most of *Donaghey*'s crew ignored the Grik and focused on saving their ship. The Grik was inshore now, and headed straight for the shoals and booming surf of the protruding point.

Garrett sat on one of the quarterdeck gun carriages, mopping his face with his hat and grimacing with pain while the Lemurian surgeon bound his wound. A large splinter had been imbedded in his thigh, and the waves of agony caused by its removal were only now beginning to subside. All around him was chaos like he'd never known. Shattered timbers and shredded sailcloth festooned the deck, and seemingly thousands of frayed and ragged lines created a nightmare web of destruction. He'd seen his share of naval combat in the last year, first against the Japanese, then against the Grik—and Japanese. But he'd always been on *Walker* when the fighting took place. He knew war was terrible, terrifying, and bloody—sometimes catastrophically so—and naval warfare could seem particularly overwhelming. Even so, he'd believed he was ready for a command of his own. Now he wasn't so sure.

He'd trained to become a destroyerman in . . . well, yes, a comparatively modern navy. He was a good gunnery officer, and managing his new ship's weaponry wasn't so different from firing *Walker*'s in local control. He could navigate and stand a watch, and he wasn't afraid to fight. Thanks to the old admiral's manual, he'd even learned to handle *Donaghey* in a fairly competent fashion. But this type of warfare—gone for the most part for a hundred years on his own world—was completely different from what he'd been prepared for. The stakes were the same, and so was the objective: destroy the enemy before he could destroy you. The results were apparently the same as well: shredded bodies, blood-splashed decks, and a stunned sense of unreality. But the *way* it happened and the pace of it all were what so disconcerted him. (He hadn't suspected splinters would be such a menace, for example.) He knew even the twenty-five-year-old destroyer he was accustomed to was far more complex, but somehow, on a sailing ship the complexity was much more apparent—particularly when it had been so horribly brutalized.

Even now, with a pause in the action, the air was filled with screams and shouts, grinding timbers, and chopping axes. The occasional gun roared, when enough debris was cleared to allow it to fire at the equally battered enemy. But above all the unfamiliar sounds of this new/old type of war, there was a deafening silence. A silence of absence. Instead of the comforting roar of the blower, and the grinding, rasping, high-pitched wheeze of the turbines, there was only the capricious wind. A wind that would drive them onto the deadly shoals as well if they couldn't quickly bend it to their will.

"Cease firing," he ground out through clenched teeth, when Chapelle approached to report. The blond torpedoman didn't seem injured, but his shirt was torn and spattered with blood.

"I just did, Skipper," he replied. "I figured the little guys had practiced enough for one day." He shrugged. "Besides, Taak took my crews and put them to work clearing debris."

Garrett nodded and struggled to rise and gaze over the nearby bulwark. The Grik was beginning to wallow, beam-on to the inshore swells.

"It won't be long before she strikes. How about the refugee barges?"

"Safely ashore," Chapelle confirmed. "I almost wish they'd stuck it out. If we get things squared away, we might be back for them in a couple of hours."

Garrett shook his head. "It was the right call for her to make. It'll be evening, at least, before we can beat back around the point—if we make it around the point." Garrett was gauging the angles as he spoke, studying the wind direction and the shore. "As hot as it is, they'd have been really suffering by then."

"We'll weather the point," Chapelle assured him, "but you're probably right. It sure is hard to get used to not having engines."

"I was just thinking that myself. It's tough getting used to a lot of things here," Garrett muttered.

Chapelle frowned. "Hey, Skipper, don't beat yourself up. You did okay." He gestured at the now clearly doomed Grik. It was rolling so violently, the masts must soon fall. With a distant, muted "crack," the main snapped off at the deck and collapsed into the churning sea even as they watched. Moments later the other masts went down as well, and all that remained was a wallowing, helpless hulk. Try as he might, Garrett could summon no compassion for the horrible creatures he knew had only moments to live.

"One against three . . . Three down and us still up. Not a bad showin', if you ask me." Chapelle chewed philosophically. "Sure, we're beat up"—he grinned—"and our brand-new ship got scratched a bit, but that's mostly because those two blew up in our face. Their guns weren't doing much harm. A few weeks in the yard, a little paint here and there, and she'll be good as new."

"Not good enough," Garrett growled. "Not nearly good enough. A few weeks sounds about right, but it'll take more than a little paint. For now, *Donaghey*'s out of the war. They have the ships to trade three to one; we don't. And . . . Damn it, Russ, they have *guns* now! Where'd they get them? How many do they have, and how fast can they make them? Damn it! Our one big advantage . . . shot!" He grimaced belatedly at the pun. "Yeah, they used them stupidly, but we can't count on that next time. We aren't exactly professionals at this kind of war either, you know."

Chapelle looked uncomfortable. "Not much doubt where they got them," he muttered darkly. "Those Jap bastards showed them how to make 'em."

Taak-Fas trotted up, weaving his way through the debris on deck. He had something in his hand.

"Cap-i-taan, we are almost ready to cut the final lines and let the mizzen fall over the side." He grinned. "You might want to be somewhere else when that happens."

"Of course."

Chapelle and the surgeon helped Garrett to his feet. One of the surgeon's assistants, covered with blood, arrived to help. Garrett shooed him away, and with a grateful nod the 'Cat raced back to whatever operation he'd been summoned from.

"As soon as it goes over," Taak-Fas continued, "the fore and main will draw much better. We'll be okay." He sounded relieved, and Garrett was too. He was also glad he had such a capable, levelheaded exec. Excited, chittering voices drew his attention back to the Grik ship. She was among the breakers now. Suddenly she heeled sharply over and performed a drunken, jerky pirouette. Waves broke over her deck, and struggling forms disappeared over the side. Garrett briefly wondered if they'd drown before the voracious "flashies" tore them apart. He still felt no pity, but was again struck by how much more inhospitable this world's seas were than those he remembered. And it could've just as easily been him and his crew dying in the surf. He shuddered.

"Let me get out of the way so we can take that mast down," he said. "Otherwise, we'll be joining them." He stopped. "What have you got there, Taak? In your hand?"

Taak-Fas raised the object and studied it curiously. "A Grik cannonball," he said. "It was rolling loose on the deck. It is about the same size as ours, and weighs much the same, I think, but it is clearly different. Here." He handed it over. "I have duties, and you must allow the surgeon to properly dress your wound. I assure you, Cap-i-taan, I can somehow manage for the short time that will take."

Garrett took the ball and laughed. Taak was right. The repairs were under control, and he was just getting in the way. Taak spoke to the surgeon in his own language; then he and Chapelle assisted Garrett down the companionway. Once they reached the wardroom, they eased him into a chair, where he sat and waited while others with more serious wounds were tended. He'd insisted as soon as he saw them. Some of the wounds were utterly ghastly: mangled limbs and terrible gashes—mostly caused by splinters, he again realized. His ship was in capable hands and his leg would keep. He looked at the ball he'd laid in his lap.

The cannons they'd helped the Lemurians create were bronze. There was plenty of copper and tin all over this region that had once been the Dutch East Indies. Iron was harder to come by and harder still to work. They desperately needed iron to make structural repairs to *Walker* and *Mahan*, and implement many of their other plans. In the short term, though, it didn't seem critical. Bronze was actually better than iron for smoothbore cannons. The elongation was better and the quality control not as critical. They made their cannonballs of copper, which flew just fine. But without a steady source of iron, and the ability to smelt and forge it in quantity, there was only so far they could go, industrially speaking. Even with their limitations, Garrett had thought they would enjoy a significant advantage over the enemy for some time to come. At least until today. As he contemplated the projectile in his lap, it suddenly dawned on him with a sickening sense of dread that the Grik had not only caught them technologically, but taken a leaping bound ahead. The ball in his lap was iron. *They're making cannonballs of iron*, he thought numbly. His thoughts immediately rearranged themselves. *They have so much iron they can* waste *it on cannonballs!*

"My God."

CHAPTER
5

*H*isashi Kurokawa, captain of His Imperial Majesty's battle cruiser *Amagi*, paced nervously back and forth in the gloomy anteroom of the Imperial Regent's palace. The regent, an imposing Grik named Tsalka, was not present, nor had he been since shortly after the disappointing setback delivered to the Grand Swarm in general, and *Amagi* in particular, by the "Tree Prey" and their American allies. He'd returned to Ceylon, where he presumably awaited either death for his failure, or a requested audience with the Celestial Mother, the Supreme Empress of all the Grik Herself, on the distant island of Madagascar where the Imperial Palace stood.

Kurokawa doubted he'd ever see Tsalka again. The regent would either be killed out of hand, or executed (hopefully eaten alive) after his audience with the empress. Even though he'd essentially been only a "passenger" aboard the Grand Swarm's flagship, and not in actual command, he'd been the highest-ranking Grik in the region. Intolerance for failure was one trait the Grik shared with the Japanese, and if the one punished was not actually responsible for the failure, it was the example that was important. Even if he wasn't killed, there was a very good chance he wouldn't survive the trip to Madagascar. Voyages across the deep water of the Indian Ocean were notoriously hazardous. Apparently, the deeper the water, the larger the predators grew. Large enough to *eat* ships such as the regent would travel in. The thought warmed Kurokawa slightly. He patently loathed Tsalka—and all things Grik, in fact—even though only Tsalka's forbearance had prevented him and all his surviving crew from being eaten in the aftermath of the "setback." Kurokawa felt little gratitude, however, since one in ten of the Japanese survivors—almost sixty men— had gone to the butchers and feasting fires of their "allies." It was nothing personal, he was assured, simply tradition. The hunter that drops his spear when the prey is brought to bay is always eaten in its stead, and the American torpedo that nearly sank his ship certainly made him drop the Grik's mightiest spear.

Kurokawa had been indignant, but since he felt no real allegiance to his men either, he'd shed no tears for those who died. They were cowards and traitors all. Particularly his executive officer, Commander Sato Okada, who constantly questioned his decision to make alliance with the Grik, and would even make an accommodation with the Americans, he suspected, if he could. He'd grown far too close to their American prisoner of late. But Okada was not unique; his entire crew had betrayed him and the Emperor with their failure. After the strange storm that brought them here, *Amagi* had been the most powerful ship in the world. He'd believed it was only a matter of time before he could use her might to gain a position of power over the Grik. The Grik were loathsome creatures, but clearly the dominant species. Once he rose in their esteem, he could co-opt, or even supplant their ridiculous "Celestial Mother" and eventually rule this world himself—all in the name of Emperor Hirohito, of course.

Amagi's worthless crew had thwarted his ambition, at least temporarily. They'd allowed the mightiest ship this world had ever seen to be grievously wounded by an insignificant American destroyer, a ship so poorly armed and obsolete even the Americans had considered her class as expendable as napkins before the war. Therefore, Kurokawa cared nothing for the welfare of his crew, except insofar as their training and experience enhanced his own value and prestige. He couldn't use them to further his aims if they were dead. He raged to admit it, but he himself would have little importance to the Grik without the skill and knowledge he commanded through his surviving crew. He therefore did his best to keep them alive and relatively comfortable.

Besides, the main reason Tsalka hadn't killed them all was that another Grik, General Esshk, had intervened. Not immune to blame himself, it was he who prevailed with the argument that the Japanese and their mighty, wounded ship might be of use. Perhaps even essential to the ultimate success of the Swarm. Esshk made Tsalka realize the old ways of war, the Great Hunt that exterminated their prey almost as sport, might not succeed against the rediscovered Tree Prey, who'd escaped the conquest of Madagascar itself countless generations before. They'd grown much more formidable than the ancient histories described.

Kurokawa had learned that when the Grik first encountered the Tree Prey, as they were called, they'd posed no more of a challenge than any other predatory species the Grik had exterminated. They usually hid in trees, of all things, and when they fought, they did so ineffectually. But unlike any other prey the Grik had hunted, the Tree Prey somehow escaped. In desperation they'd built great ships from the dense forests of their home and braved the deadly sea the Grik couldn't cross. Not until merely a couple of hundred years before had the Grik been given the gift of a seagoing ship to copy for themselves. A strange race of tail-less prey—not unlike the present Japanese, Esshk inferred—arrived in a three-masted ship with a sturdy, ingeniously planked hull. No one knew where they came from, and it really didn't matter. The prey was devoured, but the ship and technical language required to make her was copied. Educated Hij among the Grik learned to write and cipher in the strange, captured tongue, even if they couldn't form the words to speak it. More and more ships were built along the lines the captured drafts referred to as "East Indiamen." The Grik now had a fleet with which to expand their empire—although progress was slow. Even the much-improved ships the "English" prey brought were not proof against the largest denizens of the terrible sea.

It all made sense to Kurokawa. He suspected an East Indiaman had been swept to this world a few centuries before, just as *Amagi* had. Inexplicably, it was unarmed. He didn't understand that at all. Historically, British East Indiamen usually carried an impressive armament for protection against pirates, and even belligerent warships. Perhaps those long-ago Englishmen already knew something about the Grik before they were captured, and feared what would happen if "modern" weapons fell into their hands. Maybe they heaved them over the side? If so, what had they thought they were protecting? Regardless, there were no cannons aboard when the Grik took the ship. Otherwise they'd already have them and they wouldn't have come as such a devastating surprise when the hated Americans recently introduced the technology.

Kurokawa seethed. Oh, how he hated the Americans! They were responsible for his being here in the first place, instead of back where he belonged, riding the tide of Japanese victory across the Pacific. Perhaps the war was already won? The long-respected American Navy had proven ineffective, and had been unable to muster much of a defense after the devastating attack on Pearl Harbor. Nearly a year had passed since the bizarre green Squall transported him here. At the rate they'd been going, the Japanese Imperial Navy might have dictated terms to the United States from within San Francisco Bay by now. That was where he ought to be: covered in glory and recognized for his brilliance. Not here in this barbaric, perverted caricature world, where the emperor—*his* emperor—did not reign. The Americans were the cause of all that, and someday he'd have his revenge.

His value had been recognized by General Esshk, at least. The general was acting as forward vice regent in Tsalka's stead, and his quarters were in the palace of the former king of Aryaal. Even Kurokawa had to admit the palace was an impressive edifice. It was constructed of white marble, and the spired towers and spacious, arched balconies gave it a medieval Eastern European flair. It was even more striking, since it was the only building still standing within the walls surrounding the conquered city. Aryaal was "conquered" only in the sense that it no longer belonged to the enemy. The first attempt to take it failed catastrophically, and it finally came into Grik hands as a burned-out, abandoned wasteland. All except the palace that somehow escaped the inferno. Briefly, he wondered why.

Kurokawa knew the Americans had to be responsible for the scorched-earth policy that greeted the invaders when they reached the city, as well as the neighboring island of B'mbaado. He doubted their primitive lackeys were sophisticated enough to think of the strategy on their own. With the inhabitants gone, and nothing left but the palace, there was no food, no supplies. There wasn't even shelter from the terrible storms that sometimes slashed at the exposed coastal city. The Americans had managed to sour even the seizure of Aryaal, which was the one small victory the Grik had achieved. Everything they needed had to be brought by ship, putting even further strain on available resources and indefinitely delaying the buildup they'd need before renewing the offensive. Only by renewing the offensive could he prove his worth, and only by proving his worth could he renew his broken scheme for power. Captain Kurokawa continued to brood and pace.

The tapestry separating the anteroom from the audience chamber parted to reveal the terrifying form of a Grik. It looked like a bipedal lizard, except it had short, feathery fur instead of scales. Its snout and tail were shorter, proportionately, than one would have expected from a lizard, but the tightly spaced, razor-sharp teeth packing the short snout left the fiercest shark wanting. Empty, remorseless, sharklike eyes regarded Kurokawa in silence for a moment before the creature spoke.

"The vice regent will see you now."

The voice came as a series of hisses and clicks, but Kurokawa had learned to understand the words even if he couldn't speak them. Much of the meaning came from subtle sounds requiring a foot-long tongue and two-inch pointed teeth. By now a few Grik had also learned to understand English, although it was apparently even more impossible for them to speak. Most Hij could read written English. It was their technical language, and that was how Kurokawa first communicated with them: writing notes back and forth. But that was no longer necessary, and he could converse fairly normally, with Esshk, at least.

In the Japanese Navy he'd risen in, it was required that all bridge officers know and speak English, since most of the maneuvering commands were made in that language. He knew the tradition began at the turn of the century, when Japan purchased her first modern battleships from Great Britain. Even more were acquired during the Great War, when the two countries were actually allies against Germany. Since everything on the ships was written in

English—the instruction manuals were in English, and most of the instructors and advisors spoke only English—Kurokawa and his peers were forced to speak English as well. The Japanese Navy was an infant in need of traditions, and speaking English on the bridge became one. He was glad that was one tradition quickly fading back home, even if he made use of it now.

Controlling a shudder, he bowed stiffly to the gruesome messenger, straightened his tunic, and marched quickly into the vice regent's audience chamber.

General Esshk, complete with plumed helmet, scarlet cape, and shiny plate armor protecting his chest, looked for all the world like a sinister, reptilian gargoyle dressed as a Roman tribune. Mighty muscles rippled beneath his downy skin, and he carried himself as fully erect as his alien physique allowed. Even slightly hunched, he towered over the Japanese officer. Kurokawa knew that, before the recent setback, Esshk had been a favorite among the Grik elite. He was considered their greatest living general, and was actually a sibling, of sorts, of the empress. He also had an unusual reputation: he was deemed something of a philosopher. Kurokawa knew that really meant he had a keen and inquisitive mind. He was unusually open to new ideas and innovations, and seemed less entrenched in the instinctual behavior patterns and responses he'd seen in other Grik, even Hij. That was both an advantage and disadvantage, depending on the circumstances, since it made Esshk both easier and more difficult to manipulate. When working with the general, the supreme question always was, Who was manipulating whom?

Esshk noticed his arrival, and motioned another Grik he'd been speaking with to leave. He hissed a pleasant greeting.

"Ah! Captain Kurokawa! I trust you are well?"

Kurokawa bowed deeply. Visitors were expected to prostrate themselves, but he simply would not. A formal bow was as much as he was willing to compromise. Strangely, Esshk never insisted he do more.

"Well enough, Your Excellency. I do grow anxious."

"Anxious to resume the hunt? Good. That is why I summoned you here."

"There is news?"

"Actually, yes. Several days ago I dispatched three of our newly armed ships"—he bowed his head appreciatively toward Kurokawa—"to patrol the eastern approaches to the neighboring island. I hoped they might encounter one of the ships of the prey that sometimes visit the vicinity. They did."

Kurokawa contained a surge of annoyance. He'd often counseled Esshk to conceal the fact that they were arming Grik ships with guns, and to reveal the surprise only when they had sufficient numbers for a decisive blow. He was constantly amazed that a race whose only military tactic was a full frontal assault with overwhelming numbers had such difficulty understanding the principle of mass. It was an old argument by now, however, and one he had no hope of winning. Besides, perhaps the sortie had been successful. Esshk certainly seemed in a good mood.

"I take it the enemy ship was destroyed?" he ventured.

"Unfortunately not, but it was severely damaged. I congratulate you on your perseverance in training the crews to use their new weapons effectively." Esshk seemed to consider. "Perhaps even more such training is in order."

Kurokawa sighed. He did not, of course, perform any of the training duties himself. That, and other things, was what certain members of his crew were for. He'd heard, however, that teaching the semisentient Uul to do anything beyond hack at their opponents with swords was like forcing water to run uphill. He'd speak to those responsible for the training and see what more could be done.

"Perhaps. With respect, what kind of damage . . . did our . . . forces sustain?"

Esshk waved a clawed hand. "Total. All three ships were destroyed. An explosion of the black dirt that burns destroyed two. It seems a fire began." He jerked his snout upward in a gesture Kurokawa had come to equate with a shrug. "The other suffered damage to its sails and went ashore. The ship of the prey was also damaged, but managed to avoid running aground as well. It was, in fact, attempting to return to the scene when our other three ships with cannons arrived and drove it away. Perhaps they were trying to rescue some of their people left behind on the island?" He paused, considering. "I would not have thought it possible, but . . ." He looked at Kurokawa with what might have been respect.

"If I had not given the . . . unusual . . . command that some effort be made to rescue doomed crews, we would not now know what transpired in the fight, or how well the new cannons worked. As it was, almost a dozen Uul were saved from the grounded wreck. Perhaps the prey are doing the same? Trying to learn what has happened here since they left?" Esshk paused and jerked his head again. "As a further gesture, an experiment, if you will, to test the possibility you might be right yet again, I have not ordered the survivors destroyed. They were defeated, but they were not, after all, made prey. It was the ground upon which they stood that fled, not they. We will let them pass their experience to others and see what may transpire."

Kurokawa was surprised. He'd often tried to explain to Esshk how wasteful it was to kill defeated troops. All of them, anyway. Sometimes it was necessary. The Grik were perfect physical predators. Even the Uul were born with such strength and such an awesome array of personal weaponry, no creature he'd ever heard of could hope to match one unarmed. They were like cheetahs, and every other species, including man, were sheep compared to them. But with the exception of the curiously elevated Hij, the physical gifts of the Grik were balanced by some rather peculiar and apparently instinctual behavior patterns. Chief among these was a total—indeed, pathological—inability to understand the concept of defense. They comprehended only attack. Like a cheetah attacking a lamb, feeble attempts by the lamb to escape, or even defend itself, only made the cheetah attack more aggressively. As long as it was attacking, it was winning, no matter what injury it had sustained. But if the attack were ever blunted or hurled back . . . the cheetah that ran from a lamb could never be a cheetah again.

Something happened to the Grik that ran away. Something sprouted within their primitive, retarded brains, and there was not the slightest hint of its existence until the instant it took place. Kurokawa saw it after the Battle of Aryaal, when dozens of ravaged ships limped back to Singapore. They'd been advancing with the Grand Swarm, and he'd seen hundreds of Grik destroyed by their own comrades in what seemed, at the time, a mindless frenzy of wild butchery. Since then he'd given the phenomenon considerable thought and believed he knew what triggered the sudden, primordial, all-consuming urge in defeated Grik—those "made prey"—to flee, and never find it within themselves even to look back. It was panic, fear, the sudden realization that they'd encountered a predator greater than themselves. Just as the Grik attacked as a mob, they were capable of panicking as a mob if things went against them. It was a contagious thing that had to be snuffed out at once.

Kurokawa had tried to explain to Esshk that sometimes defeat in itself was not always the same as being made prey. Sometimes the heart was still willing, even when the ship beneath it could not carry on, for example. Warriors ... removed from the hunt in such a way might not always be unfit to rejoin it. He'd used this argument, in part, because that was what happened to him when *Amagi* was torpedoed on the way to Baalkpan, and he wanted to establish firmly in General Esshk's mind that Hisashi Kurokawa had *not* been made prey. It was a selfish gesture, but practical as well. If, when they inevitably resumed the offensive against the Tree Prey—and Americans!—they continued to kill or abandon their trained crews simply because their ship was sinking, they'd lose valuable resources and delay their ultimate victory. It seemed Esshk was willing to give it a try.

Kurokawa reflected momentarily while General Esshk regarded him with his intense reptilian eyes. Finally he spoke. "But the prey escaped the other three?"

"Regrettably."

"The Americans ... The prey will now know we've matched their advantage. That knowledge might be costly."

"Perhaps. But they cannot know to what extent we have surpassed them."

"Surpassed them?" Kurokawa inquired.

"Indeed. The factories your workers established in Ceylon are performing wonders. Again, you were right when you suggested they be treated differently from other Uul. They thrive with better treatment and are industrious. You

Japanese never cease to amaze me! So frail, yet so useful. And to think Tsalka wasted so many of you on his table! I am sure he has certainly changed his mind!"

"If he lives," muttered Kurokawa bitterly.

"He does. Word arrived today. That is one reason I summoned you: to tell you he not only lives, but basks in the glow of the Celestial Mother's favor. The fast ship he sent to request an audience with Her returned with Her benevolent blessings for our strategy, and instructions that he continue as your patron. She extols the virtues of the Japanese helpers of the Hunt! Just think on it, the Celestial Mother Herself knows you exist! It is a great honor!"

"Indeed," Kurokawa hedged.

"Soon all the Grik will share the benefits of these glorious cannons of yours. By the next time the moon passes into darkness, ten more ships will arrive from Ceylon, each already armed. In their holds will be more than two hundred guns—enough to arm ten of the ships we already have! A moon after that a like number will arrive, and Tsalka will accompany them at the head of another grand fleet to add to the Swarm. With your *Amagi* and over forty ships armed with cannons, and hundreds of conventional ships filled to overflowing with hundreds of thousands of Uul, the prey can do nothing to stop us! That is when we will strike!"

"A month and a half. So soon?"

Esshk peered closely at the Japanese officer. "I do not understand your face. You seem pleased, yet wary. What troubles you? Surely you do not doubt our fleet will easily sweep the prey from the sea?"

"I do not. They have few ships, and even though the large ones are formidable, they cannot maneuver. The only thing concerning me at all is the iron ship, the American destroyer. Its guns have much greater range than ours."

"*Amagi* will concentrate on the American iron ship. Surely its guns cannot outrange yours?"

"Of course not . . . I . . . I only hope *Amagi* will be ready."

Esshk's eyes narrowed slightly. "Will it?"

Right then Hisashi Kurokawa knew his very existence depended upon his next words. He contemplated the progress of his ship's "refit" so far and almost shivered in horror. The project was the most ghastly thing he'd ever seen. There was no dry dock in Aryaal, not on this Earth, as far as he knew, but somehow they'd had to get at *Amagi*'s underwater damage. After much discussion with Esshk and what passed for Hij engineers, they'd settled on a cofferdam. At low tide, weighted down by the bodies of thousands of Grik, they'd run his ship aground in the silty mouth of the river below the fire-blackened walls of Aryaal. There, a massive pile driver encircled *Amagi* with titanic beams dragged for miles through the almost impenetrable jungle beyond the plain still littered with bones from the battle fought upon it. When the framework was complete, Kurokawa's own engineers began devising ways to plank it up. Heavy, prefabricated sections were prepared and lowered into place with the ship's cranes, but they couldn't decide how to secure them to the pilings. The answer was simple: Uul warriors were ordered to jump in the water and do it by hand.

Kurokawa still lived aboard his ship, so he was there to see. As much as he hated the Grik, he was sickened by the sight. Uul by the hundreds, each covered in armor and holding a length of line, shrieked a battle cry and leaped into the water. The armor carried them down—it would be a one-way trip—and protected them slightly from the silvery fish that arrowed in from the bay at the sound of splashes. If they were lucky, they sometimes managed to tie their line before being torn to shreds. Slowly at first, but quickly growing to a nauseating pink, white, silvery roil, the water began to churn. Pieces of bodies and buoyant debris rose to the surface, only to be snatched down by ravening, gaping jaws. On command, hundreds more leaped to their doom, each clasping his piece of line. Most of the Japanese sailors couldn't watch, but Kurokawa stared, transfixed, as much amazed as horrified. Such obedience!

The second wave probably didn't fare as well as the first, but when the third command was given, the boiling water had simmered down. Perhaps the fish were sated? This time a few Grik wouldn't go. It finally occurred to their primitive minds that if they did, they wouldn't come back up. Instead of refusing or attempting to flee, however, they turned on their comrades in a wild attack. All were disarmed, but no Grik was ever truly without weapons, and they used their terrible teeth and claws on those around them. They were quickly subdued, killed, and thrown in the water, but after that first incident, there was an ever-growing number that had to be "destroyed." During this entire procedure, *Amagi*'s pumps were at work, using steam from her few remaining boilers. Finally, Kurokawa noticed that the water level inside the cofferdam was slightly lower than that outside, and he suggested a halt to further wastage of warriors.

The cofferdam was built, and within a week they began repairing his ship's underwater rents, but at such an appalling cost! Surely thousands had died. He'd learned a valuable lesson that day, besides the crystallization of his theory regarding how panic affected the Grik. He'd learned that to the Hij, all other creatures were simply tools, no matter what they said about the Uul being their "children." Life had no value beyond how useful a tool it might be. *Amagi* was just a tool . . . and so was he.

Meeting General Esshk's gaze, he finally nodded. "She can't be finished that quickly. There is still much damage to her engines and boilers, so she won't be as fast as she once was, but she'll be ready for battle."

Esshk seemed to relax, and Kurokawa did too—slightly.

"Excellent," Esshk said. "So now we may turn to another subject: the American flying machine, their 'flying boat,' you called it."

Kurokawa's cheeks burned. During the campaign against Aryaal and the abortive thrust toward Baalkpan, the damned Americans had unveiled a dilapidated PBY Catalina. His inability to prove he'd destroyed the plane still rankled. Aside from its value for reconnaissance purposes, the plane had caused a lot of damage, and the fact that it could fly higher than *Amagi* could engage it damaged his prestige.

"It must have been destroyed," he said. "I sent one of my own aircraft, an observation plane, to engage it. Since then, it has not been seen."

"But your 'observation plane' never returned, so we cannot know for certain. Perhaps they destroyed each other, as you speculated, or perhaps your plane was destroyed and theirs only damaged. If so, perhaps they do not have the . . . capacity, I think you said, to repair it. But perhaps there is nothing wrong with it, and they hold it back only until it can do the most harm. I cannot tell you how disconcerting that machine was to our Uul."

The plane, armed only with machine guns, caused an amazing amount of damage that couldn't be defended against, and the psychological effect had been profound. A shocking number of Uul turned prey merely at the sight of the thing.

"If you're still concerned about it, it's only prudent to attempt to discover its disposition," Kurokawa said, a little heatedly.

"Then do so."

"How?"

Esshk hissed exasperation, and Kurokawa knew then that the Grik general had boxed him in. It was suddenly clear who was manipulating this conversation. "Your precious aircraft, of course."

Amagi had only one observation floatplane left. One was lost chasing the PBY, and the others were destroyed, ironically, when a Japanese dive-bomber crashed into them during *Amagi*'s first encounter with the two American destroyers that somehow resulted in their exile to this place. That the plane crashed into his ship because one of the destroyers shot it down only added to his hatred. All that remained was a single Nakajima Type 95 biplane. It was old-fashioned, slow, and short ranged. Kurokawa had offloaded it before his ship began repairs. He hadn't considered it necessary to the success of the upcoming campaign, and meant to leave it behind because he didn't want to risk losing it. If he was right and the PBY was truly gone, his was the only airplane in the world. It could so easily be damaged or destroyed by a lucky shell or bullet while sitting exposed on its catapult. Also, fire had always been a big part of the way Grik made war—a sometimes indiscriminate use of fire—and the plane, and the limited fuel he had for it, was an increased hazard to his ship.

The plane had languished, floating peacefully at the dock ever since, under guard by its flight and support crew and a much larger contingent of Grik. Esshk said the guard was to protect the plane, but Kurokawa knew it was really there to prevent it from flying away. Given the treachery of his crew, that was something Kurokawa himself was a little concerned the pilot might try. He'd given strict orders that the plane be properly maintained, but the crew was not to even start the engine. He didn't want them to waste a single gallon of the precious aviation fuel—or give their captors the slightest excuse to harm the irreplaceable pilot and plane.

So far, he'd resisted every "request" by Esshk to use the plane. It was his "ace in the hole," as the Americans would say. At his orders, the Japanese sailors had cooperated with the Grik in every way. They'd given them as much technology as their primitive industrial base could exploit. He supposed that had brought them up to the seventeenth century, militarily speaking, at least as far as weaponry was concerned. But the plane represented his greatest example of truly modern technology. It was proof that, no matter how far the Grik progressed, they could never hope to match the magical powers Kurokawa possessed, and most amazing of all to the Grik was the power of flight. He was certain the PBY had been destroyed or seriously damaged. He'd even ordered the pilot of the other Type 95 to ram it if he had to, to return with his shield or on it, or his flight crew would be executed. With that threat to motivate him, Kurokawa was positive the pilot must have resorted to the final option, since he never returned, but neither had the PBY. Ultimately, whether or not the flying boat actually crashed was immaterial; he was certain it would never fly again. There was simply no way to repair it—just as there was no way to repair his own last plane if it was damaged. He therefore basked in the reflected glow of its importance while hoping he'd never have to actually use it. His reluctance was the source of growing strain between Esshk and himself.

The Grik couldn't use the plane themselves, so taking it was pointless. Even if they could be taught to fly, they couldn't physically sit in the cockpit because of their heavily muscled tails. In all the world, only the Japanese hunters controlled the miracle of flight, and that was how Kurokawa intended it to remain.

Esshk pressed him this time. "Is your plane truly so fragile it will ruin it to use it once? If that is the case, what good is it?"

Kurokawa recognized the threat in the question. In other words, what good was he?

"It is quite sturdy, Your Excellency, but we have little

fuel. Also, as I've said, if it's damaged, it cannot be repaired. We haven't the tools or materials."

"The prey flew their airplane all over the place. They must have plenty of fuel. We will capture it, and you will have more than you need. As to the other, I still do not understand. They are machines, are they not? Machines created by your folk. Surely they know how to make more. I tire of your obstructionism. You must use it! The sword that remains at the belt is of no use in the hunt."

"But the materials! I tell you we cannot repair it if it is damaged. We should wait to use it at the proper time—when it might tip the scale."

"Materials!" Esshk snarled, and Kurokawa realized he'd objected too long. He knew the conviviality Esshk greeted him with was only an act. The general began to pace, and Kurokawa remained rigidly at attention, staring straight ahead. "You mean metal? We make metal for you by the shipload! Do not toy with me!"

"I do not, Your Excellency! As I've told you, the metal we need to build more planes is called aluminum. It is . . . magical, and can be made only in the world from which we came. It is strong, like iron, but much lighter. No aircraft made of iron could ever fly."

"Then make them of something else!" Esshk raged in frustration. "You keep telling me we need to know what we face before we attack. Your aircraft is the only way to discover that and yet you refuse to use it!" Esshk glared menacingly at Kurokawa. "Reconcile this contradiction at once!"

Kurokawa stared at Esshk, his mouth open slightly. Peripherally, he was terrified of the general's behavior, but his mind fastened onto something Esshk said. *Of course!*

"General," he said calmly, "we will use the plane, and if you give me free rein, I'll make more for you. They won't be as strong, or nearly as fast, but I'll make airplanes even Grik can fly! But I warn you, it will take time. It will take more time even than the modern ships I promised, since that's what we've already begun. But I can do it for you, and because you have been such a friend, I will. But in return, you must do something for me."

Esshk's eyes widened and his nostrils flared with indignation. Then, slowly, his terrible jaws moved to form an expression Kurokawa hoped was a grin.

"A bargain? How interesting! I wonder what it is you could possibly want?" He seemed contemplative for a time, but finally waved the matter aside. "We shall see, shall we not? My power to grant a boon depends on our success, after all. In the meantime, we must concentrate on the matter at hand. You will provide me with a list of requirements to ensure your plane has the 'legs' to reach its destination and return. We must time the mission carefully, since we will open the final campaign in no more than a moon and a half. All must be in readiness by the time Tsalka returns. You will need ships placed at intervals for refueling, of course. I will order them to scout far forward after that mission is complete, to ensure the prey has no further surprises for us. Ideally, they will rendezvous with the Swarm before the assault begins." He waved a clawed hand vaguely toward the curtain. "Leave me now, and begin your calculations."

"Of course, Your Excellency," Kurokawa said with outward calm, but inwardly he seethed. "One further question, if I may?"

Esshk nodded. "Oh, very well."

"What of the enemy holdouts on B'mbaado? Will you take them seriously now? It seems to me they have evaded us too long. It's possible, if they're rescued, they might report our progress: the gathering Swarm, the pace of repairs to my ship, for example."

"Fear not. I have suffered their existence for my own purpose: to see what efforts the prey might expend to rescue them. I admit you were right, and I am surprised. I should have destroyed them sooner. But perhaps any information they have taken away has been to our advantage?"

"How so?"

"If they are spying on us, and not just huddling together on the farthest reaches of the island, then they will have seen the might we will bring against them—and more is still to come. Let them infect others with that knowledge. That terror. As for the remainder?" He sighed. "I will dispatch one of the newly arrived drafts to dispose of them. They are jungle warriors from the home province. They will make short work of them, and we shall feast upon their leaders!"

Kurokawa's stomach turned at the thought of enduring another such "dinner," but he bowed.

"Of course, Your Excellency."

Muffled machinery noises still reverberated throughout the ship, and the steel still hummed with life, but there'd been no throbbing roar from the engines for some time, and even the slight, almost imperceptible motion of so large a vessel riding at anchor was stilled. Deep within *Amagi*'s bowels, Captain David Kaufman, United States Army Air Corps, noticed the difference, but didn't understand the significance. He didn't understand the significance of much of anything anymore. He tried to do a single push-up on the cool deck plating, but just didn't have the strength. Straining as hard as he could, he couldn't raise himself from the dank, grimy floor of his cell. His jailors fed him once a day, but it was never enough, and his once powerful frame had diminished to a shadow of its former self. Tears pooled beneath his face, and he rolled onto his back, trying to control the sobs that came so frequently now. Above him dangled the single bulb that stayed on day and night. It was one small favor the Japanese officer had granted, and it was probably the only thing that retrieved him from the bottomless chasm of insanity. At least, he thought it had. He still had . . . spells, but today he could at least remember his name, and he willed that knowledge to be enough to cheer him just a bit.

The officer had granted other favors as well, when he could, and Kaufman got the impression he did so with the utmost care. A small stack of magazines was arranged carefully in the corner, opposite his slop bucket, and a couple were even in English. He didn't know how many times he'd read them—hundreds, probably. He'd memorized every word. He read the other ones too, and he'd slowly learned a smattering of written Japanese by putting the pictures in context with the curious symbols beside them. He didn't have any idea what the words sounded like, but he knew what many of the characters meant.

He rose slowly, painfully to his knees, and scooted to the overturned bucket that served as his only chair in the small, barren compartment. Easing onto it, he sat and stared at the glowing bulb for a while. It was how he passed much of his time, focusing on the bright filament until he could see it wherever he looked. His face began to twitch uncontrollably, and he tried to still the muscles and nerves by twisting his tangled beard. It never worked, but he always tried. He couldn't remember how long it had been doing that; it always started within a few minutes of his awakening from his constant, hideous dreams. Dreams of blood and screaming death, and reptilian creatures devouring people he was somehow responsible for. He couldn't remember why. He had no idea how long he'd been a prisoner of the Japanese either, but at least they hadn't eaten him.

The latch on the compartment hatch clanked, and his heart began to race. With a joy he could barely contain, he saw the Japanese officer who'd been so kind to him. How long had it been since his last visit? Months? It didn't matter. He'd feared the creatures had eaten him, but here he was, alive! The treasured face contorted into a grimace of distaste, probably at the smell in the compartment, but honestly, Kaufman didn't notice it anymore. He felt tears sting his eyes; he couldn't help it.

"Captain Kaufman?" The greeting came almost as a question, as though the officer didn't recognize him.

"Oh, ah, yes! It's me!" he croaked. It seemed strange to speak after so long, and it was pleasant to have someone confirm he was who he thought he was.

"You have not been eating!" the officer accused. Kaufman's face contorted into a grimace of contrition. He understood how the officer might think that, since he'd lost so much weight.

"But I have!" he insisted fervently. "I eat everything they bring me! Everything, I swear!"

The officer's eyes narrowed. "Then clearly my orders have been disregarded. You have my most abject apologies. I gave orders that you be fed properly. It seems that word is subject to interpretation. I will make its definition clear."

Kaufman stared at him for a long moment, mouth agape, revealing cracked, blackened teeth. "More food would be nice," he finally agreed softly, trying not to make it sound like a complaint.

"You will have it," the officer promised; then he too hesitated a moment. "I must also apologize for not visiting you more often, to see to your needs. I . . . am ashamed you have been treated so poorly by my countrymen. Necessity forced me to stay away, however. My commander has noticed my attention toward you and does not approve. He has threatened several times to return you to those despicable creatures we got you from. He does not believe you still have value as a source of information."

Kaufman felt a surge of panic. One thing he remembered very well was his terror of the Grik. But what could he say? His mouth formed a protest, but he ultimately only lowered his head. "He's right," he mumbled. "I don't know anything more than I've already told you. I guess my 'usefulness' is over." As soon as he spoke, he was shocked and terrified by his admission, yet strangely liberated as well. One way or another, perhaps his suffering might soon end. He raised his head and rested his twitching gaze on the Japanese officer. "So that's that, I guess," he said, and began to tremble. "The Grik can eat me, but I'll be free."

"Perhaps 'that' is not 'that.' Certainly not if I can prevent it, and there might yet be something you can do."

Kaufman looked confused. "I already told you I don't know anything else!"

In fact, he didn't. He'd told the Japanese officer everything he could remember, and even though he still felt a vague sense of shame, he'd left nothing out. Subconsciously he knew it was wrong somehow to do so, but he couldn't remember why. He couldn't even remember what he'd told them now, only that it had, indeed, been everything.

"That's not what I meant," the officer assured him. "Do you remember, some time ago, I asked if you would be willing to signal your old friends with a transmitter?"

Kaufman looked around as though searching for something, his expression desperate. "I . . . I think I remember you asking that, but . . . I don't know who you mean. All my friends are dead . . . but you." His gaze continued to wander. "Dead."

Commander Sato Okada's expression tensed, and he did feel a surge of shame. And hopelessness. Kaufman had clearly entered into a deep psychosis, and he didn't know if he could bring him out of it. The months of solitary confinement, sensory deprivation, and malnutrition had taken their toll. Okada had said he wasn't responsible for the ill treatment, but he knew he was. He'd given orders that the prisoner be properly treated, but what was proper? Japan was not a signatory to the Geneva Accords regarding the treatment of prisoners of war. Japanese troops and sailors were taught that surrender was unacceptable, dishonorable. Lacking detailed instructions, the ratings assigned to "care" for Kaufman would treat him as they expected to be treated in his place. He should have been more specific, and found a way to check on him more often. Now it might be too late. Okada remembered the details of Kaufman's capture and knew he hadn't surrendered; he'd been overwhelmed, so the initial dishonor was not his. Since then he'd been subjected to horrific brutality, not only at the hands of the Grik, but the Japanese as well. He eventually did surrender information, but not until his soul—and apparently his mind—had been taken from him. Okada realized he must somehow bring the aviator back from the abyss, save him from the madness he took refuge in. He was no traitor, but he'd finally decided he must risk everything to contact the Americans before it was too late. Warn them, somehow.

The Grik were evil incarnate, and *Amagi*'s captain had embraced them for reasons of his own. Even if Okada could supplant Kurokawa, *Amagi* was in the power of the Grik, surrounded, watched. At the first sign of treachery, their reptilian masters would swarm them under. The Grik dreamed of a world dominated entirely by their evil, clutched in their wicked claws. Kurokawa was blinded by his own ambitions and his obsession for revenge. He didn't realize he was but a rat taunting a mighty serpent that might make use of him for a time, but would devour him in the end. For the human race, Japanese or American, the Tree Folk, or any other sentient species inhabiting this Earth to have any hope for survival, *Amagi* and the American destroyer must find a way to work together. Any other course of action was itself madness.

But in order to plan any concerted action, he needed Kaufman's help. He cleared his throat. "Recounting your experiences might be painful," he said gently, "but we must. I will start at the beginning, as I know it."

Goddamn you, Silva!" Chief Laney snarled as he approached. "What do you mean by takin' over my machine shop without even a 'by your leave'? We were workin' on critical repairs! Even you should've been able to tell the lathe and little mill were in use; they were both set up! Hell, the setup took half a day!"

Silva turned to him with a beatific smile. He'd been leaning on the starboard rail on the welldeck, just aft of the bridge, staring thoughtfully at Mindoro—or at least what had *been* Mindoro. They were in the Philippines proper now, steaming north through the east passage of Mindoro Strait. Their old stomping grounds. In fact, Dennis suspected the distant promontory ahead should have been the mouth of Paluan Bay, but he wasn't sure, because nothing really looked the same. It took him a while to figure out what the main difference was. There were no people, no fishing villages lining the shore, and very few boats. The few they'd seen were like the other Lemurian feluccas they'd grown accustomed to, but they hugged the shallows and kept their distance from the strange, smoking ship. Several days before, they'd overhauled and spoken one of the massive Homes they knew, returning empty to Manila for more supplies. He hoped it would be full of troops when it turned back to Baalkpan.

If they were where he thought they were, they'd spot Lubang Island before nightfall, and their voyage would be nearly complete. A lot of the men had grown quiet and somber as they neared their old "home," and even he wasn't immune to a certain nostalgic sense of loss. He had, in fact, been thinking a little morosely of several young ladies in particular who'd have been glad to see him very soon in the old Cavite they'd left behind, and so, when Laney stomped up, offering an outlet for his frustrations, it actually cheered him up.

"That's 'Chief' Silva to you, Laney, you frumpy little turd." He tugged on the visored hat he now wore for emphasis. For some inexplicable reason, the Bosun had given it to him, and it wasn't even his oldest, most beat-up one, either. He just said if Silva was going to be a chief, he had to look like one. Laney wore one of Donaghey's old hats, and despite the fact that he was larger than the late engineer, it was too big, and only his ears and eyebrows held it up. Otherwise, no one else aboard would have called Laney "little," though. He was only slightly shorter than Silva, and a comment like that would once have started a fairly equal fight. Now, both were conscious of the limitations placed on them by the new hats they wore. All the same, Laney suddenly remembered another time, and he was glad they were standing by the solid rail instead of the safety chains.

"It ain't *your* machine shop, neither," Silva added. "I swear, you've got mighty uppity of late. One of your 'Cats even wants to strike for the deck." He shook his head. "Shows good sense if you ask me, but Spanky and Donaghey never ran anybody off. You always was a asshole, but you've got even worse since they gave you that hat."

"Who is it?" Laney growled. "We'll see about that!"

"Ain't gonna tell you. He don't want ordnance anyway. Ask the Bosun when we pick him up."

Laney hesitated. He couldn't afford to lose anybody, but he also couldn't go crawling to the Bosun. "Well, what about the machine shop?" he demanded. "Spanky's gonna shit worm gears when I don't deliver them parts!"

Silva laughed. "I cleared it with Spanky before we started. Besides, he said you got scads of spare pressure couplings by now; you're just doin' busywork."

"Well . . . the second reduction pinion off the low-pressure turbine is thrashed—goddamn lube oil we're getting ain't up to spec—and we gotta turn a new one. 'Sides, what are you doin' in there, makin' mop handles?"

"Matter of fact, we broke the firin' pin on number three this mornin'—all the practicin' I've had the fellas doin'—and we figured we'd make another one." He scratched his beard. "Funny, but without a firin' pin, we can't make the big, scary bullets go out the other end. I told Stites to make a dozen while he was at it. There's a fair chance we'll break another one."

"What about my pinion?"

"You gonna put it in while we're underway? That'd be a rodeo! You're a crummy machinist anyway; I don't care what your rating is. Hell, Juan's a better lathe man than you; so's the Jap. You'd be just as well using a mop handle as anything you'd turn out."

Chack was listening to the conversation with amusement a few steps away. It went on a little longer, but finally Laney stormed aft, grumbling with every step. Chack drifted over and replaced him at the rail and caught Silva chuckling.

"I swear, if he found a roach floatin' in his coffee cup, he'd turn it into a mountain fish by the time he got done yellin' at the mess attendant."

Mountain fish had dominated just about everyone's conversation the last two days. They'd finally seen one of the things—a young one, Chack assured them—lazing on the surface, taking the sun. Silva had always suspected people exaggerated their size, but now he knew they hadn't. Everyone got a good, long look through the binoculars that made the rounds, while the captain gave the creature a wide berth. It was enormous! The part they saw, just a dark hump in the distance, and a small fraction of the monster's total size, was half as long as the ship. It blew like a whale, and occasional waterspouts geysered a hundred feet in the air. Everyone was excited to see the mythical creature at last, but no one was sorry to watch it disappear astern, either. Since then, they'd spotted a couple of truly huge gri-kakka, bigger than any they'd seen before, that were as dangerous to the ship as an iceberg or torpedo, but even giant plesiosaurs paled to insignificance compared to the mountain fish they'd seen.

"Perhaps he is high-strung," Chack suggested, referring to Laney. "I've heard Mr. McFarlane say so."

Silva laughed out loud. "High-strung, and fit to snap a string, I'd say. If he's a chief engineer, I'm a Chinese fighter pilot."

They stood in companionable silence for a while, the foaming sea sluicing by beneath them. They were friends again, although there was still a measure of friction. Not enough to bring them to blows; they'd already discovered, despite Silva's height advantage, Chack's extraordinary strength—he'd spent most of his life as a wing runner or sail trimmer on *Big Sal*, after all—made them a remarkably even match, and their one altercation had left both of them uneager for a rematch. Besides, Chack was no longer certain he was mad at Silva anymore. Most of his anger had resulted from Silva's and his sister Risa's boisterously public "marriage." He felt at the time they'd done it to "get even," or humiliate him for a prank he'd pulled on Silva. He'd since learned that Silva was a *professional* prankster, who enjoyed it when somebody "got" him, but he didn't "get even." His retaliation usually consisted of gross, sometimes even dangerous escalation.

Just about everyone believed the "marriage" was a joke, but Chack still wasn't certain. Sure, Silva and Risa might have carried on so at first, just to get his goat, but since then, in several situations, he'd sensed genuine respect and affection between them. He still found the idea that they might be engaging in *sexual* relations repugnant, but he supposed if they truly did consider themselves mated, then Risa's fate could have been worse. She was a far better warrior than most males he knew, and that, as well as her own rather twisted sense of humor, had left her with few prospects for a fulfilling relationship with a male she could enjoy and respect. Silva seemed to fit that role, and even if such a match would never result in younglings—he shuddered—it might result in happiness, and he was prepared to accept that.

It was time to clear the air, though. His people had few sexual conventions, and most everyone, even Keje and Nakja-Mur, had been amused, at worst, over the possible relationship. But Chack knew the Americans were much less understanding. They liked his people a lot—more than many of their "own." They were at war with the Japanese, after all. But he'd learned an old quip: "I've got nothing against them; I just wouldn't want my daughter to marry one." He expected it was used in jest, at least when he was in earshot, but the phrase struck home. Besides, there was

Silva's alleged affair with the American nurse, Pam Cross, to consider. His people were not necessarily strict monogamists, but he knew Americans could be. Monogamy was, in fact, the norm among them. He worried that, if Silva and his sister were truly mated, Nurse Cross might try to supplant her, and he didn't want Risa hurt. He cleared his throat.

"We should speak," he said at last.

"Shoot."

"About you and Risa, and about your intentions regarding her. We must speak seriously about this at last."

"Sure."

Chack blinked annoyance, and his tail swished rapidly behind him. "I am about to muster the Marines for exercises, so I don't have a great deal of time. Will you just answer my question?"

"You ain't asked one yet."

"As hard as I've worked to master your language, you've surpassed me at being obtuse!" Chack growled.

Silva grinned, but turned to look closely down at him, and his eyes betrayed what might have been an inner sadness. "I like Risa a lot. She's a swell gal. She's a hoot, and she makes me laugh. I wish she was along with us instead of back in Baalkpan on *Big Sal*. She's the only dame . . . uh, female I could ever just let loose with, be myself, talk. I figure if things was different, she'd be about the perfect dame for me to settle down with." He paused, still looking at Chack, and was amused by the indignant blinking he saw. "Now, ain't that somethin'! All this time you've been mad at me because you thought I wasn't good enough for her; now you're mad because you think I just said she ain't good enough for me! Fact is, like I said, we're just about right for each other, even if she is a 'Cat. Trouble is, we're *too* much alike, and neither of us is ready for a rockin' chair." He laughed at Chack's puzzled expression. "You still got some work to do on our language. I mean neither of us is ready to settle down. Do I love her?" He stared back over the rail at some distant point, and when he spoke again his voice was soft, barely audible over the blower, the whoosh of hot gases rising from the funnels, and the curling, splashing wake alongside.

"Once upon a time, the only feelings I had were happy, hungry, horny, and mad. Usually they got all mixed-up. I'd get mad at a fella, we'd get in a fight, and I'd be happy. After it was over I'd wind up hungry, and probably horny too. Or I'd be happy 'cause I wasn't hungry.... You get the idea. Anyway, I had a buddy once, Mack Marvaney, who got killed by them island Griks on Bali before we met y'all, and all of a sudden I found out I had another feelin': sad.

"I don't much remember my folks; they both died when I was a sprout—about three, I guess. En-floo-en-za. It was all over the place, but Daddy might've brought it back from France." He shrugged. "I went to live with my uncle Bob, and he worked me and whupped me like a mule from then on. Got even worse after the Crash, and I had to scrape for everything we ate. He'd bring a little money home now and then, makin' 'shine, but he drank as much as he made, and one day he took a harness strap to me and I killed him with a grubbin' hoe." His jaw clenched tight. "Never felt sad about that. Anyway, I wandered around for a few years, doin' things I ain't much proud of, mostly, and when I turned sixteen I lied about my age and joined the Navy." He looked at Chack. "Now you know more about me than anyone alive ... 'cept Risa.

"I never knew what 'love' was, or 'sad' or 'safe,' or really 'happy' either, but now I guess I do." He suddenly slapped Chack on the back hard enough to take his breath. "I love you like the brother I never had, and Stites and Rodriguez, Mertz, Kutas, even Juan and all the others, 'cept maybe Laney. He's a jerk. The Mice—and Bradford!—are like the freak cousins nobody ever talks about, but I even love them too. The skipper's not that much older'n me, but him or the Bosun are the closest thing to a real dad I ever had, 'cause they keep me in line without a harness strap, and they do it for my own good." His mighty fist pounded the rail. "And I love this damned old ship that's as old as I am. She's the only real home I've ever had. She leaks, she squeaks, hell, sometimes she coughs and gags. She prob'ly couldn't hold her own in a stand-up fight against a rowboat full of Boy Scouts with BB guns, but she's my goddamn home!"

Silva quickly turned away and jabbed his fingers in his eyes, rubbing vigorously. "Damn soot!" he mumbled huskily. "Snipes must've blown tubes on one of the boilers." After a while, he turned to face Chack again with a mysterious dampness around his eyes. He made a production of pulling a pouch from his pocket and biting off a chew. Finally, when the quid was properly formed in his cheek, he spoke again.

"You wanna know if me and Risa have wrassled and romped around, and had a little fun; that's none of your damn business. Do I love her? Sure I do, and I wouldn't do anything to hurt her. She's my pal. Will I tear your heart out and eat it if you spill any of what I just told you? You can bet your life on it, brother or not."

Captain Reddy was watching the two from the perspective of the open deck behind the pilothouse. He grunted. He was glad to see that, whatever accord Chack and Silva had reached, at least they'd made up. He needed them too badly, and their strained relationship had been felt throughout the ship. Turning, he rejoined Keje, Bradford, and Adar, where they were discussing Maa-ni-la protocol on the starboard bridge wing. There wasn't that much to discuss; it was roughly the same as Baalkpan—the two land homes were related, after all—and they'd already been over it a dozen times. There'd be the initial "request to come aboard" that was a holdover from the seafaring tradition all 'Cats shared and most still adhered to, but Matt, as "High Chief" of *Walker*, must make the request this time himself. A lot would depend on how he was received by Saan-Kakja, Maa-ni-la's High Chief. *Walker* was a very small "Home," after all, and despite Matt's position, and what he represented within the Alliance, Sasn-Kakja might not recognize him as a High Chief. Nobody wanted to set the precedent that every captain of every fishing boat or trader had the same status as the leaders of the great Homes of the sea and land. Even if he was accepted, however, it'd be up to Keje or Adar to do most of the talking. Matt's Lemurian was improving, but it wasn't up to the task of serious negotiations. Sasn-Kakja was a new High Chief and an unknown, but it was a safe bet he knew no English, and Matt might as well recite nursery rhymes when he spoke. Keje and Adar already knew what to say.

He glanced at his watch and compared it to the clock on the bulkhead. It was almost time for the watch change, and he'd soon relieve Dowden, who currently had the deck.

"One thing I can't stress enough," he reminded, interrupting the 'Cats and the naturalist, "is that you immediately try to learn as much as you can about the reports of an 'iron fish.' If it's a submarine, as I suspect, I need to know as much as possible about what it looked like and where it was most recently sighted. I understand it hasn't been seen for months. It'd undoubtedly be out of fuel by now, so we'll have to base our search on its last reported position, investigate the closest islands and so forth. Hopefully, we can begin that process while your discussions are still underway, if they drag out too long. We really need to find that boat. It could make all the difference."

"What makes you so sure it *is* a submarine, Captain?" Bradford asked. "Who knows what creatures lurk in these mysterious seas? And even if it is one, what if it's an enemy vessel? The Japanese on *Amagi* have shown no inclination to aid us, certainly!"

"C'mon, Courtney! An *iron fish*? And the stories tell how strange, tail-less creatures went inside it before it swam beneath the sea! As for it being one of ours, it only makes sense. We had lots of boats in the area, more than the Japs. They might've even been enough to make a difference, but their torpedoes weren't working either. If it weren't for our crummy MK-14 and -15 torpedoes, we might've even *stopped* the Japs." His voice had begun to rise, and he stopped himself and took a deep, calming breath. "If a sub was in the vicinity of the Squall, like the PBY was, it could have been swept here just like us. Unlike us, they might've made for the Philippines, looking for a familiar face. Last we heard, we still had Corregidor, and subs were getting in and out. If they poked their scope up at Surabaya—I mean Aryaal—and saw what's there now, the next place they'd check, their only hope really, would be the Philippines. If it was a Jap sub . . . I really don't know where it would head, probably not the Philippines, though. Maybe Singapore. They've got some really big, long-range boats; they might've even tried to make Japan."

Adar shuddered. "How big would this 'sub-maa-rine' be, if it was Amer-i-caan?"

"Depends on the class; either about the same length as *Walker*, or three-quarters as long."

"Just imagine," Adar gasped, "cruising beneath the sea, and in something that small!"

Matt nodded grimly. "You bet. I always thought submariners were nuts, and that was before there were fish big enough to eat the whole bloody boat. God, I hope that's not what's happened to her!"

"You've mentioned before how . . . aad-vaan-tage-ous . . . it would be to find this amazing vessel, but despite the happy prospect of finding more Amer-i-caans, what good would it be? You have already recognized the terrible dangers of operating it, particularly underwater. I'm sure, if they live, the same dangers have occurred to its crew."

Matt nodded. "Sure, but the danger would be much less within the confines of the Makassar Strait, or Baalkpan Bay itself, and didn't you already hear me say it might have torpedoes aboard? We only have one left, and we know why they weren't working now. She might be our ultimate surprise against *Amagi*."

"I should think securing more troops than the few Saan-Kakja has already sent would be our highest priority, not finding a submarine that may or may not exist," Bradford opined.

"Probably, but that'll be largely Adar and Keje's job. If we can manage both, however—" He was interrupted by the clanging bell that signaled the watch change. "Let's just hope we can manage at least one or the other."

They could have made Manila before sunup, in the wee hours of the morning, but Matt didn't want to sneak in; he wanted to be seen. He also wanted to see the city in the light of day, gauge the reaction of its people to their arrival. Most would know what it meant, and why they were there; refugees had been crowding into Manila for months. He hoped the sight of his ship, newly painted with most of her visible damage repaired, would inspire confidence in their cause. She'd made quite a sensation the first time she steamed into Baalkpan Bay, after all. So they loitered in the mouth of Manila Bay in the dark, while swarms of fishing boats hurried past her for the morning catch. Most never saw her, or if they did they paid no heed, since her arrival wasn't a surprise. The mission had been announced over a month ago, plenty of time for even one of the lumbering Homes to bring the news. A few boats stopped, their people staring at her with their uncanny vision, but none stopped to chat. Matt wondered if that was good or bad. A few coastal traders came out with the sun, scudding before the brisk morning breeze, but they immediately went on their way. Matt cleared his throat.

"Very well. Mr. Kutas, I have the deck and the conn," he said, much to the chief quartermaster's relief. Kutas had rarely conned the ship in confined waters. "Relieve Reynolds on the helm and take us in. Carefully and politely, though, if you please." It was Reynolds's turn to gulp with relief. The young seaman had only recently been rated capable of standing a helmsman's watch.

"Aye, aye, Captain," Kutas replied. "You have the deck and the conn." He turned to Reynolds. "I relieve you, sir." Reynolds gratefully stepped aside and unobtrusively relieved the talker of his headset. The 'Cat, just as glad, scampered up the ladder with a pair of binoculars to add his eyes to the already numerous lookouts. Manila Bay was reputed to be the busiest waterway in the known world, and the last thing they needed with everyone watching was to collide with anything, even a rowboat.

They entered the bay much as they always had so many times before, back on their own world before the Japanese drove them out. They steamed up the Boca Grande between Caballo Island and the El Frailes. Just beyond Caballo—startlingly barren of the familiar Fort Hughes—was the imposing form of Corregidor. Unlike the Corregidor they remembered, there'd been no fortifications upon this one until recently. Now a great stone works was under construction. Through his binoculars, Matt saw the two heavy thirty-two-pounders Baalkpan had sent Saan-Kakja as gifts, brooding through embrasures in the hastily built walls. Interestingly, they'd been joined by several more, and he realized the Manilos were now making cannons of their own. No reason they shouldn't, once they understood the concept; their industry was certainly up to the task. It still left him feeling odd. In the past, the gift of artillery to native peoples had often been a double-edged sword.

He felt like they should salute the fort in some fashion, but the Maa-ni-los had no flag, and he wasn't about to fire a gun. They'd had few blanks, and those were given over to Bernard Sandison with all their empty shells, so he could reload them with the experimental solid copper projectiles and black powder. He settled for having their own flag dipped. Perhaps they'd understand the courtesy. He gave the order in a hushed tone, however. Even he wasn't immune to the strange emotions sweeping the men around him at the sight of the familiar, but alien landmarks.

Beyond Corregidor was the Bataan Peninsula, and there was even a small town, of sorts, where Mariveles ought to be. In the distance, barely visible in the early morning haze, stood the poignantly familiar Mariveles Mountains.

"Recommend course zero, four, five degrees," Kutas said, glancing at the compass and breaking the spell that had fallen upon the Americans in the pilothouse. Juan had appeared unnoticed, carrying a tray of mugs and a coffee urn, and when Matt glanced his way he saw unashamed tears streaking the little Filipino's face as he gazed about.

He coughed. "Thanks, Juan. I was just thinking some of your coffee would taste pretty good right now." A brittle smile appeared on the steward's face, and he circulated through the cramped pilothouse, filling the mugs taken from his tray by the watch standers. For once, none were left behind. Sensitive to the gesture, he bowed slightly.

"I will bring sandwiches, if you please, Cap-tan," he managed huskily. "It has been a long night . . . for all of us."

"Thanks, Juan. Please do." When the Filipino left the bridge, there was an almost audible general sigh, as nearly everyone realized that no matter how hard it was for them, entering *this* Manila Bay must be a waking nightmare for Juan. Looking around, Keje sensed the tension.

"What is the matter?" he quietly asked. "This is our goal, our destination. All should be glad we have arrived."

"In that sense, I guess we're glad," Matt answered, "but where we came from, this was our . . . base, before the war against the Japs. I've told you before, I was here for several months, but others were here for years. They considered it home. What you may not know is, for Juan, it *was* home. He was born here . . . there . . . whatever. We all understand the places we came from are lost to us, probably forever, but to see it with our own eyes . . . I try not to think how I'd react to see the place that should be my home near Stephenville, Texas—a place on the far side of the Earth—but I can't always help it, and neither can anyone else."

Keje refrained from pointing out the impossibility of anyone living on the far side of the Earth. He suspected Cap-

tain Reddy meant it metaphorically. Regardless, the point
was clear. "You have my deepest sympathies. I cannot imagine how you feel. I only hope time and good friendship
can help ease the pain."

They steamed northeast at a leisurely and courteous—
but awe inspiring to the natives—twelve knots against the
prevailing wind, and the closer they got to Cavite and Manila, the more surface craft they met. Most were the ubiquitous feluccas: fore-and-aft-rigged boats, large and small,
that seemed universally known and used among all Lemurians they'd met, even the Aryaalans and B'mbaadans.
Matt often wondered about that. Compared to the massive
Homes, the smaller craft boasted a more sophisticated rig:
a large lateen-rigged triangular sail on a relatively short
mast with a fore staysail, or jib, allowing them to sail much
closer to the wind than even the Grik square-riggers could
accomplish. Of course, they couldn't sail *with* the wind as
efficiently. . . . It suddenly struck him the rig might be yet
another legacy of those long-ago East Indiamen. Their
small boats and launches might have carried a similar sail
plan. Of course, not all Lemurian feluccas were open boats.
Most had at least one deck, and sometimes two, and he'd
seen several over a hundred feet long, really not feluccas
at all. Kind of a cross between a felucca and a caravel. He
shrugged inwardly. It didn't really matter. He was more
interested in the generally positive reception they were
receiving.

He'd half feared they'd be met with stony glares. Manila
was where most of their own "runaways" had fled, convinced the arrival of the Americans and their iron ship had
started the war with the Grik in the first place. There was
nothing he could say to that. Doubtless there were people
back home who thought Pearl Harbor was America's fault,
but most were more sensible. The same seemed true of
the majority of Lemurians, thank God. Those in the boats
they passed weren't exactly cheering and throwing flowers, but they appeared friendly, and even somewhat glad to
see them. They were certainly fascinated by the ship they'd
no doubt heard so much about. Some of the more daring
captains of what must have been primarily pleasure craft
even tried to pace them. It was impossible, of course; no
sailing vessel could steer directly into the wind, and even

their tight tacking maneuvers soon left them behind, but many of *Walker*'s human and 'Cat destroyermen lined the rails and cheered their efforts. It was a relief in more ways than one. There was no overt hostility associated with their arrival and the request that arrival implied, and it took the men's minds off the gloomy thoughts that had filled them.

They reduced speed to ten knots, then eight, and finally five as the bay grew ever more crowded, and they picked their way carefully through the capering boats. Matt had been warned how busy Manila was, but he hadn't truly credited it until now. Baalkpan was a major city, but essentially compact, having been hacked out of the hostile wilderness around it. Evidently Manila was a far more sprawling and populous place. Homes and small docks began to appear ten miles short of Cavite, and the shore grew more densely populated the closer they got to the peninsula that had once been the center of America's Asiatic naval power on that other world. It was a natural place for similar activity here, and a massive shipyard and repair facility dominated it even more thoroughly than they remembered. The tripod masts of a dozen seagoing Homes jutted from the yards and Bacoor Bay beyond, and more of the massive vessels were moored before Maa-ni-la.

When *Walker* first steamed into Baalkpan Bay almost a year ago, her people were impressed by the size and vitality, the riot of color, and the architectural wonder and singularity of the place. Even the more familiar, almost medieval appearance of Aryaal, with its walls and spires and arches, had not been as impressive. But Baalkpan was positively provincial compared to Maa-ni-la. When Matt asked Nakja-Mur what differences to expect, he'd been told Maa-ni-la was "a little bigger," but he now saw that had been a significant understatement. The closer they came, the more clearly he grasped that *everything* was bigger here. The exotically eastern, pagodalike structures were virtual skyscrapers in comparison, and the docks were proportionately massive. The Bosun once compared Baalkpan to Chefoo, but if that was the case, Manila was Shanghai, or some alien, chaotic, eastern-flavored Manhattan. There was no Empire State Building, of course, nothing even close to that, but everything was taller, more tightly packed, and far more densely populated than Baalkpan when they first saw it. The only thing less impressive was the massive Galla tree growing up in the center of the city. Presumably encompassed by Saan-Kakja's Great Hall, the tree wasn't as tall as the one in Baalkpan, but then again, Maa-ni-la was a younger city, closer to the shifting center of trade and commerce. There were land homes on northern Borneo now, and even in Japan. If the water was deeper and more dangerous, its coastal bounty was richer. Homes were rarely bothered by mountain fish, except for certain times of year, so they increasingly dared the deeper seas, and a place was required to build them, supply them, and trade for the rich gri-kakka oil they rendered. So even though Baalkpan prospered and enjoyed much influence, Maa-ni-la not only prospered, but grew.

Walker backed engines and shuddered to a stop two hundred yards short of the main wharf Keje directed them to. With a great rattling, booming crash, her anchor splashed into the water and fell to the bottom of the bay. Just like the first time they visited Baalkpan, Matt wouldn't tie her to the dock until invited to do so.

"All engines stop," he commanded. "Maintain standard pressure on numbers two and three, and hoist out the launch. Make sure the shore party wears their new whites."

With Baalkpan's impressive textile capacity, they'd made new uniforms principally for this mission. They were remarkably good copies, even though they were hand-sewn, and no Lemurian had ever made anything like trousers before. It took a while to get used to the feel of the strange, itchy material. It wasn't really cotton, and certainly wasn't wool. More like linen, and Matt honestly didn't have any idea what it was made of, although he was sure Courtney Bradford could go on about the process for hours. He relinquished the deck to Larry Dowden and started for his stateroom to change into his own new uniform when he had a thought. When they first entered Nakja-Mur's Great Hall, they'd carried sidearms, and the more recognizable Navy cutlasses, pattern of 1918, thinking their version of commonplace weapons might make their hosts feel more at ease. Matt had worn his now battered and ironically much-used academy sword. That resulted in a delicate social situation when he'd given the "sign of the empty hand"—essentially a wave—when his hand wasn't metaphorically empty. He'd learned the sign was customarily given only when visitors arrived unarmed. That left him with a dilemma. He knew they should have little to fear, even in the massive, sprawling city they were about to enter, but they'd suffered treachery before, and he wouldn't take any chances.

"Sidearms and cutlasses for the diplomatic mission," he said, then held up his hand before Keje could protest. "Thompsons for the detail to stay with the boat."

"Aye, sir," Larry replied, somewhat triumphantly. He'd argued strenuously that the shore party must be armed, against Adar's equally adamant disagreement. Matt turned to Keje.

"We know not everybody's on our side," he said, explaining his decision to an equal as he wouldn't have done to anyone else, "and not all the 'pacifists' are nonviolent either. I won't risk anybody in a city that large, and with that many people, on faith alone. I'll compromise to the extent that we'll leave our weapons with another guard detail before we ascend to the Great Hall. Fair?" After brief consideration, Keje nodded with a grin.

"Fair. Baalkpan has never known real crime, but in a place like this?" He waved generally toward the city. "I have rarely been here, and not at all recently. Since my last visit, the place has 'boomed,' I believe you would say. Adar will object, of course, but it is unreasonable to assume there is no risk at all. Besides, some of the more subversive elements have gravitated here, and I personally would feel much better with my scota at my side. I think leaving our weapons under guard is a fine compromise between trust and prudence."

Matt grinned back. "I'm glad you approve. Should we tell Adar the plan, or let him stew?"

In the event, they had no difficulty reaching the Great Hall. Saan-Kakja had provided an escort that led them through the teeming multitudes, swirling smells, and riotous colors of the dockside bazaar. There were ten of them, besides the four they'd left with the launch. Captain Reddy, Keje, Adar, and Courtney Bradford constituted the diplomatic mission, and Chack and Dennis Silva would ascend with them to the hall as guards of honor. Matt was dubious about including

Silva, but he and Chack were the most visibly formidable representatives of their respective species aboard the ship. Three of Chack's Marines, resplendent in their blue kilts and polished armor, would guard their weapons under the command of the Marine captain, Graana-Fas, who was the son of Jarrik-Fas, Keje's cousin and personal armsman he'd left commanding *Salissa*.

Their escort consisted of two dozen 'Cats in Saan-Kakja's livery: yellow-and-black-checked kilts, burnished silver-plated breastplates, and platterlike helmets that looked like deeper copies of the Americans', but with cutouts for the ears. A yellowish plume of something feathery flowed down their backs from a clasp on top of their headgear. Short, stabbing swords swung from their hips, again much like those the Americans introduced, which completed the martial ensemble and added a businesslike touch to their colorful garb. The curious crowd parted before them, though no command to do so was audible over the tumult, and they marched purposefully through the bustling shoppers, tradesmen hawking their wares, alien smells of cooking food, and naked younglings skittering about on all fours. The pulse of the city was vibrant and powerful, though hectic beyond belief. Much like Baalkpan, most of the commerce took place in the open air beneath colorful awnings and tapestries, but there seemed no order to it. In Baalkpan, the various services were clumped more or less together, so it was easier to find what one wanted. Here, there was no apparent attempt at any such organization, and the result was a kaleidoscope of sounds and smells and unintelligible voices that assaulted the senses from the time they left the boat until they drew to a halt at the base of the great Galla tree near the center of the city.

Like Baalkpan, the area immediately around the tree, and the Great Hall encompassing its base, was open and free of structures, permitting a park- or gardenlike effect. The area around Nakja-Mur's hall had long since been churned up by drilling troops, its original beauty sacrificed to the imperative of training an army on the only open ground available. Since then, larger parade grounds and drill fields had been established beyond the new defensive works and hastily cleared jungle, but the original effect was similar enough to inspire a sense of déjà vu. The similarity ended there, however, for the process of greeting was significantly and unexpectedly different.

Nakja-Mur had welcomed them from an opening in his elevated hall, in time-honored fashion, as if they'd approached his "ship" in an open boat. Judging by the finery of the reception committee at the base of the tree, Saan-Kakja would meet them on level ground—an honor, possibly, but something they hadn't foreseen.

Matt stared at the berobed phalanx, and tried to figure out which was the High Chief. The High Sky Priest was simple enough to identify; he was dressed exactly like Adar: younger, skinnier, and not as tall, but with the same silvery gray fur, barely revealed by the closely held purple cape flecked with silver stars. Perhaps Saan-Kakja was one of the beings standing near him? Sotto voce inquiries of Adar and Keje revealed nothing, since Saan-Kakja had risen since their last visit, and the old High Chief had been childless then. An awkward dilemma.

Decisively, Matt unbuckled his sword and pistol belt and thrust it at Silva before striding forward and holding his right hand aloft, palm forward.

"I'm Captain Matthew Reddy, High Chief of *Walker*, *Mahan*, and other units of the United States Navy, as well as Tarakan Island. I come to you in peace and friendship, representing all the allied Homes united under the Banner of the Trees, against the vicious onslaught of our Ancient Enemy, the Grik. As supreme commander, by acclamation, of the alliance, I've been granted plenipotentiary powers, and would treat with the High Chief of this Home. Do I have permission to come aboard?"

Adar nodded approval at Captain Reddy's words and interpreted what he said. For a brief, awkward moment they waited, but there was no response; then the short sky priest took a step forward as if preparing to address them. Before he could speak, however, he was jostled aside by an even smaller form that strode directly up to Captain Reddy. The Lemurian was robed as the others in the same yellow and black, but the black hem was magnificently embroidered with gold thread and sparkling, polished sequins of shell. A fringe of glittering golden cones chinked dully with every step. A matching sash, complete with cones, coiled around a wasp-thin waist, and a gold gorget, intricately chased and engraved, swayed from a ropelike chain. On its head, the Lemurian wore a magnificently engraved helmet, also of gold, reminiscent of the ancient Spartans except for the feathery yellow plume. Large hinged cheek guards and a rigid nosepiece obscured the face entirely except for a pair of brightly inquisitive but astonishing eyes. They were yellow, which was not uncommon for 'Cats, but they looked like ripe lemons sliced across their axes, and dark, almost black lines radiated outward from bottomless black pupils. A small hand rose up, palm outward, in an openhanded gesture.

"I am Saan-Kakja, High Chief of Maa-ni-la, and all the Fil-pin lands," came a small muffled voice from within the helmet. "I greet you, Cap-i-taan Reddy, High Chief and supreme commander of the allied Homes." With that, while Adar translated, another hand joined the first, and together they removed the helmet. Behind it was the fine-boned, dark-furred face of a Lemurian female of an age barely eligible to mate.

Matt was surprised. He'd suspected a youngster simply because of their host's size. But even though he'd learned to accept that Lemurians made no distinction between the sexes regarding occupation—one of the seagoing members of the alliance, *Humfra-Dar*, had a female High Chief, after all—he'd never even considered the possibility something the size of the entire Philippines might be ruled by one. Stupid. Even in human history, there'd often been powerful women, sometimes supremely powerful. He hoped with a twinge of embarrassment that he hadn't blinked surprise; he knew how to do that, at least, and he'd caught himself mimicking the Lemurian "expressions" more and more. He had to continue suppressing the reaction, because even though Saan-Kakja had never seen a human before in her life, young as she was, he detected no surprise, shock, distaste or . . . anything that might offend. Of course, she'd had that helmet to hide behind during her initial reaction, he consoled himself.

"Please do come aboard," she continued. "I have heard a great deal about you and your amazing, gallant ship, and how you came from some incomprehensibly distant place to defend our people against unspeakable evil."

"Thank you," Matt replied gravely in her own tongue. That much he could manage.

She turned slightly and nodded respectfully to Adar first, then Keje—yet another departure from protocol, since Keje was, after all, another head of state. But while Adar's status might have grown ambiguous—there'd never been a Sky Priest who, in effect, represented multiple Homes—it was certainly real, and perhaps even groundbreaking in importance. "High Sky Priest Adar, your reputation as a scholar is well remembered here, as is your knowledge of the pathways of this world and the next. I know of your oath to destroy the Grik forever, and I crave your counsel. . . ." She paused, and it seemed she'd left something unsaid, but then she continued. "Keje-Fris-Ar, you have long been renowned as a master mariner. Now you are a great warrior. I am honored to be in your presence once more, though I do not expect you to remember our last meeting." Her eyes flicked across Bradford, then lingered on Silva and Chack. Especially Chack. They rested on Matt once more. "Do come aboard, and welcome. I would prefer to celebrate your arrival in the traditional way, but the times we live in do not countenance ordinary pleasures, it seems. We have much to discuss and"—she blinked apology, while at the same time the posture of her ears conveyed intense frustration—"little time."

The entire sky was a leaden, dreary gray, unusual for midmorning over Baalkpan Bay. It seemed to radiate no malicious intent to become truly stormy, but there'd definitely be rain and lots of it. (Brevet) Captain Benjamin Mallory stalked back and forth on the beach, his arm still in a sling, watching while the huge but horribly battered PBY flying boat slowly rolled, landing gear extended, back into the sea.

"He looks like a worried mama cat whose kittens are climbing a tree for the first time," Jim Ellis said aside to Alan Letts. Both had come to observe the launching, and they'd escorted Sandra Tucker, who'd decided to join them at the last minute—probably to make sure Mallory didn't strain any of his wounds. It was a good thing too. He clearly felt inhibited by her presence. Letts chuckled, and so did

Sandra, although the nurse's laugh seemed fragile, exhausted. Letts looked at her. She'd come straight from the hospital, where she'd been working quite late or quite early, training ever more nurses and corpsmen for the looming showdown, or tending personally to a hurt beyond her students' abilities. Her long, sandy-brown hair was swept back in a girlish ponytail that belied her twenty-eight years and extreme professional competence. It accented her pretty face and slender neck, but it did make her look younger than she was. Younger and more vulnerable.

Alan Letts liked and admired her, as did everyone, human and Lemurian, but he always felt a little guilty when she was near. He was morally certain he'd married Karen Theimer because he loved her, and not, as some whispered, to snatch up one of the only "dames" known to exist. He *knew* he loved her, and they were happy together, but his very happiness inspired much of his guilt. He couldn't help thinking it wasn't right for him to be happy when so many of the men were so miserable. It had strained his relationship with the men, just as he'd expected, and Sandra and Captain Reddy predicted. As Captain Reddy's chief of staff, he was obeyed, but he'd lost a measure of moral authority, he thought. On the other hand, everyone knew Sandra and the captain were nuts about each other—*Walker*'s crew had probably known it before they had. Even so, they'd tried to hide their attraction out of respect for the feelings of the crew, and they'd never once acted on that attraction beyond a rare stolen kiss they thought no one could see. They'd both already been held in high esteem, but their poignant sacrifice endeared them to the crew even more. It was obvious their love continued to grow, and each was very much a reservoir for the other's strength, but still they didn't marry or "shack up," as the scuttlebutt said Silva and Pam Cross had sometimes done—not to mention Silva's "other" affair! They did nothing any of the surviving destroyermen from *Walker* and *Mahan* couldn't do. The men called them dopes and rolled their eyes in exasperation . . . and loved them for it. It was ongoing, positive proof the skipper wouldn't rest until he fulfilled his promise to find the other humans he believed must exist in this twisted, messed-up world. Alan Letts was in awe of their willpower, and amazed by their self-sacrificing, almost tragic nobility. It was like two star-

crossed lovers from a John Ford western had found themselves in a Cecil B. DeMille epic—complete with a cast of
thousands, monsters, and freak weather events. And every
time he saw the sad, melancholy look on Sandra Tucker's
face, he felt like a heel.

"What's the matter?" she asked, apparently noticing his
expression.

He smiled. "Nothing. Just woolgathering. Hoping they
patched all the holes and the damn thing doesn't sink." Mallory sent him a scorching look.

The plane was in the water now, fully buoyant and straining against the taglines attached to each wing and held by
forty 'Cats apiece. The current here could be fierce when
the tide was ebbing. Another hundred were sitting back,
awaiting the order to drag the plane back up the ramp.
This was merely a flotation test to see if they had, indeed,
patched all the bullet holes. A lot of other repairs had been
"completed" as well. The fuel tanks were patched and the
wings repaired. The jagged section of the port wing had
been trimmed and faired where a four-foot section had
been torn completely off when the Japanese scout plane
rammed them. Fortunately, the float was down at the time
and hadn't been carried away, but now it was secured forever in a lowered position, as was the starboard float. Ben
had decided to go ahead and cut off a corresponding length
from the other wing to trim the plane and provide enough
aluminum for repairs. The plane would lose some lift—and
a lot of speed from the additional constant drag—but it
was the best compromise he could make. Maneuverability
would suffer as well, since they'd been forced to construct
new, slightly abbreviated ailerons from the local, almost
indestructible Borneo bamboo covered with "linen" and
heavily doped.

They hadn't been able to come up with a replacement
for the shattered Plexiglas yet, either for the cockpit or the
observation blisters, but they were still kicking around a
few ideas. Beyond that, the plane was patched and dented,
and the once proud blue paint had faded and oxidized to
a general blotchy gray, but Mallory said it would fly—once
he and Jis-Tikkar finished with the starboard engine. Even
now, the plane floated with a decided list to port, the float
almost underwater, because the place where the starboard

engine should be was just a tangle of mounts, hoses, and lines, covered with a bright green tarp.

"How's she doing?" Mallory bellowed, and Ensign Palmer—formerly signalman second—poked his head out of the cockpit.

"There's a few leaks . . ." he hedged.

"How bad?"

"Just a second, Tikker's checking them now." Moments later, a sable-colored 'Cat with a polished brass cartridge case thrust through a neat hole in his right ear appeared. Sandra put a hand over her mouth and giggled as he conferred with Palmer.

"Yeah," Mallory said aside to her with a grin, "little booger doesn't want anyone to forget his 'noble wound.' I wish I had a medal for him, but I guess that'll do." He shook his head. "I still can't believe the two of them flew that plane back here after I passed out. Especially in the shape it was."

"He'll get a medal one of these days," Ellis assured him, "and he's already been made an ensign." He laughed. "Of course, he's not in the Army Air Corps. The Navy'll get to claim the first commissioned Lemurian aviator!"

Palmer shouted at them: "She's doing okay, mostly, but leaking pretty fast in a couple places. We'd better drag her out!"

Ben nodded and gave the command. A moment later the inactive 'Cats on the beach joined the others on the taglines. With a shout from a Guard NCO, they heaved in unison. He grunted. "We'll have an Air Corps someday. We have to. Even when we get *that* back in the air"—he gestured at the plane—"it won't last long."

Letts nodded grimly. "Airpower's the key; the Japs taught us that. But for now we have to concentrate on the Navy, I'm afraid. And, of course, there's the problem with engines—speaking of which . . . ?"

"We'll get it running," Mallory promised. "It's going to be rough as hell and sound like shit, but we'll get it running."

"How?" Sandra asked. They all looked at the savaged motor, hanging from a bamboo tripod nearby under an awning. Beyond was the "radio shack," a simple, sturdy, waterproof shelter erected to house the radio they'd temporarily removed from the plane—just in case it *did* sink.

The PBY's starboard motor was surrounded by benches covered with tools and ruined engine parts.

Ben shrugged. "It's almost back together. We had to take it completely apart." He nodded at Alan. "Mister Letts really came through again with that weird corklike stuff!" Ellis nodded, and Letts shifted uncomfortably before he replied.

"Yeah, well, Bradford discovered it. Some sort of tree growing in the northwestern marshes where all those tar pits are. The trees draw the stuff up in their roots and deposit it in the lower, outer layers of their trunks. They creosote themselves! Bradford says it protects them from insects."

"Whatever," Ben muttered. "Spanky said it's the best gasket material he's ever had his hands on, and you're the one who figured out the application."

Jim nodded thoughtfully, looking at Letts. "He's turned out pretty good, hasn't he?"

"Yeah," agreed Mallory, his tone turning wistful. "Married life seems to agree with him."

"So it would seem."

There was an awkward silence, but Mallory broke it before it stretched out. "Anyway, we had to take it apart so we could get at the connecting rods on the crank and take the two bad pistons out. Only one was really junked, but we lost two jugs."

Sandra smiled patiently. "And what does that mean?"

"Well . . . see those round, knobby things sticking out of the main part? The things with . . . ribs on them?"

"The cylinders?" Sandra asked. "Cylinders are jugs?"

"Uh . . . yeah." Ben smiled with relief. At least she understood that much. "Two of them we can't do anything about; they took too much of a beating. One was even shot through. We just can't fix them now. Maybe someday. Anyway, we've pulled the pistons and rods, and we're just going to plug the holes. Like I said, it'll run pretty rough, and it'll lose a lot of horsepower, but it'll run."

Ellis winced. "I guess if there's nothing else for it . . ."

"'Fraid not."

They heard a deep, dull thump of cannon far across the bay, and turned toward the sound. Another gun followed the first, then another. A square-rigged ship, the new frigate *Donaghey*, by the distant, fuzzy look of her, had finally returned from her rescue mission and was saluting the Tree Flag of the Alliance, fluttering above the ramparts of Fort Atkinson at the mouth of the bay. The fort returned the salute, but a few minutes after the last guns fell silent, a red rocket soared into the sky and popped above the fort.

"What the hell?" Ellis breathed. A red rocket from the fort was the signal for alarm. A moment later two green rockets exploded in the air. "Okay," he said. "That's a little less terrifying. The ship must be flying a signal we can't see yet, and whoever's on duty at the fort decided we needed a heads-up."

Mallory looked at him curiously. "I know what the red rocket means, but I must've missed the green rocket briefing."

"There wasn't one," Letts told him. "Jim, Riggs, and I just worked the signal out a couple days ago." He gestured at the plane, then vaguely all around. "We've all been a little preoccupied. The new system's on the roster at the fort, but not here yet."

"What's it mean?"

"One red means alarm, like always, but it's also an urgent attention getter now, too. The first green rocket after a red means 'important information.'"

"What's a second green one mean?"

"Immediate, command staff level. Basically what we just saw was somebody sending a message that says: 'Wake up! We've got important, deep-shit information. We don't have time to tell it twice, so get everybody who can do something about anything in one place right now. Damn it.'"

Ben's eyes were wide. "Those three little rockets said all that?"

"Yeah."

Mahan's general alarm began to sound, its thrumming, gonging blare somewhat muffled by the humidity and a light mist that had begun to fall, even though the ship was moored less than three hundred yards away. The sound was instantly recognizable, however.

"What the hell now?" Letts demanded. Jim Ellis was already sprinting for his ship. In the distance, also muffled, they suddenly heard an engine. An airplane engine. Ben looked frantically around at the darkening sky, his eyes suddenly focusing on an object to westward.

"This is something else!" The straining Lemurians had the plane about halfway out of the water, and he ran toward them, sling flapping empty at his side. "Get it out! Get it out! Get my plane out of the goddamn water!" He grabbed one of the lines himself, insensitive to the pain. Ed and Tikker leaped down from the cockpit and joined him. "Heave!"

"What is it?" Sandra asked Alan, still standing beside her. He wasn't wearing binoculars and his eyes were straining hard. He suddenly remembered the description of the plane that attacked the PBY, and the indistinct form didn't snap into focus, but he knew what it was: a biplane with floats.

"Oh, God!"

"What?"

Letts snatched her arm hard and tugged her toward a covered gun emplacement some distance away. "C'mon!"

"But why are we going that way? The plane, the ship ..."

"Right! They're what it's after! I'm not telling Captain Reddy I let you stand here and catch a Jap bomb!" Sandra was torn. She knew she'd be needed here if the plane inflicted any damage, but if she were dead ... She made up her mind, and in an instant she was running beside Alan as fast as she could, the engine sound growing louder by the moment.

"Run!" Letts gasped, as the two machine guns on the starboard side of the ship opened up. Many Lemurians were just standing and staring, and Letts and Sandra screamed at them to take cover. They made it under the bombproof and turned to look just as the plane roared over the moored destroyer. Plumes of spray were subsiding where the plane's bullets had struck the water, and a dark object was falling toward the ship. A huge geyser erupted just short of *Mahan*, and the harbor resonated with a thunderclap roar. The plane pulled up, poorly aimed tracers chasing it, and banked hard left, to the north. All they could do was watch while it slowly turned and steadied for another pass, this time clearly intending to strafe and bomb the ship from aft forward. Bullets kicked up white bushes of spray, and *whrang*ed off the steel of the motionless ship. There were a few screams. *Mahan* seemed helpless, but at the last instant the plane staggered slightly, perhaps from a hit, and steadied on a different course: toward the PBY and ultimately directly at Sandra, Letts, and the others who'd taken refuge with them.

"Get down," Letts shouted, but he couldn't bring himself to follow his own advice. His normally fair, freckled face was pale and drawn. Angry flashes sparkled above the cowling of the oncoming plane, and clouds of sand erupted among the people heaving on the taglines. A few Marines were shooting back with Krags, to no apparent effect, and several of the laborers pitched to the ground. Another dark object detached itself as the plane bored in, seemingly destined to land right atop the helpless flying boat. Again, miraculously, the bomb fell short, detonating close to the trees beyond the plane, and sending a greasy brown plume of smoke high in the air, along with shards of trees, timbers, and other debris that rained down on the plane and the detail still straining against its weight. A massive secondary explosion sent a roiling, orange ball of fire into the sky, consuming the barrels of ready gasoline they'd stored nearby, and more flaming debris clattered down, almost to the bombproof. Still firing its single, forward machine gun, the plane sent a fusillade into the defensive position, and bullets thunked into the heavy timbers and whirred away, showering them with splinters. Sandra clutched the dirt and burrowed even lower as the floatplane thundered overhead and pulled up, heading toward the city.

"No more bombs," Letts surmised, then coughed. "Probably going to make a leisurely recon of our defenses and just fly away. Damn-all we can do about it." Sandra looked up at him and saw he wasn't injured, just coughing on the dust and gathering smoke in the air. Others around them were standing now too, but all she saw were a few superficial splinter wounds.

"Will it come back?" she asked, rising beside him.

"I don't think so."

In an instant she was running back toward the plane and the pall of smoke and licking flames beyond. "Get some medical help down here!" she shouted, and was gone.

"Avast heaving," Mallory wheezed, wondering blearily why he'd used a nautical term even as he did it. 'Cats collapsed to the ground, gasping and coughing as they breathed the black and gray particles drifting down from the dense smoke above. It was raining now; soon it would become a torrent. His shoulder was killing him, and he absently began trying to stuff his arm back in the sling. There were moans among the workers too, but he couldn't tell the wounded from the exhausted through the burning tears filling his eyes. Ed Palmer appeared, dirty and bleeding from a cut on his brow. The ensign leaned over and put his hands on his knees when a coughing spasm took him.

"Where's Tikker?" Ben demanded. Ed gestured toward the engine, still swaying gently beneath its tripod. It seemed okay, but the awning was gone. Tikker and a dozen other 'Cats were throwing shovelfuls of sand on the burning gasoline, dangerously close to their workbenches.

"The plane?"

Ed's fit finally passed, and he spit a gobbet of dark phlegm. "We saved her, I think. A few more holes from bomb fragments, maybe." He shook his head wearily. "Nothing we can't patch. Might've sunk her if she'd still been in the water, though, and it'd have been a bitch to drag her out then." Mallory nodded. Just then Sandra Tucker joined them, breathing hard and beginning to cough as well.

"How many hurt?" she managed. Mallory gestured at the prostrate forms. "Damned if I know. Hey, you monkeys!" he shouted. "Off your asses! Anybody that ain't dead, fall in!" The workers struggled to their feet, still coughing and gasping, leaving several on the ground who were either too badly wounded or would never rise again. Sandra surveyed the scene.

"Get some first aid started here!" she instructed. "Corpsmen are on the way." With that she hurried into the smoke, closer to where the second bomb had struck, knowing there'd be more injured there. They couldn't see *Mahan* through the smoke, but her general alarm was still echoing across the water.

Mallory sighed and pointed at a group of five guardsmen who seemed relatively fit. "Well, don't just stand there; go with her! The rest of you goons check your buddies." He glanced at Ed and saw him staring at the fire as though stricken.

"God a'mighty," Ed whispered numbly.

"What now?"

Ed pointed at the fire, then fell to his knees in the sand in apparent desolation.

"What?"

"The radio shack," he whispered. "It's . . . gone."

All the top military and administrative personnel in Baalkpan had gathered in Nakja-Mur's Great Hall, summoned by the rockets—when word got around what they meant—and the attack, of course. Heavy rain still pounded the ceiling high above, and there was a cool, damp, but refreshing draft in the place. Combined with the general gloom of the few guttering lamps, the drab evening light from the open shutters, and the events of the day, however, the comparative cool served little to temper the prevailing sense of anxiety. Old Naga might have helped; part of the High Sky Priest's job was to administer to the spiritual needs of his flock, but all he did was sit by himself, chanting a nonsensical lamentation. It was inappropriate for any other Sky Priest or acolyte to speak without invitation while Naga was present. Adar could have—he'd practically been designated Naga's successor—but Adar wasn't there.

All the "battle line" commanders were there, the High Chiefs of the few seagoing Homes of the alliance. Jarrik-Fas represented *Salissa* in Keje's stead. Lord Muln Rolak commanded the third-largest infantry force, that of the displaced Aryaalans, but with Alden and Queen Maraan missing, and everyone else away, Rolak was the senior general. He couldn't hold still. Safir Maraan had been queen of his people's bitterest foe, and Aryaal had been at war with B'mbaado before the Grik came. Since then, however, he'd developed an intense fondness for the Orphan Queen. He thought of her almost as a granddaughter now—but more than that, as well. They'd fought side by side in the fiercest battle the world had ever known, and he couldn't bear the thought that she might have fallen into enemy hands. So he paced.

Commander Ellis had just arrived, soaked to the bone,

his uniform badly stained from many hours overseeing repairs to the damage the near miss had caused his ship. He looked exhausted. He joined Ben Mallory and Ed Palmer, as well as Lieutenant Riggs and Lieutenant Commander Brister, who'd just arrived from Fort Atkinson. Alan Letts and Lieutenant Bernard Sandison, *Walker*'s torpedo officer, currently serving as the ordnance officer of the alliance, were standing beside Nakja-Mur's throne of cushions where the High Chief of Baalkpan reclined, eyes darting pensively at the uproar caused by the conversations of his other advisors. None of the "principals" had spoken yet; they were waiting for another to arrive.

When Lieutenant Greg Garrett limped in, leaning on a crutch, attended by Sandra Tucker, Karen Theimer, and Keje's daughter, Selass, he was freshly shaven, and his uniform, while damp, was as crisp as he could make it, given the dingy spots where soot, powder fouling, and blood had been scrubbed away. His narrow, handsome face was pale and drawn, and he looked . . . miserable. Letts had ordered him to stop by the hospital for a checkup before appearing in person. The gist of his story was in the report he'd already submitted by courier as soon as he dropped anchor, however: a report that had spread like wildfire. Letts and Ellis crossed to him, assuring him by their solicitude that they didn't blame him for what happened, but it was clear that, no matter what they said, he blamed himself.

Nakja-Mur didn't stir from his seat. He felt no bitterness toward the young officer, nor did he blame him in any way, but so many new worries had been added to his endless list that day, he didn't trust himself to stand. Besides, ever since battered *Donaghey* entered the bay on a weak, sodden breeze, and the rockets soared into the sky—and then they heard the report of the explosions down at the shipyard and *saw* the Japanese plane soaring unimpeded over his city—he'd felt a strange tightening in his chest. Now they had some hard choices to make, choices that might lead to disaster. As much as he trusted his current human and Lemurian advisors—his friends, he felt—none of the "steadier heads"—Captain Reddy, Keje, Adar, Alden, even Chief Gray and the Japanese officer, Shinya, the ones who'd always been there for him in the past—were there.

Oh, what a terrible stroke of ill luck! He almost wished the Japanese bomb had struck the ship or the plane instead of the priceless radio!

"Is the raa-di-o truly beyond repair?" he asked almost plaintively, silencing the hubbub around them.

"I'm afraid so," Palmer replied woodenly. "Everything's gone, even the batteries."

"We lost nineteen people too," Sandra added harshly, putting things in perspective. "And it could have been a lot worse."

Nakja-Mur nodded to her, acknowledging the hit. He visibly straightened himself. Now was not the time to wallow in self-pity. He had to set an example. "Of course. While I grieve for the families of the lost, I am grateful it was not worse. I only needed to hear the words myself. In the 'bigger picture,' as Captain Reddy would say, the loss of the raa-di-o is surely a straa-tee-jik setback."

"So where does that leave us?" Letts asked remorselessly. "I'll sum it up. Two of our most important leaders are marooned, at best, behind enemy lines. . . ." Garrett flinched, and Alan looked at him apologetically. "It's not your fault, Greg; it's theirs. Damned silly heroics. Besides, you handled your ship superbly, not only in battle, but by getting her back here so quickly in the shape she's in, with such important information. My God, Grik with cannon! But the fact remains, we've left some very important people behind. If we can't get Queen Maraan out, at the very least it'll clobber the morale of her subjects here—who, I might add, constitute over a quarter of our combined army."

"Getting her out is the very first thing we must contemplate!" Rolak demanded hotly, still pacing back and forth.

"I agree. But we've got to figure out how, and we've got some other angles to consider. First, though, *how*." He turned back to Garrett. "What shape's *Donaghey* in?"

"Not good," Garrett admitted grudgingly. "Her stern was battered in by the explosion, and besides the loss of her mizzen, her top hamper's a mess. We repaired a lot, and jury-rigged more, but it'll take several days, at least, of intensive effort by the yard to accomplish the bare essentials—such as replacing the mast and stopping all her leaks."

Letts nodded somberly. "The next two frigates are nearing completion, but neither is ready for sea. The yard manager says he needs another week—and repairs to *Donaghey*'ll set that back. The rest of the 'fleet' of captured Grik ships is either still undergoing alteration and arming, or is scattered all over the place. Only *Felts* is in port, taking on more supplies for the Tarakan expedition. The Homes of the battle line are certainly powerful enough to face however many cannon-armed ships the Grik might have so far, but they're just too slow."

Nakja-Mur listened while Letts spoke, and honestly wondered if anything they did at this point would make any difference. But they had to do something. He heard the American discussing all the possibilities and discarding them in turn, just as he already had in his mind. There really was only one choice, but he waited diplomatically until the others came to the same conclusion.

"We'll have to use *Mahan*." Ellis sighed at last.

Sandra pounced. "Two things wrong with that," she said. "First, can she even do it? What kind of damage did she sustain today?"

"Two dead, and seven wounded by machine-gun fire." Ellis looked at Selass. "Saak-Fas was one of the wounded, but only lightly," he added with compassion. "He's already returned to duty. Damage to the ship consists of a few sprung plates from the near miss. Maybe some cracked firebricks in the number two boiler. We've already shored up the plates and welded them, and shut down number two. If the bricks are damaged, we'll have them replaced and be ready to steam by morning. We can take on fuel and supplies and be underway by the morning after that, I believe."

"You've still only got one propeller," Sandra pointed out. That was true. They'd tried to cast another to replace the one *Walker* had "commandeered," but the first attempt had been hopelessly out of balance. They were working on another, but it would be some time before they were even ready to pour it.

"That's right," Ellis agreed, "but *Mahan*'s still faster than anything she'll meet, by a long shot."

"Maybe, but there's still the other consideration: Matt ... Captain Reddy left strict orders that *Mahan* not do anything remotely like you're considering. He has a *plan* for the defense of this place, when the time comes, and that plan not only includes *Mahan*; she's essential to its success. Despite the imperative that the enemy never suspects she even exists!"

Rolak slapped his sword sheath in frustration. "Captain Reddy is not *here*, my lady. I am bound to obey his orders more closely than anyone. He holds my life, my very honor, in his grasp, and can do with it what he will. But he is not here, and we must deal with this situation in his stead. Knowing him as I do, I am positive he would bless this course since it is our only option—and it is a thing that must be done. Knowing him as *you* do, I am equally positive you must agree."

Sandra slowly wilted under Rolak's intense gaze, and finally she nodded. "You're right, of course." She sighed. "I only wish we could tell him. It'll be days before he starts to wonder why we haven't made our daily comm check. Even then he won't worry, not for a while. We've missed it before due to bad weather or atmospherics." She looked at Riggs and he nodded confirmation.

"She's right," he said. "And even when he does start to wonder, he won't have any reason to be alarmed. Everything was fine when we made our last report, and he knows we'd have days of warning, at least, if the Grik were on the move. He'll just think the radio's busted"—he snorted—"which it is. But that might not mean we can't get in touch with him." The hall grew silent, and he had everyone's attention. "As you know, Radioman Clancy is with *Walker*, but he, Ed, and I have been working on simple crystal receivers. There's not much to them, really, and we've got all the stuff we need to make a few. We located some galena for the crystals, which is good, but we could have done it by mixing powdered sulfur with lead. They're passive receivers and don't even require batteries. Just a little copper wire and a headset—or we might even try building some simple speakers. That won't help us right now, although they'll come in handy, but I think we can put together a simple spark-gap transmitter that might reach the captain. We'll need stuff: lots of wire, for example, and power, of course. *Mahan*'s generator would do nicely, but since she won't be here . . . I think we can make some wet-cell batteries. Lead acid. I'm pretty sure we can do it, and it shouldn't take much time."

"How much time?" Letts asked.

"We should have done it already," Riggs admitted. "We've all just been so busy, and we *had* a good radio. . . . I've been so occupied building the semaphore towers and training the operators. . . ." He shook his head. "No excuse. A week or so, I guess. We'll have to make everything from scratch."

Letts looked at Nakja-Mur. "Highest priority," he said. "Use whoever and whatever you need."

"So I guess it's settled, then," Ellis said, rubbing his scalp. "We go. What have you got for me, Bernie?"

The dark-haired torpedo officer's eyebrows rose, and he took a deep breath. "Not as much as I'd like. We've got twenty of the new projectiles cast, turned, and loaded in shells for the four inch-fifties, but we're just now gearing up to manufacture the primers, so that's it. The primers have been the hardest part, actually. Up till now we've had to make them one at a time, with a swage, and a stamp to make the anvil—not to mention some very dangerous experimentation with fulminate of mercury. We've got that sorted out now, but it'll be another three or four days before I can get you more." Ellis was shaking his head. "I know, too late. But . . . at least you'll have a few to test . . . if you need them. Remember, though, they're just solid copper bolts, no explosive, and they're loaded with black powder, so the fire control computer won't help you. I was hoping for guncotton by now—we've got all the recipes and procedures—but it's tricky stuff, and we haven't finished making the things to make it with, if you know what I mean. The reloads should work fine against wooden ships in local control, though. They ought to shoot through and through. Sorry, that's all I've got. Obviously we've been working on other stuff, but nothing's ready yet."

"What about the torpedo? Should I take it?" The only torpedo they had left, between *Walker* and *Mahan*, was an old MK-10 submarine torpedo Bernie had salvaged from a shack in bombed-out Surabaya before they abandoned it in their own world. He'd thought it was damaged somehow, since it was with others that were condemned. After exhaustive inspection, he'd determined there was nothing wrong with it after all.

"No," Letts decided. "The captain has plans for that fish. We have no real reason to suspect *Amagi*'s ready to move, and that's the only thing you'd have any business shooting it at. Besides, it might get damaged. The torpedo stays here." Ellis nodded agreement, and Letts looked around at the others. "So I guess it's settled then—except for the other 'angles' I mentioned at the start."

"Like what?"

"Like that plane didn't get here by itself," Mallory interrupted with absolute certainty. "It was a 'Dave,' just like the one we tangled with, and it doesn't have the legs to make a trip all the way from Aryaal and back. They must have rendezvoused with at least one, and probably two ships, to refuel on the way. They'll still be out there, and I bet they're the armed ones that showed up when Greg tried to go back for Pete and the queen."

"Grik always travel in threes," Ellis said, pondering. "Maybe we can catch them and destroy them on the way back to Aryaal. Maybe even get the plane, if it was damaged."

"That would be ideal," agreed Letts, "because otherwise they're going to know all about our defensive arrangements. Maybe they'll think they got the plane and the ship, which might be good, but maybe they won't. Regardless, they'll have a good idea what they'll face when they come."

"I fear the events of the last week, the attack on *Donaghey*, and the destructive scout mission, proves they will come soon. Sooner than we planned," Nakja-Mur interjected. "Why else should they do those things now? Why not wait until they are ready—unless they already are?"

"Well, we need to know that too," Letts agreed. He looked at Ben. "How soon can you fly?"

Ben was exhausted and hurting, and his brain wasn't working right, so it took him longer than usual to form a reply. "Uh, we can have the starboard engine reassembled in a day. Another day or two to install it and check it out . . . No sense putting the cowl back on; shredded as it is, it'll drag worse than the motor." He fell silent again, contemplating. Finally he sighed. "Three days, if we have plenty of help and everything works. We still need something for a windscreen, though." He looked speculatively at Ellis. "Maybe some of *Mahan*'s spare window glass?"

"Very well," said Letts, realizing he was treading on another of Captain Reddy's orders: never fly the plane without established communications. Nothing for it. "Top priority on that as well. I want you to fly to Aryaal, take a quick look, see what *Amagi* and the Grik fleet are up to, and head straight back. Can you do it?"

Ben shrugged. "It'll probably be the roughest flight of my life, but we should still be able to go higher than they can shoot. Yeah, provided the wings don't fold up on us."

"Then that's what we'll do. In the meantime, *Felts* sails tomorrow, whether Clark's ready or not. He'll warn Tarakan, in case those three Grik ships didn't head back to the barn, and then proceed to Manila. If we can't get a transmitter going, he'll be the quickest way to inform the captain the Grik are up to something." He looked at Nakja-Mur. "Yeah, I feel it too."

Brevet Captain-General Pete Alden and Captain Haakar-Faask lay in the undergrowth near the beach, taking turns with Pete's binoculars and watching Grik warriors disembark from the three ships closest to shore. Those three had no cannons they could see, but they suspected the other three, keeping station to seaward, did. The tactic was far too methodical and sensible for Alden's taste. He looked at Faask and arched an eyebrow. Faask almost snorted a laugh—he found the face moving of the humans hilarious—but he understood the gesture, even if he had little English. Fortunately, Alden had picked up a functional 'Cat vocabulary by now. "I think they're through messing around with us," was a rough translation of what he said.

Two weeks had passed since he and Queen Maraan were marooned with the rest of the refugees, long enough for the three Grik ships that drove *Donaghey* away to return to Aryaal with news of the battle, prepare this expedition, and return. It was also past long enough for *Donaghey* to make it to Baalkpan, damaged as she was, and another relief force to be dispatched. The problem was, with the allied navy scattered from here to the Philippines, could they even scrape together a force large enough to come to their aid?

He had no doubt that, eventually, help would come. If nothing else, Garrett would return as soon as his ship was repaired, but that might be a while. In the meantime, the better part of a thousand Grik warriors were about to start beating the brush for the less than three hundred souls left in Faask's and his care, mostly males by now at least, but mostly civilians too. Less than a hundred had ever borne arms, but ever since he'd been left behind, Faask had been training all the refugees, females and younglings included, for just this eventuality. Fortunately, most of the latter had already been rescued. There were still a few, those who wouldn't leave their mates, or females who'd been separated from their younglings and still hoped against hope they might turn up. A few elders had remained as well, too old and frail to wield a sword or spear, but who wouldn't leave until everyone else was rescued. Many were ill, due to either malnutrition or exhaustion. That left Alden's "effectives" at just over two hundred.

His scouts had discovered a force of two thousand or more closing from the west-northwest, pushing them back from observation points overlooking the bay they'd used to such good effect, and now this blocking force was landing in their "rear," cutting off their egress to the sea.

"We better get back to the rally point and tell the queen what we've seen," he said. Motioning a pair of pickets to maintain their positions and keep tabs on the enemy advance as long as they could, Alden and Faask slithered down the embankment and hurried off through the jungle.

Queen Maraan awaited them, anxious for their news. "Is it true?" she hissed. Pete and Haakar-Faask both nodded, and her eyes turned to slits. "What will we do?"

"We must keep you safe, Your Majesty," Faask replied.

"How? Would you have me slink off into the jungle, dig a hole, and crawl into it?" She gestured around at the refugees, huddled under makeshift shelters against the rain that had begun to fall. "What of them?"

"With respect, Majesty—" Faask began.

"No! I will not skulk around, leaving my people to be slaughtered!" She stared levelly at Alden and Faask. "We will fight! All of us! You two are probably the greatest generals this world has ever known. In different ways, perhaps, since you come from different backgrounds, but that should give us an insurmountable advantage, not a disadvantage. Surely, between you, you can devise a plan that will, if not give us victory, at least deny it to them! All we need is time, my friends. Our allies will not abandon us." She grinned. "We are too important, are we not?"

"But they are simply too many!" Faask protested. "They outnumber us fifteen to one!"

Alden scratched his beard. "Yeah," he agreed, "if they were all in one place, that would be true." He knelt to the soggy ground and swept the leaves and brush away, revealing a bare spot of damp earth. The rain was already tapering off—another short squall—and he selected a small, pointed stick. After he scratched a rough outline of the island, he drew a line across the top. "This is the main Grik force. There're many of them, but they're stretched across the entire width of the island. If we mass our forces here"—he pointed to the south—"we can strike their right flank and probably have numerical superiority, at least locally. We hit 'em like maniacs and break through into their rear. Even against a 'normal' enemy, that'd leave them dangerously exposed. With any luck, they'll go nuts—like we've seen them do before—and we roll up their flank, killing as we go." He grinned. "We might even set the whole army to flight, but probably not. Sooner or later our guys'll get tired and the attack'll run out of steam. That's when they'll hit back."

"I agree so far," Faask said, "but what good will that do? It will be a glorious end, but it will not protect the queen."

"Sure it will, because we don't let our 'army' run out of steam. We pull back to here"—he pointed again with his stick—"where we take a breather while the Grik center turns to attack us on their right. Where we *were*. When they do that, we hit 'em again, on their new *left* flank!"

Faask was silent for a moment, studying the impressions in the dirt. "But that's . . . brilliant!"

Pete grinned. "Of course it is! We just have to make sure our coordination works like clockwork, and we have signals that work and are obeyed instantly."

Faask stroked his own beard. Alden was more used to the sea folk, who generally kept their facial fur clipped short, but on the veteran warrior the beard seemed appropriate somehow. "And the tactic should work equally well against the Grik far left, if they have not, as you say, gone 'nuts' already. It would be the greatest, most audacious victory of the age!" He looked at Alden with renewed respect, then frowned. "But what of the blocking force? Our warriors will be exhausted, even if we are successful."

Alden gestured toward the sea. "It'll take them a day to get their shit together. We know where they are, but they don't have a clue about us. They'll figure it out pretty quick, but by then we'll already be headed toward the main force. That ought to confuse them. I figure we'll have a day or so to rest before they catch up, and they'll be at least as spread out as the first bunch by then."

"And we do it again!" Faask shouted triumphantly.

"And then we do it again," Alden confirmed.

Queen Maraan coughed. "All very inspiring, noble generals. I am impressed. I knew you could do it, and it seems an outstanding plan . . . only remember the single greatest lesson I have learned from both of you: no plan may ever be entirely relied upon, once the battle has begun!"

Warm sunlight filtered through the delicately woven curtains draped across the doorway to the balcony, and Matthew Reddy opened his eyes and blinked. He'd slept late again, he realized with chagrin. That was two days in a row. All his life he'd risen with the sun—or before—but lately ... He shook his head and rubbed his eyes. Rolling off the great, mushy cushion that served as a mattress, he stood and walked to a water basin on a table near the door. He submerged his face for the count of ten, then rubbed it briskly with his hands. Rinsing, he parted the annoyingly long hair and combed it from left to right across his scalp, and looked intently into the polished silver mirror above the basin.

"Starting to look like a hobo," he growled, remembering the ones he used to see wandering around the stockyard train station when he was a kid. "Acting like one too. Waking up when I feel like it—damn, I bet it's nearly oh eight hundred!" He glanced at his watch: 0750. He frowned, shaking his head, then looked at the mirror again. His hair was halfway down his ears, and starting to curl a little against his collar in the back. It also had a little gray in it all of a sudden. The stubble on his face seemed as much salt as pepper, and he was only thirty-three. He needed to hit Juan up for a haircut, he thought with a grimace, but then, with a twinge of satisfaction, he remembered he still controlled his razor, at least.

He shaved as carefully as he could. Most of his old Asiatic Fleet destroyermen had long since ceased shaving. He wouldn't force them to, with razors so scarce. The main reason he still did it himself was that the men expected it. He'd kept his face clean shaven, to the best of his ability, throughout all the trials they'd come through together, and even though it was a little thing after all, sometimes it was the little things that made all the difference in the end. It was a symbol of continuity they all could cling to, even him. It was a stubborn statement that not everything they knew before the Squall was lost forever. The skipper still shaved his face. He had to admit it was a rather pathetic affectation, but they'd lost almost everything else.

Stepping to the little closet, he selected one of his new uniforms and put it on. As always, it took a few moments to get used to the itch. He didn't mind. The new uniforms were amazingly well made, and he thought it important that all his people, human and Lemurian, continue to wear the uniform of the navy they were part of: a uniform they were accustomed to, and associated with their duty. The battered shoes and hat contrasted with his new clothes, but there was nothing he could do about that. Finally he buckled the belt supporting his holstered M-1911 .45 automatic, and his hard-used academy dress sword. The sword was polished and well cared for, but the sweat-stained grip and notched blade attested to far more service than he'd ever imagined it would see when he purchased it for his graduation.

Belatedly prepared to face the day, he stepped onto the balcony. The apartment shared by the small allied diplomatic mission to the Maa-ni-los occupied an entire level of the Great Hall, and the balcony went all the way around it like a giant wraparound porch. Despite the hall's robust construction and the massive trunk of the Galla tree that anchored it, as high as he was above the ground, there was still an almost imperceptible sense of motion. Unfortunately, the motion of the diplomacy they'd been engaged in was almost imperceptible as well, scandalously so, according to Keje and Adar. Ever since that first unusual, hopeful meeting with Saan-Kakja, when there'd seemed to be such commonality and unity of purpose, the Maa-ni-lo High Chief had been kept away from them by officious underlings under the pretext of "propriety." That was a bunch of crap, according to Matt's Lemurian friends.

Propriety had nothing to do with it, they said; factional

politics was to blame. Both felt grievously insulted, not only for themselves, but for him. Matt was willing to put up with much; they needed the Maa-ni-los' help too badly, and as long as there was any hope at all, he'd wait a little longer. But it wasn't easy. There was so much to do, both back "home" in Baalkpan and otherwise, that he couldn't shake the frustration gnawing him. He'd grown so used to the constant stress of his position, the combat and preparation for it, that to become essentially a tourist on vacation was about to drive him nuts. He had nothing critical to do, and he was too keyed up to relax.

As he'd been every morning for the five days they'd been in Manila, he was greeted by the awesome sight of the vibrant, chaotic, prosperous city. The sights, sounds, colors, and smells blended together to mount an overwhelming assault on his senses. Much like Baalkpan's, the morning activity was centered around the waterfront, where vendors hawked the early catch, but there was more native industry than he was used to as well. More than Baalkpan boasted before he and his people arrived, at least—back before the war became all-consuming. Open-air ropewalks were laid out between the great chandlery buildings, where hot, smoky pitch was daubed on heavy new cable, destined for hawsers or stays aboard the massive ships. Sailmakers toiled under awnings, sewing bolts of fabric together with quick, deft stitches. A singsong, chittering chantey reached his ears on the same breeze that carried smells of savory cooking, boiling pitch, and animal excrement. Less intense, but far more familiar, was the waterlogged, rotting-wood, fishy-salty aroma of any harbor and the sea.

Much of the excrement came from a species of stunted, domesticated brontosaurus, similar to those they knew from other places. Some came from the myriad packs of shrieking younglings scampering heedlessly—and apparently unheeded—about, who'd not yet become shackled to the remarkably refined running-water privies that allowed life to flourish in the densely populated city. The privies were not so different from those aboard *Walker*—water rushing under a hole with a board across it—but unlike in early human cities with similar arrangements, the soiled water passed through mounded ducts, like road-level sewers, instead of open-air gutters. It did, ultimately, find its

way into the bay, but the scavenging fish and other creatures were more prolific, and far less picky, than those on
that other Earth.

Some of the indiscriminate heaps were deposited by
creatures he'd never seen before. One looked a little like
a brontosaurus from a distance, although it was smaller,
and had a shorter—if beefier and more muscular—neck,
and a much shorter tail. The head was larger, with short,
palmated antlers. It was also covered with fur—real fur—
and Bradford excitedly insisted the things were herbivorous marsupials, of all things. Matt wondered why no one
ever imported them to Baalkpan; they were obviously
more sensible draft animals than the ubiquitous brontosaurus. Probably smarter and more biddable as well, from
what he'd seen. He found himself wishing for some to pull
his light artillery pieces. Perhaps they could even be ridden, although he hadn't seen anyone doing it. They were
called "Paalkas," but Silva had immediately dubbed them
"pack-mooses."

There was an animal the Maa-ni-los did ride, but he'd
seen only a couple. They looked like long-legged croco-
diles that ran on all fours, as they should, but their legs
were shaped more like a dog's. They ran like dogs too, and
the only time he'd seen them, they bore troops in Saan-
Kakja's livery on some apparent errand. The crowds gave
them a wide berth, and Matt noticed their jaws were always
strapped and buckled tightly shut. The 'Cats called them
one thing, he couldn't remember, and Courtney Bradford
had made up another name he couldn't pronounce. Whatever they were, he'd have to find out more about them.

It was all very fascinating, but profoundly frustrating as
well. Strangely, he liked this Manila a lot better than the
old, in a way, but he was becoming almost frantically anxious to complete his mission and get back. He missed Sandra terribly—missed everybody—and there was still the
iron fish to consider. Each day they spent here, dithering
over details and placating the endless stream of dignitaries
and counselors, was one less they could spend looking for
it. And another thing was troubling him too: they hadn't
heard a peep out of Baalkpan in days.

"Mornin', Skipper."

Matt noticed that Silva had joined him during his reverie. The big gunner's mate had no official standing as far as the diplomatic mission went, other than that he had, somewhere along the line, taken personal responsibility for Captain Reddy's welfare. He'd stepped into Chief Gray's self-appointed role as Matt's senior armsman, and he commanded a detail of enlisted humans and Lemurians who'd volunteered for the duty—knowing full well that the man they were bound to protect didn't always make it easy. Like that of Juan Marcos, their job had just . . . evolved. Unlike Juan, the "Captain's Guard" had become an official posting at the urging of Keje and Adar. Silva knew the job was Gray's whenever he was able to resume it, but he'd have been protecting the captain anyway, and he'd been making a real effort to behave. His restriction to the ship had been only provisionally lifted, and if he was stuck on the ship, he couldn't do his job. Matt was beginning to suspect Silva was the sort of person who rose to meet expectations. All his life he'd been expected to be a screwup—so he was. Now everyone, himself included, expected more, and so far he'd delivered. Matt harbored no illusions that Silva had completely reformed; the best-trained, most trusted dog still crapped on the floor now and then, but if Matt needed a guard dog, Silva was the best he could ask for, absent Gray.

"Morning, Silva. Anything on the horn?"

Dennis shook his head. "Just came from the ship," he said, and Matt noticed the big man already had sweat circles under his arms. "Still no word. Clancy says it's not on our end. There just ain't anything to receive." He saw the captain's worried frown. "No big deal, Skipper; it's prob'ly nothin'. Last report, everything was fine. Besides, you know what a klutz that Palmer is; he prob'ly popped a tube with a wrench, or maybe the damn airplane sank. Lieutenant Riggs'll get it sorted out, or he'll make a whole new bloody set."

"I know. It's just . . . Everything was fine before Pearl Harbor too," Matt said, immediately regretting the display of uncertainty. Silva had no response to that. "Well," he said, clearing his throat and straightening, "let's see what kind of Kabuki dance the 'Cats have ready for us today. Besides, it's breakfast time." He paused, suddenly decisive. "Run back down to the ship, or send somebody, and inform Mr.

Dowden to make preparations for getting underway. The Maa-ni-los are going to help us or not. Hanging around and pestering them probably won't make any difference. It's really Saan-Kakja's decision, anyway. But I've had just about enough, and one way or another, this is our last day here."

"Aye, aye, Skipper," Silva replied with his usual unnerving lopsided grin.

Breakfast was a lavish, quiet affair, but Matt immediately got the impression that, today, things would proceed differently. Perhaps word had slipped that *Walker*'s people were fed up and about to leave. Matt suspected Silva of the leak, but maybe that was best. As badly as they needed the Maa-ni-los, the Maa-ni-los needed them too, and if that was what it took to get the ball rolling, so be it. He was seated at one end of a long table, a position of prestige, and at the other end, in a place of equal honor, was Saan-Kakja. It was the first time he'd seen her since their arrival. All the negotiations had been conducted by underlings. Now, few of those underlings were present and Matt expected, as a result, things would move more swiftly. One way or the other.

Saan-Kakja sat on her stool across from him, locked in a posture of tense precision, lifting careful spoonfuls of fluffy yellow eggs to her mouth. Her short, silken, gray-black fur was carefully groomed, and glowed with the luster of healthy youth. Around her neck hung the golden gorget of her office, and occasionally her short, delicate fingers strayed between her small breasts and absently stroked the metal. It dawned on Matt, despite her noteworthy greeting, that she might not yet be comfortable in her exalted role, and he felt his heart go out to her. They'd learned a few things about her through back channels during the negotiations, and what they knew explained a great deal—particularly about her behavior. She really didn't know how to proceed, and she'd delegated much to her High Sky Priest, who Adar thought was a "jerk," to use a charitable translation. Her father had been Saanga-Kakja, which explained a little of the initial confusion. Keje and Adar had known him long ago, but not as High Chief. They'd hoped to be dealing with a person they knew. A widower like Keje, he died mere months earlier of a long illness. All his older offspring, from another, previously deceased mate, had already moved on: one as High Chief of a newly built, seagoing Home, and two others who'd established land Homes on the southern Fil-pin Islands. All that remained to assume the mantle of leadership was Saan-Kakja, the young child of his young, much adored, and deeply lamented second, and final, mate. Some believed he actually died of sorrow, since he joined his beloved in the Heavens such a short time after her passing.

Regardless, he'd left his daughter—at the tender age of fourteen—ill-prepared to rule, and her understandably tentative approach, and willingness to delegate, undermined her authority. Lemurians matured much quicker than humans, but she was still considered a youngling even by her own people. She'd been through a lot, and was clearly aware she had a lot to live up to, but based on his first meeting with her and looking at her now, Matt suspected she'd do all right if she had the right kind of help and support. Safir Maraan had risen at a younger age, and look how she'd turned out. Of course, the cultures were different, and she'd always had Haakar-Faask to back her up. Apparently there was no Haakar-Faask for Saan-Kakja. There was only her Sky Priest.

The Sky Priest in question sat on Saan-Kakja's left. He was called Meksnaak, and despite Adar's opinion, Matt didn't really know what to think of him. He seemed dour and suspicious, and couldn't have been more different from Adar. Adar was seated in his customary place beside Keje, even though he was Sky Priest to more than just a single Home. His example and personality—not to mention his early recognition of the greater threat—had done much to smooth the waters between the Americans and the various factions that ultimately formed the alliance. He'd shamelessly waved the bloody shirt of *Revenge*, the allies' first "prize ship." Her loss, and the loss of her integrated crew in a struggle against impossible odds, had provided a shining example of honor and sacrifice to the technically amalgamated, but increasingly Lemurian, "U.S. Navy." The two species had both been somewhat ethnocentric when they met, but even given their mutual need for allies, there'd been surprisingly little friction. Maybe they were so physically different, there was no real basis for racial resentment. Each looked equally "funny" to the other, but each had recognizable strengths the other lacked. The battle resulting in the loss of *Revenge* set the ultimate precedent of coequal status among the two species, and began a growing tradition of "equal glory or a shared death." Matt reminded himself the Maa-ni-los were not yet part of any such tradition.

He cornered the last of his eggs between his spoon and a strip of fish, and when he ate them both he realized the others had mostly finished. He cleared his throat. Recognizing the gesture, Saan-Kakja laid aside her own single utensil, an instrument like a broad-bladed, concave knife that also served as a kind of spoon or scoop. It was gold, like so many other Maa-ni-lo devices. Matt hadn't seen as much gold in his life, certainly not among other Lemurians, as he had in the last few days. The thing was, it didn't seem to have any value other than that it didn't tarnish and it was pretty. The High Chief . . . tess?—absurd, they didn't think like that. Their word, U-Amaki, transcended gender. The High Chief dabbed daintily at her mouth with an embroidered napkin and sat even straighter, if possible.

"Cap-i-taan Reddy," she began. "I must begin by begging you to forgive me for neglecting you so inexcusably." Meksnaak blinked furiously and opened his mouth to speak, but she darted a look in his direction that Matt couldn't read, and his jaws clamped shut. "I have wasted much of your time," she continued, "and I fear in doing so, I have squandered valuable time we may all remember with wistful regret." Matt waited patiently for a full translation, even though he got the gist of what she said. "You come here seeking alliance against the threat posed by our Ancient Enemy, an enemy as implacable and relentless as the very sea. It may be deceptively calm for a time"—she looked back at Meksnaak—"but eventually, inevitably, the Strakka strikes with unbound fury. I am . . . a young High Chief who has seen little of life, and learned even less of what is expected of me, so I was persuaded to delegate the task of treating with you on this subject." Her voice became hard. "That was a mistake. It was rude and irresponsible, and I apologize." She blinked sincere regret and lowered her head. When she looked up at Matt, her remarkable eyes were gleaming.

"I have heard much about your adventures and battles against the scourge from the west, and I am inspired. I allowed myself to be convinced, however, that my excitement was that of an emotional youngling, and here we are safe from attack. Better to stay uninvolved—beyond learning as much from you as we can, and helping you in small, safe, material ways. There are . . . factions in Maa-ni-la that thrive on contention and intrigue, and are obsessed with their own petty concerns. They counsel that we let you, Baalkpan, and the other allied Homes stand alone against the Grik, while we remain safely uninvolved. We are prosperous, happy, stable, and untouched by the distant threat. Even if Baalkpan falls, the Grik will be content to remain far away, and in the meantime our trade, industry, and prosperity will flourish even more." Her ears flattened with contempt. "Of course, there are also the ones you call 'runaways,' who counsel that, even if the Grik do someday come here, we can flee once more as we did in the ancient tales of the Scrolls; that we have grown too comfortable, too fixed in place, too reliant upon the land."

Matt nodded. Those were the same arguments he and Nakja-Mur had faced when they first suggested defiance. Most people on the seagoing Homes couldn't comprehend their cousins' attachment to *places*, or understand their un-willingness to leave them. Keje did, and so did the other members of the alliance. They knew there'd be no escape this time. The world was a smaller place, and now the Grik had oceangoing ships of their own, albeit tiny in compari-son; they had so many, the terrible sea was no longer the protector it had been. It was like the old scorpion and ta-rantula in the jar. The tarantula wasn't well equipped to cope with the scorpion, but sooner or later he had to deal with his deadly, aggressive adversary, because he couldn't avoid him forever, and there just wasn't anyplace else to go. It was always a toss-up who'd win.

"I understand you grow impatient," Saan-Kakja resumed, "and I do not blame you. Your most powerful ship is here, and you languish in comfort and are free from want, but all the while the enemy may be massing against you. You are frustrated by our intransigence, and don't understand our hesitation to join you." She shook her head. "Honestly, I am as frustrated as you, and my patience is possibly even less. I do know what causes it, however. My people are comfort-able and free from want. That is a condition any good ruler desires, but there are times, such as this, that that very condition makes it difficult for such a ruler to convince those comfortable people they must put that aside and face the unpleasant reality of the harsher world beyond their sight." She sighed and turned again to Meksnaak.

"What of the proposal I put before the counsel? That we join the alliance to destroy the Grik threat forever, and send whatever we may in the way of troops and supplies to their aid?"

Meksnaak shifted uncomfortably. "My dear, it is . . . unwise to reveal our private discussions in the presence of strangers—particularly when those discussions involve them." He hastily turned to Captain Reddy with a glare. "No such decision has been taken!"

"The decision has been taken by me," Saan-Kakja retorted.

Meksnaak shook his head sadly. "You are powerful, High Chief, and your *opinions* have great weight, but even you cannot engage us in full-scale war on your own authority. The clan chiefs must speak."

"Then let them speak! So far, none has done any speaking but you and other members of the counsel who represent those with the most to gain by inactivity!"

"There are legitimate objections," Meksnaak insisted, "not only to going to war, but to any association with these Amer-i-caan . . . heretics!" He blinked outrage at the thought of the Americans' Scrolls. He'd never seen them, but he'd been assured they were . . . extraordinary. His initial concern that their existence represented heresy was not dispelled when Adar told him with glowing eyes that the American Scrolls almost perfectly mirrored their own, except they were even more precise! Meksnaak accepted that. Adar was a Sky Priest of extensive renown, and Meksnaak was willing to take his word in that respect. But the knowledge did not make him admire the Americans, or soothe his concerns about their spiritually corrosive behavior. If anything, it made him resent and fear them even more. If their Scrolls were so much more precise than those of the People, they must be holy indeed. Could they even be the very originals from which all others were copied long ago? Scrolls formed under the hand of the Great Prophet Siska-Ta herself? And what of the rumors that the Americans possessed Scrolls no one else had ever seen? Scrolls depicting mysterious lands far beyond the world known by the People? And Adar assured him they displayed their precious Scrolls in the open, for any and all to see—even to *handle*! How could the Americans be so careless and . . . irresponsible? Incredible. He'd asked the question of Adar during one of their meetings, and was shocked that one so highly regarded could harbor such liberal views.

"I was as troubled as you, at first," Adar had confessed, "but that is because I had grown set in my ways, ossified and concerned about a diminution of my precious prerogatives. After much consideration, I changed my mind. Are the Scrolls to be kept secret, and viewed only by those such as we? Surely the great Siska-Ta never intended that; otherwise why write them at all? It was her goal to teach, to enlighten, to share the knowledge of the past and the heavens and the pathways of the sea and sky—not create an exclusive club reserved for only a select few!"

Now Adar stood and spoke with heat. "They are *not* heretics; I told you that already! They have different beliefs, surely, but they do not seek to trample or transgress upon our own! And regardless of their differences, the very Scrolls you would use as examples of their heresy prove we share more similarities of thought than differences, and *they*, at least, gladly aid us against our Ancient Enemy!"

"An enemy made stronger with the aid of others of their kind!" Meksnaak retorted.

Adar took a strained breath. "Perhaps their enemy does collude with ours, but they didn't know that when they joined us, and it has not altered their commitment. That you, a Sky Priest, would counsel inaction during our current, collective crisis, when our race faces extinction at the very hands that drove us from our sacred, ancient home—as described in the same Scrolls you profess to revere—makes me question *your* commitment!"

Meksnaak sputtered for a moment, then spat: *"Ser-vaabo fidem summo studio!"*

"Suspendens omnia naa-so! Usus est ty-raannus, usus te plura docebit!" Adar replied scornfully. *"Cucullus non facit monachum. Cul-paam maiorum posteri luunt!"*

"Gratis dictum. Honos haa-bet onus, maag-naavis est conscientiae."

"Oh, Lord." Bradford sighed. "I do hate it when they do that!"

"What're they saying?" Matt demanded.

"Let me see, I've brushed up my Latin a bit of late, from necessity, but their pronunciation is quite bizarre. Hmm. Well, as you know, Latin is somewhat difficult to translate literally even when spoken well—which makes the Lemurian capacity for it doubly fascinating, since they are so literal-minded! Their own language . . ."

"Courtney?"

"Umm? Well, it seems their Meksnaak has said he only keeps the faith, while Adar says he's shackled by it, and his people will pay the consequences. Meksnaak says that's ridiculous, and he has an obligation to his people."

The argument continued.

"*Medium tenuere be-aati,*" Adar scoffed sarcastically, "*mihi cura futuri. Quousque tandem abutere paa-tientia nostra? Recovate aa-nimos! Aude saa-pere. Stant belli causa, belli lethaale . . . belli internecinum. Timor mortis morte peior!*"

"Oh, dear," Bradford said with real alarm.

"What?"

"Adar has admonished Meksnaak to remember the cause of the war . . . and I think he called him a coward!"

Matt coughed politely before Meksnaak could respond. "We consider it rude to carry on in a language others can't understand." He glanced at Saan-Kakja, and she nodded. Adar resumed his seat with a huff, and Meksnaak blinked insincere apology. Courtney Bradford couldn't entirely stifle a sigh of relief, and Meksnaak's eyes narrowed irritably.

"If the . . . plodding pace of our discussions is so unsatisfactory, you can always go aboard that . . . smoking iron abomination of yours, and leave us as we were."

Bradford leaned back in his chair and arched an eyebrow. Now Matt began to rise, his face red with indignation.

"Meksnaak . . ." began Saan-Kakja.

"No. With respect, child, I grow weary of the constant complaining of these . . . foreigners. Maa-ni-la has prospered in peace for over eighty years, and will be doing so long after our spirits have gone above. If you ask my opinion, I tell you we neglect our own people's interest by

even contemplating the risky adventure these . . . others . . .
propose. And honestly, this extraordinary meeting and the
pointless haste in which it was convened is . . . unseemly."
Meksnaak glared at Bradford, but continued to speak to
his High Chief. "I remind you, child, my friend, your father,
did not rush to war when first he heard of this unlikely
threat!"

There was an uncomfortable silence, and all eyes turned
to the young, smallish . . . well, girl. That was the only word
that really seemed to fit, as far as the humans were concerned. But Matt could only wonder if he was the only one
that saw the wide, striated eyes suddenly become pools of
molten iron. When she spoke, however, her voice was under
firm control.

"My lord Meksnaak, I know you were my father's friend,
as well as his most trusted advisor. That is, after all, one of
the primary duties of all Sky Priests to their chief. I honor
you for that service and friendship." She slowly turned her
head to look at the older Lemurian, and Meksnaak must
have seen the same thing Matt had, because he visibly
blanched. "I am High Chief of Maa-ni-la now, by acclamation as well as birth. I am my father's daughter. Although I
do not doubt your devotion to my father, I begin to doubt
your wisdom. I say this not to hurt you, but because you
will not *see*. You and I cannot know what it was like for
our guests to face the Ancient Enemy, the terror of all our
nightmares. Neither of us can fully understand what that is
like. But because I love my people and yearn for them to be
forever safe and free, I fairly chafe to go myself to the aid of
our western friends. I *yearn* to send them aid, because only
then can we harry the Grik vermin from the sea, and ultimately from our dreams and our ancient home as well!"

For just a moment Meksnaak held her gaze, but then
came the long, slow blink of abject apology. "You shame
me, child."

"No. You shame *me* with your impolite behavior." Her
hand swept outward in a gesture encompassing all those
seated at the table. "You have been impolite to my guests
and to me. I am no mere youngling to be dismissed at the
table of adults, any more than . . ." She paused, and her mes-
merizing eyes fell upon Chack. "Any more than the noble
Chack-Sab-At, of whose exploits I have heard so much!

He is little older than I, yet he has faced our enemies many times. Tell me, Master Sab-At, are you a youngling?"

Chack, uncomfortable with being forced to speak under the circumstances, glanced at Captain Reddy and saw his confident nod of approval. He stood with as much dignity as he could muster.

"I have seen my former Home, *Salissa*, ravaged by the Grik, and I fought them with all my might, though I was not yet a warrior. I joined the Amer-i-caan clan and learned not only to fight more efficiently, but also to lead. I have participated in five boarding actions now. . . ." He paused and regarded Meksnaak. "I truly cannot convey how horrific that can be. If you saw the aftermath of such a thing only once, you would not doubt our cause. The Grik carry our people as cargo . . . live provisions aboard their ships. . . ." His tail swished impatiently, and he shook his head. "I was in the great Battle of Aryaal, where we slaughtered twenty thousands of our foes and lost many of our own. It was after that we came to know that, no matter how many we killed, it was but a tithe against their total strength. I saw *Amagi* pound *Nerracca* into a sinking inferno. We rescued as many as we could—hundreds—but thousands were left to burn or drown or be taken by the fish." For a moment he closed his haunted eyes while he spoke, and no one doubted he was seeing again the events of that terrible night. "I saw Tassana, daughter of *Nerracca*'s High Chief, younger even than you, Saan-Kakja, help cut the tow cable that connected her helpless, sinking Home to the wounded Amer-i-caan destroyer trying to drag her to safety. She did it because her father knew Captain Reddy, and feared he might wait too long, hoping to rescue more. As it was, damaged and leaking, *Walker* nearly sank under the sheer weight of the survivors she managed to save."

Not a word was uttered in the chamber while he stood silent, contemplating his next words. "I was a youngling before all this started, if not in years, then certainly in experience. Now I am a bosun's mate, a captain of Marines, and I guard some of the most important leaders of our alliance." He stared hard at Meksnaak. "Do you dare call me a youngling, or offer further insult to those I protect?"

Saan-Kakja took a breath and realized she'd been holding it. She looked around the table, surprised how much

Chack's words had changed her perceptions of the people there. Particularly the Amer-i-caans. She'd heard the tales, of course, but they'd been told dispassionately. To hear Chack tell them, in his own words, made them real. She pierced her Sky Priest with another molten stare.

Meksnaak's apologetic blinking was constant now and, from what Matt had learned of Lemurian expression, sincere. He even felt a little embarrassed for the Sky Priest, but he also knew Saan-Kakja needed to get this sorted out. He thought she had. She and Chack had. The new High Chief of Manila might be young, but she was no "youngling." Not anymore. She finally spoke again, and when she did her voice had lost much of its fury.

"You may one day earn the right to be rude to me, Meksnaak, but you will never be rude to my friends again. They have earned our respect and gratitude. Besides, none of us have the luxury of being rude to *anyone* who will help us in this fight. Yes, we need their help as much as they need ours. This is our war too. The Grik have come as if our most horrible dreams have been made flesh, and they come to devour us all! Our only hope is to destroy them first, and we must have friends to do it. How can we expect to make those friends when we can't even be polite at the breakfast table?"

"Hear, hear!" Bradford said, banging his coffee cup on the table for emphasis. It wasn't quite empty, and much of the remains wound up on his sleeve. "Saan-Kakja for queen, I say!" He looked at the suddenly wary Sky Priest. "She certainly settled our hash! I suppose we'll have to keep our little arguments more private from now on." Meksnaak hadn't had much contact with humans, but he'd learned a nod was still a nod. He nodded now and forced a small smile.

"If that is the will of my chief," he said quietly.

"Surely she can't object to a little debate between two scientific beings, though?" He arched his eyebrows once again, and Saan-Kakja couldn't restrain a giggle. Like the cats—and lemurs for that matter—they so closely resembled, Lemurians had an extraordinarily limited range of facial expression. They were *very* expressive, through eye blinks, ear positions, and body posture, and their tails added an emphasis to their emotions and attitudes that humans couldn't hope to match. A grin was a grin and a frown was a frown, but other than that their faces hardly moved at all. Humans, on the other hand, used comparatively little body language, and it took quite a while for Lemurians to understand that much of the true meaning behind their words was conveyed by a bewildering array of inimitable facial contortions. Courtney Bradford had discovered early on that 'Cats sometimes found these contortions amusing. Particularly when wildly exaggerated. He made good use of that knowledge now, bouncing his bushy eyebrows up and down like a pair of spastic caterpillars. Even Meksnaak couldn't resist, and he suddenly broke into a grin after an explosive snort. Bradford looked at Chack, who'd resumed his seat, but was now barely able to stay on his stool. His eyes were clenched shut, and he was making a kind of high-pitched, hacking sound.

"What?" demanded Bradford in a voice of purest innocence. A moment before there'd been a dangerous tension in the room. Now . . . there wasn't. Matt congratulated himself again for bringing the Australian along.

"Mr. Bradford," he said, shaking his head with a grin, "I think you've made your point." He nodded respectfully at Chack. "As has our captain of Marines. Now . . ." He looked at Saan-Kakja, who was gaining control of herself. "With your permission, perhaps we might proceed?"

"Of course."

Walker steamed southwest under a cloudless, hazy sky through the treacherous waters of the Visayan Sea. Lookouts were on constant alert for shoaling water and the little islets sprinkled about. Through Adar they'd acquired copies of Lemurian Scrolls for this portion of the trip, and Meksnaak was partially mollified to discover that, regardless of the detail American Scrolls possessed, they depicted a slightly different world, where conditions weren't entirely the same. He'd also pinpointed the area, west of wild, largely unexplored Mindanao, where fishing boats of the southern clan colonies last reported the "iron fish."

They departed Manila with Saan-Kakja's promise her personal Guard of a thousand troops would depart immediately aboard one of the "supply" Homes bound for Baalkpan. Chack's Marine lieutenant remained behind to give rudimentary training to the levy, before taking ship with the Guard, whom he'd train as much as possible on the way. More would follow. It wasn't as much or as quickly as Matt had hoped, but it was more than he'd begun to fear they'd get. As it was, they still had a few days left of the time he'd allocated for looking for the submarine, even if he'd begun to begrudge it. They still hadn't heard anything from Baalkpan, and they had to assume, at the very least, that the radio was out. He didn't want to think about other possibilities, no matter how far-fetched or unlikely.

Those possibilities were beginning to affect the crew, however, and Chack was becoming openly worried about Queen Maraan. Somehow he sensed she'd done something foolish, and he couldn't get the conviction out of his head. Matt tried to soothe his nerves (and his own) by assuring him the problem was probably just some glitch with the radio—yet another piece of equipment they'd relied so heavily upon had let them down. Regardless, he was anxious to complete their quick sweep and head for home.

They saw plenty of gri-kakka, and even hit one again. This specimen wasn't nearly as large as the plesiosaur they struck in the Java Sea, so there was no damage. The coloration was peculiar, however, and Mr. Bradford's insistent demands obliged them to heave to briefly and compare the dead creature to others they'd seen. He didn't have much time. Being back in relatively shallow water, the flashies made an immediate appearance, drawn by the blood, and soon the water churned with such violence he was forced to abandon his investigation. In the short time he had to study it, though, he documented a few distinct variations.

Land was never entirely out of sight, and strange, flying creatures dogged them constantly, swooping among the signal halyards and roosting on the number one funnel and generally shitting all over the ship. Chack had a constant detail plying hoses and mops, but it made little difference. Most of the creatures were familiar variations of the lizard birds they were used to, even if the colors were generally different. Some "birds" looked like actual birds, with real feathers, and they shrieked and cawed right among the others. On the amidships gun platform, Silva was pitching small morsels in the air, and the off-duty crew were bet-ting on which creatures would slaughter the others to get them.

Matt was leaning on the bridge wing rail with Spanky and Keje, watching the entertainment, and was surprised to see Gilbert and Tabby participating. He raised an eyebrow at the engineer.

Spanky shrugged. "They've been getting out more," he confirmed. "Weird. It's like we had three trees growing off the same root, and when we cut one down, the other two took off." He shook his head. "I wonder how Isak's doin'. I know it sounds selfish, but I hope they all get along when we get them back together." He grinned. "They still do their jobs, but I don't get as much extra work out of them as I used to, what with them hanging around in the firerooms off watch."

Matt saw Silva stiffen suddenly, his predatory eye fixed like a cougar on its prey. He shoved his way forward through his bewildered audience, scooping the large, slimy quid of "tobacco" from his cheek. Pausing by the rail next to the ladder, he waited for his chance. Below him, Chack and a couple Marine "deck apes" were working their way aft. Chack was grousing loudly about something, probably all the "bird" crap. Like a bombardier, Silva took careful aim at his objective and, when he judged the moment was right, released his payload. It struck the deck directly in front of Chack with a resounding, viscous *splap*, and the 'Cat quickly looked skyward, searching for whatever creature was capable of creating such prodigious droppings. Instead of an unprecedentedly large flying reptile, however, his eyes fastened onto Silva's bearded face, leering happily amid the sound of raucous laughter.

"Oh, Lord." Spanky sighed.

Matt's first instinct was to shout a reprimand. Instead he stifled the impulse and laughed. He caught Spanky's questioning, almost indignant look. "Oh, don't worry; he'll clean it up. He's become 'responsible'! I'm just glad to see his practical jokes have moderated with his increase in rank."

Spanky shook his head. "But have Chack's?" he wondered aloud.

Lieutenant Dowden joined them with a smirk. "You know, right now we've got half the deck division spraying bird crap off the ship, while the other half is encouraging the damn things to squirt more on it." He shook his head when the others laughed.

"Is this a ... met-a-for? A metaphor for human behavior?" Keje asked, and joined in when the laughter redoubled. In spite of their worries about the radio, everyone felt a certain lightness now that the greater part of their mission had been achieved. Baalkpan would be reinforced. It would take a while, but they should have the time.

"Maybe so," Matt conceded, "but there're plenty of 'Cats doing it too. Maybe we're too much alike for our own good." He sobered and looked at Spanky. "How's our fuel holding up?"

"Okay, so far. We made a slower run out than planned, so we saved a little there. We're kind of pouring it on for this little side trip, holding twenty knots, but we'll have to slow down again in the Canigao Channel. We'll be taking the Surigao Strait in the dark, so we ought to keep it slow.... Plenty of fuel for a return trip like the one we came out on. Where are we looking first for this sub?"

Matt stepped around the charthouse and stared down at the copied Lemurian Scrolls rolled out under the Plexiglas on the chart table. The others joined him there. "Last reliable reports have it in this vicinity," he said, pointing at Davao Gulf and circling his finger south of Mindanao. "Fishing boats from Saaran-gaani—used to be General Santos, where one of Saan-Kakja's brothers set up house— saw it pretty often for a week or two, from the reports Meksnaak finally coughed up, but nobody's seen it for a year now, which would be about right." Matt frowned. "I know Meksnaak finally made all nice, but I still don't know about that guy. I'm pretty sure he's still convinced it's a sea monster of some sort. Anyway, given that it must have gone through the same Squall we did, and the fuel it must've had, it couldn't have made it much farther than that. By the time they made it here, they must have realized something was seriously out of whack." His finger traced the western coastline of Mindanao, paused at the bay where Mati should be, considering, then swept around Cape San Agustin and into Davao Gulf. "If it was anywhere near Saaran-gaani, or beached on the coast anywhere along here, Saan-Kakja's brother would know about it. We'll look, of course, especially in that bay, but I don't think we'll find it there. No one's reported it, and I understand the local wildlife is even more extreme than usual. If they tried to land along there, I bet they didn't stay."

"Maybe it's just gone, Skipper," Dowden said. "Sunk."

"Maybe . . ."

"Where, then?" Keje asked.

Matt's finger roamed south about a hundred and fifty miles to Talaud Island and drew a circle, encompassing the tiny islands around it. "Here, I think, if they had the fuel. These islands are . . . were Dutch. Maybe they hoped to find *somebody* home."

Keje studied the chart. "Deep water. Deep water all around."

"Yeah. Nobody in their right mind would go monkeying around down there. No reason to, besides. Dangerous water and nothing to catch. If they're there, they could've easily gone a year without anybody noticing." He looked at Keje and their eyes met.

"I have seen those islands," Keje said softly, "many years ago. I did not go ashore—that was not our purpose—but the land on the big island, this Taa-laud, is lush, and could sustain them if they were not eaten by predators—and if they made it across the deep waters in the first place. The island is also founded upon a burning mountain, a 'vol-caano' that rarely sleeps. I have heard the earth moves often, and the very sea sometimes behaves strangely."

Matt straightened, decision made. "We'll work south along the coast of Mindanao, checking every nook and cranny, but then, if we haven't found it, we'll cross to Talaud."

"What if it's not there either, Skipper?" Spanky asked.

Matt shrugged. "We go home."

*I*t was overcast, but not raining this time when Sandra waved good-bye to yet another destroyer. Now *Mahan* was steaming toward the mouth of the bay, looking just like *Walker* from a distance, and fingers of dread clutched Sandra's heart. *Mahan* was following in the wake of a pair of fast feluccas that had departed the night before. They'd serve as scouts at first, then transports if the need arose. Nobody really knew how many people remained on B'mbaado—trapped now behind enemy lines.

Selass was with her, come to say farewell to her mate, Saak-Fas. He'd been leaning on the rail, staring, as the ship moved away, but if he saw her in the throng he made no sign. Now the ship had almost vanished against the dreary, light gray sky. They saw a wisp of smoke, a sense of ghostly movement. Otherwise all that marked her passage was a flicker of color at her masthead as the Stars and Stripes streamed aft in the sultry air, stirred only by the ship's motion. Sandra watched the flag slowly fade with mixed emotions, an elusive memory of something Matt once told her rising to the surface. Something he'd seen a doomed British destroyer do in the face of impossible odds, and then *Exeter* did the same thing before her final battle. She strained to remember, sure it was important.

"Do you think they will return?" Selass asked quietly.

"They must. We'll need them desperately when *Walker* returns."

"I meant *Walker*," Selass almost whispered. "I feel so guilty. I find myself almost hoping *Mahan* will fail. That would mean the end of Queen Maraan, but then I might have a chance when Chack returns. It would also probably mean the end of Saak-Fas as well." She paused, then almost pleaded, "But that is what he wants, is it not?"

"I suspect so," Sandra replied, saddened for her tragic friend, though not shocked that her thoughts had taken such a turn. "If that's the case, if he truly wants to die, he'll likely get his chance." She sighed. "Jim Ellis is a good man and an excellent officer, but I'm not sure he should be commanding this mission. He still blames himself for losing *Mahan* when Kaufman shot him and took command. He thinks his ship's honor is stained—*his* honor too. He feels he has something to prove. Nobody like that should ever command a mission like this, with so much at stake. I know Jim, and trust him, but I can't shake the fear that he'll take chances with himself and his ship, hoping to remove that stain, when his most important objective is to get himself and his ship back in one piece."

She lowered her head in thought as they walked back through the bazaar in the direction of the hospital. They entered the textile section, where colorful tapestries and fine fabrics swayed gently in the light air. A matronly Lemurian female, with hard-used, pendulous breasts, was perched on a high stool, embroidering a smock with an ornate design, and Sandra paused to admire the work. Then it hit her.

"Excuse me," she said excitedly. "Your embroidery is beautiful, but do you also sew fabric together?"

"Of course! What a silly question . . ." The female grunted rudely, then looked up and hastily added, "Esteemed healer!" She stood and bowed low. "My apologies! Indeed, I must first make these garments before I embroider them."

"Excellent! I know you're busy, but could I commission you to make something for me?"

"For you, anything! You healed one of my daughters, badly wounded at Aryaal. Nothing will take precedence. I will begin work today! What would the esteemed healer have me make?"

Sandra took her precious notebook and pen from her shirt pocket and began to draw. Curious passersby stopped to stare, and it occurred to Sandra that she'd probably doubled the old seamstress's business by choosing her. She displayed the sketch and said how big she wanted the finished product.

"I have seen that before," the matron said. "Everyone has. Certainly I can make it, but so large?" Sandra nodded emphatically. Then, thinking of the female's embroidery skills, and her own Virginia heritage, she scribbled some more on the drawing. "And I want that on it too."

Tarakan Island had changed dramatically. Chief Gray had finally taken Silva's advice and burned half of it off. They took extreme care to make sure the prevailing winds confined the blaze to only half the island; still, Gray knew Bradford would be livid. There'd been nothing for it, though. The dense foliage simply couldn't be cleared in the time they had, and the priority, after all, was the well. Besides, it was a dangerous place. They'd lost two more 'Cats surveying the site—killed this time—and the Bosun wouldn't sacrifice another life for every tree on the island. Even so, he'd been surprised how well the place burned. He hadn't even been sure they could light the wet, waxy undergrowth, and when it went up like kerosene-soaked wood, it was a scramble to contain the blaze and get everyone clear. They even had a battle on their hands, of sorts, down on the beach, when swarms of wildly unlikely creatures stampeded from the forest. Fortunately, Shinya had already begun defensive positions, and a lot of the fleeing beasts simply leaped the entrenchments the workers and Marines scrambled into. Some of the terror-maddened creatures wanted to fight, though, and some of his people suffered a few injuries—none serious, fortunately, but they were well supplied with meat for a couple days before it began to spoil.

Work on the well proceeded rapidly after that, surrounded by a surrealistic landscape of fire-blackened stumps and a jumble of fallen trees. At least the workers were no longer in peril from predators, although nighttime brought a variety of scavengers anxious to pick the cooked victims clean. Soon even they lost interest, and before long one could walk from the beach to the well at any time of the day or night in relative safety.

Shinya and Gray had a falling-out over the burn, but not for environmental reasons. Shinya wanted to leave a belt of jungle as a fallback defensive position. Gray even tried to arrange it, but the fire took off quicker than anyone expected. Angry, Shinya accused Gray of deliberately disregarding his advice, and, just as angry, Gray told him to go to hell. They coexisted even more uneasily than usual after that, and each concentrated on his own area of responsibility. As a result, both probably did a better, quicker job than they would have otherwise, but they drove their work crews unmercifully. By the time Isak brought in the well, everyone was exhausted.

The upside was, that left little strenuous labor for anyone to do. The storage tanks were erected and emplaced, and a pipeline had already been run to where the new refinery would be once *Felts* returned with the equipment. Shinya had overseen the construction of impressive works down at the beach, with multilayered defenses anchored on the impenetrable jungle on one flank, and a rocky mole extending into the sea on the other. The storage tanks were just outside the secondary defensive perimeter, but the wellhead was protected.

Gray sat on the edge of his cot under a makeshift shelter the Marines erected. It was a sturdy affair and would probably survive a moderate blow. It wasn't big, but at least he had it to himself. All the workers and Marines shared similar structures with ten or more. He heard a loud *crack* and glanced up from the journal he was keeping, pen poised over the paper. He had a good view of the beach, and experienced a nostalgic moment when he realized it looked just like any other island beach he'd seen—like those in the Keys where he took the Boy fishing when he was on leave—before his wife got fed up and took the Boy away. He hadn't seen him more than half a dozen times after that, so he'd been shocked to run into him, all grown up, in a bar in Cavite. The Boy was in destroyers then too, but he'd received a transfer. They had a few beers, talked about things, and then went to the beach and fished until the sun came up. The next day, the Boy shouldered his seabag and boarded an oiler bound for Pearl. From there he'd hitch another ride to the States and spend a few days with his mother before joining his new ship: the USS *Oklahoma*.

When things started getting hot with the Japs, the Pacific Fleet—and *Oklahoma*—moved to Pearl. Gray had been planning on taking some leave to get together with the Boy, but a little over a year ago now, on December 7 . . . The letter he got said the Boy was "missing and presumed lost." He figured his ex got one just like it, but he never wrote to find out. There wasn't any point. He closed his eyes and rubbed his face.

There was another *crack* and he focused on the cause. Down by the water a group of 'Cats was gathered around a man, and Gray did a double take. He snorted with amazement. He'd seen dinosaurs, monkey-cats, flying lizards, and Grik, but nothing rivaled this: Isak Rueben was teaching the 'Cats how to swing a baseball bat. Gray was shocked that he even knew how. The Mice had always scorned the ship's team, back when there was one, and never even watched the games. While Gray stared, Isak tossed another of the softball-size, inedible nuts they'd discovered on the island into the air, and with a confident flourish twirled the bat and whacked the nut far out over the water. It disappeared with a splash, lost in the sound of the surf.

"I'll be damned," he muttered, a grin creeping across his face. It vanished an instant later when he heard the insistent clanging of the general alarm bell. The bell was little more than a hollow bronze pipe, but its sound carried amazingly well when it was vigorously struck. There was only one reason for anyone to do that. Tamatsu Shinya appeared in the entrance to his hut, breathing hard, almost coming to attention.

"We have visitors," he said, very formally.

Shinya and Gray stood on the beach surrounded by their "staff," consisting of two Lemurian Marine captains, their four lieutenants, and a Guard captain in charge of the project company. His lieutenants were organizing his workers into squads and arming them, while the Marine NCOs directed their troops into their fighting positions. Signalman "Mikey" Monk, from *Mahan*, and Shipfitter Stanley "Dobbin" Dobson from *Walker*, were also there, and, for some reason, so was Isak. Gray lowered his binoculars and grudgingly handed them to Shinya.

"Three Grik ships—you can just see the red of their hulls—working up from the south. There's another sail, southwest and farther away, but coming up fast. She's got a better wind."

"You reckon it might be *Felts*?" Isak asked, uncharacteristically curious. "She's due back."

"Could be," Gray answered. "Whoever it is, they're by theirself. If she's ours, maybe she'll get here in time to intercept those Grik bastards." He grinned wickedly. "I wonder how they'll like her guns."

A blue-kilted staff sergeant scampered up and saluted. "The Marines are in place, sirs." His tail twitched. "The Guards soon will be. I sent first squad, second platoon, to help them get sorted out." The Guard captain bristled, but said nothing.

"Very well," Shinya replied. "Once they're in position, have them stand easy. It will be a while before the enemy arrives. Make sure there is plenty of water and the ammunition is distributed."

The ammunition was mainly arrows and crossbow bolts, although some of the NCOs had Krags. There were also the two field guns they'd brought ashore, six-pounders, now emplaced halfway from the center to each flank, where they could sweep all approaches.

For the better part of the morning, the group stood rooted, watching the approaching ships. A single, towering cloud appeared and lashed the sea with a vicious squall before vanishing entirely. The Grik ships continued their relentless advance. So did the other "sail," and before long they saw the white stripe between her gunports. *Felts*.

"This ought to be a pretty good show," Gray surmised, and indeed, he was right. *Felts* slanted down, Stars and Stripes streaming to leeward, and crossed the bows of the tightly packed enemy squadron. A single, billowing white cloud erupted along her side, and long moments later a dull thumping sound reached them over the surf.

"Give 'em hell, Mr. Clark!" Mikey growled.

They couldn't see the effect, if any, of the initial broadside, but *Felts* wore around and punished the enemy with her portside guns. They saw splashes of debris, and a mast toppled into the sea. Cheers erupted behind them. The Grik squadron's precise formation fell into disarray, and two of the ships slewed around, beam-on to their attacker. Then, with disbelieving eyes, those on the beach watched sporadic puffs of white smoke gush from the sides of the red-hulled ships.

"Holy *shit*!"

Round shot kicked up splashes, skipping across the wave tops in the general direction of the beach, and a few of the staff cringed involuntarily.

"Holy shit," Dobbin murmured again. "Where'd they get *cannons*?"

"Same place we did, idiot," Gray growled more fiercely than he intended. "The bastards made 'em."

Felts didn't wear this time; instinctively Clark must have known it would expose his vulnerable stern. Instead, the sloop hove to and held her ground, pounding away at the enemy.

"Gonna be a better show than we thought," Gray said ironically.

Felts's gunnery was far better, and she hacked away at the red ships. She finally fell away before the wind, to keep the Grik at arm's length, and took a pounding then, but when the now crippled squadron re-formed for the advance, she hove to once more and raked them again and again. The damage she inflicted was exponentially greater this time. Rigging and stays, weakened by the previous fire, parted, and shattered masts teetered and fell, taking others, less damaged, with them. One enemy ship was a wallowing, dismasted wreck, and the other two weren't much better, but their gunnery was improving at the point-blank range of the duel, and *Felts* was suffering too. Over the next hour they watched while the battle raged on the sea, and *Felts* maintained the same tactics: pouring withering fire into her foes until they got too close, then gaining some distance again. The dismasted, sinking Grik ship fell far behind, but the remaining two learned to present their own broadside whenever *Felts* moved away. It was difficult for them, since they could barely maneuver, but the American ship had finally lost her foremast and maintop as well.

"Mr. Clark is fighting his ship well," Shinya observed politely.

"He's a brawler," Gray conceded, "but he's fighting stupid. *Felts* is faster and more maneuverable, and her gunnery's obviously better. He should be taking advantage of that. He's gotten sucked into a slugging match, and that's the Grik's kind of fight." The ships were close enough now that there was only the slightest pause before they heard the sound of the guns. The tearing-canvas shriek of shot passing nearby was more frequent too, but the staff no longer flinched. "He needs to get out from between us and them. The tide's out, and he'll run out of water pretty soon." Sure enough, while they watched, *Felts* heeled slightly, righted herself, then heeled sharply over as she went hard aground, beam-on to the advancing swells and the enemy.

"Dumb ass. Give the kid a ship and what does he do?" He shook his head. "Mr. Shinya, get a platoon of Marines into the boats and pull for *Felts*. Those Grik bastards draw more water and they'll be aground too, I expect, but they'll send boarders. I doubt they'll fool with us while they've got the ship right in front of them. We have to keep them off her at all costs."

Shinya saluted. "Very well." He looked at the commander of First Platoon. "With me."

Even aground, *Felts* kept up a withering fire, but the Grik remorselessly advanced. Inevitably, they too struck, and then it became a race to see whether the Marines or the enemy boarders reached *Felts* first. Another of the Grik ships, holed repeatedly, filled and heeled over on her side in the shallow water. Most of her crew were already in the boats, however, and *Felts*'s guns churned the sea with canister, splintering boats and scything down their crews. Before long, though, they were under her guns. At their upward angle they just couldn't be depressed far enough, and when they gained her side they swarmed up and over the bulwarks. They were met by a withering fusillade of arrows and more canister from the guns that were loaded and waiting. Mangled bodies rained into the sea, and the "flashies" quickly went to work, thrashing the water beside the ship into a white, pink-tinged froth.

The Marines pulled as hard as they could, oars dipping and straining, with Shinya in the foremost boat, waving his modified cutlass and exhorting his troops to greater effort. They almost made it. They would have made it, Gray thought bitterly as he watched. The fighting was dying down, the first onslaught repulsed, when *Felts*'s own boats dropped to the water, and her crew, wounded and hale, scrambled into them. Dense smoke poured from the bowels of the grounded ship, and soon flames were licking up her masts.

"Goddamn it!" Gray seethed. "That better have been an accident, or I'll have that useless bastard shot!"

Shinya paused his advance, resting his Marines while the abandoning crew joined him. Then, at a more leisurely pace, the flotilla of boats returned to shore. Behind them, *Felts* became fully involved, flames soaring high into the sky, still-loaded guns occasionally booming from within the inferno. The mainmast toppled amid a cloud of gray smoke and swirling sparks, about the time the first boats nudged ashore through the gentle surf. Guardsmen sprang forward to assist the wounded, and Marines and uninjured sailors mingled on the beach, sorting themselves out, while Shinya escorted Lieutenant Clark before Gray and his impatient staff.

Clark's uniform was stained and bloody, and his hair and face were scorched. He'd clearly been the last to leave his ship. His cutlass was in its sheath, blood trickling down the side where it scraped from the blade when he thrust it in. He drew himself up before Gray and saluted. If either was struck by the irony of an officer saluting a noncom, neither commented on it; there was no question who was in charge.

"What happened?" Gray snapped.

"Why, well, we fought a hell of a fight!" Clark retorted after a brief hesitation, clearly surprised by Gray's tone. "The bastards had cannons! We knew it was possible, of course, but we didn't really expect it."

"What do you mean, you knew it was possible?"

"That's right," Clark replied, "you couldn't know." He quickly outlined recent events while Gray stood, listening with growing rage.

"Let me get this straight," Gray said at last. "Queen Maraan, Pete, and who knows who else are stranded behind enemy lines, *Donaghey*'s laid up, the rest of the new construction's not ready for sea, *Mahan*'s gone—against orders—to rescue the queen, the goddamn Griks are gettin' frisky and they have *cannons* now, the radio's busted so we can't even tell the captain"—he gestured out at the inferno—"and you just burned our only way home! You better convince me real fast why I shouldn't have your sorry ass shot!"

Clark shook his head in astonishment. "Mr. Gray, there

were *three* of them! We whittled them down to one, killed most of the boarding party they sent against us, but another was forming from the other, mostly undamaged ship. There was no way we could repel another attack."

"The Marines were almost there!"

"Yes, sir, and maybe that would've helped, but I didn't see any point losing more lives over a wrecked ship."

"Was she wrecked?"

"She was hard aground!"

"Sunk? Leaking bad?"

"Well, not really, but . . ."

"But the goddamn tide's out! We could've held her until it came back in and refloated her!"

"But . . ." Agonized realization dawned across Clark's blistered face. "Oh my God."

"Yep. You screwed up by the numbers in each and every category. We bett—"

Isak poked him in the ribs with his elbow. "Griks is comin'," he said, motioning out to sea. Gray looked past the burning ship at the mass of approaching boats.

"We better get ready," he growled. "Mr. Shinya?"

"Sir?"

"See to our defenses. Arm the sailors if they lost their weapons, and if we have anything extra." He looked back at Clark. "If they're true to form, there'll be six or seven hundred of 'em. With your boys, we'll have about two hundred and fifty. Looks like this'll be the Grik's kind of battle too."

"At 'em, boys!" Alden bellowed as he dropped his shield and sprinted into the clearing from the cover of the dense forest. Others surged forward to join him: dozens, then nearly a hundred. Fortunately most didn't follow his exuberant, somewhat irresponsible example by throwing their own shields aside. The disorganized Grik line was caught completely by surprise. This time an even larger number turned on their fellows and began hacking away. Some even dropped their weapons and simply ran—something Pete had never seen. Quite enough Grik to satisfy him reacted in a more predictable fashion: they charged to meet the attack.

He emptied his Springfield into the mass, then slashed

with the bayonet at its muzzle. Knocking a sword aside, he skewered what appeared to be an "officer," if Grik infantry had such things. The "troops" under his command maintained a relatively cohesive front when they slammed into the enemy with their handmade shields and spears of sharpened wood. Enough of them, Alden's personal guard and B'mbaadan warriors, had real spears to do most of the killing, while those on the flanks funneled the enemy toward them. There came a crash from the center when the disorganized remnants of the Grik mob slammed into the interlocked shields and those shields pushed back. Spears bristled and jabbed, and Pete's little army fought with everything they had, from swords to garden tools. Some of these Grik had no weapons either, the earlier surprise sweeping them away before they had a chance to grab them, but even disarmed, the Grik were deadly with their terrible claws and teeth. Therefore, brief as it was, the fight was still unimaginably fierce. Finally, all the Grik that charged the line were dead or writhing on the ground, with the exception of a trickle that ultimately ran away as well. Gasping after the sharp fight and aching after the long morning of exertion, Pete took a drink from his canteen.

The sun hadn't been up long, but the battle had raged since before dawn. With their amazing eyesight, Lemurians could see fine in the dark, where apparently their enemy couldn't. The Grik had no "taboos" or anything against fighting at night, but they weren't very good at it. The local 'Cats preferred not to either, for religious reasons. Therefore, aside from his huge numerical superiority, it must've never even occurred to the Grik commander he might be in danger even as he slept. The sight of the enemy army asleep, totally off guard, was too much of a temptation, and Pete kicked off the attack ahead of schedule.

The killing had been almost wanton, and those that survived the initial onslaught broke and ran in all directions. Pursuit was unthinkable, though, and Alden gathered his force and withdrew to his secondary position. The enemy reacted quickly, sending reinforcements against the thrust. Like most highly specialized predators, however, Grik seemed to key on motion even in the daylight, so they were completely surprised again when they ran right into Haakar-Faask's force that Pete's had retired behind.

Savaged again by the stalwart B'mbaadan general, the Grik reeled back in the direction of their own lines. That was when Alden's rested troops struck them again on the flank. It appeared this element of the Grik advance, at least, was shattered beyond reclamation.

Alden wiped his bayonet on his pants leg and snapped it back on his rifle. Taking another long drink, keen eyes glancing all around, he spit and began thumbing slender .30-06 rounds back into his empty magazine. He was already out of stripper clips, and had only the dozen or so loose rounds in his pocket.

"All right," he said, closing the bolt, "let's pull back. Easy does it; don't get split up in the woods. We'll re-form with General Faask, and see what kind of hornet's nest we've stirred up. Stretcher bearers, get our wounded out of here."

The wounded would be carried back to the "reserve" commanded by the Orphan Queen, whose primary responsibility was guarding the younglings and noncombatants.

He glanced at the sun, now clear of the treetops overhead. "It's gonna be a long day."

"So this is your 'surprise' for the mountain fish," Keje observed.

"One of them," Matt confirmed. "At least, I hope so. Took Sonarman Brooks long enough to get it working again, even though we had all the parts." He shrugged. "We just never saw any point in it at first. It's meant to find submarines underwater, and we had no reason to suspect we'd need it against any of those. I've heard active sonar plays hell with whales back home—our version of mountain fish, even if they're a lot smaller—so maybe it'll kick these big bastards in the head too."

"Why are we going"—Keje grinned—"so slow? I thought you wanted to cross to Taa-laud as fast as possible."

"I do, but I want to see if this works. We can't get a return at anything much over fifteen knots. If we can get a return, Brooks ought to be able to tell us what effect it has on the big devils by how they react to it."

They waited for the better part of an hour, crowded in the charthouse behind the nervous sonarman's chair, while he listened intently through his headset. The constant, eerie pinging continued uninterrupted.

"Contact!" Brooks suddenly shouted, unaware his voice was so loud. "Bearing one nine five! Probable sub . . . probable mountain fish! Range fifteen hundred yards, down Doppler. Wait! Return is narrowing. Either he's turning toward us, or away."

Matt leaned out the hatch and caught the talker's eye. "Sound general quarters," he said calmly.

Knowing the cause, the talker gulped. "General quarters, aye!"

During *Walker*'s refit, much was repaired, but somehow they'd overlooked her ill-sounding general alarm. There'd been no emergency aboard since they began the mission, but daily exercises—something Matt insisted on—still took their toll. The musical, insistent *gong! gong! gong!* had gradually been replaced by something more like a loose guitar string being brutally plucked. The alarm was still referred to as "Gee-Kyoo" by the crew, but the act of setting it off had become: "Somebody up there's (on the bridge) stompin' on a duck." Abused duck or not, the alarm still had the desired effect, and within seconds reports started coming in. Finally, the talker looked at the captain.

"All stations report manned and ready, Captain."

"Very well." Matt looked back in the charthouse. "Well?"

"He's moving away, Skipper! First he was running straight away; now he's on a bearing of two one oh, and picking up speed!"

"Let's hope the neighborhood just got too noisy for him."

"Captain," shouted the talker, "lookout reports 'something' surfacing astern!"

He looked aft, but couldn't see past the amidships deckhouse, so he scrambled up to the fire control platform. "Mr. Campeti," he acknowledged as the new gunnery officer directed his gaze, and Matt raised his binoculars. It was a mountain fish, all right, a different one. It had risen directly astern, and was giving chase. Matt suddenly realized this "surprise" had one small weakness: *Walker*'s sonar was directed primarily forward.

He'd known, intellectually, that mountain fish were big; he'd been told so often enough. But to actually *see* one this close! *Jesus*, he thought, *the damn thing's* huge. *Now I know what it feels like to be a grasshopper in a stock tank full of bass!* "All ahead flank!" he shouted, knowing the order would be passed along. "Mr. Campeti, have the number four gun commence firing in local control! Stand by to roll depth charges!" It looked like they'd get to try all their "surprises" today. It would be a few minutes before they accelerated to their maximum speed. In the meantime, the thing was gaining on them! "Set your depth at fifty feet!" Any shallower and they ran a serious risk of damaging the ship.

"Depth charges report set at fifty feet,'" Campeti reported a moment later. "Ready to roll at your command!"

Silva was on the aft deckhouse, watching, while the crew of number four made ready. His new exalted status was liberating in a way; he wasn't a gun captain anymore, so he could pretty much pick where he wanted to be during general quarters, but it also left him feeling like he had nothing to do at times. Lieutenant Dowden, a few feet distant, probably felt the same way, manning the auxiliary conn. It was his duty to conn the ship if the bridge or its personnel were disabled. In the meantime, he didn't have anything to do either, except watch the god-awful, humongous fish come swimming up their skirt. All they could really see was an enormous, rounded hump, pushing displaced water like a rogue tsunami. Occasionally it blew a mist of atomized water high in the air from an indistinct hole that closed immediately after. Its massive flukes, or tail, or whatever drove it, never broke the surface, and it did look for all the world like a big, rounded, barnacle-encrusted . . . island, chasing them to beat sixty. The stern crouched down suddenly, and Silva felt the ship accelerate, but the damn thing was fast! Realistically he couldn't imagine the fish maintaining its nearly twenty-knot surge for any length of time, but realistically it shouldn't exist at all. He wasn't sure they'd get clear in time.

"Commence firing!" shouted the talker beside the gun, and an instant later the pointer stomped the trigger pedal. There was an earsplitting *boom!* and the gun jumped back, vomiting its empty shell to clang on the deck. Another shell went in and the breech slammed shut, while a 'Cat ordnance striker chased the empty shell with outstretched gloves, trying to catch it before it went over the side, and keep an eye on the approaching horror at the same time. *Boom!* The breech clanked open, spilling another empty, and the shell man slammed another home. *Boom!* Three high-explosive four-inch shells disappeared into what had to be the thing's head and detonated with enough force to scatter gobbets of flesh hundreds of yards. A massive, gaping wound as big as a car had appeared where the shells struck home, and the wave it pushed had taken a pinkish tinge from blood coursing down. Suddenly, much closer than they expected—less than a hundred yards astern—another hump rose up, clearing the water and exposing monstrous ivory teeth. The thing emitted a roar like a hundred whales being electrocuted, and surged in for the kill. They hadn't been shooting at its head at all!

"Out of the way, goddamn it!" Silva shouted, yanking the 'Cat pointer out of his chair and sending him sprawling on the deck. He jumped on the metal seat and looked through the eyepiece in front of him. He barely heard the shouted, "Roll two!" command and the muted splash of the depth charges. "Clear!" he roared, making sure no one was behind him, and he pressed the firing pedal with the crosshairs centered far back in the roof of the creature's mouth. *Boom!* The overpressure of the gun's report was like a lover's embrace. "Load!"

The water beneath the monster's upper jaw spalled suddenly, and two enormous spumes of water obscured their vision. There was a sense of massive motion, and then what seemed like tons of seawater deluged the men and 'Cats on the stern of the ship. Silva wiped his eyes and searched frantically for the target. For an instant he felt disoriented, and started to yell at the trainer, thinking he'd spun the gun out to one side. But wait, there were the depth charge racks right below him. He stared again, squinting, and realized it was true: the monster was gone. All that remained as *Walker* continued to accelerate away was a giant field of churning bubbles, harsh against the cerulean sea, and in its midst, like an oil slick, an expanding stain of black-red blood.

"Goddamn!" Silva whooped, joining the cheers around him. "I sunk him!"

Lighting a third boiler, and keeping a steady twenty-five knots, *Walker* managed to outrun anything her sonar didn't scare away for the remainder of the transit. By midafternoon, Talaud Island was drawing near, as well as a group of smaller islands off the port bow, and Matt finally gave the order to reduce speed as the water shoaled rapidly closer to land.

"Which way, Skipper?" Dowden asked. They'd raised the island on its northeastern coast, and there was nowhere immediately apparent even a small boat—much less a submarine—might find shelter. Now they must decide whether to steam west, then south, to inspect the rest of the northern part of the island, then its western flank, or explore the eastern flank first. Matt glanced at Bradford, leaning on the rail, "his" binoculars glued to his eyes, oblivious to the question. He'd been morose when they'd been forced to injure and possibly kill one of the enormous mountain fish, and scandalized that he hadn't been able to at least view its corpse—if there'd been one. Now his earlier petulance was gone, as he prepared for yet more fantastic discoveries. This would be the first time they'd visited a landmass far enough from any other and surrounded by deep and hostile enough waters that there'd have been little, if any, dissemination of land-dwelling species. He was excited by what he'd seen so far, even from a distance, and occasional happy chortles escaped him.

There were plenty of "birds." Already they'd begun littering the deck again—and actual birds seemed to predominate. Bradford believed that, even if they weren't as fiercely armed as their leathery competitors, they were lighter and probably had a longer range. Therefore, more species of feathered birds might make it to this isolated place to diversify and thrive. Perhaps the ones they saw before were even migrants from here? There were still plenty of lizard birds, but not in comparison, and most were larger than their northern cousins. In any event, Bradford was in no position to offer constructive opinions regarding which direction to go. He didn't care.

Matt conferred quietly with Keje, and finally nodded in

agreement. "We'll explore the western flank first, Mr. Dowden. If we don't find them there, or in the south or east, we'll be in position to check out the smaller islands over there"—he gestured—"before heading home."

"But ... Captain, there're still lots of other places they could be."

"Possibly, but we don't have time to look. It's time we headed back, regardless." He paused a moment, considering. "Have Mr. McFarlane secure a boiler of his choice. We'll reduce speed to one-third, but let's keep a close sonar watch, shall we? Helmsman, make your course two six zero, if you please."

"Aye, sir, making my course two six zero."

For the remainder of the day they cruised sedately on a calm, gently rolling sea. They saw nothing in the north and when they turned south it looked like more of the same at first: dense, impenetrable jungle growing right down to and beyond the shore, by means of a mangrove-type root system. It was unlike anything Matt had ever seen on such a large and isolated island, and always, in the distance, a large volcano loomed menacingly from the jungle mists enshrouding its flanks. Jets of smoke or steam curled from vents in its side. Eventually they began to notice irregularities in the shoreline, and they slowed to a crawl so they could glass them more carefully. Still, no true inlet was apparent, or even a beach. There was no sign of life at all, in fact, besides the ever-present, swooping, defecating birds. Even Courtney began losing interest by the time the sun edged toward the horizon.

"I say, Captain Reddy, shouldn't we speed up? Hurry along, as it were? Surely the eastern side of the island is more hospitable and, well, easier to land upon."

"We can't know that, and we're only looking once. If we 'speed up' we might miss something. It'll soon be dark anyway, and we'll have to anchor. I want to do it in the shallowest water possible, and right now there's less water under our keel than we've had all day." Making up his mind, he spoke to the talker. "Pass the word for Chack; have him call the special sea and anchor detail. This is as good a place as any."

Lightning lit the night, slashing the sea in all directions, but there was little thunder, and the wind and sea remained calm and placid. It was an almost surrealistic spectacle, and nobody got much sleep. Earl Lanier went fishing—as was his custom whenever the ship was at rest. For once he didn't whistle tunelessly or snap at others standing by the rail, watching the silent display. He didn't catch anything either. Every time he lowered a hook, something immediately snapped his line. What's more, things in the water evidently began associating the bait with the ship, and an unnerving bumping and . . . sliding . . . commenced against the hull. Campeti had the watch and ordered Lanier to hang it up before whatever was down there got any friskier. For once, Earl didn't argue.

Before dawn, the anchor detail sprayed the heavy links with water as the chain came aboard, booming and rattling into the locker below. The crew stood to their battle stations as they did every morning when the ship was most vulnerable to observation, silhouetted against the graying sky. The practice had even taken on a more conventional feel. They knew they were looking for a submarine, and conventional wisdom said it was American. But they didn't *know* it was American. Besides, even if it was, and even if it was out there, it might not know *they* were Americans, and after a year on this God's nightmare of a world, it might have an itchy trigger finger.

In the pilothouse, holding his steaming "Captain's" mug, Matt didn't try to lighten the fresh tension around him. He knew there was almost no chance the iron fish would even be at sea, much less stalking them, but after the tiring night they'd passed, heightened awareness was a good thing. He gulped Juan's coffee and didn't even grimace. Bradford clomped up the ladder behind him, yawning loudly, followed by Adar and Keje. One way or another today would solve the mystery, at least so far as it was in their power to solve it, and they'd either find the elusive submarine on Talaud's eastern flank or the little islands to the northeast, or they'd turn for home. Either way, everyone was anxious to get about it. The sense of "something's not right" at Baalkpan had become a palpable thing, and every day they remained away added an exponential layer of anxiety. Even Bradford seemed resigned when Matt told him that unless they saw some evidence of the submarine, there'd be no excursion ashore.

"Anchor's aweigh, Captain," Dowden reported quietly in response to the shrill call of the bosun's pipe on the foc's'le. Matt nodded. He'd been wondering how 'Cats could toot on a bosun's pipe when they couldn't make a sound with a bugle. They'd learned at the Battle of Aryaal that they needed something like bugle calls to pass commands on the battlefield. Maybe they could adapt something like a giant bosun's call. Use whistles or something? He shook his head. He'd have to ask someone. All he could make a bugle do was fart.

"Very well. All ahead slow; make your course zero seven five. Extra lookouts to port."

When they rounded the island's southern tip and headed north, they began to discover beaches. Visibility was excellent, and the rising sun penetrated the shadows of the suddenly less dense forest, and they caught glimpses of a few animals here and there. Most, beach scavengers probably, scampered quickly under cover at the sight of them, but one creature the size and shape of a rhino-pig, but with a powerful neck as long as its body and a head like a moose—with tusks—stared insolently at them as they passed. It occasionally even rushed the surf, as if warning them away.

"Oh! You're a nasty fellow, aren't you!" Courtney giggled happily. "Oof! Oof! Orrrrr!" There were chuckles in the pilothouse, and Matt stifled a grin.

By late morning the distant humps of the small islands to the northeast appeared through the haze, and everyone knew they were about out of luck. There'd been a couple of promising lagoons, but they turned out to be little more than crescents eroded into the island by the marching sea, and they could see clearly to their termination. Another such lagoon, or the point at the mouth of one, was coming up, and all were grimly certain it was their final chance. They'd almost reached the point where they'd initially turned west.

"Captain," called Reynolds, "lookout reports this one's deeper than the others. Maybe better protected."

"Very well. We'll stick our nose in and take a look. Pass the word for the lead line. Dead slow when we round the point, consistent with the current, of course."

They passed the point and *Walker* slowed, Norman Kutas inching the big wheel ever so slightly to bring the bow around. The long swells pushed them toward the cove, and a series of constant adjustments were required.

"It *is* a deep inlet," Reynolds confirmed, passing the lookout's observations. "Surf's a little gentler inside."

"What's our depth?" Matt asked.

"Seven fathoms, coming up fast."

Reynolds looked up, eyes wide, and holding his earphone tight against his head as if not sure he'd heard correctly. "Uh, Captain, lookout says—I mean reports . . . there's something on the beach, high on the beach, twenty degrees off the starboard bow. It looks sort of like the pictures you showed them."

There was a rush to the bridge wing.

"Five fathoms!"

"Left full rudder," Matt commanded, "port engine ahead two-thirds, starboard back two-thirds!" *Walker* eased to a stop and the stern began swinging right. The ship pitched uncomfortably on the rollers for a moment, then began to roll. "Drop anchor. Mr. Dowden? How's the tide?"

"Low ebb, sir, about to turn."

"Very well. Leadsman to the stern. Prepare the launch." Only then did Matt go to the bridge wing, shouldering his way through the onlookers, and raise his own binoculars.

"I'll be damned," he said with a sinking heart. "Jesus, there she is . . ." He lowered the binoculars, but continued to stare. One of his questions had been answered. The stern continued coming around until *Walker* rode at anchor, pitching against the incoming sea.

"Stern lead reports three fathoms."

Matt raised his glasses again and studied the object of their search, the object of so many secret hopes. "Well," he said, his voice neutral, "stand by to lower the launch. Have Silva prepare a full weapons load for a shore party of twelve. Food, water, and medical supplies as well, in case there're survivors." He sighed. "As for the sub, we won't be getting her off *that*. Not this trip, anyway."

They took "Scott's" barge, named after the dead coxswain. It was the biggest, and still the best maintained. Besides Matt (Lieutenant Dowden hadn't even tried to talk him out of going this time), the barge carried Bradford, Adar, Keje, Spanky, and Gilbert Yager. Also aboard were Chack,

Silva, Stites, and three Marines. Stites did a creditable job as coxswain as he conned the burbling boat through the rollers into the calmer water protected by the northern point of the lagoon. They were so fixated on the beached submarine, they hardly noticed the flashies bumping the hull with their bony heads, and the closer they came to shore, the more disheartened they became.

The submarine wasn't only beached; she was high and dry. Even the incoming tide wouldn't float her. It would barely reach her. It would've taken a severe storm indeed to leave her that high on the beach, and there was absolutely nothing they could do with the time and manpower available to get her off—not that there seemed much point. She lay at thirty degrees, keel toward the sea, and rust streaks ran from her cracked, peeling, faded gray paint. It was an old S-Boat, as Matt suspected all along. There'd been quite a few of the obsolete submarines attached to the Asiatic Fleet, and this one was clearly a *Holland* class, based on its unique stern configuration and distinctive sow-belly shape. Matt quickly reviewed what he knew about *Holland* boats in his mind: a little over 200 feet long with 20-foot beam, somewhere around a thousand tons, with two diesels and electric motors. Top speed of fourteen or fifteen knots on the surface. Four torpedo tubes, a four-inch-fifty deck gun—just like *Walker*'s main battery.

"S-19," Spanky announced when the weather-ravaged numbers on her hull finally came in view. They couldn't see the larger numbers on her conning tower at the angle she lay. "I know that boat," he continued. "She was trying to clear Surabaya the same time we were. Having trouble with one of her diesels or something, and awaiting special orders. Battery trouble too, if I remember right. I talked to her chief, and he was run pretty ragged."

"We all were," Matt reminded him.

"True, but that boat's even older than *Walker* and *Mahan*. And to think fellas would go *underwater* in it. Gives me the heebie-jeebies." Another detail about S-Boats came to Matt's mind as the barge scrunched onto the sandy beach and the shore party scrambled ashore: they had a crew of about forty officers and men. So far they'd seen no sign of them.

Stites and one of the Marines secured a line from the

barge to the submarine's port propeller shaft, and joined the others fanning out to inspect the environs. The Marines and Bradford had their Krags, and Silva and Stites both carried BARs. Matt and Keje were the only ones with Springfields, and Adar wasn't armed at all—beyond a short sword at his side. Keje had become quite a marksman, but Adar wasn't any kind of fighter. Heavens knew he wished he was, but he thought he'd be more dangerous to his friends than to an enemy with the powerful American weapons. He didn't mind the little sword, because he could use it to hack brush—and he probably couldn't hurt anyone with it but himself.

"There are many tracks in the sand," Chack observed, and Bradford and Silva stooped to examine the impressions.

"Indeed there are!" Bradford exclaimed. "Some quite unique! I've never seen them before." He pointed. "Here's one that might have been made by one of those unpleasant buggers we saw earlier today!"

"I'm more interested in human tracks," Matt replied, also stooping, "like these." There was a large, well-beaten path leading from the submarine into the jungle. The tracks ran both ways, and some were relatively fresh. One very distinct set of tracks left him puzzled, however; the impressions were human, but only about half the size of the others.

"Jumpin' Jesus!" Silva exclaimed. "There's Grik tracks if I ever saw 'em! Lookie here, Skipper!" Matt hurried to where Silva stood, swatting sand off his knees.

"You're right," he confirmed darkly. "Everyone, there's definitely Grik on this island, so keep your eyes peeled." He stared at the trail leading from the submarine for a moment, then looked at the source. "I'd rather we all stuck together, but I'd also rather we didn't waste any time. Spanky, Yager, and I will inspect the submarine, see if there's anything we can salvage immediately. Maybe we can at least dig up some more four-inch-fifty ammunition. Stites'll remain topside on the sub as security while we go inside. Chack, you and Silva lead everyone else up the trail and search for survivors. Keep an eye on Mr. Bradford." He looked at Adar and Keje. "Would the two of you prefer to stay or go?"

Both Lemurians looked dubiously at the sharply leaning submarine.

"Fascinating as it might be to crawl inside that ... contraption," Keje hedged, "for myself, I would prefer to stay in the open."

"I as well," Adar agreed fervently.

"Suit yourselves. Can't say I blame you. I'm not wearing dolphins for a reason."

A cargo net hung from the shoreward side of the submarine, and they scrambled up without much difficulty. The deck was a little rough to stand on, since there were few stanchions, and S-Boat decks were notoriously slender to begin with. Only the area around the gun was very wide, where it swelled abruptly to give the gun crew footing when it was traversed. Matt eyed the gun greedily. If they couldn't salvage the sub, he at least wanted that gun someday, and it looked more and more like he'd have it. Onboard, the sub looked even worse. The wooden strakes were rotting and a few had collapsed. They had to be careful not to fall through to the pressure hull below. One of the periscopes was badly bent, and the hull plating was washboarded like one would expect after a severe depth-charging. They climbed up to the conning tower hatch, and Spanky undogged it easily enough. He stuck his hand out to Gilbert, who fished in a pack and produced a pair of battle lanterns. Spanky briefly shone one down the hatch, and then slid down the ladder. Matt followed him, and Gilbert brought up the rear.

"Stinks in here," Gilbert said, joining the others in the cramped compartment. "Ow." He'd jabbed himself with something. Matt had been aboard submarines before, and knew they weren't made for people as tall as he was. He had to crouch everywhere he went, and there was always something, a valve handle or pipe or who knew what, waiting to conk his head or poke his ribs. With only the light of the battle lanterns, it was even worse.

"Ow," he echoed.

"Always stinks in a pigboat," Spanky said. "That's why they call 'em that."

"There's something else," Matt said.

"Yeah," answered Spanky, "smells a little gassy." He cocked his head. "A little smoky too."

They descended another ladder to the control room. There was slightly more space, but the protuberances were even more aggressive, particularly at the angle the boat lay. Spanky shone his light at something.

"I wonder," he murmured, and flipped a switch. Much to their surprise, an eerie red light flickered to life, glowing dully in the compartment. "Night-light," he explained. "So there's a little juice, anyway."

"Which way?" Matt asked the engineer, leaving the decision to him. It was stiflingly hot, and he knew they couldn't stay below long. "Forward or aft?"

"Torpedoes would be forward, engines aft. What's our priority?"

"Torpedoes."

"Ain't as thick as most jungles I've vacationed in lately," Silva noted, swiping at a vine with his cutlass as the group of eight marched inland.

"This side of the island is more exposed to extreme weather," Bradford explained. "Saplings are often swept away before they take root, I should think."

"Mmm."

There were still areas that were quite dense, but occasionally the trail opened into clearings, of a sort, where strange pine/palmlike trees stood tall with little undergrowth. Whenever they came to such a place, Silva covered Chack and his Marines while they split up and scouted ahead, in case someone or something intended to use it for the excellent purpose of laying an ambush. Super lizards weren't the only creatures that knew clearings were well suited for that. When the Marines were satisfied no threat existed, the party moved on. Currently the trail was clear, but the foliage was dense on either side. Up ahead another clearing opened, however. Silva advanced slowly, BAR at his shoulder. When he reached the edge of the opening, he'd scan it for obvious threats before the Marines cast ahead once more.

"Leapin' lizards!" he hissed. Standing in the center of the clearing, about thirty yards away, was a Grik. It was broadside-on, motionless, nose sniffing the air. The light filtering from the canopy above made it a perfect target. Even as Silva's finger automatically tightened on the trigger, his subconscious mind noticed several startling things: the Grik was an entirely different color from any he'd seen, kind of a stripey, orange-ish-black—like a tiger—and its tail seemed longer. It wore no armor, only a ridiculous, uselessly oriented leather breechcloth. A pouch hung at its side. The most outlandish thing about it, however, had only an instant to register before Silva's instinctual reaction to shoot it fully manifested itself. Maybe the subconscious realization threw his aim, or maybe he sensed something creeping up on *him* even as he fired. Whatever the reason, he knew the shot was bad even as the deafening bark of the BAR shattered the silence of the forest and a number of things struck him at once.

First, something *was* creeping up on him—rushing, in fact. The second thing to strike him was a club of some kind, moldy-soft on the outside, but with a core as dense as iron. Third, even as he staggered from the blow and heard high-pitched shrieks accompanying it, his subconscious mind screamed out the shocking detail he'd half missed about the Grik: it was carrying a musket.

He fell to the ground, too stunned even to defend himself, much less strike back. For a moment he had no idea what was on top of him, shrilly shrieking and landing blow after blow. As his head cleared from the initial strike, he realized whatever had "ahold" of him wasn't very big, it wasn't eating him, and the incessant blows didn't really hurt. He also understood the hysterical screaming—as well as the hysterical, chittering laughter accompanying it. He opened his eyes. There, straddling his chest, was a nymph-size fury, jade eyes wide with rage, lips skinned back from perfect, if yellowed teeth, long, wildly disheveled hair revealing glimpses of the golden radiance beneath the filth.

"Oh, you monster! Vile, loathsome, horrible beast!" it ranted, still pounding him with little fists.

"Goddamn it, fellas! It's a *girl*!" Silva almost squeaked, to a fresh round of laughter.

"Don't you use such language in front of *me*, you filthy murderer! You . . . you *bastard*!" The blows resumed with renewed fury.

"Get this wildcat offa me! Chack, you little turd!" Silva yelped, but Chack couldn't move; he could barely breathe. He was paralyzed by the sight of a clearly human youngling beating the stuffing out of the mighty Dennis Silva. Silva finally resorted to simply immobilizing the girl in a tight embrace. She struggled mightily, but there was no escape. Finally her shouts became desolate sobs.

"Listen . . . girlie . . . I ain't gonna hurt you none—nobody is—but you gotta leave off whuppin' on me, see? It ain't polite."

Courtney Bradford shook off the shock of the moment and raised a restraining hand to Chack's Marines. Keje and Adar weren't laughing. They'd instantly realized the possible significance of their discovery.

"Chack!" Keje rumbled. "If you cannot control yourself, or your Maa-reens, I will do it for you!" Keje might no longer be Chack's personal High Chief, but the young Lemurian still respected him tremendously. Chastened, he and the three Marines sobered.

Bradford knelt down. "There, there, child. Please do compose yourself," he said gently. The small girl was filthy, and dressed in rags. Clearly she'd suffered a terrible ordeal. Perhaps she was unhinged. What else might motivate her to attack Silva that way?

"Yeah," Silva grated as softly as he could. "If you'll cut it out, I'll turn you loose." The grimy, tear-streaked face nodded, and Dennis let her go. Instantly she scrambled to her feet, and bolted toward the Grik on the ground. Silva jumped up, snagging his rifle. "Shit, girlie," he yelled, "are you nuts? The damn thing might still be alive!"

"I certainly hope he is, for your sake, you vicious, murdering villain!" the girl shouted back. Unable to shoot even if it was, with the girl in the way, Silva ran after her. So did the others. When they arrived at her side they were in for another shock. The girl had collapsed, sobbing, beside the writhing Grik. It moaned piteously and she stroked it with the utmost tenderness.

"Lawrence!" she cried tearfully. "Oh, Lawrence, you mustn't die!"

The evil jaws opened slightly, and a long, purplish tongue moved inside them. "Hurts!" it said. The humans and Lemurians looked on, stunned.

"It spoke!" jibbered Bradford.

"Of course he spoke, you silly man! This is Lawrence," she snarled, "my friend!" Looking up, she seemed to notice for the first time that they weren't all humans, and her eyes went wide again, but with something besides rage. "My God!" she said, hushed. "You are not all people!"

Adar hesitantly stepped forward and bowed to the girl. If he was affected by the bizarre irony, he managed to conceal it. That must have taken considerable effort, since few loathed the Grik as much as he. "I am Adar, High Sky Priest of *Salissa* Home, and currently Steward of the Faith to the various members of the alliance under the Banner of the Trees. We are indeed 'people,' just a little different. Where we come from, creatures such as your 'Lawrence' are vicious predators, intent on exterminating us. Our Amer-i-caan friends have explained their concept of 'pets,' however, and though I consider it foolhardy and . . . astonishing . . . you have chosen such as this as your own, I . . ." He started to say he was sorry, but simply couldn't manage it. "We would not have harmed it had we known," he concluded gently, but with little conviction.

"Lawrence isn't my pet, you furry imbecile! He's my friend!"

"Rend!" confirmed the Grik with a gasp.

Adar tried to reply, but ultimately he could only blink.

"Goodness gracious!" Bradford breathed, then cleared his throat. "My dear, I'm Courtney Bradford, and these are my friends." The girl looked at him, zeroing in on his accent, strangely similar to her own. "If you guarantee your . . . friend's . . . good behavior, I think we may repair him. He's most fortunate, actually. Mr. Silva's usually a remarkably good shot. You cannot know how glad I am his aim strayed just this once! We have a doctor, of sorts, aboard our ship. . . ."

"Ship?"

The word came from behind them, and Silva and the Marines whirled to see a variety of weapons pointed in their direction. They'd been so focused on the girl and the Grik, they'd never sensed the strangers' approach. Most of the weapons were Thompson submachine guns, or 1911 Colts, and they were held by men dressed in remnants of garments once issued by the United States Navy. One man, dark skinned, with a huge mustache drooping over his beard, held a sawed-off musket in his one hand like a pistol. It was he who'd spoken.

"S-19?" Silva challenged.

One of the apparent Navy men lowered his Thompson slightly. He was short, with a scruffy red beard and long, thinning hair poking from under a battered chief's hat. "I really am in hell," he muttered, "and here's the devil himself!"

"In the flesh," Silva said absently, staring hard at the speaker. "Billy Flynn! It *is* you, you redheaded Irish ape! You owe me seventeen dollars!" The tension evaporated, and all the weapons were lowered except the musket/pistol held by the dark, mustachioed man. Silva regarded him appraisingly, recognizing a fellow predator. He nodded slightly before returning his attention to the others. "Who's with you, Billy?" he asked, then added for his companions' sake: "Billy's the sub's chief of the boat—sort of like the bosun, in a slimy pigboat sort of way."

"We've lost some guys," Billy acknowledged, "but we've preserved most of our passengers." He nodded at the girl, the Grik, and the one-armed man. "Picked up a couple too," he added enigmatically. Then his fierce visage disintegrated into an expression of open joy. "I never thought I'd say this, but damn, am I glad to see you!"

"You know this guy, Chief?" one of the others asked.

"You could say that." He paused, gesturing at the Lemurians. "What's with the monkeys? You friends of theirs?"

"Yeah," Silva answered, a hint of threat in his voice, "good friends. Why?"

"We ran into one of their ships once. Great big bastard. Damn thing launched giant spears at us!"

Silva laughed. "That's how we knew you were here! They thought you was a metal fish! Don't take it personal; I'm sure you know there's bigger fish than yours in *this* sea!"

Billy's expression became grim again. "Tell me."

"Tell *me*," insisted the dark-haired man, still holding the gun, "about your ship!"

Silva bristled, then slowly grinned. "USS *Walker*, DD-163, at your service!"

Mahan stood off the B'mbaado coast, numbers one and three guns covering the beach, in the general vicinity of where *Donaghey* had fought her battle with the three Grik ships. Now another enemy ship was aground, burning fiercely, and two more were on the bottom of the Java Sea. There hadn't been a fight, really, merely an execution, and they didn't even know if the ships had been armed, since *Mahan* destroyed them well beyond their own possible range. The telltale column of smoke from the burning ship was regrettable, but it wasn't like they could put it out now.

Jim Ellis was on the port bridge wing, watching a small boat approach. Four adult 'Cats were at the oars, and a number of younglings filled it to overflowing.

"Lower the whaleboat," he ordered. "Tow them in. We don't have all day."

Shortly, both boats were alongside, and willing hands helped the younglings to the deck. One of the adults raced to the bridge, accompanied by Lieutenant Steele.

"What's up, Frankie?" Jim asked when they arrived. Steele waved at his companion, who spoke English. He was one of the Marines who'd gone ashore with Pete.

"Cap-i-taan Ellis, Gener-aal Aalden sends his compliments. Our scout saw your approach and reported your presence."

"What's the situation?"

"Complicated and desperate," the 'Cat conceded, but there was pride in his tone. "Gener-aals Aalden and Faask defeated a large enemy force advancing from the city, but we took many casualties. They then turned on the force those ships landed"—he gestured at the burning wreck—"and struck their left flank, cutting a gap to this beach. Even now, Queen Maraan leads the wounded and noncombatants here. We have the boats of the Grik landing force, but if you can tow them out as you did us, it would help."

Ellis nodded. "Of course, but what of General Alden?"

"His force now numbers little more than a hundred. He is 'rolling up' the enemy flank—a tactic that has worked very well—but he is ... significantly outnumbered. When the enemy stiffens its spine, he will try to hold them long enough to complete the queen's evacuation. The difficulty is, besides the numbers before him, it would seem the force approaching from the city has been reconstituted and reinforced. It will soon flank him in turn."

Ellis looked thoughtfully at the shore. The battle couldn't be far away, though he couldn't hear anything. That was still so weird!

"How long before the second force arrives?" he asked.

"An hour. Perhaps two."

"Very well." He looked at Frankie. "Here's what we'll do. You stay here, and be ready to support us with gunfire." Steele tried to protest, but Ellis continued talking. "Keep an eye out for more ships too. I'll take a company of the First Marines ashore"—he nodded at the Lemurian—"if this gentleman will be kind enough to lead us. We should be able to hammer the enemy hard enough to let Pete break contact; then it'll be hell-for-leather back to the boats." He frowned. "That means you'll have to have all the queen's people aboard, and the boats back ashore, before we need them."

"It's gonna be tight," Frankie observed.

"Sure, but . . ." Jim's eyes got a faraway, haunted look. "It'll give us . . . and *Mahan* . . . a chance to do something right for a change."

Boats plied back and forth, carrying survivors and salvaged equipment to *Walker* from the beach, while Matt listened to Silva's and Chack's reports and spoke to S-19's chief. More Marines guarded the perimeter. Even if the girl's strange pet was the only Grik on the island, there were plenty of other dangerous animals. Bradford, Keje, and Adar were still present, as was the strange one-armed man, and Matt certainly had a few questions for him, but he wanted to hear Flynn's story first. Work proceeded under Spanky's supervision while they talked. There was little heavy equipment they could take from the sub; it just wouldn't fit through a hatch. Besides, they couldn't disable it further if they hoped to salvage it later—something Matt still hoped to do. She wouldn't need her ammunition, though, and they'd discovered close to a hundred four-inch-fifty rounds.

To Matt's bitter disappointment, there'd been no torpedoes. S-19 carried only two when she left Surabaya—there just hadn't been any there, as Matt well knew—so that still left only the single MK-10 they'd scrounged. Besides, the sub had needed space for her "cargo," and couldn't have carried many more torpedoes anyway. She'd fired the two she had at a Japanese transport that blundered across her path and even got a hit, Billy claimed, but they got worked over by the transport's "tin can" escort for their trouble.

That was when their problems began. The sledgehammer blows of the depth charges cracked a battery and popped a bulb, causing an explosion in the forward battery compartment. The forward crew and officers' berths—as well as the radio room—were incinerated. They shut the hatches to the torpedo room (S-19 had only one, forward) and the control room, but six men died, either burned or suffocated by chlorine gas, created by seawater flooding the damaged batteries.

Their "cargo," twenty children—mostly of diplomats and highly placed executives, as well as four nannies and a nun who'd been sent to care for them—spent several terrifying hours isolated in the torpedo room while S-19 lay on the bottom of the Java Sea, a hundred feet below her test depth. Finally, the Japanese destroyer lost interest. Pressurizing the half-flooded compartment, S-19 slowly rose to the surface after dark to vent the gas and pump out the water. Still trying to reach Fremantle (and avoid enemy planes), they barely managed to submerge the following day. That was when they heard the thrashing screws and heavy detonations of *Walker* and *Mahan*'s battle with *Amagi*. They had no idea what was going on, of course—the search periscope had been damaged by the depth charges—but that must have been what they heard, because soon after that their screws ran away and they shut the motors down. Unlike the two American destroyers' traumatic experience on the surface, that was the only effect of the Squall they felt.

Of her crew of forty-two officers and men, only twenty-six remained—and none were senior officers. The highest-ranking crewman was an ensign, who'd wisely deferred command to the more experienced chief of the boat. The rest were killed during her various attempts to land in different places, or by the local predators over the last year.

Matt could only imagine what it must have been like. He and his people had figured out pretty quickly that things were out of whack, and they'd also made some friends. S-19's people had spent the last year living on the edge, never really knowing what had happened. Except for the moment when the screws ran away, there hadn't even been a "transition event" to blame. They just went underwater on one world and came up on another. Their first idea that that might be the case came when they met fish as big as their boat. Matt shuddered. *Walker* wasn't much bigger than the sub, but she was higher out of the water and a hell of a lot faster. It didn't *feel* as much like swimming with the sharks.

"My dear Mr. Flynn," Bradford puffed, wiping sweat with his sleeve, "a dreadful adventure indeed." He peered at the one-armed man. "But who might you be, and the young lady, of course, and where did you find her fascinating ... friend? We've tried to capture them before, you know, but ..." He shrugged. "They simply won't surrender, you see."

The man saw them all staring at him, expecting answers. Matt noticed even Flynn appeared curious. Why would that be?

"I'm O'Casey," he said at last. "Sean O'Casey." He paused, considering, glancing at the destroyer riding at anchor in the mouth of the lagoon. "The lass's name is ... Becky. We was shipwrecked an' these ... fellas was good enough to pick us up. As for her 'friend,' the beastie was a maroon hi'self. We found 'im on a little isle where nothin' could survive." His voice was deep, with a kind of lilting accent that stressed unusual syllables. It was almost as if he spoke a different language, and his awkward insertion of words like "fellas" were substitutes he'd picked up.

"Found 'em floating in an open boat, drifting with the current, when we crossed from Mindanao to here," Flynn supplied. "O'Casey was almost dead. Bad fever from a recently severed arm."

Matt put his hands on his hips. "That tells us who you are, Mr. O'Casey, but not what you are, or where you come from." He looked at Flynn, who shrugged.

"He never would say, Captain. Once he got well, him and the girl sort of kept to themselves. The ... 'beastie' was friendly enough, even if he's scary as hell, and to be honest, he prob'ly brought in more than his share of game. But the girl never played with the other kids, and O'Casey didn't talk much. Carried his weight, though, even with one arm, and after a while that was all that mattered, you know?"

"I do know, Flynn, but that's changed. It matters a lot—before I let him on my ship." He scrutinized O'Casey. "So far, I've had a better character reference for an animal whose species we're at war with. You're not a shipwreck survivor from our world at all, are you?"

"Of course he is not," Adar said, his face inscrutable, but his ears quivering with excitement. "He is a descendant of the Others, the tail-less beings that came before! The ones who taught the ancient tongue to the Prophet, Siska-Ta, then sailed across the Eastern Sea."

Conscious of Captain Reddy's veiled threat, O'Casey nodded reluctantly. He didn't think for a moment these Americans—more Americans! how much more twisted could the world his ancestors left behind have become?—would leave the girl behind, but there was a distinct possibility they'd leave him, and he wanted to get to know them better despite his need to be circumspect.

"There's old . . . tales of folk such as ye," he admitted to Adar, "an' our founders did pass through yer seas."

"I knew it!" Adar exulted. "As soon as I saw the youngling! There is so much about our early history we can learn from you! So many missing pieces of the puzzle! Where did you ultimately go?"

"East," he said vaguely. They knew that already. "Some islands. I'll tell ye what I can, but ye must respect the fact that I know as little of ye as ye know of me. I may tell ye more as me knowledge of yer intentions . . . an' capabilities grows."

"Fair enough," Matt conceded. "You can come with us, but I'll expect further revelations." He noticed that Silva's attention had been diverted, and saw the "nannies" climbing aboard one of the boats with the remaining children. He'd spoken to them briefly. One was British but the others were Dutch. All spoke English, as did the nun. The children were about half Dutch and half English, with a young Australian boy thrown in. Dennis had pronounced one of the nannies an "old frump," but the others were young. One was even attractive, as was the young nun. She'd managed to keep her habit fairly well preserved, even her bizarre hat. The women doubled the number of human females they knew about—not counting the children—and even the "frumpy" one would probably be the object of more attention than she'd ever known. He shook his head. He'd have to speak to them again.

The whaleboat was coming back, its coxswain really laying on the coal. It smashed through the marching rollers, throwing spray, until it gained the calmer water and accelerated to the beach. Clancy leaped out and hurried to him, a message form in his hand. He looked a little green after his wild ride, but his expression was grim and purposeful.

"Captain!" he said urgently. "We picked up a faint transmission in the clear! You need to see it right away!"

A tendril of dread crept down Matt's spine as he took the sheet. "Excuse me, gentlemen," he said, walking a few paces away.

THESE SPACES FOR COMM OFFICE ONLY

TIME FILED   MSG CEN No   HOW SENT

MESSAGE
(SUBMIT TO NAVY DEPT. IN DUPLICATE)

No   DATE

TO

TO CAPTAIN REDDY FROM CAPTAIN KAUFMAN   X   AM CAPTIVE ON JAPANESE BATTLECRUISER AMAGI   X   MINORITY ELEMENT HERE BELIEVES COOPERATION AGAINST GRIK ESSENTIAL   X   CANNOT REPEAT CANNOT GUARANTEE COOPERATION X   YOU MUST EXPEDITE OR ABANDON WALKER RESCUE MISSION B'MBAADO   X   GRIK SWARM UNDERWAY   X   AMAGI ALMOST READY FOR SEA AND WILL FOLLOW WITHIN DAYS X JAPANESE AIR NO THREAT   X   OB PLANE DAMAGED BOMBING BAALKPAN X   ONLY OPPORTUNITY FOR WARNING   X   DO NOT REPEAT DO NOT RESPOND   X   SORRY ABOUT MAHAN   X   TRANSMISSION ENDS

OFFICIAL DESIGNATION OF SENDER   TIME SIGNED

SIGNATURE AND GRADE OF WRITER   *Clancy*

"God*damn* it!" Matt swore. He looked at Silva. "Tell Lieutenant McFarlane our scavenger hunt's over. He's to be in the next boat back to the ship, and I want number three lit off."

"What's up, Skipper?"

"We're out of time."

"Hurry up, damn it!" Ellis shouted as half his surviving, exhausted Marines streamed back through the open ranks of the other half. Close on their heels came whickering arrows and a roaring tide of Grik. They'd fought all day, and the late-afternoon sun glared mercilessly upon them. They'd made the beach at last, and all the refugees were safely aboard ship except Queen Maraan, Haakar-Faask, and the tiny knot of remaining Guardsmen. Pete was still there as well, woozy from fatigue and loss of blood, but he wouldn't leave before the queen and his new friend, Haakar-Faask, and *they* wouldn't leave while anyone else remained. Idiots! Jim was tempted to knock them all on the head and have them carried to the boats.

Mahan's guns opened up, now that they knew exactly where their friends were, and massive concussions burst in the trees beyond the beach, sending shrapnel and blizzards of splinters into the greater mass of Grik infantry. Tracers arced overhead toward the enemy as well, and the weight of the assault began to ease. There were still the berserkers out front, however.

"Second rank, present!" Ellis yelled, voice cracking. *"Fire!"* The volley staggered the enemy, and a cloud of fine sand erupted when dozens of bodies hit the ground. "Fire at will!" he commanded, and the staccato report of thirty-odd Krags competed with the explosions in the trees. He whirled to those he'd come to save, angry at their stubbornness. "The time's come for you to act responsibly! We need to get off this beach, and there're people dying so you can satisfy your 'honor' and be the very last ones! That's not going to happen." He looked at Safir. For the first time since he'd met her, she looked utterly spent. Her garments were torn, and her silver breastplate was tarnished and splashed with blood. "We didn't just come get you because we gave our word not to leave anyone behind; we came because we *need* you!" His gaze slashed Alden, who was covered with blood from many superficial cuts. "*All* of you! This'll have been for nothing if you get your asses killed now!" He pointed where the other Marines were forming in front of the boats. "This isn't just about you; it's not your decision. Winning the war's a lot more important than this pissant little fight!"

Faask whispered urgently to his queen, and finally she jerked a tearful nod. Grabbing Alden's bloody shirt, she pulled him toward the boats, leaving behind Faask and the dozen real warriors he had left. Ellis looked at him, and Faask grinned back.

"You will not leave before the last of your Marines, will you?" Ellis didn't answer, and Haakar-Faask laughed. "You are important too, you know. When you finally enter the boats, someone must keep them away." He drew his sword and looked at the notched, blood-encrusted blade. "To talk of 'winning the war' is very well. It is also true. But I am old, and I have seen my world collapse. I think this 'pissant little fight' will be enough for me."

Jim was the last to climb the rungs to *Mahan*'s deck. He was sick with sorrow at what he'd seen, but also filled with pride. The Orphan Queen's tear-soaked face was the first he saw, and on impulse he embraced her briefly. When he stepped back, he saw her looking at the beach where hundreds of Grik, no longer galled by *Mahan*'s guns, capered gleefully over the scattered corpses. One waved a severed leg above its head, bloody teeth still chewing.

"I'd love to bust those bastards up!" growled number three's gun captain, just above his head on the amidships deckhouse.

"No point," Ellis replied. "Save your ammunition."

A 'Cat signal striker raced up. "Skipper!" he said. "Lookout says sails to the north! Many, many sails!"

Dowden, Campeti, and *Walker*'s other officers were waiting when Matt and the last of the shore party came aboard, already laying plans. The sun lay on the horizon, and the long day was nearly spent. Menacing clouds roiled in the east, and the rollers had a distinct chop. All except O'Casey saluted the colors, but no time was wasted on ceremony. Many of the crew stood watching, wide-eyed.

". . . I *think* we've got the fuel for it, but . . ." Spanky continued, joining Matt on deck. He looked around at the many faces and stopped. Swearing, he shook his head and disappeared down the companionway, bellowing for Laney. Matt's eyes found Dowden's.

"Plot a least-distance, least-time course for Baalkpan, via Tarakan. Consult Spanky and determine our best speed, without getting home completely dry. We might show up in the middle of a battle. Have Clancy transmit 'on our way, *Walker*' over and over. Standard code. Maybe they can hear us, even if we can't hear them."

O'Casey was staring around at the ship, as curious about it as about the sudden activity. He'd been offended when they took his antique weapon away, and resisted giving it up—until Silva and Stites had "insisted." Stites had discovered several more muskets at the castaways' camp, and, never one to abandon any weapon, he'd brought them along. O'Casey wasn't overawed by the ship, exactly, but he did seem amazed. And envious. He stiffened when he heard the word "battle," however. Silva was watching him at the time, and noticed the reaction.

"Aye, aye, sir," Dowden answered. "Uh, Captain, I've taken the liberty of putting the children and their chaperones in the chief's berthing spaces, and moving the chiefs to available officers' and enlisted berths, based on seniority. I've also begun entering S-19's survivors in the books. We'll have to see who fits where best; they're not destroyermen, after all."

"Of course." Matt knew when Dowden was beating around a bush. It was his job to sort out everything he'd reported, and unnecessary for him to report it. "What else?"

"Well, sorry, Skipper, but there's two things, actually. First, the girl with the pet Grik won't berth with the other kids. Says she'll only berth with Mr. O'Casey here, and she won't leave the damn lizard till we have a look at him and promise not to hurt him."

Matt looked at Bradford, still puffing from his climb. "Go have a look. You're our expert on Grik anatomy. Have Jamie give you a hand." He paused. "Silva?"

"Skipper?"

"Go with him. Damn thing may be tame as a puppy, but if it even looks cross-eyed, blow its head off."

"Aye, aye, sir!"

Silva and Bradford clambered down the metal stairs.

"I will accompany them," Adar proclaimed. "I am curious about this 'tame' Grik, but I would get to know the youngling better."

Matt nodded. "Me too. See what you can find out." He looked back at Dowden. "What else?"

"Well, Skipper, it's the nun. Says they all appreciate being rescued, but she'd like to speak with you again. She hopes . . . you won't be so 'rude' next time."

"*Rude?*"

Dowden shrugged, and Matt rolled his eyes.

"Maybe later. Chack?"

"Sir?"

"Assemble your sea and anchor detail, and prepare to pull the hook. We're getting underway."

"Aye, aye, Cap-i-taan."

All that remained were Keje, and *Walker*'s officers. Captain Reddy turned to O'Casey.

"We're about to leave your island resort behind, and I've made good on my part of the deal. We're all going to the pilothouse now. Things are going to be busy while we get underway, but as soon as I have a free moment, you'll be standing right there, ready to pay your passage. I have some questions and you're going to answer them."

"Very well, Captain. I've a few questions of me own, if ye please. Ye say we might be headed fer a battle. Might I ask who you expect to fight?"

Ignoring O'Casey, Matt turned and strode purposely toward the bridge, leaving his surprised entourage hurrying to catch up. Taking the steps two at a time, he arrived in the pilothouse, preceded by his own shouted, "As you were!" Facing the startled OOD, he announced: "I have the deck and the conn. Make all preparations for getting underway." He looked speculatively back at O'Casey, as the one-armed man reached the top of the stairs.

"We're at war with creatures like your young lady's pet, and they're on their way to attack our . . . our home. Maybe a few hundred thousand of 'em. The first thing I want to know is how you made friends with one."

Silva, Courtney, and Adar slid the green wardroom curtain aside. Silva had handed his BAR to Stites, who'd recover the rest of the shore party's arms. All he had was his .45 and cutlass, but the Colt was in his hand. The lizard lay on the wardroom table, moaning as the rolling ship caused him to shift back and forth under the lowered operating light. The girl sat beside him on a chair, petting him reassuringly, and glaring at the new arrivals. Jamie Miller, former pharmacist's mate, and now *Walker*'s surgeon, nervously gathered his instruments and laid them out.

"Critter give you any trouble, Jamie?" Silva gruffed.

"No . . . it's just . . . Shit, Dennis, it's a Grik!"

"Noticed that myself. So what? Ain't you got a hypocritical oath, or somethin'? Patch him up."

"Hippocratic," murmured Bradford, moving raptly toward the creature. The girl stood unsteadily, but hovered protectively near. "We won't hurt him, child, I assure you. You must understand; I've never been this close to a *live* one before that wasn't trying to eat me." The girl jumped at the rush of iron links flooding into the chain locker forward. "There, there," Bradford soothed, "nothing to fear, the racket is quite normal, I'm afraid. Please do sit again, before you fall and hurt yourself. We're old salts, and quite used to this abominable motion."

Silva smirked.

"You said his name is Lawrence?" Bradford continued, ignoring the big man.

The girl nodded. "I named him that," she said.

"And you're Becky? How interesting. Charmed, of course, and very pleased to make your acquaintance."

Soon the ship came alive beneath their feet, and the nauseating pitching motion became more bearable as *Walker* accelerated into the swells. Becky finally sat, but continued glaring at Silva.

"I don't want that evil man in the same room with my poor friend," she insisted. "If Lawrence is to die, I prefer it not be in the presence of his murderer!"

"Now see here, girlie!" Silva protested.

"My name is *not* 'girlie'!"

"Calm yourself, child!" Bradford pleaded. "Mr. Silva cannot leave; he has his orders. Besides, he didn't mean to injure your friend; it was a dreadful misunderstanding!"

"He did too," the girl fumed. "And my name is not 'child' either!"

"Of course, my dear. I apologize." Bradford glanced hurriedly at the wounded Grik. "I think your friend will recover well enough. The wound is painful, certainly, but not fatal, if my memory of his anatomy serves. The bullet passed cleanly through his left pectoral muscle, left to right, and if you allow us, Mr. Miller has some salve that should accelerate the healing process and prevent infection. It will also ease his pain. May he proceed?"

Becky sighed. "Of course, but please hurry!"

Jamie advanced hesitantly with the Lemurian antiseptic, analgesic paste, made from fermented polta fruit, on a wooden spatula. The creature seemed to understand the conversation, as well as Jamie's intent, and lay docile, waiting for him to apply the medicine. Jamie gulped and did so. Within moments the creature's tense, straining muscles began to relax, and it sighed in evident relief.

"Do you feel better now, my dear?" the girl crooned.

"'Etter. Thank you."

"Well . . . good," Silva gruffed, strangely moved. His world had been turned upside down yet again. Here was a Grik, a member of a species so terrible it almost defied comprehension. Yet lying there with a child stroking its brow, it looked almost vulnerable and benign. What was more, not only did it understand what they said, but it could speak. It was even polite! He scratched his beard sheepishly, glancing around. "Sorry I shot you. Maybe there's good Griks and bad Griks, just like good people and Japs."

"I not Grik," it said, almost dreamily now, another effect of the paste. "I Tagranesi, on islands east-south. I lost, like 'riend 'Ecky." Its eyelids fluttered. "I sorry you shoot too."

"He'll sleep now," Bradford assured the girl. "Mr. Miller will bind his wounds."

"Uh . . . I don't want to bug him," Jamie almost sputtered. "Why don't I wait until he *is* asleep?"

Bradford rolled his eyes. "He's quite harmless."

"I wouldn't say that," disputed Silva, then paused. After a moment he dropped his pistol in his holster and buttoned the flap. "But maybe he ain't dangerous, if you know what I mean." He looked at the girl again. "I'm sorry to you too. I never would've figgered it. You want somethin' to eat?"

Becky started to flare at him again, but caught herself and just sat, looking disoriented.

"I . . . I suppose. Yes, thank you . . . Mr. Silva."

Once summoned, Juan brought a tray of sandwiches and bowed. "It is a great pleasure," he said, "to have a young lady as beautiful as you grace our poor, drab ship. It has been too long!" He looked her over. "I will see if I can find more suitable clothes to replace those rags."

Becky paused before taking a bite of one of the steaming sandwiches. "Why . . . thank you. You are very kind."

"De nada," Juan said, and departed.

"Was that Spanish?" the girl asked, shocked.

"Sorta," answered Silva, surprised. If she was one of these "Others" Adar always spoke of, where'd she learn to recognize Spanish? he wondered. "He's Filipino. You know who they are?" Becky didn't answer, but dove into her sandwich. They munched companionably, seated around the unconscious lizard. Everyone was famished, and the stack of sandwiches soon disappeared.

"My dear—" began Adar.

"Young lady . . ." interrupted Bradford.

"Whoa!" said Silva. "Damn, fellas! She just ate. Give her a while." He looked into her large, jade eyes. "You tired?"

"Not especially." She saw the light dimming beyond the porthole. "I suppose I should be; this is the time of day we usually prepared our defenses for the night."

"Mmm," Silva replied. It must have been tough living on that island, fighting off nightly incursions by predators, both by land and from the trees. The shore party hadn't encountered anything dangerous, but Flynn had described some particularly terrifying creatures that dropped on them at night from above. They'd quickly learned to keep to the clearings. "Don't have to do that tonight, doll. Yer safe as can be! How about a evenin' stroll? I'll show you around the ship!" He caught Adar's eye and winked.

"I really shouldn't . . . Mr. O'Casey . . ."

"O'Casey'll be busy talkin' to the skipper till who knows when."

The girl stood and, with a final glance at her sleeping friend, nodded. "Very well then, if it isn't any trouble. I must admit to an intense curiosity about your ship." She paused. "I must also admit I misjudged you, Mr. Silva. I still dislike you, but perhaps that may pass as well. I apologize for attacking you."

"Good thing you did," Dennis admitted, also looking at her friend. "I *would've* killed him if you hadn't."

"Just so. Very well, then, please do lead the way."

They left the others behind, mouths agape like beached fish, and climbed the companionway to the open deck. Silva described the various features of the ship visible from where they stood: the back of the bridge, the funnels, the amidships deckhouse. He noticed she was particularly interested in the four-inch guns atop it on either side, fascinated by the rifling at their muzzles.

"What are those twisty grooves for? I've seen many cannons, but nothing like them."

Silva blinked, hesitating, then laughed. "Why, they spin the bullets. Makes 'em fly straighter."

"Oh."

Her tone sounded like he'd satisfied a long-burning question. Surely she'd seen the gun on the sub? Maybe she'd never asked the pigboat pukes. O'Casey'd probably told her not to. Silva remembered Flynn telling them she never played with the other kids, and suddenly realized that despite O'Casey, she'd probably been very lonely indeed. They passed under the platform and walked by the galley, ignoring Lanier's strident criticism of his assistants. Standing between the port and starboard torpedo mounts, the small girl got her first look at the passing sea.

"My goodness!" she declared. "This is a very fast ship! How fast can it go?"

"'Bout twice as fast as this, give or take." He looked at her. "How old are you?"

Her eyes never left the surging wake. "I'll soon be ten," she answered absently.

"Lordy. You look six and act twenty!" His tone prevented her from taking offense. "You on that island a whole year with them submariners?"

"Indeed. They picked us up at sea after our ship was destroyed by a leviathan. It was terrifying."

"If 'levy-than' means what I think it does, I know what you mean," he agreed. "Them big boogers scare me to death!"

She glanced at him with a tentative, impish smile. "I cannot imagine you frightened."

"Mmm. Well, I was. A little. Least I sunk one of the bastards!"

She giggled. It was such an unusual, forgotten sound it almost broke his heart.

"Did not! What a villainous liar you are! Besides, I asked you before to control your language."

"Did too!" Dennis insisted, willing away the strange, fluttery sensation in his chest. "With the four mount! Shot him right in the mouth! Course, the depth charges might've helped, but that don't matter." He looked at her. "Besides, you called me a 'bastard.' I figgered I could say it."

She giggled again, and held her hand over her mouth. "I *am* sorry. What would Master Kearley say?" Her expression grew sad. "Poor man. He knew he was doomed, but he saved my life, as did Mr. O'Casey."

"Master Kearley?"

"My tutor. He . . . didn't make it off the ship."

"How long were you adrift?" Dennis asked gently.

"Something over four weeks. I'm not certain. We had plenty of provisions—just two of us in a boat meant for twenty. Still, it was terrifying. There are few silverfish in the deep waters to the east, but there are other things." She shuddered.

Silva took a pouch from his pocket, loosened the string at the top, and removed a plug of yellow-brown leaves. He bit off a wad and worked it for a moment until it formed a bulge in his right cheek. Seeing her watching him, wide-eyed, he graciously offered the pouch. "Chew?" Revolted but intrigued, she shook her head. "Suit yerself," he said, and pulling the string tight, he returned the pouch to his pocket. "Where'd you come up with Lawrence, anyway? Flynn said he was in your boat."

"He was. We found him on an island we landed upon, searching for a place with food and water closer to . . . where our people might search for us. There wasn't any, but he'd been there several days, a castaway as much as we. All he had was a dugout canoe, and no idea which direction to head! His species is not unknown to us, a few meetings on isolated islands southeast of my home somewhere. But I'd never seen one before!"

"Peaceful meetings?" he asked, apparently astonished.

"I believe so, yes."

"I'll swan. Where's home?" Dennis ventured.

She started to answer, then caught herself. "Are you interrogating me?"

"Yep."

Hands on hips, she looked up at him. "How rude! A gentleman never pries into the affairs of a . . . a young lady!"

Silva shrugged, a twisted grin on his face. "I ain't no gentleman, doll. 'Sides, whose rules are those?"

"Why . . . they're society's rules—the rules of civilization."

"Land rules."

"Not just 'land' rules!"

"There's other rules, you know. Sea rules. When somebody rescues castaways, either adrift or ashore, he can ask 'em anything he wants."

The girl became pensive. "Truly?"

"Yep."

"Must one always answer such questions?"

Silva laughed, a deep, booming laugh that drew the attention of those working nearby. "Not always, doll, but it's sorta rude not to."

"Do you have to answer my questions too?"

"No, but I will. I already have, some."

She pointed at Chack, supervising a deck crew lashing covers over the fireroom skylights. Silva was expecting a blow, and it looked like the skipper was too. "What are those creatures?"

"'Cats. Cat-monkeys, monkey-cats—Bradford calls 'em 'Lemurians,' and I guess that's stuck, but most fellas just call 'em 'Cats. They have another word for theirselves—can't remember it—that means 'People.' They're good folks, too: smart as a whip and twice as strong. Hell, Adar—that's the fella in the wardroom—and Keje are prob'ly the smartest fellas I know. Them and the skipper."

"Skipper?"

"Captain Reddy, to little girls."

"He mentioned a battle, and several times people have acted afraid of poor Lawrence—and you shot him, of course! What is that about?" She seemed genuinely curious, so Silva told her. He wasn't used to talking to kids, especially ones who acted so grown-up, so he didn't pull any punches. When he was finished, she just stared at the wake. They'd moved to the rail while he spoke, and she was leaning on it now. "So you Americans are fighting for the freedom and safety of others, essentially. You yourselves could simply leave, if you wished."

He spit a yellowish stream over the side, and she shuddered. "Well, sure. But where would we go?"

"You could ..." She stopped herself again, and shook her head. "It makes no difference. You wouldn't leave even if you could. You are engaged in a noble war, a holy war. A war against absolute evil." In a small voice she added, "I think Father would approve ... almost envy you that." Her face was suddenly stricken. "Oh, Lawrence will be so upset to discover others of his kind behave so!"

"That's okay. There's others no more different from us than he is to Griks, helpin' 'em. Buncha Japs, with a great big battle cruiser. Could eat us alive, like one o' them 'levy-than' things."

"Yet still you stay?"

Silva shrugged. "'Tween the Japs and Griks, I've lost 'most every friend I ever had. It may be a 'noble holy war' to some, but to me—and the Skipper too, I think—it's plain ol' simple revenge." He was almost shocked out of his wits when he felt her warm, tiny hand crawl into his massive paw.

"You have a new friend now, Mr. Silva, even if you are a disgusting beast. I don't dislike you anymore at all. I have another question, though."

"Shoot," he said, still rattled.

"Why do you call me 'doll'?"

He was silent a moment, watching the lightning off the starboard quarter; then he sighed. "You don't like 'girlie' or 'child,' and you don't look like a 'Becky' to me...." He shrugged. "You look like a doll. A fragile china doll. Dirty, shaggy haired, with raggy clothes, and you need a good washin', but underneath, you're a beautiful china doll." He growled incoherently and shook his head. "Say, while yer all dirty, you wanna see the engines?"

Later, in the wardroom, Silva made his report. He stood as if he didn't notice the deck heaving beneath his feet, and he probably didn't. The ship was pounding through the rising swells of the Celebes Sea at twenty-two knots, and the storm that had stalked them for the last couple days in the east was chasing them now in earnest. It was a godsend, in a way; it kept the monstrous fish from basking in the surface sun, and the lashing sonar chased away those lurking in their path. Their speed outpaced any that rose behind them.

Every officer was present except Campeti, who had the watch. Flynn and his nominal superior, Ensign Laumer, sat beside the captain. Adar, Keje, Bradford, and Chack were also there, as were a couple of Chack's senior Marines. Silva felt awkward being the center of attention in such a . . . respectable way . . . and also felt uneasy recounting his conversation with the girl, as if he were betraying her confidence. Still, despite the girl's obvious attempts to conceal certain things, he'd gathered a lot of information the captain needed.

"We already knew their ship was wrecked by a mountain fish," he began, "an' they were the only survivors. Girl had a tutor named Curly er somethin' who didn't make it, so I figger she's sorta 'somebody.' I thought that anyway 'cause of her name. She just don't seem like a 'Becky' to me. That might be a nickname, er part of her real name, but I don't think she's used to goin' by it."

"I got that impression too," Matt murmured thoughtfully. "Please continue."

"Yes, sir. Anyway, she said they'd drifted on the current four or five weeks from the 'deep water to the east' and went ashore on an island close to their own shipping lanes. They had to leave 'cause there wasn't no food er water, but that's where they picked up their lizard. She'd never seen one, but knew about 'em. Said they came from islands to the southeast of her home, and there'd been contact with the critters before. She also didn't seem to think it unusual for it to be friendly. Said her friend'd be upset how vicious 'our' Griks are."

"Good God!" Bradford exclaimed. "If there was no food or water on the island, why was the creature there, and how did it survive?"

"'Marooned' too. Showed up on a dugout canoe."

Adar and Keje exchanged significant glances, and Bradford sputtered: "By canoe on such a sea! But that certainly explains much. I've often wondered why the 'aboriginal' Grik seem so prolific from one land to another, when other creatures don't. I've studied our sleeping guest, and though there's no question he's the same *species* as our enemy, he's clearly an entirely different *race*—as different as Europeans from Polynesians! Perhaps his race evolved a different sociology—less violent! Oh, I can't wait to speak to him!"

Silva shrugged. "Could be. Maybe we could raise a regiment: Comp'ny A, First Stripey Lizards!"

Matt scowled, looking at Adar's disgusted blinking. "Mr. Silva . . ."

"Oh. Yes, sir. I picked up some technical things too. Granted, she's only ten, but she was very int'rested in our guns and engines. Not shocked, she *knew* what they were, just amazed by what they could do."

Matt nodded. "I got the same sense from O'Casey, though I admit you picked up more information than I did. How'd you do it?"

Dennis grinned. "She's a kid, Skipper. So am I. Just a great big kid."

Matt sipped his coffee and rubbed his chin. "Well, between us, we learned a lot. Almost as much from what they didn't say as what they did. They obviously don't want us to know where they're from. Normal reluctance to reveal too much before they get to know us, or societal paranoia?" He paused. "Either way, they're from the east. Adar suspected as much as soon as he saw the girl, and then we learned they weren't part of S-19's 'cargo.' Now we're sure. They're descendants of the 'Others' that passed through here before. Looking at a map, we could probably extrapolate a pretty good estimate of where their home is.

"They know about guns—witness the muskets— although according to Mr. Bradford, they're virtually unchanged from those the original East Indiamen would've carried. The girl said they have artillery as well, even if it's not any more advanced. That tells us something right there. In all this time, they haven't had any reason to improve their weaponry, so they never did. In our own history, flintlocks reigned supreme for two hundred and fifty years, and reached a level of refinement that couldn't be improved upon. Only constant wars with equally well-armed opponents spurred the innovations we made in the last century.

So wherever they are, they must be on top of the heap, and there must not be any really dangerous animals. Steam power's something else they must have. Like Silva said, they're impressed by how fast we can go, but not shocked we do it without sails."

He drummed his fingers on the tabletop the Grik-like creature had lain on most of the afternoon. "All fascinating mysteries I look forward to solving, and it's good to know, at long last, that there *are* other humans on this world. Right now, though, we have more pressing concerns." He opened the note he'd received from Clancy and read most of it aloud. They already knew the gist, but each point needed discussion, and he wanted it fresh in their minds. He slapped the table with the message form. "I have no choice but to believe this is genuine. Kaufman's apology at the end, while also probably genuine, is clearly meant to convince us he is who he says he is."

"But how in hell did the bas . . . did he get access to their comm equipment?" Spanky grumbled dubiously.

"With the help of the disaffected 'elements,'" Dowden speculated. "Probably wouldn't be too hard; it's not like they have a lot of folks to talk to. Most likely just a comm watch to see what *we're* saying."

"But what of the rest of it?" Adar demanded heatedly. "This warning to *us*! A warning that the enemy moves, and we must complete or abandon our 'rescue' attempt? How could they know of that?"

"Simple," Matt answered grimly. "Kaufman's not talking to *us*. He thinks he is, because *Mahan*'s disguise has fooled them. For whatever reason, Jim's taken her to B'mbaado."

All those present, except the submariners, knew that was against Matt's direct orders. They also knew that if Jim Ellis went against those orders, there'd been a damn good reason.

"I've felt something was wrong ever since we lost communications. Felt it in my bones," he confessed. "They must've taken out the radio with this bombing the note refers to." He rubbed his eyes. "Damn! We should've headed back two weeks ago!" Glancing at Flynn and Laumer, he allowed a wry smile. "Sorry. I'm damn glad we found you, but we may not have done you any favors."

"I don't understand, Captain," Laumer replied. The

lanky ensign was very young, and probably hadn't been out of submarine school for a month before the war started, back home. As S-19's sole surviving officer, he'd shown unusual maturity by letting the more experienced chief take the lead. He clearly wasn't a coward, and Flynn continued to show proper deference and respect even if he was making the decisions. Matt suspected Laumer would shape into a good officer.

"We probably just dragged you out of the frying pan, into the fire. With us." In response to their blank expressions, *Walker*'s people began to explain.

The storm was a bad one, and it lashed them with its fury throughout the night, even though they caught only the edge. By morning the worst had rumbled into the south-southwest to slam against northern Celebes. Tabby had been seasick again, but not debilitated this time. She'd spent most of her life aboard *Salissa*, barely noticing any but the most severe storms, and the first she'd weathered on tiny *Walker*—a Strakka at that—left her unable to do anything but moan and wallow in vomit. She must finally be getting her "sea legs," as Gilbert called them, and this time it hadn't been so bad. She could only shudder at the thought of the misery she'd have endured if the storm hit them full-on, however.

The sky was still gray, the sea still choppy when she and Gilbert went to the galley for a late breakfast. Lanier complained, of course, about "snipes wandering in any old time, whenever they felt like it," to eat, but they paid him no heed. The griping was desultory anyway; Lanier was in a pretty good mood, since the Coke machine had weathered the storm, still chugging away, cooling the empty space inside. Tabby still didn't understand why that was cause for such celebration, but if the irascible cook was happy, the food would be better.

She and Gilbert munched egg sandwiches under the gun platform protecting them from a persistent drizzle and looked around. Something had the crew's attention forward, under the pilothouse deck. They moved over to see what it was, and were stunned to discover a tiger-striped Grik reclined on a mattress pad, with a semicircle of men and 'Cats gathered around. Bradford was there, sitting on a chair, as were Silva, Adar, and several small children.

"Holy smokes," Gilbert said. "A Grik!"

"He's tame," Stites said, hearing him. "Didn't you know he was here?"

"No. We been workin'. Where'd all the scudders come from?"

Stites looked at him. "You need to get out more."

"I been tryin'!" Gilbert replied, almost plaintively.

Stites shrugged. "We took him, the kids, and a couple dozen pigboat pukes off Talaud." He leered. "Got a couple new women too, but, except for some nun, they ain't showed their faces yet. The nun keeps tryin' to pester the skipper."

"You don't say?" Gilbert scratched his ear and pointed at the "Grik." "Bradford gonna di-sect him?"

Stites laughed. "Hell, no! He's friendly as a hungry pup. The Aussie's been talkin' to him just like he was a person. Silva shot him and he's a little sore, but I swear, sometimes you can even understand what he says! Talks a little like one o' you Georgia crackers, though."

"I ain't from Georgia, you damn Yankee!"

Stites shrugged again. "All you snipes sound the same to me."

"What about Spanky? You understand him fine."

"He ain't from Georgia."

Gilbert shook his head. Everyone "on deck" talked weird as far as he was concerned; so much of their language was salted with archaic nautical terms. He was more accustomed to technical and mechanical jargon.

"Laney's a snipe and anybody understand him," Tabby pointed out. "All he do is cuss." They applied their attention to the bizarre conversation taking place in front of them.

"South of the overhead sun!" Bradford gushed. "How exciting! Do you think you could point out your home on a map?"

"What is . . . 'ap'?" the creature replied.

"Oh, dear. Well, a map is like a picture of the world. It shows where places are." The creature looked blank. "Never mind, I'm sure we'll sort it out. Tell me, though, why on earth were you paddling around the open ocean in a canoe?"

"I grow . . . turn into adult. It time I leave nest, show I adult."

"A rite of passage? Face the dangers of the world and prove you're no longer a . . . a child?"

"Essentially. To ha', to take . . ." He struggled for a word. Bradford had learned there was no limit to the creature's vocabulary, but there were some words he simply couldn't say. Anything requiring the use of lips, for example, was impossible. He understood the words; he just couldn't form them. "To ha', to earn right to . . ."

"Mate?" Bradford supplied.

"Yess! 'Ate! I show strength, courage, I return." He looked down. "I never return, now."

Bradford blinked. "Don't be so downcast. Perhaps you will. This dreadful war can't last forever!"

Becky stirred and looked at Bradford. "Perhaps I should explain. Listening to you two hash this out is excruciating! I've had much longer to get to know him." She looked at those gathered around, particularly the other children. "Mr. Silva has told me castaways should answer questions, but must poor Lawrence do it in front of so many superfluous persons?" One of the little girls sat up straight and sniffed. Becky glared at her. "You have always taunted him as a beast! He has no obligation to unburden himself to you!"

"Not me! I think he's fascinating!" exclaimed a scruffy-looking boy in an incongruous upper-crust English accent. Becky rewarded him alone with a small smile.

"You are always so mean!" squealed the haughty girl. All but the boy loudly agreed.

"Children!" protested Bradford. He turned to Silva. "Surely the crew has other duties," he suggested, "and perhaps these children have had enough fresh air?"

"You bet. Move along, fellas, before somebody gives you work. Kiddies, I think Stites'll take you back below."

"But it stinks down there!" a Dutch girl complained.

"Honest sweat," Stites proclaimed piously, "won't hurt you." Amid whining complaints, he shooed the children down the companionway, while the other observers slunk off.

"You mind if we stick here, Dennis? Mr. Bradford?" Gilbert asked.

Becky glanced at them and did a double take. "Good heavens, that one's female!" Silva laughed, and the girl glared at him.

Gilbert was startled, then looked at Tabby. She was wearing a T-shirt at least, but it was soaking wet. "Yeah, well, I guess."

"There are many others aboard, my dear," Bradford said. "Our allies have unusual mores. Please think nothing of it."

"Think nothing of it . . . ?" Becky shook her head. "Unusual indeed. I thought I'd noticed a couple on deck wearing nothing but kilts, but believed I'd imagined it."

"Can we stay?" Gilbert persisted. "We been in the fire room and ain't seen ya'll yet."

"Very well," Becky replied, still shaking her head and looking at Tabby. "Let me see, as best I understand it, Lawrence's people are quite wild when they hatch—from eggs, you know—and run loose on an island near their home until they reach a certain level of maturity. Not age, necessarily, but a level of self-awareness. They are guided and taught by adults the whole time, but there is little supervision. Just enough to keep them from reverting to savagery. When they do become self-aware, the instruction becomes more intense until, ultimately, they are judged fit to enter society. They demonstrate their ability to reason and use tools by building their own boat in which to return, but they must do so by way of a more distant island, where they must face a final test of courage and resourcefulness. Poor Lawrence completed his test, but a storm took him far from his return course. When we found him, he was dying of thirst and hunger."

"What was the final test?" Courtney asked.

"He won't speak of it. To do so with others who haven't completed it is forbidden."

"I see. Hmm. Fascinating . . . and informative. I have just a few more questions. Obviously Lawrence's species, like the Grik and, well, us, I suppose, are predators. I assume they hunt?"

Becky looked at Lawrence, who said, "O' course."

Bradford blinked. "Oh, please do forgive me; I'm afraid I've fallen into talking as if you're not here."

"It's all right," Lawrence assured him. "'Ecky?"

The girl frowned. "Well, of course. As you say, his people are predators. They hunt, but they also raise domestic livestock of sorts, though we've never discussed what kind."

"Fascinating!" Bradford beamed. "But I hoped he might describe *how* his people hunt."

Becky seemed troubled by the line of questioning. "Well, he's spoken of a vague understanding of how his culture allocates labor—you must remember he had not yet joined 'society' as it were—and did not yet know his place within it. But evidently there are different castes among his people; some are herders, some hunters, others are artisans—boatbuilders and the like."

"But he received some small instruction in the basics of each of these?"

"Yes."

"So, how was he taught to hunt?"

"Cooperatively. Much like our own people would, if they had to for survival, and weren't just 'sport shooting.'"

"Are there other predators his people must compete with?"

Becky looked blank, and Lawrence answered for her: "Yes. Shiksaks. Dangerous, scary creatures. They take our li'stock. O'ten kill Tagranesi. Tagranesi hunt. Lots hunters against single Shiksak; Shiksak hard to kill. Shiksaks go sea and land. Thrice size Tagranesi."

"Indeed? Tell me, Lawrence, do your people ever hunt these creatures for sport?"

Lawrence managed an expression of surprise. "S'ort? Insane."

"Hmm. Sounds as though it would be, yet you can never be entirely rid of them if they're amphibious. And so large! I'd love to see one!"

Lawrence shook his head. "See alone, you die."

Bradford's eyebrows furrowed. "So you do understand theoretical situations then. Marvelous! Tell me, if one of these 'Shiksaks' were making a nuisance of himself and your hunters went after him—had him cornered—and another 'Shiksak' suddenly attacked without warning, by surprise, what would they do?"

"Not . . . can't occur. Shiksaks hate each other. Not hunt together."

"Glad to hear it, but what if they did?"

Lawrence blinked, clearly contemplating the possibility. "Hunters scared?" he finally answered. "Run a'ay."

Bradford realized he'd been leaning forward, anticipating the answer. When it came, he eased back with a sigh. "Quite understandable. Very well. I have only one more question: are your people violent at all? I mean, do they fight others of their kind . . . or any other sentient species, perhaps?"

Lawrence turned to Becky. This was a subject they must have discussed.

"They sometimes fight invaders from other islands," she confessed guardedly. "They do not attack others."

"When they fight, do they ever . . . eat their enemies?"

"No!" interrupted Lawrence. "Disgusting thought! Never eat others . . ."

"They never *eat* other intelligent beings!" Becky finished for him. "What a revolting and insulting question! I might ask the same of you!"

Bradford breathed. "I apologize. We and our allies do not, of course, do such things, but"—he pointed at Lawrence—"the others of his kind, whom we fight, most certainly do. They even eat each other. It was a question I had to ask." He stood. "Now, if you'll excuse me, I must tinker with my journal, write a few things down, you see."

C hief Bosun's Mate Fitzhugh Gray sat on a charred stump—about all that remained of his quarters. His face was soot blackened, streaked with sweat, and spattered with blood. His new uniform was destroyed, and it hung on him in rags. A bandage encircled his wrist, and the viscous purple of the Lemurian paste oozed from underneath it. The usual westerly breeze had stalled, as if deciding whether to come around out of the east, and smoke hung over the island like a pall. So did the stench. Their Lemurian dead were already gathered for their pyre, but there was nothing left to burn them with. A few colonists from the mainland, graw-fishers, had sailed out last night and, after viewing the scene with a horror beyond their isolated experience, solemnly promised to return with wood.

Three American dead were buried early that morning, Lieutenant Clark among them. Gray felt responsible for that. He'd severely reprimanded the young lieutenant, and he'd deserved it, but maybe he'd been too severe? As if to atone, Clark had put himself forward in the terrible fighting, and it cost him his life. All young officers make mistakes, and Clark's had been a doozy, but he'd had the makings of a good commander. He'd just been too young and inexperienced for the position he'd held, and then been too immature to accept his mistake and learn from it. The other two humans had died fighting as well, but they hadn't practically courted death as Clark had done. Now three lonely graves, and a marker for the Lemurian dead, would forever bear witness to the price they'd paid for this place.

Hundreds of Grik still lay where they'd fallen, covered with buzzing insects and strange-looking crabs. They didn't know what to do with them; they couldn't just throw them in the surf. Flashies didn't come that shallow, and they'd just wash up again. The surviving Marines and Guardsmen were too exhausted to bury them, though. Maybe when they'd rested a bit, they could heap them on the barges and tow them to deeper water. It would take a lot of trips. . . .

A few days earlier it would have seemed very strange if Gray and Shinya even said "good morning." Now, when the equally bedraggled Japanese officer sat heavily beside him and offered his canteen, Gray nodded his thanks.

"Mr. Bradford will scold us cruelly," Shinya said softly. Gray grunted and took a sip. The island's jungle was gone now, all of it. He wasn't even sure what had set the fire, but there'd been no stopping it this time, not in the midst of battle. He hacked hoarsely and spit dark phlegm.

"I guess he shoulda taken specimens while he was here after all," Gray deadpanned.

In reality, most of the island's species would survive; enough escaped the conflagration to the beach to ensure that. It wouldn't take long for foliage to return with almost daily rains. The herbivores would take a serious hit, and when they grew scarce the carnivores would too, but enough would survive. Lightning, if nothing else, had surely burned the island before. The important thing was that the well was mostly intact, even after being struck by a few round shot, and Isak and his crew were repairing it. Also, somehow, the Stars and Stripes still floated above the island on a makeshift spar, salvaged from the mostly intact Grik ship beached in the shallows. Rooting the last enemies out of it was how they lost Clark.

The Battle for Tarakan had been a desperate, grisly affair. For the first time Lemurians had stood under a terrifying, if mostly ineffectual bombardment. Then the enemy swarmed ashore. They'd been outnumbered at least three to one, and the fighting had been almost as bad as Gray remembered on the plain below Aryaal's walls. Almost. This time they'd had prepared defenses and trenches, making it possible to reinforce weak spots. Still, it had been bad, and their own losses were nearly thirty percent. Nothing compared to the Grik, whose losses were total, but that didn't matter at all like it might if they'd been fighting a human foe . . . or any foe that deserved the slightest speck of compassion. When the attacking force was destroyed, the exhausted Marines mounted an assault of their own on the ship in hopes of taking it intact, and predictably, as before, the cornered Grik fought like fiends. But the stranded ship was flooded, and all they'd accomplished was the capture of some Grik armaments.

"Their cannons are incredibly crude," observed Shinya, as if reading his thoughts. "The bores are rough, and so is the shot. No wonder so many burst when fired."

"Yeah, and they're made from crummy iron too. But it is iron, damn it. We sure need to be working on that."

Shinya nodded, then spoke reflectively: "They relied heavily on those guns. We've given them an appreciation of artillery, at least. I believe they expected theirs to perform as well as ours. That might have made the difference. There were far more of us waiting to greet them than they expected."

Gray matched Shinya's predatory grin. Both men had fought hard, and the battle *had* been desperate; hand-to-hand at times. More than once each had now saved the other's life. They'd both been through the crucible of Aryaal, but they hadn't been back-to-back then. They might never be friends, but they'd finally developed a bond of respect, trust, and shared commitment that could form only in battle. For the first time since they met, there, amid the detritus of bitter strife, they felt . . . comfortable with each other.

The general alarm began sounding again, and Gray saw Shinya close his eyes briefly before rising.

"First Marines," he yelled, "stand to!"

Gray painfully rose to join him while exhausted, bandaged 'Cats shuffled into formation as quickly as they could. "What the hell now," he growled, looking at the distant 'Cat atop the makeshift tower.

A runner sprinted to them, gasping. "More sails," he reported breathlessly, "in the north."

"North?! How many?" Gray demanded.

"Four, sir."

"Well, that tears it," Gray spat disgustedly.

"Perhaps not," Shinya observed. "Our one major advantage over the Grik is their tactical inflexibility. Their strategy can be cunning, but they seem unwilling to change basic procedures. Four, did you say?" The runner nodded. "Most unusual. The Grik usually come in multiples of three—I have no idea why; ancient hunting traditions, perhaps? Regardless, with few exceptions, we've always seen them in groups of three, or in their hundreds. Four seems atypical."

Gray looked at him thoughtfully. "Maybe. I hope so. One way or the other, we'll know before long."

"I'll be goddamned," Gray murmured. The four ships approached rapidly, the fitful breeze giving way to a stiff easterly, but they'd been coming up fast already. Columns of gray-black smoke pouring from tall funnels between their masts explained how. That alone was sufficient proof they weren't Grik, or if they were, the war was already lost. They were long and black with sleek clipper bows, and Gray had seen others just like them as a kid: old then, and obsolete, but occasionally still in use. They were transitional ships, much like the next generation the Americans planned, relying on both sail and steam, and paddle wheels churned the water at their sides. What attracted his attention more than anything, however, were the flags at their mastheads. He wasn't a historian like the skipper, or a knowledge nut like Courtney, but he'd heard enough of their conversations with their 'Cat allies about the "tail-less ones" of old or "the Others who came before" to catch some details now and then. One such detail had been what flag the ancient East India Company visitors would have flown. That was how he knew what he was looking at now: a flag with red and white stripes, strangely similar to his own, but with the familiar Union Jack where forty-eight stars ought to be. "I'll be goddamned," he repeated.

"Friends of yours?" a Marine lieutenant asked hopefully.

"No," Gray said absently, "never seen 'em before."

The ships hove to while they watched, and the largest lowered a boat into the sea. It was filled with red-coated soldiers, and some others in white coats. Probably officers. "No," he repeated, "but let's see if we can keep them off our list of enemies. Spruce up your Marines and form a detail, about a dozen or so, that don't look too scruffy and worn-out." He looked meaningfully at Shinya. "Have the rest return to their fighting positions and stand easy, but no goofing around. We'll meet our 'guests' on the beach."

The reception awaiting the boat was as smart as possible under the circumstances. The lieutenant and Shinya chose the hardest, most powerful-looking 'Cats, wearing the fewest bandages, and whose blue kilts were the most easily cleaned. They stood on the beach in two ranks of ten (Shinya expanded Gray's request just slightly), Krags at port arms, bayonets cleaned, fixed, and gleaming in the sunlight. When the boat rasped ashore, the redcoats stowed oars and leaped into the surf, dragging it farther until the bow was mostly out of the water. Their red coats had yellow trim and looked like something out of a Revolutionary War movie, but their hats were white-painted canvas tricorns, and they wore short white breeches and sandals that seemed infinitely practical under the circumstances, and contrasted sharply with their sun-bronzed legs. Finishing with the boat, they grabbed *muskets*, and assembled to either side of their craft on the beach, facing the Lemurian Marines, muskets held awkwardly high on their shoulders. The "white-coats" picked their way gingerly forward, and exited the boat onto the damp sand below. Their coats and breeches looked like heavy white canvas, lightly stained and yellowed, with bright yellow double-breasted facings, collars, and cuffs. Gold braid bordered the yellow to varying degrees, and adorned the black, low-crowned, shako-like hats they wore.

The man with the most braid also had a gold epaulet on each shoulder, and sported a large, sun-bleached, blond mustache, braided at the tips. His well-tanned face wore a calm, curious expression as he gazed at the Marines, the Grik corpses, and the expanse of the fire-blackened island. There was no question he recognized the aftermath of a fiercely contested fight, and he stared curiously at the now proudly streaming Stars and Stripes for a long time before resting his penetrating eyes on Gray and Shinya. An awkward moment ensued.

"So, who's in charge here, then?" he asked, vaguely condescending, in strangely accented English.

"I am," Gray answered, stepping forward. "Chief Bosun's Mate Fitzhugh Gray, United States Navy." He gestured at

Shinya. "And this is my second in command, Lieutenant Tamatsu Shinya, late of the Jap Navy, and currently brevet major commanding these Marines. Who are you?"

If the man was confused by the contradictory ranks he'd been presented, or Gray's brusque manner, he took it in stride. "Captain—well, Commodore, actually—Harvey Jenks," he answered, "commanding this squadron, and His Supreme Imperial Governor's frigate *Achilles*. At your service, I'm sure." He added the last with a smirk.

Even as Gray felt his temper rise, he wondered briefly how many wars had been started by such a simple facial expression. "Pleased to meetcha," he said as amiably as possible. *Control!* his subconscious insisted.

A thought seemed to dawn across the stranger's face. "You must be the 'Amer-i-caans' we've heard about! Where is your astonishing ship?" Jenks glanced around again at the wounded, the dead, the distant drilling rig, and finally the stranded Grik ship. "I certainly hope that's not it."

"Americans," Gray corrected, "most of us. Some of the 'Cat Guards are allies, and Shinya's a Jap. Our ship's not here." He nodded at the Grik Indiaman. "That and two others brought our enemies, the Grik, and we killed them." He paused, examining Jenks. "How'd you hear about us? And for that matter, where're you from? We haven't heard doodly about you."

"We have sources," Jenks explained vaguely, looking at the flag once more. His face and tone reflected growing incredulity. "And we spoke one of your Philippine allies' amazing, massive ships a few days past. Fascinating vessels! Dreadfully slow, however. Once we introduced ourselves, they described your predicament. The ship bears reinforcements for your city of Baalkpan, I believe. I hope they arrive in time to aid you." He paused, shaking his head with a little snort. "Pardon me, but that *is* a flag up there, is it not?"

"It's a flag," Gray replied through clenched teeth. "Have you come to aid us?" he asked as neutrally as possible.

" 'Fraid not. We're engaged in a rescue mission: searching for survivors from one of our passenger ships that went missing. They may have been swept this direction on the current, if any did, in fact, survive. Other elements of our navy are searching elsewhere even now. We were told your iron-hulled steamer was on a similar mission, to find other

'Americans,' and we hoped they might have rescued our castaways."

"You're welcome to hang around and ask, when she gets here," Gray replied, "but we ain't seen anybody. 'Sides, you still haven't told me where you come from and why we haven't heard of *you*."

"That's simple enough. The location of our homeland is none of your business; I'm sure you understand. As to why you haven't heard of us, I doubt that's entirely true. I admit there has been little recent contact, but the Ape Folk we met had a rather . . . flattering historical recollection of an earlier visit by my people. Gratifying, indeed, to be remembered so fondly and reverentially, don't you agree? Now, although my government has historic claims to all this region, we have not exercised control for quite some time. There are traditional and pragmatic reasons for that, but suffice to say we have no aims here, and pose no threat to you or your 'alliance.' We welcome its existence, in fact, as a more powerful buffer than the simple fragmented tribesmen that once stood between us and the western menace—against which you, sadly, must contend."

"You haven't come around for, what, two hundred years? And now here you are, out of the blue. The people you're looking for must be pretty important."

"That also is none of your concern," Jenks replied tightly. "We wish only to retrieve them, if, again, any have survived."

Gray was already smoldering over the man's apparent derision toward his flag, and his evasion and superior attitude only fanned the embers. "Fine," he snapped. "You do that. Like I said, you can wait for our 'iron-hulled steamer' here, or look for her where she is, which is the Philippines, last we heard. But for the record, you should show a little more respect for the flags around here, because you got *no* claim to anything here now. Look for your 'castaways,' and if you find our ship, USS *Walker*, and go aboard, you damn sure better salute that flag"—he gestured at the streaming bunting behind him—"because she flies the very same one. If you act like you have here, Captain Reddy's liable to scatter fragments of your puny little fleet all over the sea. He ain't as sensitive and forgivin' as me about such things."

Jenks's mustache worked as his jaw clenched tight.

"And another thing," Gray growled. "If you hang around here, you best watch yourselves, because if you're not here to help us, you won't get any help in return. There's a shit-storm of a fight coming against those things"—he waved at the Grik bodies—"that'll make this look like a picnic spat. You don't want to get caught in the middle of it."

Jenks took a step back, his surprised expression clouding to anger. "Is that a threat, sir?"

"No. Just fact. And a word of advice," Gray said, looking at the Marines. "These ain't 'Ape Folk,' or the simple 'tribes-men' your granddaddys abandoned to fend for themselves against a threat they knew would come someday."

Jenks stroked his mustache and regarded Gray more carefully. The contradictory ranks *had* confused him, and the mostly white-haired, powerfully muscled man in torn, bloodstained khakis and a battered, floppy hat must have significantly greater status among these . . . Americans than boatswains did in his own navy. Amer-i-caans—Americans! Colonials from the far side of the world! Ridiculous! He hadn't put it together before. And what were these "United States" the man referred to? Still, he clearly spoke a warped version of English. Could it be the sacred Mother Country on that distant, long-ago world had allowed her squabbling American colonies to pretend they were a nation? Impossible, yet . . . evidently true. He considered himself something of a historian, and he'd always been fascinated by the histories of the pre-Passage world their founders left behind. Yes, he could see a parallel between how his own empire had abandoned this region of savages and how that other empire might have done the same. Might that not have made the "simple" American "tribesmen" into something more formidable one day? He wondered briefly if it might be better to destroy this "buffer" than leave it in place.

"Very well, then. I can see we shall be the *best* of friends. I take my leave and wish you joy in tidying up after your 'spat.'" Captain Jenks tossed a casual salute at the flag and turned back to his boat.

Long after the oars began propelling the boat back through the surf to *Achilles*, Gray stood trembling with rage.

"Well," said Shinya at last, "that is just how I would have

recommended keeping them off our 'enemies' list. Perhaps we can cement our friendship with some parting gifts. Some round shot, perhaps?" Gray thought he was mocking him until he saw Shinya's deadly serious expression.

Captain Reddy wiped sweat from his eyebrows with his sleeve and took a long gulp of cool water. Juan had brought a carafe to the bridge, filled from the refrigerated scuttlebutt on the side of the big refrigerator on deck. It was unbearably hot, and ever since the wind came around out of the east, there was only the slightest apparent breeze—even as they charged west through the Celebes Sea at twenty-five knots. Keje and Adar stood beside him on the bridge wing, panting like dogs, and Bradford fanned himself manically with his ridiculous sombrero. Flynn was with them, newly shaved face and close-cropped hair exposing already sunburned bright pink skin. With the dark tan around his eyes, he looked like a raccoon. They'd been talking about Bradford's interview with their Grik-like guest, and comparing what he'd learned with what they knew of their enemies. There were a few similar behavior patterns that seemed to support their theories about the Grik—behavior they hoped to exploit—but there were a lot of differences too. One glaring difference was currently on display.

They were watching Silva, Becky, and Lawrence on the amidships deckhouse, playing with the number two gun. Men and 'Cats stood around watching, but the trio didn't seem to notice. Becky was in the pointer's seat, spinning the wheel that elevated the muzzle, while Lawrence, who couldn't sit like a human, stood to the right of the gun, gleefully spinning the trainer's wheel, moving the gun from side to side. His wound had to hurt, but you couldn't tell to look at him. Silva was pointing at a low cloud far abeam, giving them a target.

"Amazing!" Courtney gasped, stilling his frenzied fanning for a moment. "I declare, Captain Reddy, what a fascinating sight. And your man Silva reveals new depths all the time!"

"He does, doesn't he?" Matt agreed absently. He blinked. "Put something to kill in front of that gun and he'll revert quick enough, I expect."

"As will we all," Keje agreed, and Matt could only nod.

The mission had been a success, as long as the promised troops arrived in time. They'd even found the submarine. But the avalanche was loose, and he was beginning to feel the old pull, the impatient, almost yearning for the "game" to begin. If they believed Kaufman's cryptic message—and they had no choice—they'd beat the advance elements of the Grik swarm to Baalkpan by mere days. Perhaps longer if this wind held. Once again he'd be back at the center of the maelstrom with every life he held precious under his command: his responsibility, and there'd be little time for contemplation, only quick, decisive action. Time would compress to the size of an egg, and frenzied activity, chaos, and terror would prevail both inside and out, all trying to crack the egg at unpredictable points. Within the egg were his people, his friends, his love—maybe even the future of civilization on this twisted world. Outside was *Amagi* and the Grik, and all the horrors the shell must protect against, and it was fragile, fragile. In many ways *Walker* represented that shell: old and frail and held together by imagination, but she was just the outer, rusty layer. Without her destroyermen to reinforce her, to give her strength with their bodies, their character, and courage, she was nothing. With her crew she was a living thing, weak perhaps, but game and ready to do what had to be done, and for that she needed a mind. Captain Reddy was that mind, and he was fully aware of the responsibilities and implications. It was a heavy burden. He feared, ultimately, that the primary part of the shell was himself, and he'd made too many mistakes that cost too many lives to be confident he'd keep it intact. He feared and dreaded the great test to come, even as he planned for it, prepared his crew with more frequent drills, and tried to prepare himself. He loathed himself as well, because even greater than the dread was the craving. His hatred of the Grik and their Japanese helpers was so intense he could barely wait to get at them. He'd have to guard against impetuous impulses.

He missed Sandra more than he could say. He missed her face, her insight, her soft voice, her touch . . . and the steadying influence those things had over him. The trip had been a welcome rest, and he'd been able to step back, for a time, from the War and all the stress and urgency that went with it. For a while he was just a ship's captain, a destroyerman once again. But soon the trip—the escape—would end, and he grew increasingly anxious. He knew he'd "revert" just as quickly as Silva, and he needed Sandra's influence to make sure he didn't screw it up.

"That beats all," Dowden said, joining them on the cramped wing. "When that girl came aboard, she would've killed Silva with a bar of soap. Now they're best friends." He paused, seemingly at a loss for words. "And the Grik too."

"Tagranesi," Bradford corrected, flapping his hat again.

"Whatever. Anyway, all the other kiddos stick with their elusive nannies, who act like the ship's full of pirates ready to ravish them on sight. . . ."

"It is," Kutas muttered bleakly from the wheel.

Dowden spared him a glare. "But she sticks to him like glue whenever O'Casey lets her out of his sight. Where is he, anyway?"

"With Chack and Spanky in engineering," Matt answered. "He might be helpful when we build our own reciprocating steam engines. He knows how his people do it, and since turbines are out of the question for the foreseeable future . . ." He shrugged.

"He does seem to know much," Adar conceded sourly. "Apparently he is an engineer, a sailor, a soldier . . . he speaks of his experiences, but only vaguely, and according to Silva the girl doesn't know much about him either. Almost as if he hides himself from her as much as us."

Matt looked at the Sky Priest thoughtfully. "You may have hit on something," he said. "I need another little talk with Mr. O'Casey, it would seem."

They raised Tarakan late that afternoon, and thought at first they were mistaken; it bore no resemblance to the tropical jungle isle they'd left behind a few weeks before. What remained was a barren, blackened tangle of charred trees and brush, with a heavy pall of gray smoke still rising above. Only the flag and the ragged, cheering people on the beach convinced them it was the right place. Not long after they hove to and let fall the anchor, Gray was clambering up the side from a boat. He was grinning when he saluted the colors and turned to salute Matt.

"Permission to come aboard, Skipper?"

"Granted! God, what happened here?" Others climbed aboard while Gray told his tale. All were covered in soot and dried blood, and several were bandaged, including Shinya and Isak Rueben, who stood blinking with his arm in a sling. Matt glanced at each appraisingly, returning their salutes, but continued listening to Gray. His eyes moved to *Felts*'s blackened timbers, protruding from the sea, and on to the stranded Grik ship. Flynn, Laumer, and O'Casey were staring at the aftermath of battle with almost identical expressions of concern and calculation, but he suspected the thoughts behind their eyes were somewhat different. He looked back at Gray. "Sounds like you had a tough fight, Boats," he concluded. "What was the bill?"

"Not too bad, considering they had cannons. Good thing their gunnery's not up to par. Otherwise, they just came on in 'the same old way.' Our casualties were about thirty percent, which sounds pretty bad, but most of the wounded'll make it."

"Cannons?!" Bradford gasped incredulously.

"Oh." Gray shook his head and blinked. He was clearly exhausted, and honestly, as hard as it was to remember sometimes, he wasn't a young man anymore. "I guess I left that part out."

Shinya continued the report. "Yes, Captain Reddy, they had cannons. Naval guns, much like those we equipped *Revenge*, *Felts*, and the other prizes with. Not as good as our new construction; not even as good as our first attempts, really, since theirs were not only crudely formed, but poorly bored, and made of what Mr. Gray called 'crummy iron,' prone to burst."

"Still . . ." Matt murmured, contemplating the implications.

"Yes, 'still,'" Shinya agreed. "How many do they have, how many of their ships have them, and how will this affect our defensive plans?" he said, stating the obvious questions. "There's another matter we must report," he added. "This morning we had some curious visitors."

"Oh?"

"Indeed. Human, singularly rude. Spoke English with a strange accent." Matt's eyes leaped to O'Casey, but aside from a sudden tenseness, he made no response. "They had four armed sailing steamers, and claimed to be on a 'rescue mission.'" The surprised reaction of those nearby was matched by those from the island when Silva pushed his way through the crowd with a small girl perched on his shoulders. Following close behind, like a devoted pet, was an unusually colored, bandaged Grik. Shinya stepped back, and Gray snarled, going for his cutlass.

"As you were!" Matt said, his calm, firm voice having greater effect than any shout. He glared at a grinning Silva, who'd probably timed his approach for maximum shock effect. "Don't be alarmed, gentlemen. May I present"—he paused—"'Miss 'Becky,'" he continued with a trace of irony, "and her friend Lawrence." He pointed at the rail beside Flynn. "And that's Mr. O'Casey, another acquaintance of hers. You may notice when you speak to them, they have unusual accents as well."

"I'll be damned," grumbled Gray. "That bastard Captain Jenks said they were looking for shipwreck survivors. I guess you found them." He glanced around and saw other unfamiliar faces. "And the sub too." He spotted Flynn, whom he knew, and nodded.

"Jenks!" squealed the girl.

"You know him?" Matt demanded. The contrast between Becky's reaction and O'Casey's couldn't have been greater. The girl was animated with happiness, while the one-armed man slumped, in apparent dejection, against the rail.

"Oh, yes! He's a famous naval captain and explorer! Did you hear, Mr. O'Casey? We are rescued!"

"He's also a asshole!" Gray barked.

"Yes, he is!" The girl giggled. "But a very good one. Don't you see?" She patted Silva energetically on the head. "With his help, you should have no trouble with these terrible, vicious Griks of yours!"

Matt looked at Gray, who shook his head. "He's a asshole, Skipper, beggin' your pardon. He's lookin' for *them*. He ain't here to help us, and he won't—not that he'd make much difference. His ships are wooden-hulled paddle wheelers. Probably mount good guns, but they ain't worth more than four or five of the enemy each. Twenty Grik ships won't make a difference one way or the other."

"It might if that's all they have guns on, and they might be worth a lot more that aren't armed."

"Don't matter," Gray snorted. "He won't help."

"Certainly not now," Shinya added wryly.

Matt glared at them both. "What did you do?" he demanded.

"Nothin', Skipper, honest! Like I said, he's a asshole." Gray shrugged. "Maybe we were kinda assholes too, but he was one first!"

Eyes clenched shut, Matt shook his head. "Are we at war with them?" he ground out.

"I don't think so," Gray answered honestly, "but he carried on about how all this area was theirs, but it was okay if we squatted here as a 'buffer' against the Grik and such . . . then he was a jerk about our flag, and I got kind of riled."

The girl's expression of glee had turned to confusion, as if she couldn't understand their doubts about Jenks. "I'm not sure whether it will be up to Captain Jenks whether he helps or not," she said cryptically, then turned to Gray. "He's headed for Baalkpan?"

The Bosun glanced at the captain, then faced the strange girl. "Not necessarily. Said they passed a 'Cat Home out of the Philippines loaded with troops. That's who told them where to look."

"Well, that's good about the troops," Matt mused. "No reason they shouldn't have told him, either, and it might work to our advantage."

"I, uh, doubt it, Skipper," Gray interjected. "Like I said, Jenks has no intention of helpin' us, and when he asked where you were, I told him the Philippines—which I thought you were. Last we saw, his squadron was headed northeast along the coast. You coming in from almost due east, it's no wonder you missed 'em."

Matt shook his head and glanced at the setting sun, perhaps lamenting a lost opportunity. Finally he took a deep breath. "Listen, we'll bring you up to speed, but right now all you need to know is that the Grik are coming. I want all your people aboard and us underway by dark. Leave the tools, equipment, and brontosarries behind. When this is over, we'll come back and finish the job . . . or we won't."

Chack bellowed commands, and his whistle whirred insistently. *Walker*'s borrowed boats went over the side and prepared to run for shore. Signal flags fluttered up the halyards, and rapid preparations commenced on the beach.

Amid all this activity, Isak Rueben stared at Gilbert and Tabby—staring back.

"You hurt bad?" Gilbert finally asked.

Isak flapped his arm. "Naw. Nary a scratch in the fightin'. Stayed out of it, mostly. I ain't no good with no sword, an' I loaned my rifle to Clark. He got killed, though. I got this while I was dumpin' a load. Grabbed a burnt tree, squatted back, an' snap! Tree broke, an' I fell an' poked myself on another one. Think they'll gimme a medal?"

Gilbert shook his head with a concentrated frown, just as he always had, but his time without Isak had wrought subtle changes. Where before, the dry banter might continue endlessly, neither of them truly recognizing the humor, this time something in Gilbert's expression cracked. Tabby watched with blinking eyes as the crack turned into a grin, and something like an indignant skuggik's call escaped his lips.

"You laughin' at me?" Isak asked, astonished, while Gilbert's unaccustomed sounds became a recognizable cackle.

"Yeah . . . I am!" Gilbert replied, and he and Tabby both exploded into uncontrolled hilarity. Isak shook his head, eyes wide. For a moment he wondered if his friends had been filching torpedo alcohol, but the way they were laughing, barely able to breathe . . . he saw the stunned expressions or blinking of those standing near, and the absurdity of it all: his wound, his and Gilbert's seclusion, the stagnant, cloistered life they'd led, struck him like a blow. He'd enjoyed being off the ship and doing something else for a change. He'd even made a few friends, sort of. Evidently the separation had been good for them all. Without really realizing it, at some point he'd begun laughing too. Tears streaked his face as he gave himself over to whatever possessed the others, and he didn't know if they were tears of mirth or despair.

Seaman Fred Reynolds sat on the uncomfortable chair in *Walker*'s radio room. He had the midwatch radio watch until 0400, and was almost out of his mind with boredom. The earphones emitted only a steady, uninterrupted hum as he monitored the guard frequency listening for . . . nothing.

Something was obviously wrong with the PBY's transmitter in Baalkpan. Clancy said it might have been bombed! But the captain had decreed that somebody continue to monitor their own receivers, just in case, and tap out, "We are coming," at least four times every watch. Clancy was the only radioman aboard and couldn't do it all the time, so the tedious chore fell to just about everyone on a rotation basis.

Reynolds had lied to join the Navy—twice, actually. He'd known no one would believe he was eighteen, so he claimed to be seventeen and forged his parents' permission. He'd still been surprised his stunt was successful, since he'd been only fifteen at the time, and probably looked twelve. Now, actually seventeen at last, he was probably the only human on *Walker* still listed as "seaman," since he hadn't struck for anything. He just couldn't decide. He'd become a good bridge talker, and he liked that okay, but anybody was supposed to be able to do that. The exec said he'd probably be an ensign soon, if he'd just pick something and learn to do it well. He'd thought about striking for ordnance, but he wasn't very big. Any thought he'd had about striking for radioman or signalman was losing its appeal. Maybe navigation? It was time to make a decision.

He leaned back in the chair, considering, his eyes sweeping across the clock on the bulkhead. It was time. Sighing, he shifted forward and tapped out the string of memorized dots and dashes. He began to lean back again when he almost lost his eardrums to the intensity of the unexpected reply. Tossing the headset down, he dashed through the hatch to get Clancy.

Matt stared at the vague shape of the message form in his hand with mingled relief and concern. Keje arrived on the bridge, followed by Adar and Shinya. Dowden brought up the rear, escorting a still-drowsy O'Casey. The dim red light in the pilothouse provided barely enough illumination for the watch to move about, and the starboard wing where Matt waited was almost totally dark, a heavy overcast blotting out the stars. "We've finally heard from Baalkpan," he announced without preamble, with a touch of irony. They'd be there in a few hours.

"That is good news," Adar said.

"Very good," Matt agreed. "Mr. Riggs constructed a broadband spark-gap transmitter pretty quickly evidently, but he couldn't power it. The batteries are going to take longer than he thought. Trouble making sulfuric acid. Anyway, *Mahan* finally came crawling in yesterday, and they used her generators."

They didn't like the sound of that. "What happened to her, and why did Mr. Ellis disobey you?" asked Keje.

Matt told them about *Donaghey*'s fight, and how Queen Maraan and Pete Alden got left behind. It all made sense now; with *Donaghey* under repair, and the other frigates incomplete, *Mahan* was the only ship that could have pulled off the rescue against cannon-armed Grik. But it had been a terrible risk. It hadn't gone all her way, either. Baalkpan already knew the Grik were coming; *Mahan* had run the gauntlet of their fleet. She'd expended most of her remaining ammunition and destroyed as many of their cannon-armed ships as she could, but she'd been severely punished in return. Matt had it on good authority now: the crude Grik shot could indeed punch through his old ships' rusty sides at point-blank range.

"Was she badly damaged?"

"She had some casualties—hard not to, as packed as she was, and she lost a boiler. Good thing the wind's in the enemy's teeth, or they might've caught her."

"And Queen Maraan? Aal-den?" Adar asked urgently.

"Safe. They lost Haakar-Faask, it seems, but no details."

"Most unfortunate," Keje rumbled. "I did not know him well, but he had great honor. I trust his end was noteworthy." He hesitated. "Have you told Chack?"

Keje approved of Chack and Safir Maraan's relationship, but he also wanted happiness for his daughter, Selass. It was a tough situation, but one Selass had brought on herself, as far as he was concerned.

"Yeah, I expect he's in the fire rooms now, pestering them to step on it."

"What of *Amagi*?" Shinya asked, carefully neutral.

Matt looked at the Japanese officer. Shinya had been given considerable time to resolve his inner turmoil concerning *Amagi*, maybe too much time. Now he must quickly decide where he stood. The luxury of time for contemplation was over for all of them. Matt felt a pang of guilt, however. He'd read only *most* of Kaufman's message to his assembled officers, and suggested Kaufman might have subverted a single sailor to let him send it—which might be the case. He'd deliberately withheld the possibility that there might be widespread contention aboard the Japanese ship. It would only make the issue more difficult for Shinya, and if *Amagi* attacked anyway, it wouldn't make any difference.

"Jim didn't see her, so she hadn't sailed with the enemy vanguard, at least."

"Oh four hundred, Skipper," Dowden interrupted.

"Very well. Sound general quarters."

The alarm reverberated through the ship, and the relative peace was shattered by frantic activity. Most of the crew was already up, anticipating the daily ritual and eating breakfast, so there was literally no delay before Campeti and his fire-control team scampered up the ladder behind them, and Silva—and now the Bosun too—began loudly exhorting their divisions. Even in the dim light, Matt saw that O'Casey was impressed by the discipline.

"That leaves us with you, Mr. Sean O'Casey ... if that's really your name. You didn't seem as pleased by the prospect of 'rescue' as the young lady did. Is there some reason you don't want this Jenks to find you?"

"Ye ... might say that."

"Well. The last thing we want right now is war with your people—the war we already have is quite sufficient! But if Jenks is as big a jerk as the Bosun says, we're liable to have one if you don't tell me what I want to know. They're obviously looking for you, or more probably the girl, and they've gone to extraordinary lengths to do so. Each of those 'rescue' ships might have suffered the same fate as yours. That's a hell of a risk to take on such slim odds, and I have to know why. Is Jenks a threat? Now, you may not believe it, but this single ship, battered as she is, could slaughter his entire squadron without working up a sweat." He glanced at the others and shook the message form. "Hell, according to this, *Donaghey*'s repairs are complete and the new frigates *Kas-Ra-Ar* and *Tolson* will join her and the guard ship, *Big Sal*, currently on duty." Keje formed a predatory grin. If plans had gone apace, his Home, *Salissa*, had become even more formidable during their absence. "Jenks can hurt my frigates, and it'd probably be a hell of a fight, but based on

Gray's estimates I'm confident they can take him. So, do I send those frigates after him, or keep them here, where we really need them?"

O'Casey slumped. "All right. I may be on the run, but I'm no traitor—although Captain Jenks might disagree. I've told ye nothing of the location of our homeland, an' won't, because that's been pounded into us since birth: safety from secrecy. Aye, 'tis a tradition passed down from our ancestors who first came to this world. They knew of the Grik, and the Ape Folk, as they called them, but assumed that eventually the first would conquer the second, an' they didna want anyone knowin' where ta find us. They set a colony on some secluded islands in the middle o' the Pacific, what the Ape Folk—Lemurians—call the Eastern Sea. Over the last two-hundred-odd years, their colony's grown into an empire, the 'Empire of New Britain Isles,' an' now includes many islands, as well as larger lands. It's become prosperous an' powerful but, over time, tyrannical as well. The governor-emperor is a good, kindly man, as have been most of his predecessors, but the company has supplanted the Court of Proprietors an' the Court of Directors to such a degree, he has little power now."

"The 'company'?" Shinya asked.

"Aye, the Honorable New Britain Company," O'Casey answered with a sneer. "They've won their power on fear o' the threats surroundin' us, and kept it by suppressing the lower classes—descendants of lascars and transportees—that gave them power in the first place, in the Court of Directors—like the old House of Commons—who then cemented it in the Court of Proprietors—like the old House of Lords." He paused, a wry smile on his face. "Ye see, I know me pre-Passage history well, though they suppress that too, now. Because I object to the current system, I'm a traitor, a subversive, as far as they're concerned, but in fact, I'm a patriot who supports the governor-emperor wi' all my heart. I'm a soldier, sailor, and an engineer ... but I also led a wee mutiny, ye see, an' when it was crushed—not enough arms!—I took ship for the western colonies, the 'buffer zone.' I didna think they'd find me there." He paused, apparently considering whether to go on.

"When we were wrecked, I saw the girl! I couldna believe she was aboard! She'd kept to her cabin, I suppose, an' I never, ever knew it. But don't ye see? Savin' the girl proves me word! She's a darlin' creature, an' I like ta think I'd'a tried ta save her regardless, but would a true traitor ha' done so, she bein' who she is?"

The sky was beginning to brighten aft, and there was enough light in the pilothouse to see Captain Reddy blink. "Who is she?" he grated, although he'd already begun to suspect. How much more complicated could their situation become?

O'Casey confirmed his fears. "Why, she's the governor-emperor's daughter, of course!"

Matt took a deep breath. "And this Jenks, he's a 'company' man?"

"Nay, he's Imperial Navy through and through, but he follows orders," O'Casey said.

"Issued by a company-controlled admiralty, I shouldn't wonder," Courtney Bradford grumped. Matt hadn't even noticed him join them, and he wondered if he'd heard it all.

"So," Dowden spoke thoughtfully, "is he actually here to rescue her, or to make sure she's gone for good?"

O'Casey shook his head. "I despise the man, but he wouldna harm the child. He may have company wardens aboard he doesna even know of, though. They wouldna miss the chance."

Matt struck the rail in frustration. "Goddamn it, we don't need this right now!"

Bradford looked at him in alarm. "Indeed."

"All stations manned and ready, Captain," Dowden reported quietly.

Matt brooded in silence for a considerable time. Finally he straightened his shoulders and looked them each in the eye. "This stays between us for now, clear? Anybody else we tell only on a 'need to know' basis, and I'll decide who needs to know."

Three distinct pyramids of off-white canvas appeared in the hazy, muggy morning air. An even greater mass of sail signified *Big Sal*'s mighty presence, on guard at the mouth of Baalkpan Bay. Home. Beyond, the jungle-choked entrance was broken only by the long southern beach, and the imposing shape of Fort Atkinson overlooking the eastern

approach. Hove to in line of battle, the three rakish frigates flew the Stars and Stripes, and Keje's colossal Home
anchored the center of the line. However meager it might
ultimately be, it was a stirring, impressive sight.

"Thank God!" Bradford exclaimed, echoing everyone's
sentiments. "At least we're here in time!"

Matt ordered smoke so everyone would see his ship approaching against the gray day. *Mahan* was out of sight,
as ordered, already undergoing repairs. He looked back
at O'Casey. "You'd better round up your young charge. I
recommend you tell her the whole truth and explain why
you're not going with her, if Jenks shows up here." He
paused. "I'll give you asylum with us, but you're damn sure
going to earn it. And if I find out you've lied to me . . ."

O'Casey nodded sadly. "Thank ye, Captain Reddy."

O'Casey found the girl leaning out over the rail, pointing
excitedly at the graceful ships and the massive Home. The
big man, Silva, was with her—as he always seemed to be
lately—and Lawrence lay coiled on the deck like a dog,
head up, sniffing, staring at the other children, and even the
women, who'd finally ventured on deck. They were the center of much attention, even dressed in the variety of naval
garb they'd taken in exchange for their ragged clothing. All
except the young nun. She still wore her battered habit,
standing a little apart from the other women, looking about
with an impatient, frustrated expression. O'Casey caught
her eye and shrugged sympathetically. He knew she was
still waiting to speak to Captain Reddy. He nodded at Silva
as he approached, then spoke to the girl.

"Young miss, may I have a word?"

"Of course, Mr. O'Casey! I owe you my life!"

He gently steered her away from the others, though he
was conscious of Silva's unwavering eye. "Miss . . . Your
Highness . . ." he began softly. She looked quickly around,
but he made a shushing sound. "No need to fear; no one
can hear. Besides, I've told their captain who ye are. No
choice . . . for I canna go wi' ye if yer Jenks should come
for ye. In fact"—he sighed—"though I hate ta ask ye ta lie
yet again, I must beg ye not to reveal my part in yer affairs
these past many months."

Tears formed in Becky's eyes. "But . . . *why*? Certainly

you'll be knighted, at least, for what you have done. I will see to it!"

"Nay, me dear," O'Casey said. "I'm a wanted man, and I'll certainly be hanged for what I've done." He put his broad hand on her small shoulder. "I've risen against the company, ye see."

She did see, or thought she did, and her eyes went wide. "All this time . . . and you are a traitor?"

"Nay!" he said firmly. "No traitor ta ye or yer father, but perhaps a traitor ta those who subvert ye. Yer father's a good man . . . long ago he was even me friend, but the company's made a stuffed shirt o' him, an' I would change that if I could . . . I tried . . ."

She gasped. "The Mutiny!"

He nodded. "Aye, the Mutiny. It was never against the Empire, er him . . . er you! God knows! It was against the way things have become. We tried ta right a terrible wrong, an' we didna succeed. I'm sorry for that, but not for tryin'."

She still seemed stunned. "So you will stay with these people? Fight with them?"

"Aye. Theirs seems a cause worth fightin' for, after all, an' hopeless as they make it sound, it isna over yet." He lowered his head. "Me last cause is finished, an' there isna any hope a'tall."

"Perhaps," she hedged, still uncertain. "We shall see. In any event, I shall not betray you. If Captain Jenks arrives, I shall tell the entire truth of our ordeal, but at first I shall not reveal you live. Enough?"

He nodded. "Enough, Your Highness. Thank ye."

Silva had drifted over. "What the hell's all this 'Highness' shit?"

Captain Reddy appeared, dressed in his finest, academy sword at his side. "Yes, Mr. Silva," he said quietly, looking at the girl. "You've been associating with royalty all this time, and never even knew it. None of us did." He glanced around. He'd already decided to include Silva in the circle of those who had the "need to know," and he made sure no one else was near enough to hear. "And for now, that's the way it stays. Tell no one. From now on, if, and until her own people collect her, she's your responsibility: yours and Mr. O'Casey's, of course. Her safety's in your hands." He paused. "Highness?" The girl nodded. "Well. Perhaps a proper introduction is in order at last?"

"Becky" cleared her throat. "Rebecca Anne McDonald will suffice, I think," she answered. "As Mr. O'Casey just pointed out, my various titles are rather meaningless anymore. Only one might pertain to the current situation"—she glanced at Silva with a grin—"and I might just trot it out someday, if I get the chance."

Just then she perceived a clattering, rumbling drone unlike anything she'd heard before, growing louder by the moment. She looked up.

"Damn that idiot!" Matt declared. "Who gave him permission to fly?" He paced to the rail and watched the battered PBY approach from the south. It looked decidedly odd with its shortened wings, and the engines sounded like they'd mixed rocks with the oil.

"I can't believe he got it up again," Gray confessed, joining them.

"Ol' Benny's a whiz with gizmos," Silva stated, "an' pretty sharp for an army aviator."

"It's an airplane!" Rebecca squealed excitedly. "Oh, it is, it is! Mr. Flynn told me about them, but I confess I scarcely believed him! Oh, look! Is it going to land upon the sea?"

The Catalina staggered past *Walker*, banked delicately, and flew toward the open sea still separating the destroyer and the picket force. Two hundred yards away it thumped exhaustedly onto the calm sea and wallowed to a stop. Gunning the port engine, the pilot began his approach.

"Oh, look, oh, look!" chanted the girl, almost hopping.

When the plane was within a hundred yards, the pilot—it must be Mallory—turned the plane away from the ship and cut the engines. The ensuing silence seemed almost more intense than the previous racket. A moment passed; then Signals Lieutenant (JG) Palmer appeared on the wing.

Matt spotted Stites leaning on the rail near the whaleboat. "Don't just stand there," he shouted. "Go get him!" He looked at Silva and O'Casey, then glanced at the impatient nun. "Carry on," he said. "I'd better get to the bridge."

"Captain!" shouted the nun, her Dutch accent clear. Grimacing, Matt paused while the woman strode quickly toward him. "Captain, I must protest! I have been asking to speak with you for days!"

"My apologies, uh, sister . . ."

"Sister Audry. I appreciate you rescuing us from our previous . . . circumstances, but now I understand we are steaming directly toward a battle? Have you not thought of the children in my care? Is it possible you will expose them to further risk? I must insist you provide for their safety!"

Matt gritted his teeth. "Lady . . . Sister, I haven't got time for this now, but you have my word those kids'll be as safe as I can make them. If I could drop them, and you, off someplace safe, I would, but there *is* no safe place. I'll do what I can, but for now you must excuse me." He turned and continued on his way, leaving the nun wearing a stormy expression.

Shortly the whaleboat returned, with Palmer standing in the prow. When it came alongside, the signalman scurried up, saluted the flag and Gray, and raced for the pilothouse. "Skipper!" he said with feeling, saluting again. "Am I glad to see you!"

"The feeling's mutual, but what's the meaning of this?" Matt gestured at the plane.

Palmer's face took on a haunted look. "Yeah, well, jeez. Believe me, Skipper, we wouldn't have gone up in that death trap if we didn't have to. It flies, but I think that's only because it hates floating even more." He gathered himself. "Mr. Letts sent us. You were right; the Griks are on the move. They handled *Mahan* pretty rough, but we thought that might've just been a stab at catching her. No go. It looks like the real deal."

"Any sign of *Amagi*?"

"Not with the advance force. Looks like a hundred-plus ships, even after *Mahan* tore 'em up. We might've seen smoke way to the south, but we didn't want to push the old girl, if you know what I mean." Palmer shuddered. "I hate to say it, Captain, but I think it's time we stripped her for the metal."

"Probably right," Matt mused sadly. "We might need her to fly once more, but after that . . ." He shrugged. "How long before the enemy arrives?"

"The wind's against them," Palmer replied, "but by late tomorrow morning, surely."

"Very well. How are the preparations I mentioned to Mr. Sandison proceeding?"

"They haven't started yet, sir. We just now got all *Ma-*

han's holes patched. They could commence tonight, but Sandison says we should wait for daylight."

"Quite right," Matt mused. "We'll just have to slow the enemy advance then, won't we?"

"Yes, sir."

Matt turned to Dowden. "We'll go in and off-load nonessential personnel and refuel. We're running on fumes. Signal the 'fleet' . . . prepare for action."

Isak Rueben ran a proprietary hand along a feed pipe in the aft fire room. He stopped at a gauge and tapped it. "So," he said to Gilbert and Tabby, "I guess you managed to keep my babies lit while I was away."

"Sure did," Gilbert answered. "Course, the refit didn't hurt none. Boilers are in better shape than they've been in twenty years. Didn't have to do nothin' but feed 'em oil an' air an' water the whole trip."

"Didn't even need me," Isak muttered.

"Well, it wasn't like the run outta Surabaya, or after our fight with the Japs, but there's always a little somethin'," Gilbert hastened to add.

"Like what?" Isak asked, interest flaring.

"Number two smoke-box uptake is leakin'," Tabby supplied helpfully, "keeps smokin' up for'ard fire room, and tubes in number three is all coked up." She spat on the slimy deck plate. "Damn green snipes is battin' burners too big. Makin' smoke."

"Laney's been real jumpy too," Gilbert added. "Keeps forgettin' there's only been two of us to do all our work, an' his too. An' there you was, takin' yer ease on a tropical island."

"At least you guys didn't have to fight a bunch of Griks! All you did was run around gatherin' up pigboat pukes an' a buncha kids an' dames. An' what's the dope on that pet Grik the deck apes got?" He gestured at Tabby. "Hell, they got the first 'Cat that came aboard. It ain't fair, I tell ya."

Tabby and Gilbert both laughed, and a grin spread across Isak's face; another real one. "Boy, it's sure good to be back, but it was sorta fun too, you know?"

As soon as he saw her, Chack leaped the remaining distance between the ship and the fueling pier and flung himself into Safir Maraan's arms. Wolf whistles from the ship and cheers from the assembled crowd accompanied the feat. The dignified queen showed no restraint on this occasion. Not to be outdone, Silva mimicked the leap (across a much narrower gap) with a wild whoop and a great show of boisterous exertion. Waiting for him were Ensign Pam Cross and Risa-Sab-At, who, as Active Guard training instructor for *Big Sal*'s combined clans, had been ashore helping train the allied armies. There was a collective gasp of expectation as everyone waited to see what would happen. Silva was onstage, poised to commit a blatant act of public misbehavior, and he knew it. Evidently, so did the "girls." With an exaggerated look of alarm, then an even more exaggerated attempt to make a decision between the two, Silva stood on the pier looking from Pam to Risa and back again. Finally he enfolded them both in his powerful arms and raced through the crowd bellowing, "Gangway! Time's a'wastin'!" The crowd erupted with laughter, and there were hoots and catcalls from the ship.

"Secure those lines!" roared Gray over the tumult. "The next man . . . 'Cat . . . or I don't care what else, jumps ship is a deserter!"

Dowden shook his head beside Captain Reddy on the port bridge wing. "That crazy bastard! I'll have Silva polishing brass from one end of this ship to the other—with his toothbrush!"

Matt barely heard him. Alone, it seemed, of all *Walker*'s crew, his mood remained unaffected by the stunt. His attention was fixed on a small, slim form, standing a little apart from the others, long, sandy-brown hair unclasped for once, flowing in the stiffening breeze. "Don't bother," he said absently, the words ringing hollow. "I said he could. Everybody needed a laugh."

Dowden chuckled uneasily, then followed his captain's gaze. Lieutenant Tucker wore an anxious, sad smile as she stared back across the impossible gulf the others had simply hopped over, with a sharply focused message of love, welcome, and . . . pain that almost broke his heart. He looked back at Matt. Now he knew why the captain had dressed in his best—and why he wasn't laughing.

Matt stepped briskly back from the rail. Nearby, snugged to the old fitting-out pier, was *Mahan*, looking somewhat the worse for wear. Her crew was waving and calling across the distance, their shouts lost in the wind. A loud *toot-toot* and a jet of steam escaped her forward stack. Her new paint was blotched with rust, and there were patches welded here and there. After her long trip, Matt doubted *Walker* looked much better. He noticed the other destroyer already sported her old number again, 102, and the fresh paint contrasted sharply with that around it. He'd transmitted permission to the request early that morning. The deception didn't matter anymore; with any luck the enemy would never see *Mahan* again, and he was glad *Mahan*'s crew—and Jim Ellis—was proud of her once more.

"Commence refueling at once," Matt commanded. "Off-load our 'passengers' and all nonessential or specified personnel, as well as small arms, ammunition, depth charges—you know the list."

Dowden nodded. "Aye, aye, Captain."

"Maybe, if we have time, we can tear out the other stuff we talked about tomorrow night. In the meantime"—he glanced at his watch, 1310—"try to let as many guys as possible go ashore for an hour or so. We can wait for *Big Sal* to follow us in and tie up, but I want to be underway by nineteen hundred." He looked around. "Now take over, if you please. I have someone . . . some people to see."

They gathered for the staff meeting, perhaps the final one, in Nakja-Mur's Great Hall. Lieutenants Letts, Brister, and Sandison, as well as Lord Rolak and Queen Maraan, of course, had met Matt on the pier, so he and Sandra hadn't had a single moment alone. They stood together now, however, and if they weren't holding hands, they stood close enough for their arms to touch and make that vital connection: a warm, tingling, electric circuit both of them needed to draw strength from the other. For now it had to be enough; neither of them knew what the next few days might hold.

Her Highness, Rebecca McDonald, Sean O'Casey, and Ensign Laumer stood with them, the first two introduced as shipwrecked survivors of the fabled earlier "tail-less ones"—which caused quite a stir at first. But old Naga wasn't there; he hadn't been seen in days. Adar was, but having been included among those with the need to know, he hadn't resolved the dogmatic challenges to some fundamental interpretations of the ancient Scrolls they represented. He'd chosen not to "make a big deal" of their presence until he sorted things out in his own mind. The specter of bitter controversy loomed, controversy that might prove distracting at the worst possible time. There was no telling how—or if—different historical perspectives on ancient events might conflict with their own, and if they differed wildly, how might they be reconciled? It was a perplexing problem. He expected no challenge to the most basic unifying gospel of his people, however: reverence of the Sacred Heavens. So for now, he'd concentrate on his sworn task: defeating the Grik. Only with victory would he have the leisure for theological contemplation, not to mention possible "adjustments" to many of his people's most closely held beliefs.

Ensign Laumer was clearly out of his depth, and it showed in his expression. There just hadn't been enough time for him to grasp all that was going on. His previous situation had been far enough beyond his experience, but his slowly growing understanding of *this* situation left him overwhelmed. Matt knew the kid wasn't ready to lead his men in battle, but he knew he'd have to figure out *something* for him to do or he might be ruined. O'Casey was stony-faced, observant, apparently curious about how he could help. That was what he'd asked the captain, but Matt wasn't sure. He'd introduced him to Letts and told the lieutenant to figure it out, as long as O'Casey, Silva, or now—apparently—Sandra was with the girl at all times.

Sandra became one of Rebecca's "protectors" almost at first sight. Rebecca was a virtual (smaller) twin to the nurse, and each had recognized herself in the other at once. Both were willful, intelligent, accustomed to getting their way, but profoundly empathic as well. Sandra was impressed by the girl's resilience, her capacity to cope with the hardships she'd endured and remain so self-possessed at such an early age—not to mention her devotion to such bizarre and disparate "friends" as Lawrence and Dennis Silva. When they were first introduced, Rebecca was still seething with revulsion and indignation over Silva's behavior at the pier and Sandra recognized an anger founded on affection at once.

She also instantly realized the girl harbored a great secret that wasn't for public discussion.

Rebecca saw in Sandra a mirror image of her mother, but an image—much as she loved her—her mother could never reflect in action. She'd already seen a huge difference between how Lemurians and her own people perceived a female's role, and now she saw a similar stunning difference in the way the "Americans" treated their women. She sensed they were extremely protective of them, which made sense when they were so few, but there was no condescension or disdain, and the protectiveness was of a different sort; it was not of the type extended to property. She'd been immune to that sort herself, considering who she was, but knew it was pervasive among her people. Here, despite their scarcity, women had real power and status—equality—and Sandra Tucker epitomized that equality with her every word, her bearing, and her most casual gesture. Here was a woman like Rebecca had never seen, who, while wholly feminine, demanded and received respect. Not because she'd been born to it, but because she'd earned it.

At the same time, the girl also sensed a sadness, a vulnerability separate from Sandra's professional self, and knew the woman held a great secret of her own. Even Rebecca, a child of ten, quickly realized what it was.

Now she stood, her small hand in Sandra's, eyes wide as she took in the sights, smells, and . . . terrifying momentousness of the proceedings within the Great Hall she was but a spectator to. She missed Lawrence's comforting presence, but knew he'd been left aboard the iron ship for his own protection. The hall was filled with the tension of a looming battle of unimaginable proportions against creatures far too similar to him.

Captain Reddy was talking, describing the voyage they'd returned from. Occasionally Sandra squeezed her hand uncomfortably tight when he spoke of some tense moment. Once she gasped, not sure if it was from pain or because she'd become so caught up in the tale, and Sandra knelt and murmured soft, fervent words of apology. Captain Reddy paused and glanced their way, and in that instant Rebecca caught a glimpse of him she hadn't seen before: a gentle, almost boyishly wistful tenderness, haunted by something lurking beneath a fragile facade. She imagined she sensed a titanic conflict between howling terror and a capacity for unimaginable violence. She blinked, recoiled slightly, and it was gone, leaving only a benevolent expression of mild concern.

Matt turned back and resumed, speaking to all, but generally directing his words to Baalkpan's High Chief. Nakja-Mur looked terrible. His once massive arms had seemed actually frail when he wrapped Matt in the usual awkward greeting embrace. "You cannot know," he'd said low, "how glad I am you have returned." His eyes had even been misty. The stress he'd endured the last few weeks had been grueling, and if it hadn't sapped his will, it had wracked his body. Since his greeting, he'd retired to his cushions and spoken little.

". . . so," Matt continued, "we'll sortie tonight with the frigates. Try to meet this advance Grik element and bust it up before it gets too close. That'll leave time for Mr. Sandison and *Mahan* to prepare our final surprises." He looked at Bernie Sandison. "I can leave you Silva and Chief Gray to supervise the detail. I wish I could leave Campeti, but I'll need him at fire control."

"Thanks, Skipper. I didn't expect Silva or Gray. We'll get the job done."

"What about *Amagi* and the main force?" Pete Alden asked, speaking for the first time. He still looked haggard after his ordeal.

"Day after tomorrow, I expect." Matt shrugged. "That's what Mallory thinks—if that was her smoke he saw. I think it probably was; why else come now at all? All the same, they must've really rushed her repairs to get her to sea this quickly. She's their wild card. Normally she could blast Baalkpan to dust without even entering the bay. Her shells are a lot more effective falling on top of a target than hitting it from the side. If she shoots right at something, she either hits—and trust me, it's a hell of a thump—or misses completely. That's why ships like her usually don't get in too close." He was trying to demonstrate ballistics with his hands as he spoke. "Thing is, if she stands off, she has to see the target herself, which she can't do here, or have forward observers correct her fire. They could stash one on a Grik ship, I suppose, or even send one ashore, if they have radios to spare. But regardless, if they use indirect fire"—his hand described a high arc in the air—"they're still going to miss a lot. My bet is, they won't want to waste the ammunition." He glanced at Sandison, then looked at Nakja-Mur.

"We're almost out of ammunition ourselves," he admitted. "We picked up some from the submarine, and Jim says the copper bolts shoot fine, but have 'limited destructive capability.' In other words, they just punch holes. But they do work, and they're better than nothing. Someday we'll make explosive shells. It'll be a lot harder for the Japs to do that—to make more of their big shells, that'll not only take rifling, but also blow up. Without their explosive force, they're not much more dangerous than our copper bolts. They'll make a bigger hole, but against our defenses here they'll just make bigger holes in the dirt." He grinned crookedly. "And you have to wonder if even the Japs would show the Grik how to make something that might blow a hole in their *own* ship. Regardless, for now, they've *got* to be feeling the pinch—especially after they wasted so many destroying *Nerracca*. They must've thought they had us— that it'd be worth it to go for broke—but it didn't work that way." He paused, remembering that fearful night before continuing. "What I think they'll do is come right up into the bay, use their secondaries as much as they can. That's what we've planned for, and that's what we *need* them to do. Our whole defense relies on it, and I think that's our only chance to kill her." He looked at Keje. "Trouble is, if they do that, the Homes'll be slaughtered."

Keje blinked. "I'd rather avoid the 'slaughter' of my Home," he said dryly.

"Me too," said Matt. "That's why *Big Sal* and the other Homes should leave now. Tonight."

"But we've sworn to fight!" Ramic protested loudly. "I for one have a score to settle! I will not leave!"

"Nor I," said Geran-Eras.

"I'm glad to hear it, but you misunderstand. Your warriors'll fight on land, as they did at Aryaal, but I think the Homes themselves should sail immediately for Sembaakpan, near our new fuel depot at Tarakan. It's a crummy anchorage, but that'll take them out of *Amagi*'s reach. If we faced only the Grik, using the Homes as floating batteries would make sense. We could tear the hell out of them. But if *Amagi* comes in, they won't stand a chance. Second, they could carry away more of the Aryaalan and B'mbaadan younglings *Fristar* and the others didn't wait to take—besides our own recently acquired 'noncombatants.'" He paused, catching sight of Ensign Laumer. The young officer still looked lost. Matt understood how he felt. "Laumer?"

"Sir?"

"I want you and half your submariners to go as well. Continue providing security for our noncombatants. Besides, if we fail here, it'll be up to you to continue the fight, keep helping our friends in technical matters." Laumer straightened, glad to have something to do. Something he *could* do, while he got his feet under him.

"Aye, aye, sir."

Matt turned back to Geran-Eras. "I understand there's a small Baalkpan settlement at Saangku. They may need evacuation as well, if things go poorly here." There were a few thoughtful nods in the crowd. Matt pressed on. "If that happens, then the Homes will serve yet another purpose. If Baalkpan falls, we'll retreat north through the jungle, and the Homes'll be waiting to take us to safety." He smirked. Everyone knew how dangerous a trek of that distance through the Borneo jungle would be—particularly with the Grik snapping at their heels. Perhaps some would survive. "Not much of a backup plan, but it's better than nothing."

The High Chiefs of the three remaining homes spoke rapidly among themselves. Excited conversations erupted throughout the hall. Matt remained silent, watching, while Keje, Geran, and Ramic made up their minds. Finally they stood ready to speak, and Nakja-Mur touched the gong for quiet.

"Very well," Keje announced. "It's agreed. *Humfra-Dar* and *Aracca* sail immediately for Sembaakpan, with enough people to trim the wings and work the guns, if necessary. The High Chiefs will remain to command their warriors."

Matt nodded reservedly. "Good," he said, "but what about *Big Sal*?"

"*Salissa*, like her sister, *Walker*, will remain here." Keje blinked utmost resolution when he spoke. "That, my brother, is not open to discussion. You conveniently omitted the fact that *Walker* and *Mahan* will face the same 'slaughter' as our Homes. They will not face it alone. *Salissa* will be your floating battery as long as she can."

The hall was silent while everyone considered the implications of Keje's words. Matt didn't know what to say.

"One problem I can see," Ellis interjected, "is their damn observation plane they bombed us with. If it shows up again, it could throw a major wrench in the works. Japs could stand off and pound us—just like you said—and there'd be nothing we could do."

Matt knew Jim wasn't very happy with *Mahan*'s assignment, and his tone actually sounded a little confrontational. Matt glanced at Shinya, then looked his former exec—his friend—in the eye.

"Good point, but I have it on ... good authority ... the spotting plane won't be a factor."

"How ... ?"

"Our radio wasn't busted, remember? We picked up a transmission, in the clear, that the plane was damaged. Must've been right after its attack."

"Well ... okay, but that's just one example of how easily the plan can get thrown out of whack."

"I thought you liked the plan. If you didn't, why didn't you say something when we were making it?"

"Because I did—*do*—like it!" Jim admitted in frustration. "No, I take that back. I hate the damn plan, but it's probably the best we could come up with under the circumstances. What I disagree with now, that maybe I didn't before, is that the plan leaves *Mahan* out of the fight. By all rights, she ought to have *Walker*'s job!"

Matt shook his head. "She's too vulnerable. It'd be suicide. *Amagi* has to *see Walker*, which means she's going to get to shoot at her. With one good boiler and only one screw, *Mahan*'d be a sitting duck."

"*Walker*'s not much better off than *Mahan*," Jim insisted stubbornly.

"But she *is* faster," Matt stressed. "And as soon as *Amagi* gets a good look, we're going to make smoke and run like hell. After she sees *Walker* run away, she won't worry about her anymore. That's when *Mahan* does her job. It's an important job, Jim. Besides"—he grinned wryly—"you already changed your number back."

Jim snorted. "All right, Skipper, but next time *Mahan* gets to play target while *Walker* puts the sneak on 'em. Fair's fair. The boys are starting to feel left out—and sort of coddled." Jim chuckled softly, but Matt knew his old exec was more serious than he seemed. The *Mahan*s didn't want to die any more than anyone else, but they did want to do their part. Many still felt tainted by the Kaufman incident, despite their recent success.

"You bet, Jim. Next time."

"I guess it's really come down to this, hasn't it?" Sandra asked bitterly. Everyone looked at her questioningly, surprised by her tone. "You know, 'win or lose, live or die'— probably die even if you win?"

"It's been that way from the start," Matt said gently. "Ever since the Squall. In our old world, maybe it wasn't so black-and-white. I guess you could always surrender—even to the Japs—but that won't work here." He took a breath. "So, yeah, it's down to that, and it's just that simple."

Sandra shivered in the warm hall. She knelt and gathered Rebecca in her arms. "Maybe, but it seems even worse when you joke about it."

Nakja-Mur cleared his throat, and everyone looked at him. "Well," he said, "that's decided, and well-done. I do have a request, if you will permit me, Cap-i-taan Reddy."

"Of course."

"Before you depart, would you share with us again your *not* 'backup' plan?"

CHAPTER
10

*T*salka glared across the water as Kurokawa's launch returned to his ship. "You know, General, I still detest that creature."

General Esshk hissed agreement. "But he is useful. His iron ship is still slowed by damage, he says, but at least it floats evenly now." He hissed amusement, remembering Kurokawa's stormy indignation and fury toward their enemies after they blew another hole in his mighty ship almost four moons ago. "He is also highly motivated," he added cryptically.

"Their iron ship is wondrously powerful," Tsalka agreed. "I will never forget the concussion of its great guns, and the damage it inflicted on the huge ship of the prey. Magnificent!"

"Most impressive," Esshk hedged. He gazed at the lumbering iron monstrosity. Black smoke belched from its middle as it burned the coal that somehow pushed it along. Despite its amazing power, he must not forget that the Tree Prey had friends who could damage it. It was ensconced deep within the protective embrace of the main body of the "Invincible Swarm" (as opposed to the previous, ill-fated Grand Swarm) to protect it from another surprise enemy attack. Nothing could get through the impenetrable cordon of almost four hundred ships.

"He still entertains somewhat grandiose illusions of his own importance," Tsalka declared. "He is impertinent and grasping."

"True," Esshk agreed, "but he is also too often right, concerning the methods of the prey. He was right about the importance they placed on retrieving their castaways from Madura, and I confess I did not see it until too late. An opportunity was lost there, I fear." He hissed a self-depre-cating sigh. "He also seems right about sparing some Uul, particularly those with valuable experience, when a ship—or even an army—is beaten. Not all fall prey, after all, and it does seem to harden them somehow. Besides, their valu-able experience is not then lost. It is difficult starting over with mindless Uul every time we suffer a reverse."

"A most dangerous precedent, I will say it again," Tsalka objected. "Our Way has worked well for millennia. It is not for us to make changes on a whim." He sniffed. "Your 'philosophical hobbies' will place you in grave danger one day, General; mark my words. You will strain your familial relations with the Celestial Mother too far, and even she will not indulge you."

"Perhaps," Esshk agreed, "but our Way has struck a snag this time, it seems. Improvisation is often dangerous, but I do command here, Excellency. I will take Kurokawa's ad-vice, follow his 'tactics,' give him his head, to a degree. For now. I can always cut it off at my leisure. Consider it an experiment. If I am wrong"—he hissed the equivalent of a shrug—"I will destroy myself."

"If you are wrong, dear General," Tsalka replied, "I doubt you will be allowed that honor, and neither will I."

Walker steamed away from the pier shortly before dark to join the frigates in the Makassar Strait. The next morn-ing, as soon as the sun was up, the Catalina clattered its way into the sky on what, it was hoped, might be its final flight. At the old fitting-out pier, two huge barges had been brought alongside. One was equipped with a respectable pile driver—even by Navy standards—for driving pier pil-ings into the bottom of Baalkpan Bay. Both it and the other barge were crowded with empty casks and great long posts, like telephone poles. Yard workers and a large force of un-skilled laborers scurried about on each, making final prepa-rations and casting off lines.

Chief Gray and Dennis Silva were on yet a third barge, along with Dean Laney, Randal Hale, Sandy Newman, Pack Rat, and six other Lemurian helpers. This particular barge was attached in tandem to the others by a long, thick cable ultimately leading to *Mahan*'s fantail. When the final lines were taken in, Gray sent a signal to be relayed up the awkward train. Ever so slowly *Mahan* strained against the weight, and one by one the barges began to move. The third barge had to wait longer than the others, since its cable was twice as long. The reason was its cargo. Securely lashed to the broad, flat deck were all but twenty of *Walker*'s and half of *Mahan*'s MK-6 depth charges. Both ships had been blessed by a full allotment of the antisubmarine weapons when they fled Surabaya, and until now, except as "anti-mountain fish" weapons, no one had thought of a way to use them.

Unlike the MK-6 magnetic torpedo exploder they'd had so much trouble with, there was nothing at all wrong with the MK-6 depth charges. They were ridiculously unsophisticated weapons, and had remained virtually unchanged since the Great War. Each consisted of a can roughly the size of a forty-gallon drum, filled with six hundred pounds of TNT. Hydrostatic pressure detonators activated when they reached a preselected depth. Their very simplicity made them remarkably reliable weapons—at least as far as their designed function was concerned. The only problem was, when used against a submarine's tough pressure hull, they had to sink to within twenty yards just to damage the target, ten yards or less to have a serious chance of destroying it. In practice, against a radically maneuvering submarine, they were extremely inefficient. Gray often compared their use to a blindfolded man shooting at bats with a pistol.

Theoretically, the detonation of six hundred pounds of high explosive underneath a *surface* target would have more gratifying results. That was, after all, the desired effect of the MK-6-equipped torpedoes. Therefore, Lieutenant Sandison had been charged with the task of inventing a way to make the depth charges do what the torpedoes wouldn't.

"This'll never work," Silva proclaimed grandly as the line of barges eased into the bay. He was sitting atop one of the sixty cylinders clustered together on the barge. "'Ash cans' are supposed to *blow up* when they go in the water." He arched an eyebrow and looked at those around him. "We're all gonna die."

"Shut up, you maniac," Gray growled. "Besides, what does it matter to you? At least you'll die happy." Silva hadn't returned until morning after he disappeared with Pam and Risa the previous afternoon.

"Yeah," grumped Hale. "The dame famine's bad enough without you making it worse. Two of 'em's already taken. That leaves only two left, well, 'sides the new ones. But they left last night on *Humfra-Dar*."

Silva regarded him with feigned astonishment. "Why, whatever do you mean?"

Laney stepped in front of him, fists at his side. "Silva, if you don't shut the hell up, I'm gonna stuff your hatrack."

"Lighten up, Laney," Silva said. "If you're that hard up, get yourself a 'Cat gal. You'd be surprised how adventurous they are!"

Laney blinked at him. "You just never quit!"

Silva arched his eyebrows again.

"You're one sick bastard, Silva," Randal Hale said, shaking his head, but there was speculation in his voice.

"That's enough!" Gray commanded. "We got enough unnatural things to worry about today—like turnin' depth charges into mines!"

"How are we gonna do that, anyway?" Newman asked.

"See those big posts on the first barge?" They nodded. "We'll drive 'em into the bottom with that pile driver, and tie a depth charge to it a few feet underwater. If any of the post is still sticking up, we'll cut it off. Then, if a ship runs into it, hopefully it'll snap off and the charge'll sink. When it gets to twenty feet, *boom*! Got it?"

Silva cocked his head. "What are we gonna do in the main channel? Too deep to sink poles."

"We'll hang a charge underneath however many of those barrels it takes to keep one up, and anchor the whole thing to the bottom."

"They'll see them, won't they?" questioned Hale.

"Maybe," Gray agreed. "But what are they gonna do about it? We'll rig it so's they can't squeeze between 'em without hitting another. Top it off by putting out way more barrels than we have depth charges too. It'll be just a matter of tying an anchor to 'em and heavin' 'em over the side. That's how we'll leave a clear channel for *Walker* to come back through, without it lookin' like there is one."

Newman looked thoughtful. "Might work," he said. "Now I know why we're on such a long cable, though. I guess we're the ones setting the charges?"

Gray nodded. "With this box of bombs, if one of 'em slips after we set it, the flashies won't even find enough to make it worth their while."

Pete Alden stood on Nakja-Mur's balcony with the High Chief of Baalkpan, Letts, Shinya, Bradford, and Sandra Tucker. The kid was off with O'Casey. The balcony made an ideal observation post from which they could see the vast panorama of the city's bristling defenses in the late-afternoon sun. The regiments had been moved into their positions, and *Big Sal* was now moored by the shipyard dock. She had a spring in her cable so she could fire her augmented battery into the flank of any force trying to land there, or anywhere along the waterfront. Her sails were stowed, and like all the defenses, she held plenty of water barrels ready to defend against firebombs. Because it was such an obvious place for them to direct the battle, they'd already made plans to abandon the Great Hall if *Amagi* came into the bay. Even with high-rise dwellings all around, the Great Hall and its Sacred Tree stood out quite prominently. It would be a prime target for the battle cruiser's initial salvos. Nakja-Mur was horrified that the Sacred Tree might be damaged, but there was nothing they could do to prevent it. Secondary command posts had been established in strategic locations.

Karen Theimer had worked wonders setting up a central hospital and ambulance corps, and the surgeons and nurses who'd learned their trade with the Allied Expeditionary Force were now fully integrated into the system. Sandra was in overall command of the medical effort, from the central hospital. Karen was her exec, and the other nurses would supervise the two main field hospitals in north and south Baalkpan. Smaller aid stations were established near every defensive position, supervised by talented veterans such as Selass. Sandra hated that she wouldn't be with *Walker* during the coming fight, but there was no question where she'd be most needed. Jamie Miller could care for any casualties the ship might have. Other than her personal feelings, she had no excuse to be aboard.

Without *Mahan*'s generators to run the new transmitter, it had been stowed in a deep, safe bunker. *Walker* would remain in constant contact through light and flag signals, as well as the crystal receivers Riggs had constructed, which required almost no electricity. The experimental batteries they'd built had plenty of juice for them, so Matt could keep overall strategic command even while fighting his ship. Hopefully. Even if everything went exactly according to plan, however, *Walker* would be fighting for her life. Her exposure to the enemy was *the* part of the plan everything else depended on, so that was where he had to be. Sandra still wished she could be with him. The frustration of the evening before had only heightened her longing, as well as her conviction that they *had* been a "couple of dopes" all along. She envied Karen her happiness and her ability to show open, natural affection for the one she loved.

She suddenly realized someone had spoken to her. "What was that?" she asked, shaking her head.

"Do you have any questions or requirements, Lieutenant Tucker?" Letts asked. Gone was the tongue-tied suitor of short months before. Alden would have command of the "land battle" they expected, but Letts was still acting as Captain Reddy's chief of staff.

"Uh, just the disposition of the child, Becky, and Mr. O'Casey."

"I thought you might keep the girl at the central hospital—what's the dope on her, anyway?" Only Bradford and Nakja-Mur knew, and they didn't answer. "Well, if you'll do that, I'll keep O'Casey with me. I'd like to see what he's made of."

Sandra nodded. "Other than that, then, everything's under control," she said.

"Good. Mr. Alden?"

Pete shrugged. "We're about as ready as we can be without reinforcements. *Mahan* signaled a few minutes ago that they're nearly finished laying the mines." He shook his head. "It's a miracle nobody got blown up doing that. Otherwise, the only thing I have to add is that Lieutenant Riggs is finally satisfied with the visibility of the semaphore tower in Fort Atkinson. His guys on the southwest wall couldn't see it through those last few trees and they cut them down. Oh, yeah, I sent Lord Rolak and the First Aryaal to reinforce the two hundred Sularans, and Mr. Brister's artillery-men in the fort. I also think Shinya should command the independent force we talked about."

Letts nodded agreement. "That's what the captain said too."

Pete looked at Shinya. Ever since he returned, not only from the trip to Manila, but from Aryaal with the AEF, Pete's friend had been very quiet. "I want to deploy the First Marines, the Tenth Baalkpan, and the warriors from *Aracca* to a forward position defending the south and west approaches against any enemy landing." He held up his hand. "You're *not* to pull a Custer's Last Stand, or some Jap equivalent! I don't want you getting tangled up in anything you can't handle. I mainly want you out there to keep some small force from coming ashore and cutting us off from the fort."

"The First Marines are under strength," Shinya said absently. "They had losses at Tarakan and B'mbaado."

"Yeah, well, maybe we can fill 'em out with rifle-trained guys from the Second. Will you do it?"

Very seriously, Shinya nodded, and Pete peered intently at him. "Say, you aren't going to cut your guts out or anything if you have to pull back, are you?"

Tamatsu chuckled. In spite of his mood, he was surprised by the question. "Not unless you tell me to. We don't have the luxury of engaging in such selfish gestures. Besides, that would only increase whatever dishonor I might earn by retreating. It would give aid and comfort to the enemy by contributing to their commissary." Everyone laughed at that, including Shinya. But then a strange expression crossed his face and he grew silent again.

"So that's it, then?" Letts asked skeptically. Alden looked speculative but didn't reply. "Nothing at all?"

"Well, yes, actually," said Courtney Bradford. He motioned to himself and Nakja-Mur. "What about us? What shall we do?"

Letts looked at him, surprised. "I just assumed you'd help in the hospital. The way you're always dissecting stuff—you certainly know how to handle a knife."

Bradford drew himself up. "My dear sir, as I've made no secret, I fancy myself something of a naturalist. It's a hobby. I've a great deal of experience cutting things up, but virtually none putting them back together. Certainly you understand the difference? Of course you do!" He shook his head. "No, just give me a rifle—point me where you need me most, I say. Besides, my recent observations about Grik behavior might prove crucial."

"Trust me, Mr. Bradford, everybody's up on your 'observations,'" Pete interrupted. "But no offense; if things get bad enough we need your one rifle, we'll all be bugging out! I'll give you a Krag—but I'd consider it a personal favor if you'd use it to help guard the hospital. I'm sure Captain Reddy would appreciate it as well. Will you put yourself at Lieutenant Tucker's service?"

Bradford pursed his lips. "Well, if you insist on putting it like that . . ."

"That still leaves me," said Nakja-Mur. "I've grown old and fat, but I was a warrior once. Not much of one, I admit. This is the first time in the memory of the Scrolls that Baalkpan has ever faced war, but I should be defending my people."

"You are," Letts assured him. "You're leading your people, and your courage is an example to them, as well as us. Besides, I need you beside me throughout the battle. I may need your advice or skill at dealing with people. Also, if something happens to me, you're the only one who can see the whole picture. You'll have to step in as Captain Reddy's chief of staff."

"Very well," Nakja-Mur said somberly. "I accept. I will watch you closely to know what to do if that unfortunate event comes to pass. I pray it does not."

"Me too," Alan Letts fervently agreed.

One by one, Sandra, Bradford, and finally Nakja-Mur left the balcony to continue their preparations. Only Shinya and Alden remained. Pete suspected Tamatsu had been waiting to talk to him alone.

"I will be honored to command the independent force," he said at last, "but I wanted you to know I have been engaged in a struggle of . . . honor."

"I know," Alden said simply. "Adar told me."

Shinya looked surprised. "And yet you still trust me to do this thing?"

"Sure. Otherwise I wouldn't have brought it up. Why, don't you trust yourself?"

Tamatsu only shook his head in amazement. "You Americans. You assume a great deal. Even I didn't know, until a few moments ago, which side of the struggle would prevail. And yet you had no doubts?"

"Nope." Alden sighed. "Look, you said whatever was eating you was a matter of honor, right? I know you pretty well by now, I think. The honorable thing to do in this situation is pretty clear—as long as you're not going to commit Harry-Carry."

A ghost of a smile crossed Shinya's face, but he shook his head. "It isn't that simple. I gave Captain Reddy my parole, and I've since engaged in numerous activities for the common good, I think. That wasn't inconsistent with my concept of honor. This . . ." He paused. "This is different. If I continue to help you, even to the extent of aiding you against my own people, I will be committing treason in their eyes—and mine. Whatever the reason, and wherever we are, my people and yours are at war, Sergeant Alden." He took off his hat and scratched his short hair. "However . . ." He stopped again. "Such an interesting word, don't you think? 'However.' I wonder if it was ever intended to be so vague, yet so profound at the same time," he mused darkly. "However, for whatever reason, *Amagi*'s commander supports the side of purest evil in this war. There can be no honorable explanation for that. On its face, that would seem to make my decision simpler, yet it does not. My people do not have the freedom to choose which policies of our government we will support. As far as *Amagi*'s crew are concerned, ordinary seamen and junior officers—men like me—*Amagi*'s commanding officer is the direct representative of the emperor. Whatever has befallen them, they will follow him because of that, whether or not they believe he is right." He searched Alden's face for understanding. "You see it as misplaced obedience to a corrupt commander, and perhaps it is. But to my people, a commander's dishonor does not reflect upon those under his command, as long as they follow his orders. Regardless of the commander's motive, obeying him is the honorable thing for *them* to do. Do you see now why I have had such difficulty with this decision? Through their captain, the crew of *Amagi* have become tools of the Grik. Through their honorable service, they are assisting in the commission of evil. That's the most tragic irony of all.

"So you see, I have not been agonizing over which side is in the right; even from my different perspective, that is obvious. The decision I faced was whether to revert to my status of noncombatant parolee, or openly betray my people, whose honor has already been betrayed by their leader." He took a deep breath. "I have made that decision. Perhaps my long association with Americans has corrupted me, but I begin to see that blind obedience to a dishonorable command can't obviate the final, greatest responsibility of honor: to do the right thing. I grieve for my countrymen who have not realized that yet, but I cannot stand idly by."

"You Japs are so weird," Alden said quietly. "No offense. What made you make up your mind?"

Shinya considered. "First, it was my realization that, if the roles were reversed, and *Walker* had somehow come into association with the Grik, Captain Reddy would never have aided them as *Amagi* has. If he tried, the crew wouldn't have supported him. The way the crew of *Mahan* finally decided they could no longer support Captain Kaufman, regardless of rank, is a good example. Then, when King Alcas ordered the surprise attack on *Walker* that killed Mr. Donaghey, Captain Reddy hanged the saboteurs. I saw no injustice there. They were only following orders, but to do such a thing while negotiations were underway—and after we saved them from the Grik—collective guilt couldn't fail to stain the perpetrators."

Alden nodded. "Now you know why we were so mad about Pearl Harbor."

Shinya grimaced. "Perhaps." He looked out over the wind-ruffled bay. In the far distance was *Mahan*'s battered outline. The low-lying barges and toiling men and Lemurians were barely visible. Preparing.

"In any event, as I said, I will be honored to command the independent force, if you still desire it. The duty will be heavy, should I face my countrymen. I cannot deny that. But it is also, clearly, my duty." He paused. "As it is my duty to ask for the Second instead of the First Marines. You will need the riflemen as a reserve, whereas if I have to fight, it will be the shield wall and spears."

"All right," Pete agreed, "and you're right. Just remember your promise not to gut yourself if anything goes wrong." They shared another small smile. "You know what you're supposed to do. If things get too hairy, pull back to Fort Atkinson or the Baalkpan wall." He shrugged. "They may not put anyone ashore there at all; flank attacks don't seem their style. We rolled up their flanks time and again on B'mbaado, and it always took them by surprise. That stuff Mallory said about Tjilatjap keeps coming back to me, though, so keep your eyes peeled."

The sun was near the jungle horizon when the last cluster of barrels went into the dappled sea. As powerful as he was, Silva hurt all over from the backbreaking chore of man-handling the heavy depth charges. He tried to use his grimy T-shirt to wipe the burning sweat from his eyes, but the shirt was so soaked it only made it worse. He glanced at the mouth of the bay. He was surprised *Walker* hadn't returned and was struck by the irony of that. On the world they came from, she'd been an insignificant, expendable asset, a relic of an almost ancient war—in terms of technological advancement. She hadn't been in the same league with her smallest modern counterparts in the Japanese Navy. Most of her sisters weren't even frontline warships anymore; they'd been converted to seaplane or submarine tenders, minelayers, transports, even damage-control hulks. . . . Now Dennis was surprised she wasn't already back from facing maybe a hundred enemy ships, with only three sailing frigates to assist her. Nobody else seemed to think it was a big deal either, and he guessed that was really more of a testament to their faith in her captain than the dilapidated ship herself. Still . . .

Several times during the afternoon, they thought they heard the faint booming of *Walker*'s guns, and duller, rippling broadsides of muzzle-loading cannon. Maybe not. The wind was wrong, and the fighting had to be closer than they'd expected if it was so, but regardless, *Walker* and her little fleet were doing their job: buying the time they needed to finish their little surprise.

He looked at the evidence of their hard day's work. Across the lightly choppy water, hundreds of clustered barrels bobbed from the shallows on one side of the channel to the other. Some supported a deadly cargo. Beyond the barrels, and even mixed with them where they could, they'd set the posts supporting even more explosives. The minefield looked more impressive than it was, and the first storm that came along would carry it away. Eventually the barrels would leak and the depth charges would sink and detonate without warning. That was one of the main reasons they'd waited so long to prepare the "surprise"; so it would be fresh and ready when the enemy came. He noticed there was a kind of vague pattern to the floating shapes, and it occurred to him the pattern was broken along the side of the channel they were on. It'd be obvious to anybody— especially some Jap lookout in *Amagi*'s top—there was a free pass right through the minefield. The other side looked tight, but that was where they'd deliberately set most of the dummies so *Walker* and the frigates would have a safe path to return. He looked tiredly around. There were still ten depth charges left, but all the barrels on the barges were gone.

"Hey, Bosun," he said, getting Gray's attention. "I think we missed a spot." Before Gray could answer, a growing, clattering drone approached from the southwest. Looking up, they saw the abbreviated outline of the PBY. "Coming back," Silva muttered. "I wonder how far behind our ship is?"

Another drone was approaching. He looked toward *Mahan*, loitering a safe distance from the semicircle the barges had formed, and saw a launch drawing near. A few minutes later it bumped alongside, and Lieutenant Sandison hopped onto the barge carrying a large, canvas-wrapped object in his hands.

"Is this the last of them?" he asked.

"Yes sir," Gray replied.

"All right. I want you to set them all for, oh, say, a hundred and fifty feet; then we'll tie a cable off to one and put it over the side."

"One fifty?" Gray asked, surprised.

"You heard me."

"But the water here's only about eighty feet deep."

"I know. Trust me; you're going to like it." Securing one end of the rope to the barge, they dropped the depth charge attached to the other over the side.

"Now," Sandison instructed, "rig all the rest to slide down the rope so they'll rest together on the bottom. All except one. Chief? I might need your help with this. I'm a torpedo guy, after all."

"Well, I ain't no depth-charge man," Gray growled. "We ought to have Campeti." He paused, pointing, while Sandison unwrapped his object. "What the hell's that?"

"It *used* to be a MK-6, magnetic torpedo exploder. It's the one we took out of that fish we put in *Amagi*—the one that went off. We worked it over, and now it's been redesignated the Silly Six, Sandison Surprise."

"Silly's right. What the hell's it good for?"

"Well, as you can see, there've been a few modifications." He held it up. "First, the contact-exploder mechanism has been entirely removed—leaving just the magnetic trip mechanism . . ."

"Okay."

". . . which is now just a glorified magnetic switch." There was a loud splash behind them as another depth charge rolled over the side. Half a dozen men and Lemurians held the rope taut as it sank. "I will next put the switch back in this waterproof shell canister, with the battle-lantern battery for company. . . ."

"I'll be damned!" Gray muttered, realization dawning.

"Almost certainly," Sandison agreed. "You'll see there're two long wires trailing out of the canister? I want the canister secured tightly to a rope by its handles, the other end of the rope wrapped around the depth charge. Make the distance about sixty-five feet. When you do that, we'll wrap these two wires around the cable—loosely, with lots of slack—until we get to the charge."

"But how are we going to set it off?" Gray asked. "If we try to run those wires in through the hydrostatic fuse, the damn thing'll leak."

Sheepishly, Bernie fished a hand grenade from his pocket. Two more wires ran out of the top where the fuse had been, and it was carefully sealed around them. "I got this from Reavis. He had the duty."

"Why that little . . . !" Silva began, gasping from exertion.

"Don't be too hard on him, Dennis. Spanky gave me a note."

Gray just shook his head. Another heavy splash. "So," he

said, pointing to another object. "What's that? It looks like a big-ass cork."

Sandison nodded. "It's a float for a Lemurian fishing net. Buoyant as hell. I can't remember what they call it; ask one of your guys." He gestured around. "Whatever it is, I think it's 'Cat for 'big-ass cork.' It'll hold our trigger up."

Gray stared, hands on his hips. "You know? If that crazy gizmo works, it'll probably be the first time in the history of the war against the Japs one of those magnetic bastards did anything right."

"Maybe," Sandison agreed; then he pointed to the open lane in the minefield that led to it. "But if it doesn't, we'll have even more reason to curse them—only we probably won't be able to."

Gray nodded as another depth charge splashed over the side. "Yeah. Thank God this ain't the main deal. I'd hate to think everything was riding on it."

Silva stopped heaving on the next depth charge in line and wiped his brow. "What the *hell* do you mean, this ain't the main deal?" he demanded between gasps for air. "We been doin' all this work for a *sideshow*?"

Shortly after 2100 that night, the new construction frigates, USS *Tolson* and USS *Kas-Ra-Ar,* displayed the proper lantern-light recognition signals, and were allowed to pass under the guns of Fort Atkinson. *Mahan* was waiting for them, having returned the barges to the yard. Now she signaled them to heave to and wait for a launch to bring a pilot to take them safely through the minefield. As the ships passed in the night, Jim Ellis saw they'd taken quite a pounding, and though their masts still stood they didn't look new anymore. Of *Walker* and *Donaghey* there was no sign for almost another hour. Finally a flare went up, declaring an emergency, and *Walker* appeared, towing the wallowing, dismasted hulk of Lieutenant Garrett's ship. The launch took Gray across so he could guide the two ships inside the bay. With her searchlights sweeping the surface of the water, the old destroyer picked her way into the clear, where *Tolson* took up the tow so she could move her battered sister to the new fitting-out pier that served the frigates. Reunited with *Mahan*, *Walker* and her own sister steamed back toward the city.

Matt yawned and rubbed his face while Gray sipped the coffee Juan had given him, and finished his report on the mining operation. It sounded like they'd managed a better job than expected. Like Gray, Matt was dubious about the last mine they'd set, but agreed it was worth a try. He thanked the Bosun and leaned back in his chair, stretching his shoulder muscles experimentally. They ached, but not much worse than the rest of him. He thought about how hard it must have been for the detail that set the mines, and imagined they were much sorer than he was. It had been a long day for everyone.

Walker and her little squadron had indeed met the advance enemy force, and Matt now suspected their hundred-ship estimate had been conservative. He also believed they'd engaged the cream of the Grik fleet that day: most of their cannon-armed ships. One had been larger than the others, painted white, just like the curious ship Ben said had grappled with *Revenge*. He wondered what their significance was. He blinked his tired eyes. Not that it mattered as far as this one was concerned: *Walker* had destroyed it, along with as many others as she could, given the restriction Matt had placed on ammunition expenditure. Campeti had tried to destroy mainly gunships, to spare their frigates, but there'd still been plenty to occupy the new ships. *Tolson*, *Kas-Ra-Ar,* and *Donaghey* fought splendidly, savaging their foes with spectacular results—but there'd just been so many.... Lieutenant Garrett, in particular, fought his ship brilliantly—he had the most experience, after all—and maybe a little recklessly too. His ship wound up surrounded, where *Walker* couldn't support her, fighting both sides at point-blank range. It had been a stirring, frustrating scene—the way it must have felt to watch Hawkins hurl himself at the Spanish Armada. In the end, *Donaghey* managed to destroy her tormentors, but Garrett's ship was so badly damaged she might never fight again. Garrett survived—somehow—unscathed, but his sailing master exec, Taak-Fas, was dead, along with almost half his crew. Torpedoman Chapelle, his "master gunner," was lightly wounded.

The battle ended near dark, uncomfortably close to the clustered Balabalangen islands and the bay. The sea was littered with derelict Grik ships, but those that could—about twenty—uncharacteristically fled back the way they'd come, and the destroyer didn't pursue. The enemy retreat was surprising enough, but it was also well coordinated, and that set off warning bells in Captain Reddy's mind. There was no smoke on the horizon that would indicate *Amagi* was near, but he felt the prickly suspicion of a trap nevertheless. It was as if, even as they tried to hold the enemy away, the Grik were attempting to force them back, to shrink their scouting range. Their mission, to prevent the enemy from approaching close enough to discover or interfere with the placement of the minefield, had been accomplished. But the Grik might have accomplished their objective as well, and Matt had to wonder who'd actually won the battle. Mallory flew over several times during the day, but with no radio they had to rely on spotty visual signals. As night fell and his Morse lamp became more visible, Mallory did confirm sighting the main enemy force northeast of Pulau Sebuku, clustered protectively around the battle cruiser. The news wasn't unexpected, although it was dispiriting. Deep down Matt had continued to hope that, given enough time, *Amagi* might still just roll over and sink. For a fleeting instant he had a poignant thought of his father and the scorn he'd have heaped upon such wishful thinking. He sighed.

Wishful thinking wouldn't solve their ammunition problems, either. *Walker* had sortied with another twenty of the "new" shells, reloaded with a solid copper projectile and black powder. As Ellis reported, the projectile worked okay, after a fashion. They went off, and even flew reasonably straight, but with a much lower velocity than the targeting computer was accustomed to, so local control was the only way to go. It also took every one they had to sink six ships. It went without saying that the copper projectiles would be worse than useless against *Amagi*. Sandison hadn't been pleased to learn how the rounds performed when Ellis first told him. He, Garrett, and Campeti had plenty of ideas how to improve them, but they just didn't have the time. They'd have to fight with what they had. He shook his head.

Looking out to starboard, Matt made out *Mahan*'s outline in the dark as the other ship closely paced them. It occurred to him that this was only the second time they'd steamed together since being reunited at Aryaal. That other time was only a brief foray when they'd played tug-of-war for *Mahan*'s propeller. Now, even if they were making only ten knots, Matt felt a sudden exhilaration. The sound of the blowers so close together, and the swish of the sea as they parted it between them, left him with a sense of companionship he'd missed. Jim Ellis was over there, on that other bridge, and Matt wondered what he was thinking. Maybe the same thing. He suddenly wished it were daylight so the people they defended could see the two destroyers steaming side by side in the bay. The sight might bolster their morale—at least until they saw what they were up against.

Without warning, Matt had a chilling premonition that this was the last time *Walker* and *Mahan* would ever be in formation again. As hard as he tried, he couldn't shake the thought. It was as though the swishing sea were a ghostly voice warning the elderly sisters to say their final farewell, because one, at least, was doomed. Which one? he wondered with a heavy heart. Or would both face destruction when *Amagi* steamed into the bay? The moment ended when they neared the dock, and both ships reduced speed. *Mahan* went first to the fueling pier, where her bunkers were quickly filled. Then she moved briefly to the dock, where over half her crew went ashore, leaving fifteen human and twenty Lemurian volunteers aboard—just enough to operate her during the short part she would play. Half her remaining ammunition was off-loaded as well. It had been agreed that *Walker* would need it more than she.

In less than an hour, *Mahan* cast off once more, just as *Walker* was beginning to fuel. As she crept away from the lights on the dock, the jury-rigged Morse lamp on her port bridge wing quickly flashed: "Good hunting. Farewell." Ellis emphasized his message with a long, harsh toot on *Mahan*'s steam whistle.

"Send, 'Good hunting, God bless,'" ordered Matt. While *Walker*'s Morse lamp clacked, he watched *Mahan* fade into darkness, until she was visible no more.

Near the end of the midwatch, Dennis Silva was supervising the transport of vital tools and machinery from the torpedo workshop to their—hopefully—temporary storage, in hardened bunkers ashore. Everything that could be spared—the lathe, mills, cutters and bits, extra torches and acetylene bottles, their meager supply of spare parts—was

being off-loaded . . . just in case. Dowden and a small detail had carried all the ship's papers, logs, charts, manuals,
and other documents ashore a short time earlier. Even the
conduits and bundles of long-bypassed wiring were being
stripped from the ship to save the copper wire. Earl Lanier, Ray Mertz, and Pepper gravely removed the restored
Coke machine themselves. All told, it was a difficult task,
and even though Dennis appreciated the necessity and approved the captain's foresight in ordering it, the implications were ominous and disheartening.

He'd never been so tired. It had been a grueling day, and
even his apparently inexhaustible and irrepressible energy
had limits, it seemed. Laney would soon replace him with
the morning watch, however, and hopefully he'd get a few
hours' sleep. The captain had already told them the morning general quarters alarm wouldn't sound. He stopped
on the pier, shuffling back from the bunker, and looked at
the ship for a moment. She seemed strangely fuzzy in the
humid, hazy air, and ephemeral sparks flew like fireflies
from last-minute repairs. Her weirdly diffused searchlights
beamed eerily downward, illuminating her decks and casting long, twisted shadows. They made her glow like some
unearthly, mournful specter, and completing the surrealistic scene, a lively tune squeaked vaguely from Marvaney's
phonograph. Silva felt a sudden chill, and sensed he was
moving toward his grave. He shuddered.

"She does look rather 'creepy,' as you would say," came
a girlish voice from the gloom, and the mighty Dennis Silva
nearly pissed himself.

"What're you doin' here, goddamn it?" he demanded
more harshly than he meant to.

"I came to see you."

"Me?" He stopped, peering down at Rebecca's tiny
form. "What for? Why ain't you with O'Casey or Lieutenant Tucker?"

"I 'gave them the slip,' and each thinks I am with the
other. Besides, you are my other protector, and I'm perfectly safe."

"Sure, you're safe as can be around here, even without a
watchdog. Least for now. 'Cats are swell folks. But what'd
you wanna see me for?"

Rebecca sighed. "Dennis Silva, you are the most vile,

crude, wildly depraved creature. . . . I never suspected such as you might even exist. The spectacle you made of yourself when we arrived! I would scold you for your shamelessness if I suspected you understood the concept of shame, but somehow"—she took a breath and shook her head—"I have come to care for you . . . to a small degree. I never had a brother, and have always been thankful for it—properly so, it seems—for I find myself thinking of you more and more in that unsettling role. My sense of propriety demands I despise you—and I do!—yet . . . I also find, like a brother, I suppose, I can't help but love you just a bit as well." She grimaced, as if at the foul taste of the words.

Silva cracked. Perhaps it was exhaustion or indigestion, or perhaps some soot from *Walker*'s stacks got in his eyes, but suddenly his face was wet with tears, and he'd gathered the girl in a tight embrace. "I'm a rowdy old scamp," he agreed huskily into her hair. "Can't help it. But I'd be proud to take you on as my little sister, if you make me. Maybe you can teach me a little about that word, 'shame,' you mentioned. Right now, though, you got to run along. I got to get that old ship ready for a fight, and pretty as she is, she's got a quirk or two ol' Silva's got to straighten out."

"You are unloading things from her in case she sinks!" Rebecca cried, suddenly tearful as well.

"Naw, she can't sink. We're just gettin' a buncha loose junk out of the way. You'd be amazed how cluttered a place can get with nothin' but sloppy guys livin' there."

"You're lying. You need me, you and poor Lawrence as well. I can't help but think something dreadful will happen to you both without me to watch over you—and just think how terrified he will be: his first battle, and no one to comfort him. . . . I don't think anyone really likes him, you know."

"I like him, even if he is a lizard," Dennis assured her. "I already said I was sorry for shootin' him."

"It's not the same. I must spend the battle aboard your ship. . . ." She paused, desperate. "You need me! You will need me before the battle is done; I know it!"

"Now, now, little girls underfoot is the last thing we need in a fight. Lieutenant Tucker's gonna need you, though, and that's a fact." He set her down, wiping his eyes. "An' one thing I need you to do, if it comes to it, is tell my gals I love 'em all. Would you do that? It's Pam and Risa. I know you don't approve, but I do love 'em both." He smiled. "And you too, doll . . . I mean . . . sis."

Rebecca burst into tears again, and clung to him like a rock in a confused, breaking sea.

"Now run on. I got stuff to do, or the Griks won't have to get me; the captain will."

"Very well." She sniffed, releasing him. "Please tell Lawrence—"

"I will. So long now."

She watched him turn and walk tiredly—dejectedly, it seemed—to join a group of Lemurians who'd passed them while they spoke, and together they crossed the gangway onto the ship. Still sniffling, Rebecca stood in the shadows for quite a while, looking back and forth. Eventually, convinced there'd be no more arrivals, she strode purposefully in the direction she knew she was supposed to go.

Lieutenant Perry Brister, *Mahan*'s former engineering officer, was standing on the southwest wall of Fort Atkinson before the sun came up. It was dank and humid and totally dark. There was no moon, and the stars were obscured by a heavy, drizzly overcast that had moved in during the night. The fort was entirely exposed to the elements, and there was no higher promontory nearby to protect it from the wind or shade it from the sun. If a Strakka ever directly struck it, the damage would be severe. It did enjoy the highest elevation for miles around, strangely enough, and the best view of the strait. It was strange, because, like other little geographic things now and then, Perry didn't remember the elevation on the point where the fort was constructed being quite this high in "the old world." He wasn't complaining, but it often struck him as odd. Everyone always said the planet was the same, just everything living on it was different. That wasn't always the case, according to Bradford's "ice age" theory, and Perry agreed that whatever was responsible for all the big differences probably had something to do with the little ones too. Whatever the reason, Fort Atkinson was a lot better situated than it would have been built on the same stretch of ground back home.

He fiddled nervously with his binoculars. He wanted to raise them and take a look, but it was too early for that. By doing so, he'd only confirm his unease to the defenders gathered nearby. He cleared his throat and clasped his hands behind his back.

"Good morning, Mr. Bris-terr," greeted Muln-Rolak from the gloom. The elderly Lemurian held two cups of "coffee." His English was still barely understandable, but Brister had become fairly fluent in 'Cat. He replied in that language.

"Morning, Lord Rolak," he said, accepting one of the cups. He looked curiously at the other. "I thought you guys didn't like this stuff. Only use it for medicine?"

Rolak chuffed. "I need medicine today."

Perry nodded. He took a tentative sip and grimaced. "If bad taste is the measure of an effective dose, this stuff ought to cure you."

"I need it to wake me up," Rolak confessed. "I didn't sleep well last night." He scratched at an eye with one of his clawed fingers. "I've been a warrior all my life, and have fought many battles." He blinked. "I've not always won, but I've usually enjoyed myself—and I always survived. Until the Grik came to Aryaal, I never faced the fear that I might not." He uttered a grunting laugh. "Now I face that fear every day." Subconsciously, Perry was fingering the binoculars again. Rolak gestured around them. "These warriors feel it too. All of them. They wouldn't be sane if they didn't." He made a coughing sound that passed for a wistful sigh. "This is not a fun war." He glanced ruefully at Brister and pointed at the binoculars. "So take a look if it makes you feel better. I doubt anyone will notice."

Perry felt himself blushing. "You did," he said.

Rolak blinked with humor. "But that is because I am drinking coffee."

Slowly the sky began to brighten, and nervous, eager eyes stared hard at the strait. The sun would rise behind them—at least that was the same—so there'd be no silhouettes. They'd have to wait until the sun actually illuminated the water below.

"I see them!" came a shout, and Perry did look then. He squinted hard through the binoculars and adjusted them with his thumb.

"Where?!" he shouted in reply.

"Right *there*!"

He quickly looked up and saw a 'Cat pointing down toward the very mouth of the bay, and he jerked the glasses back to his face.

"My God."

The squiggles he'd seen and written off as wave tops suddenly resolved themselves into scores of ships packed impossibly close. He'd been looking mostly at the horizon, beginning to emerge. Looking too far. The thing he'd dreaded to see in the distance was already *here*.

"Load your guns!" he shouted at the top of his voice. "Batteries A, B, and C! Remember your training, and choose your targets!" He snatched a bleary-eyed 'Cat who'd appeared behind him. It was one of his runners. "Quick, to the semaphore tower! Have them fire the flare to signal the city the attack has begun!" He turned back to the front. Beside him was one of the massive thirty-two-pounder guns, resting on a naval carriage like the ones they'd developed for the Homes. The weapon's crew was in the final stage of preparing it to fire. A gunner poured priming powder into and on the vent, and another 'Cat stood ready with a smoldering linstock. Perry looked at Rolak and shook his head with frustration. Then, tilting it back, he opened his mouth.

"Commence firing!"

Matt raced to the bridge, still tucking in his shirt. For once he hadn't bothered to shave. In the distance, through the windows, he saw stabbing flashes of fire as the guns of Fort Atkinson hurled their missiles down upon the still-unseen targets below. He felt and heard a deep, shuddering thunder, and the glass panes in the pilothouse rattled with each report.

"Sound general quarters! Tell Mr. McFarlane to light off number two. Where's Gray? Pass the word: single-up all lines, and prepare to get underway!"

Campeti relayed the commands into the talker's headset. Reynolds had gone to the head, and he raced back up the ladder and snatched the set from Campeti's hand.

"Sorry, sir," he mumbled. Matt didn't even notice. He was still issuing orders.

"Signal Mr. Alden—send a runner too—and make sure HQ's aware the attack's underway!"

"Aye, aye, Captain."

Chief Gray was heard on the foredeck, bellowing at the line handlers.

"What's our pressure?"

"Two hundred pounds on three and four, Captain. All night long," Campeti quickly replied. "Just as ordered."

"Very well."

Suddenly there was a bright flash of light in the mouth of the bay, and burning debris soared high.

"Whoo-ee!" shouted Norman Kutas, standing behind the wheel. "Something just blew the hell up!"

"Quiet on the bridge!"

"Captain," came Reynolds's voice, "all stations report manned and ready, except torpedoes! Mr. Sandison has placed his division at the Bosun's disposal—except the smoke generators, and they're manned and ready."

"Very well. Cast off all lines."

Juan Marcos appeared on the bridge, accompanied by a haggard Lieutenant Garrett. Instead of the usual carafe, Juan held a large, wrapped bundle in his hands.

"Mr. Garrett, what are you doing here?" Captain Reddy demanded.

"Sir," Garrett replied formally, "my command is incapacitated, out of the fight. I've moved her to a safe anchorage—I hope—and request permission to resume my previous post here, for the duration of this action."

Matt glanced at Campeti, who shrugged.

"No complaints from me, Skipper. He's a better gunnery officer than I am. 'Sides, we might need more than one before this is over."

"Very well, Mr. Garrett, you have my permission." Matt looked at Juan. "What are you here for?"

"I promised to bring you this, Cap-tan," he replied with quiet dignity. "Lieutenant Tucker sent it out a short while ago. I did not want to wake you."

Matt began to send Juan away, but something in the steward's manner made him reconsider. Instead he took the bulky package and curiously peeked under the folds. He blinked in surprise and glanced back at Juan, a soft look of wonder on his face.

"Lieutenant Tucker commissioned it," Juan explained. "She said you once told her we had seen such a thing, and you admired it greatly. The one who made it would take no payment."

"That was . . . generous," Matt said huskily. Gingerly he

handed the package to Garrett. "Have this run up, if you please. On the foremast halyard."

Pete Alden was on the balcony of the Great Hall again, but this time with a far larger group: official gawkers, for the most part, who should have been at their posts. In spite of all their preparations, the attack had come so swiftly and unexpectedly, a measure of confusion was inevitable. Letts was shouting for them to disperse. From Alden's perch, much of the mouth of the bay was obscured by the south headland, and even as the day began to brighten and the overcast burned away, he could see only the mast tops of the enemy ships. It reminded him of a forest of toothpicks. Fort Atkinson was invisible as well behind a shroud of dense white smoke gouting continuously from the active guns and drifting lazily toward the city. It was accompanied by a constant rumbling sound. *It must be hell for the gunners*, he thought: gasping and choking and going deaf in the dense, sulfurous haze. He didn't know how they could even see their targets. Somehow they could, evidently, because even as he watched, another geyser of flames erupted among the clustered masts.

"The fort's really pounding them," Letts observed beside him. Most of the gawkers had finally fled, although Pete saw many Lemurians still crowding the nearby dwellings, trying to catch their first glimpse of the enemy.

"Not hard enough," Pete growled, pointing at the part of the bay they could see. A phalanx of Grik Indiamen had appeared around the headland.

"They'll be in the minefield soon," said Letts. "Too soon. Do you think it'll stop them?"

Pete shrugged. "It might slow them down. Bunch them up. That'll give the fort more time to hammer their flank."

"Look!" cried Nakja-Mur, pointing westward, toward the middle of the bay. Under the brightening sky, *Walker* lanced across the placid water at a flat sprint. Gray smoke streamed aft from three of her rusty funnels, and white water curled from her bow beneath the proud, faded numbers and churned along her side. She was rust blotched and streaked, and all the patches and welds gave her once-sleek hull a leprous look, even at the distance from which they viewed her. But her sad, frail appearance wasn't nearly enough to offset the impression of bold determination she managed to affect. Straight out behind her high foremast, brilliant and new in the first rays of the sun, streamed a huge American flag. Alden raised his glasses and saw words embroidered on the broad stripes: *Makassar Strait, 1st Java Sea, Escape from Surabaya, 2nd Java Sea (Salissa), The Stones, B'mbaado Bay, Aryaal,* and simply *Nerracca.* The names of *Walker*'s major actions.

"Now, isn't that just the damnedest thing you ever saw?" Letts managed to say. Pete only nodded. With the size of the lump in his throat, he didn't trust himself to speak.

Another, different rumbling boom came from across the bay. They watched a dirty gray upheaval of water and debris gush skyward from among the leading Grik ships. The red-painted hull directly over the explosion lifted bodily into the air, breaking its back. It sank quickly beneath the settling spray. Several ships nearby looked mortally damaged, and masts plummeted into the sea or fouled other ships as they listed.

"It worked!" Letts shouted, clapping his hands. "My God, what a mess!" Nakja-Mur clasped his paws together in a gesture of thanks.

"Yeah," muttered Alden, "but they're still pushing through. Look at those coming up behind. They're not even stopping for survivors!"

Letts nodded, his joy draining away. "The captain—and everybody with the AEF, for that matter—told me the Grik show no concern at all for losses. I guess I didn't really believe it. Only at the end of the Battle for Aryaal, when all was lost, did they finally break."

"It's like they think they're winning, no matter what, as long as they're on the attack," Pete agreed, remembering Bradford's observations. Another depth-charge mine exploded, causing similar destruction to the first. The Grik sailed inexorably forward. *Walker* was nearer the enemy now, well within range of her guns. She slowed to a near halt short of the minefield and turned to port, presenting a three-gun broadside. Four, if one counted the three-inch gun on the fantail. In this instance, even it would have effect.

"She's at point-blank range!" Letts said excitedly. "She can't possibly miss from there, even with the new shells!"

With simultaneous puffs of white smoke, *Walker* opened fire. Copper bolts slashed into the approaching ships near their waterlines. Another mine detonated, and more Grik ships and warriors were swept away. The entire center of the enemy advance had been thrown into disarray by the mines and the lonely four-stacker with the huge, streaming flag. Fort Atkinson continued its uncontested slaughter as well, firing down into the ships that waited to push forward. The semaphore tower was barely visible through the smoke, but a runner arrived with a hasty report. Brister had sent that many of the heavy copper balls were crashing completely through and out the bottoms of their victims, and the closer reaches of the entrance to the bay were clotted with settling hulks. In spite of the initial uncertainty, it looked like the battle was under control.

Another runner appeared, her yellow eyes wide and blinking with excitement and fright. "The Grik are landing on the south coast, east of the fort!" she gasped. "*Amagi* has been sighted to the south, accompanied by another large force!"

"Very well," Pete replied without inflection, but his chest tightened with the news. *Under control, my ass,* he thought. *It hasn't even started yet.* He turned to Letts and Nakja-Mur. "I ought to be down on the south wall, the way things are shaping up."

Letts shook his head. "Not yet, Sergeant. The landing in the south might be a feint." Alden raised a skeptical eyebrow. He didn't believe the Grik were that subtle. "Even if it's not," Letts persisted, "sooner or later they're going to get past *Walker.* She doesn't have the ammunition to hold them forever. When that happens, it might get hairy on the waterfront in a hurry. The only way you can be two places at once is if you're right here, where you can direct all the defenses." He shook his head again, apologetically, looking at the man almost twice his age. "But you're the Marine. I'm just a supply officer."

A rueful grin spread across Alden's face as he looked at the fair-skinned . . . kid, in front of him. "You're right. I *am* a Marine, and this standing around is kind of tough to do. But you're not just a supply officer anymore; you're the god-damn chief of staff!" His eyes twinkled. "So the next time I start to go off half-cocked, just keep yankin' my leash!"

*   *   *

Perry Brister could barely talk. His voice was hoarse, and his throat hurt from all the yelling. Not that it mattered to most of the crews manning the big guns on the south and west sides of the fort; they were probably deaf as posts by now, and no longer needed his direction anyway. Their task was simple, if physically exhausting. As long as there were Grik ships below, they'd keep blasting them apart. They couldn't get them all, of course—there were just too many—but there was no question the Grik knew they were in a fight. As the supply of ready ammunition dwindled, and more had to be brought from the magazines, their rate of fire inevitably fell off, and an ever-increasing number of the enemy slipped through the gauntlet of fire. Also, the guns of the fort simply wouldn't reach clear across the mouth of the bay, and the enemy seemed to have realized that at last. More and more hugged the distant shore. Still, the slaughter Fort Atkinson had worked so far was beyond anything Brister had expected, and the sea frothed with flashies around the burning, sinking ships.

Brister's most pressing concern, however, was what was taking place on the other side of the fort. Scores of small boats plied to and fro between half a hundred Grik ships and the shore. The guns on that side were smaller than those facing the sea—twelve-pounders—and were emplaced to defend against a landward assault. So far they'd been silent. Now those that would bear began firing at the boats full of warriors as they neared the beach. The range was extreme, and they had almost no chance of hitting the anchored ships, but an occasional lucky shot spilled a score or more Grik into the deadly surf. In spite of that, a truly terrifying number of the enemy had begun assembling onshore, their garish banners flapping overhead.

"Look!" cried Lord Rolak, pointing. A peninsula of the thick, impenetrable jungle running east and west between the coast and Baalkpan City had been spared the axes of the defenders, all the way up to the Fort Atkinson road. On the other side of the road, across a wide avenue allowing the movement of troops, as well as visual communications between the city and the fort, an isolated island of vegetation called the Clump had been allowed to remain. Now, as intended, the jungle acted as a formidable obstacle preventing a rapid advance from that direction. The only clear avenue of approach lay through a narrow gap between the jungle and the fort itself. What aroused Rolak's attention was the disciplined column of Lemurian troops marching up the road out of the drifting haze.

Even as Brister raised his glasses, he saw a battery of four field pieces manhandled forward of the column, deploying in the gap. He felt a surge of sympathy for the gunners. The only large domestic animals the local Lemurians used were the pygmy "brontosauruses." They were ideal for leisurely, long-distance transportation of heavy burdens, including artillery, but wholly unsuited to rapid tactical maneuvers. They were surprisingly quick in a sprint, but had no endurance. Besides, they were difficult to control. When frightened or confused, they were at least as dangerous to their owners as to the enemy. Rolak told him Aryaal had maintained a small number of them as warbeasts, and Captain Reddy himself had actually ridden one into battle. Perry was skeptical, and even Rolak admitted they weren't much good for anything beyond mobile observation points. In any event, he wished there were some local equivalent of a horse. By the time the guns were in position, their sizable crews were clearly winded.

"Cease firing on the boats!" Brister croaked. "Target the concentration on the beach!"

"Perhaps we should hold fire until they are closer?" Rolak suggested. "I believe the main assembly area is nearly a thousand tails distant."

"Yeah. But they're so bunched up, all we have to do is shoot in among them. We'll get a few with every shot—even with solid shot. Maybe it'll make 'em think."

"I doubt it," Rolak remarked. "It's gratifying to slay them even at such a great distance, however."

"Sure is. The farther the better."

North of their position, Major Shinya's force began deploying from column into line, a short distance behind the guns. At the sight of them the Grik on the beach uttered a collective ululating shriek and surged toward the gap, even while others continued landing behind them. "Here they come," Brister breathed.

"I agree completely with your previous statement," Lord Rolak remarked. "Farther was better." He stepped back from the wall and drew his long, curved sword. "First Aryaal! Sularan volunteers! Stand to!"

The devastation and slaughter on the bay was beyond incredible. The minefield had worked better than anyone hoped, and flames leaped high and spread from ship to ship. The debris and shattered timbers were so dense in the water, Matt was becoming concerned for *Walker's* screws as she cruised slowly back and forth, firing into the mass of enemies. *Tolson* and *Kas-Ra-Ar* had finally joined the destroyer and added their guns to the massacre. The entire center of the Grik advance had ground to a halt. Dozens of ships were hopelessly entangled and had created a massive blockage in the channel. Only a few of these carried cannons, and their return fire was wild and desultory. So far, *Walker* and her consorts had suffered only superficial damage. Occasionally enemy firebombs arced out of the wreckage of ships, but the American squadron stayed beyond their range. The effort to use the things was far more dangerous to the Grik themselves. Matt was bitterly convinced that, with enough ammunition, his little squadron could stop this prong of the invasion all by itself.

They didn't have enough, however. All the new copper bolts they'd taken aboard last night had been expended, and they'd dipped dangerously into their reserve of high-explosive shells. They'd discovered their star shells were highly effective against the wooden hulls of the enemy, able to penetrate and then set them afire when they burst. But they had only about ten salvos left, and they might need them for illumination when darkness fell. There were still a fair number of armor-piercing rounds in the magazines, but they'd been even less effective than the copper bolts against wooden-hulled ships. They just punched a four-inch hole in one side and out the other, and almost never exploded. It was better to save them for later. Riflemen and machine gunners fired at the barrels floating among the enemy ships. Many were decoys, of course, and a lot of ammunition was wasted sinking them. Silva tried to remember which ones were which, and concentrated only on those he felt sure supported a depth charge. Occasionally he was rewarded by a resounding blast and another expanding column of debris and spray.

The center, for the moment, was secure. The chaos and frustration there had become so intense, Grik could be seen actually fighting *one another* from ship to ship. It was on the flanks that things were getting out of hand. Ship after ship managed to squirm past the blockage and make its way into the clear. Some fell victim to the shallow water mines, but others got through. On the east side of the bay they came under the guns lining the southern waterfront, and a terrible destruction was heaped upon them. Regardless of losses, the Grik bored in, literally running their ships aground on the open beach between the Clump and the southwest wall of the city. Even as the warriors leaped into the surf and were shredded by the terrible fish, mortar bombs fell on the ships and set them ablaze. And *still* they came. What was more, an increasing number of the enemy were making it ashore. Whether because there were just so many of them or the carnivorous fish were strutted with their flesh was impossible to say. Whatever the reason, the road to Fort Atkinson was in growing danger of being cut.

Matt couldn't do anything about that. If *Walker* moved closer to the waterfront, not only would she interfere with the gunnery from the city wall, but she risked accidental damage herself. Steel or not, the old destroyer's thin skin wouldn't stop a thirty-two-pound ball. She could do something about the Grik squeezing through the open lane in the channel, near the west side of the bay, however. Signaling the two frigates to hold where they were, she altered course and sprinted in that direction. An agonized, droning noise rose over the sound of the blower, and the PBY flashed by overhead, a depth charge slung beneath each wing, set to detonate at its minimum depth. *Just one more flight*, Matt hoped fervently as she passed. *Just one more* . . . With luck, Mallory would continue to contribute to the devastation in the center, while *Walker* raced to secure the flank.

With the snarling, hissing sound of a raging sea, the mass of Grik warriors crashed against the shield wall of the Second Marines and the Tenth Baalkpan, deployed across the gap. Still more lapped against the base of Fort Atkinson itself. Sheets of arrows and bounding round shot had torn at them as they charged, and still they came. At three hundred yards, canister and grape from the field battery, as well as the fort, scythed down great gaping swaths of the berserker horde, and still they came. Crossbow bolts and arrows from both sides passed one another in midair, to drive home in shields and flesh. With their smaller, less effective shields, the Grik were savaged by this final fusillade, but even then they didn't falter. The clash of shields, the shrieks and screams, the bellowed curses, and the ring of weapons merged into a single cacophonous thunderclap of sound when the armies came together. The Lemurian line sagged in two places: first in the center, where the heaviest blow fell, where the walls of the Marines and the Guards came together. Second was at the point where the Guard right was anchored to the fort. Shinya bolstered the center by wading into the fight with his own guards and staff. It was, effectively, the only reserve he had. The pressure on the right was relieved when the two hundred Sularans under Lord Rolak's command sortied from the fort behind the line, and drove a wedge into the brief gap the Grik had created.

Shinya's modified cutlass parried and slashed across the top of the shield in front of him. Gaping jaws clamped down and tried to wrench it away, and a spear wielded by one of his staff drove into the top of the creature's head. Tamatsu crouched down and slashed beneath the shield at feet and ankles on the other side as the wall began to stabilize. His wrist jarred painfully when the blade struck bone, and he was rewarded by a muted wail. A foot slammed down on his sword, pinning it to the ground. With all his strength he twisted the blade and wrenched it back, sharp side up. If there was a scream that time, it was drowned by others. His arms were already throbbing with pain. His left was in the shield straps, and the unending blows were starting to be felt. The awkward angle at which he was using his sword sent fire into his right chest and shoulder. The initial defiant yelling of the Lemurians had all but stopped, to be replaced by the panting and grunting of disciplined troops holding the wall, and heaving against the weight of ten times their number. Their only words were cries of instruction or encouragement to those behind, and the spears of the second rank remorselessly thrust and jabbed.

"Major Shinya!" came a cry behind Tamatsu. He spared a glance in that direction and saw an American shoulder his way through the second line. Without another word, the man rested the muzzle of a BAR atop Shinya's shield and held the trigger down for a magazine's burst, sweeping it back and forth. Then he dragged someone forward to take Tamatsu's place. "C'mon, sir! You got more important shit to do!"

Without resisting, and still a little numbed by the fighting and the close report of the automatic rifle, Shinya allowed himself to be dragged out of the wall. Behind the spearmen, he looked at the sailor. He'd seen him before, he supposed, but they'd never met.

He'd called him sir.

"What are you doing here, ah . . ."

"Torpedoman First Russ Chapelle. USS *Mahan*, originally. *Donaghey* now." He had to scream to be heard over the roar of battle. "I said I was bored, and Alden sent me and Flynn and some of his sub pukes up the Fort Road. I'm such a dumb ass. We barely made it! Lizards is landin' hand over fist!"

Flynn joined him, panting. "God, what a snafu! Except there's nothin' 'normal' about *this* situation! Captain Reddy wasn't kiddin' when he said he'd pulled us out of a fryin' pan just to throw us in a fire!"

Shinya whirled and looked at the hell below the fort, but couldn't see beyond the Clump to tell what was happening to the north. "I left Ramic and his warriors from *Aracca* to guard that approach," he insisted.

Russell nodded. "They're moving up here. There's nothing they could do. Goddamn lizards took us by surprise—started runnin' their ships right up on the beach. Ol' Ramic never even had a chance to deploy."

"We're completely cut off?"

"Looks that way. There's no way back to the city with the lizards between us and there. If we hit 'em in the rear we might get through, but the Baalkpan guns would have to quit shooting or risk hitting us." He shrugged and pointed past the shield wall, beyond the fighting and screaming and blood. "Besides, I don't think they're gonna let us disengage."

Shinya agreed. His eyes flitted back and forth, between the fort, his own force, and the road. Ramic's column was approaching at the double-quick. Individually, the warriors from *Aracca* Home couldn't have looked less like soldiers, with their multicolored pelts and bright kilts, but together the *Aracca* regiment moved like the crack veteran infantry they were. "All right then, Torpedoman Chapelle, Chief Flynn," he said with a sharp nod. "This is what we're going to do. . . ."

Some of Shinya's staff managed to extricate themselves from the fighting and gathered around. Several were bleeding. Ramic hurried up, gasping for breath. He seemed oblivious to the swarms of crossbow bolts falling around him until he got behind the protection of the shield wall.

"I'm sorry," he said simply. "I had no choice but to join you here."

Shinya nodded. *Nobody* hated the Grik more than Ramic—not after the loss of *Nerracca* and his son. If there was anything he could have done to prevent the landing, he would have. Tamatsu was just glad Ramic hadn't sacrificed himself and his warriors in a hopeless attempt. "Of course," Shinya said. "Now, as soon as you shake out of column, the *Aracca*s will directly reinforce the shield wall. Relieve as much pressure as you can."

"Yes! We *must* hold here!" Ramic agreed. The others nodded, but Tamatsu sighed.

"Impossible. We have only three regiments. If we had twice that, and the rifle company, we could hold forever, no matter what the Grik send against us—but the troops weary already." He shrugged. "And the rifle company is in reserve in the city. We'll bleed them awhile yet, but then we must fall back on the fort. The left flank will begin to collapse backward, refusing the flank as it does." He looked at them nervously. "I know we've never practiced anything remotely like this, but the Tenth did very much the same against the walls of Aryaal, so I know we can do it. The Grik will try to get around the flank as it moves, and we must not allow that." A crossbow bolt skated off his helmet, and he shook his head irritably. "We'll pull the guns out of the line to cover our flank. Hopefully the pressure will ease when we no longer block the road."

"Yes." Ramic snorted. "We will have opened the gate to their objective!"

Shinya looked at him. "Perhaps. But our new objective must be the preservation of the fort so it can remain a thorn in their side." He gestured at the bay. "Perhaps you've not seen, U-Amaki, Ramic-Sa-Ar! Fort Atkinson has already avenged *Nerracca* manyfold!"

Ramic blinked his rage and suppressed frustration, and replied through clenched teeth, "My revenge won't be complete until the Grik are *extinct*, and the iron ship that aids them lies at the bottom of the sea!"

Nakja-Mur was numbed to silence. So great was his shock over what he beheld, he'd been unable to speak for some time. He still stood beside Letts and Alden, and outwardly he was calm, but his claws dug deep furrows in the balcony rail. The slaughter was incredible—and so utterly alien. As he told his companions earlier, he'd received training as a warrior in his youth, but Baalkpan had forever been at peace. He'd known, theoretically, that he might one day have to fight, but the possibility seemed so remote he'd never truly contemplated what war might be like. The training sessions were viewed as rough, structured play by himself and his young companions, and little more than a way to vent excess energy by his parents. Now he saw war for the very first time, and the scale and scope and violence of it all were appalling.

The nature of the enemy added yet another dimension to the overall horrific effect. They came as inexorably as the tide, entirely oblivious to loss. Baalkpan Bay was a cauldron of destruction and fire, and the air was thick with choking smoke that completely blocked the midday sun. *Kas-Ra-Ar* was burning, and *Tolson* stood by, collecting her crew and spitting hate at the tangled swarm threatening to overwhelm her. *Walker* couldn't be seen, and if not for regular reports from the magical crystal receivers, they'd have no idea if she even yet lived. Beyond the southwest wall, more and more Grik streamed ashore. Propelled by the freshening breeze, they deliberately crashed their ships onto the beach. That was yet another act entirely alien to Nakja-Mur, and one even his American friends hadn't foreseen.

The Grik that made it to the beach were destroyed as effortlessly as insect pests by the cannons, arrows, and mortars of his people. Even from his distant perch, he saw their mangled corpses lying in dark, grotesque heaps. Yet still they came. Driven by some incomprehensible, maniacal madness, the Grik forged through the storm. There were just too many to stop them all. It was like holding back the sea with a fishnet. He caught occasional glimpses of a sizable force through the haze, beginning to assemble in the jungle cut on the Fort Atkinson road. Beyond that, the fort itself was invisible through the smoke.

Nakja-Mur looked at his human companions. He was still unable to judge their emotions by the confusing face moving that they did. A grin was a grin, and a snarl was a snarl, but their eyes—so expressive among his own people—told him nothing. And, of course, they didn't have tails. The tension in their unmoving stance was clear enough, however. Suddenly, even over the tumult, they heard a deeper, prolonged rumble. It was more like an earthquake or distant volcanic blast than anything else he could imagine. They glanced at one another uneasily. A different female runner approached them. "The road is cut!" she cried in near panic.

"Calm, child!" Nakja-Mur soothed, none too calm himself—at least inwardly. "You must not show fear, lest it spread to those around you!"

The young female lowered her eyes and blinked. "Of course. I am shamed."

"Not at all!" Nakja-Mur retorted. "Now, what is your message?"

"Tower one reports a signal from the fort: Major Shinyaa has withdrawn within its walls. His force is mostly intact, and they continue to engage the enemy, but the landing force is free to move on the city. The fort is under heavy attack, but Lew-ten-aant Brister believes they can hold for now."

"Did they estimate the size of the landing force?" Alden demanded.

The runner nodded, eyes wide. "Sixteen to twenty thousands—but the landings continue."

"Very well—thanks." He turned to the others. "As soon as they join the ones in the cut, they'll probably come right at us."

"You don't think they'll wait for further reinforcements?" Letts asked.

Pete shook his head. "Not their style. The first try, anyway. I think now it *is* time for me to go."

Letts nodded. "By all means."

"What of the threat from the bay?" Nakja-Mur asked nervously.

"You two will have to handle it. The defenses are stronger there, and the lizards'll have to land right in their teeth. It'll be very difficult to consolidate their force. They already have in the south. I think that's where the main threat lies."

Alden turned back to the runner. "First Marines, Fifth Baalkpan and Queen Maraan's Six Hundred will prepare to advance to support the south wall."

"Reserves already?" Letts asked.

Pete shook his head. "Do the math. The First Baalkpan and the few Manila volunteers are all we have on the south wall. That's about twelve hundred, counting artillery. There's no way they can stand against twenty or thirty thousand. I wish the rest of the Manila troops had arrived in time! We'll pull the Second Aryaal off the north wall and add them to the central reserve." He cocked his head to one side when the strange thundering sound resumed. Realization struck.

"Son of a bitch! *Amagi* must be in range. She's shelling the fort!"

⸻

"Thank you, Lieutenant Brister," said Shinya between deep, ragged breaths. "You timed that perfectly, I believe."

Brister waved his hand and grated, barely above a whisper, "Your withdrawal was what was perfect. I never would have believed it."

Shinya had to strain to hear him. "We lost two of the field pieces," he brooded. "Their crews managed to spike them, but . . ." He shook his head. "It was that double load of canister from each of your guns just as we came over the wall that kept them off us long enough to re-form."

"Later you may admire each other's prowess," Rolak growled tersely. His own part in the successful maneuver had not been inconsiderable. "Right now there is still a great battle underway."

The fighting along the north and west walls of the fort was

still fierce, but the pressure was easing. It was as if, sensing greater prey ahead, the majority of the Grik were content to leave the fort isolated and continue their push toward the city. Beyond the fighting on the wall, the seething mass sluiced through the gap and down the road. Midage younglings scurried behind the lines, distributing bundles of arrows. Guns barked, spraying their deadly hail into the flank of the mass, mowing great swaths through the rampaging mob, but for all the attention the bulk of the enemy paid them, they may as well not have bothered. "Cut off and bottled up," Chapelle grimly observed.

Brister's runner returned. "The message got through," he announced with evident relief. "The tower confirmed receipt."

"At least Baalkpan knows what's coming." Brister sighed hoarsely.

A high-pitched, deepening shriek forced its way above the din. It sounded like a dozen locomotives barreling directly toward them with their whistles wide open.

"Holy Christ!" Perry blurted, eyes going wide. "I forgot about the Japs!" He threw himself to the ground. Even as he fell upon it, the earth rushed up to meet him and the overpressure of titanic detonations drove the air from his lungs. Clods of dirt, jagged splinters, and various debris rained down, and a heavy weight fell across his back. For a moment he could only lie there, trying to draw a breath. Finally he succeeded, but the air was filled with chalky dust, despite the damp night before, and he coughed involuntarily. The weight came off and he was dragged to his feet. Chapelle's face appeared before him, looking intently into his eyes. Then it disappeared. Brister shook his head, trying to clear it, and looked around.

A smoking crater was less than forty yards away, and bodies were scattered in all directions. One belonged to the runner who'd just spoken, and most of his head and part of his shoulder had simply disappeared, as if a super lizard had snatched a bite. Another shell had landed on top of the north wall, leaving a big gap surrounded by dazed and broken troops. He wondered why the Grik weren't already pouring through, and lurched toward the wall and climbed to the top. "Form up! Form up!" he rasped over and over to those standing near. He doubted they could hear him. Even to himself he sounded as if he were shouting through a pillow. Rolak joined him, clutching his bloodied left arm to his side, and together they stared beyond the wall.

Ironically, most of the shells had fallen on the Grik. More smoking craters, surrounded by dripping gobbets of steaming flesh and shattered bone, formed a rough semicircle beyond the fort, extending about two hundred yards into the gap. Many of the enemy closest to the impact points were stunned into motionlessness, while others tried to force their way back through the press in panic. Those were mercilessly slaughtered.

"That's something to see," Brister muttered. "Panicked lizards."

"Understandable under the circumstances," Rolak agreed. "But few seem affected."

"Yeah. But remember Bradford's theory, and the way they acted at the Battle of Aryaal—you were there! When they were suddenly and unexpectedly attacked by overwhelming force, they flipped."

Rolak nodded.

"Interesting. Friendly fire indeed," Brister mused. He looked at Rolak. "Shinya?"

"Alive. He ran toward the west wall to see what damage there was. A Jaap bomb fell there."

More shells began to fall.

"Quick!" Brister grabbed Rolak, and together they tumbled into the crater in the wall. Several defenders fell in on top of them, just as massive explosions pounded the fort again. Only one shell fell among the Grik this time. Brister brushed away debris and peered out of the hole. Most of the enemy were drawing back from the fort. In spite of the terrible damage they'd taken, they knew what *Amagi*'s true target was. Perry was up and running.

"Where are we going?" the old Lemurian asked, struggling to keep up.

"They're trying to silence our guns! I have to make sure they think they have; otherwise they really will!" They came to a stop near the center of the fort to find the signal tower shattered.

"Damn!" Brister swore. He ran toward the west wall again. "Cease firing, cease firing!" he shouted with his damaged voice. He could see one of his guns already destroyed.

Another tearing-canvas shriek sent everyone to the dirt this time. The concussion was so great it literally hurled him onto his back. Gasping, he sat up. With everything left to him, he shouted at the top of his lungs, even while debris was still in the air.

"Cease firing!"

With unspeakable gratitude he heard the command repeated, and the surviving crews stepped haltingly, dazedly from their guns. Another was wrecked by the most recent salvo.

"What are you doing?" Shinya demanded harshly, suddenly standing before him. "If you think you can surrender—"

"Surrender, hell!" Brister somehow managed. "*Amagi* doesn't want to waste shells on us! She's only trying to knock out our guns! If she thinks she's succeeded, she'll leave us alone!"

Shinya crossed his arms in front of him, face very stern. "This fort has a mission! You cannot accomplish it by hiding from the enemy! Lieutenant Brister, I had thought much more highly—"

Perry scrambled to his feet. "Now listen to me, you Jap bastard . . . !" he croaked.

Lord Rolak and Russ Chapelle managed to keep them apart.

"What have you in mind?" Rolak asked in a reasonable tone.

"Listen!"

"What?"

"Just listen! What do you hear?" Brister walked to the wall beside one of the guns and peered over it. In the middle distance *Amagi* was clearly visible, surrounded by her grotesque brood.

"What do you hear?" Rolak asked, and Brister sighed.

"Nothing. It worked. They've stopped." For the moment the only sounds were the screams of the wounded, the crackling of fires, and the surflike noise of the Grik flowing past the wall. He pointed at the bay for Shinya's benefit. "Look down there. We've sunk everything in range! Nothing else can even come into this part of the bay without running onto the wreckage of their friends. The battery's done all it can! Despite all our shooting, the enemy's getting past us now by hugging the far shoreline. That's *not* in range, although the guys have been giving it hell. If we keep firing, all it'll accomplish is to get us slaughtered." He paused and looked at their faces. "Together, counting my gunners, we have close to three thousand troops in this fort. We may all die anyway, but I have an idea that might make it more worthwhile than just standing and getting pasted."

A shout rose up from the other side of the fort.

"It would seem our friends are preparing to return," Rolak stated dryly.

"Swell. Can the guns on *that* side of the fort keep firing?" Chapelle asked.

"God, I hope so," answered Brister. "Just don't shoot at the bay anymore!"

"I still don't know what you hope to accomplish by this!" Shinya hissed low, as they trotted back across the center of the fort.

"Maybe nothing," Brister replied. "Maybe everything."

Pete Alden's new forward command post occupied a multistory dwelling belonging to one of Baalkpan's more affluent textile merchants. Like many of her class, she hadn't originally been a member of the "run away" party, but she'd joined it quickly enough when *Fristar* abandoned the defenders. Pete didn't care. All that mattered was that the dwelling afforded an excellent view of the entire south wall. The enemy facing it continued to swell far beyond the initial force that landed north of the Clump and occupied the fort road. Ever since the fort was cut off, thousands upon thousands of lizards had poured through the gap, up the road, and out through the cut, where they deployed into a mile-wide front with their backs to the jungle. Round shot bounded through their ranks from across the killing field the People had cut with such effort. Each shot killed some of the enemy, plowing through their densely packed ranks, but the fire had a negligible real effect. Pete thought it was probably good for the gunners' morale, though, faced as they were with what stood before them. If the Baalkpan defenders had a wealth of anything, it was powder and shot for their guns. Let them shoot.

He'd have been happy to let the mortars fire as well, and they might have wreaked some real havoc, but they didn't

have as many of the bombs, and the range was a little far—
for now. His reserve mortar teams were rushing from the
center of the city, and when they arrived he'd have thirty
of the heavy bronze tubes at his disposal. He hoped the
copper, pineapple grenade–shaped bombs would dilute the
force of the Grik assault when it came, preventing it from
hitting his defenses as a cohesive mass. Canister ought to
blunt the spearhead; hopefully the bombs would shatter
the shaft. Now all he could do was wait and listen as the
reports flooded in.

Chack and Queen Maraan scaled the ladder behind him
from the level below. A signaler escorted them to his side.

"The First Marines have deployed in support of the Manila volunteers," Chack said, saluting. As always, the powerful young 'Cat wore his dented helmet at a jaunty angle,
and a Krag was slung over his shoulder.

"The Six Hundred and the Fifth Baalkpan are in place
as well," Safir Maraan reported in a husky tone. She was
dressed all in black, as usual, and her silver armor was polished to a high sheen.

"Good," Alden murmured. "We're going to need them."

"It's certainly shaping up to be a most memorable battle," the queen observed.

"And how," said Chack, using the term he often heard
the destroyermen use. He stood on his toe pads and peered
out over the wall. From across the field beyond came the
familiar strident, thrumming squawk of hundreds of Grik
horns, and the hair-raising, thundering staccato of tens of
thousands of Grik swords and spears pounding on shields
commenced. "I think they're about to come," he said, turning to Pete. "With your permission?"

"You bet. Give 'em hell."

For just an instant, as he passed her, Chack paused beside Safir. Reaching out, he gently cradled her elbow in his
hand. They blinked at each other, and then he was gone.
The Orphan Queen's eyes never left him until he disappeared from sight.

"Gen-er-al Aal-den?" she asked.

Pete nodded, still looking at the enemy. "Yes. Go. I think
Chack's right." He turned to look at her. "Be careful, Your
Highness. I expect I'll be down directly."

*   *   *

"The waterfront's in for it," Dowden observed, peering through his binoculars. The cork in the center of the enemy advance was out of the bottle, and dozens of red-hulled ships were streaming toward the docks. Most of the mines were gone. Clusters of barrels still floated in the bay, giving the impression that mines remained a hazard, but the Grik avoided those that they could. *Kas-Ra-Ar*'s smoldering wreck had finally slipped, hissing steam, beneath the water of the bay, and Matt had ordered *Tolson*, the last shattered, leaking frigate, to disengage. Her captain, Pruit Barry, signaled a protest, but Matt repeated the order and *Tolson* was retiring sluggishly, reluctantly, from the fight. She'd given a good account of herself, surely destroying the last of the gun-armed enemy ships in the center, but she'd paid a terrible price. Her sails were tattered rags, and her foremast was gone. Matt only hoped she'd reach shallow water before she sank. The heavy guns of the waterfront defenses opened up as the enemy approached and tore them apart, but unlike the plunging fire from the fort, fewer of the hits were immediately fatal or disabling. In their same old way, the Grik just kept charging through.

"Can't be helped," Matt ground out. Her ammunition nearly exhausted, *Walker* had only two objectives left. First, she had to prevent any Grik ships from probing the west inlet of the bay. Not many had tried so far. The lure of the city, as expected, kept most of them drawn in its direction. Mainly, though, *Walker* had to remain visible in the bay until *Amagi* arrived. So far the Japanese battle cruiser was taking her own sweet time. That was as they'd hoped, from a naval perspective, thought Matt, glancing at the setting sun. They'd savaged the Grik fleet without *Amagi* to protect it, and *Walker* would be a more difficult target in the dark. But in the meantime people were dying. There'd been no word from Fort Atkinson since it was smothered beneath several ten-inch salvos. Smoke still rose from there, so fighting clearly continued, but the guns overlooking the entrance to the bay were silent.

A continuous, impenetrable pall of smoke obscured the south side of the city as well, and no one on *Walker* could tell what was going on from her station across the bay. Matt now knew he'd been naive to think he could control the battle from his ship. He could transmit, and presumably someone could hear him, but he couldn't see any of his friends' signals at all. It was beyond frustrating, and there was nothing he could do but trust the people on the spot. They were good people, and his presence probably wouldn't make any difference, but it was nerve-racking all the same. Letts had managed to get a single message to him by means of a small, swift felucca. Several major assaults against the south wall had been repulsed so far, but the last attack had been costly, and actually made it past the moat to the very top of the wall. Most of the casualties suffered by the defenders came from blizzards of crossbow bolts, but the enemy was also employing a smaller version of their bomb thrower they hadn't seen before. Several Grik would carry the machine between them, and once it was emplaced they could hurl a small bomb about the size of a coconut almost two hundred yards. The weapon had little explosive force, but like the larger ones it dispersed flaming sap in all directions when it burst. It was a terrible device, and the Grik had an endless supply.

Most of the reserve had already been committed, but more Grik continued pouring through the gap and up the fort road. Letts had been forced to strip defenders from unengaged sections of the wall, even as the invading army lapped around to the northeast to threaten there as well. With this new attack on the waterfront, things would get tight.

"Send a message to HQ. Tell them they're going to have a lot of company along the dock, and there's nothing we can do about it."

"They probably know that already, Skipper."

Matt shrugged. "All the same . . ." The rattling drone of distressed motors distracted him, and he looked again toward the wreck-jumbled harbor mouth. The PBY was returning from somewhere beyond, its latest load of depth charges gone. Gray smoke streamed from the starboard engine, and the plane, less than a hundred feet in the air, clawed for altitude.

"Mallory must've tried to drop on *Amagi*," Larry said. "Crazy bastard. Now the plane's shot to pieces! I thought you told him to stay away from her."

Matt nodded. He had. He also knew Mallory's view of the battle was better than anyone else's. Only Ben Mallory knew exactly how the enemy was deployed, and he must have thought things were desperate indeed to try to tip the balance single-handedly. *Amagi* must be getting close, and Ben must have thought the defenders couldn't take it.

The plane rumbled by, heading for the north inlet, where a backup landing ramp and fueling pier had been established. Up close now, Matt saw it was riddled with holes, and a wisp of smoke trailed the port engine as well. Ben obviously had his hands full just keeping it in the air. The navigation lights flashed Morse.

"*Amagi*," Dowden said.

As they watched, orange flames sprouted around the port engine and leaped along the wing, consuming leaking fuel. Black smoke billowed.

"Oh, no," Matt breathed.

The plane turned into the failing engine, but with an apparently herculean effort, Ben managed to straighten her out with the big rudder and claw for the nearest shore.

"Come *on*!" someone murmured.

Even as the lumbering fireball fought for altitude, however, throttles at the stops, the fight ended with a suddenness as appalling as it was inevitable. The port support struts gave way, and the plane staggered in agony. An instant later the wing around the engine, weakened by fire, simply folded upward. Flaming fuel erupted, spewing from the sky with a heavy, distant *whoosh!* and the brave PBY Catalina and its gallant crew plummeted into the sea.

"Get a squad of Marines into the launch to look for survivors," Matt said huskily. By his tone he didn't expect them to find any. "Then you'd better resume your station, Larry," he added, referring to the auxiliary conn. With only the Grik to fight so far, he'd allowed Dowden to remain on the bridge.

"Aye, aye, Captain," Larry said, still staring at the erratic plume of smoke hovering above the burning, sinking wreckage of the plane. He took a deep breath and looked at Matt. "Good luck, sir."

"You too."

Keje-Fris-Ar paced the battlement spanning the width of his Home, his fond eye tracing details he'd so long taken for granted. Even if all went well, his ship—his Home—

would likely be reduced to a smoking, sunken wreck in the shallow water off the fitting-out pier. The distant sound of battle in the south had become a living, gasping, thundering throb, and the guns behind the fishing fleet wharf had begun booming as the Grik drew ever closer to his beloved *Salissa*. They were so densely packed he couldn't even count them. Far to the west, he saw *Walker* beneath her massive flag, racing to intercept a red ship that had strayed too close to the inlet. Tiny waterspouts erupted around the Grik as one of *Walker*'s machine guns came into play. In spite of his dread of what lay in store for his own ship, he felt a surge of guilt, mingled with gratitude for all *Walker* and her people had done for them. What they had yet to do. He sent a prayer to the Heavens for their safety, and added one for *Mahan* as well. The thick smoke had prevented him from seeing the PBY go down.

He knew some still believed the Amer-i-caans had brought this upon them, that the horror they faced was somehow connected to the arrival of the slender iron ships. He also knew that was ridiculous. The Grik had always been there, and today was but a reenactment of that terrible, prehistoric conflict that fragmented and exiled his people. This confrontation had been preordained, inevitable, building to this point over countless generations. The Grik were a scourge, a pestilence, the very embodiment of evil, just as the Scrolls had said. Only distance and the hostile Western Ocean had preserved his people this long. But the Grik managed to cross that distance at last, just as they'd once crossed the water between that distant place the Amer-i-caans called Aa-fri-caa, and the ancestral home of the People.

Keje would never have known that much if *Walker* hadn't come. They'd already done so much for his people, from that first time they helped save his ship until now. If it hadn't been for their timely appearance, the People might already have been scattered again. Keje would certainly be dead. Far from being a party to the evil that descended upon them, Keje believed the Amer-i-caans were a gift: deliverers sent to aid them in this terrible time. That was all very well as far as the People were concerned, but it was terribly unfair to the deliverers. Whatever force for evident good had sent them to this place, its dark counterpart balanced that act by sending *Amagi* to their enemies. Fleetingly, he wished he were facing this battle beside his friend in *Walker*'s pilothouse, underneath that great colorful flag. Keje knew he was where he needed to be, however. His duty to his people—his family—dictated that he make this fight here, upon his precious Home.

He felt a presence behind him and turned. There stood his daughter, Selass, holding forth his polished armor. He already wore his finest embroidered jerkin and his old, heavy-bladed scota at his side. Reaching for the armor, he saw that the fur around Selass's eyes was matted with tears, and for the first time in so very long he saw the true face of his daughter once more. Gone was the rebellious arrogance and air of condescension she'd so carefully honed. In its place there remained only a sad, wistful softness. He knew of her friendship with San-draa Tucker, and her dutiful attempts to help the tragic, tormented Saak-Fas come to terms with his ordeal. He also knew of her hopeless love for Chack, the one she'd once spurned. Now she'd lost them both. Saak-Fas had gone to *Mahan*. By all accounts he performed his duty, but Jim Ellis told him that he rarely spoke. Chack had earned distinction and the favor of an exotic foreign queen. The only things Selass had left were her Home and her father, and she stood on the brink of losing them as well. Keje's heart shattered within him, and he took his daughter in his arms.

"Never fear," he told her as softly as his gruff voice allowed. "All will be made right." He squeezed her tight, then gently pushed her away. Behind her stood Adar. "I thought you were ashore," he accused. "Go, take her with you. She belongs at the aid station, not here, and we have 'medics' enough. Besides, this will be a fight for the cannons. Our warriors are behind the fortifications."

"I am going ashore, my lord." Adar gauged the distance to the approaching enemy. More guns along the wall were firing now, and splashes rose among the ships. "We have a moment yet." That said, he spoke no more. He just stared at his lifelong friend.

"You're likely to have a larger 'official' congregation before this fight is done," Keje observed uncomfortably. "I hear Naga has climbed the Sacred Tree."

"To the very top," Adar confirmed. "He prays to the Heavens above the din of battle, so he might be heard."

Keje grunted. "How did he get up there?" He shook his head. "Never mind. He knows the Jaaps may target the tree and the Great Hall?"

"He does. Suddenly he seems aware of quite a lot. He hopes his prayers will protect them."

"Do you think they will?"

"No."

Keje nodded. "Then surely mine won't do much good," he muttered wryly. He looked down. When he spoke again, his voice sounded sad, almost . . . desolate. "Will you pray with me now, Sky Priest?"

Adar blinked rapidly, overcome by emotion. "Of course." Together with Selass and the few others on *Salissa*'s battlement, they faced in the direction the sun had set and spread their arms wide. As one, they intoned the ancient, simple plea:

"Maker of All Things, I beg Your protection, but if it is my time, light my spirit's path to its Home in the Heavens."

The traditional prayer was over, but before they could complete the customary gestures, Adar's voice continued: "I also beseech You to extend Your protection beyond our simple selves to include all here who fight in Your name, even those with a different understanding of Your glory. Aryaalans, B'mbaadans, Sularans, and the others, all perceive You differently, but they do know and revere You . . . as do our Amer-i-caan friends. Our hateful enemy does not. I know it is . . . selfish of me to ask You to deny so many of Your children their rightful, timely reward in the Heavens, but Maker, we do so desperately need their swords! I beg You not to gather too many in this fight, for even should we be victorious, the struggle must continue, and it will be long, long. Instead, let those You spare be rewarded later, with a brighter glow in the night sky, so all will remember the sacrifice they made!" he lowered his head. "I alone ask this of You. If it is Your will to deny my own ascension in return, so let it be."

The rest of those present stared at him, shocked by the bargain he'd made, and Keje's red-brown eyes were wet with tears. Following Adar's example, together they crossed their arms on their chests and knelt to the deck, ending the prayer at last.

"You take too much on yourself," Keje insisted.

Adar blinked disagreement. "I only wish I had more to offer than my own meager spirit."

"Then you may add mine as well," Keje said, and Adar looked at him in alarm. Once spoken, the bargain could not be taken back. "Idiot. Do you think I would be separated from you in this life or the next, brother? The boredom would destroy me." He paused. "Two last things; then you must leave. First, if we are victorious but I do not survive, send my soul skyward with wood from *Salissa*." He grinned. "Perhaps the Maker did not hear me. Finally, I will trust you to give Cap-i-taan Reddy my thanks."

Adar embraced him then, wrapping him in the folds of his cloak. "I shall."

"I say," exclaimed Courtney Bradford. "I believe the buggers are hitting the docks!"

The central hospital had been reestablished beneath a long block of elevated dwellings and shops, half a mile southeast of the Great Hall. The sheltered area covered almost six acres, and as the hours passed the space was filling with wounded. Nothing of the battle could be seen from where he stood, gazing westward, but the noise was overwhelming, even over the cries of the wounded.

"I think you're right," Sandra said tersely. "Now put that rifle down this instant and help me with this patient!"

Self-consciously, Bradford leaned the Krag against a massive "bamboo" support and peered at the limp form placed before her. All around them, other nurses and Lemurian surgeons fought their own battles to save the wounded, even while ever more arrived. Many had terrible, purplish red burns, and their fur was scorched and blackened. Others had been slashed by sword or axe, and many were pierced by the wicked crossbow bolts with the cruelly barbed points. There were few minor wounds. Those were tended by medical corpsmen right amid the fighting, or in one of the several field hospitals or aid stations. Those who were able returned to their posts with a bandage and some antiseptic paste on their wound. Only the most severely hurt were brought before Sandra. In spite of the fact that she was, after all, still just a nurse, she'd become the most experienced trauma nurse in the world. An orderly passed by, lighting lamps with a taper.

"I'd love to help you, of course, but I fear there's little point," Bradford said. Sandra spared him a harsh glance, then looked at her patient's face. The jaw was slack and the eyes empty and staring, reflecting the flickering flame. "Dead, you see," Courtney continued bleakly. "Perhaps the orderlies would be good enough to fetch us another?"

Sandra closed her eyes and held the back of her hand to her forehead. It was a classic pose, and for a terrifying instant Bradford feared she would faint, leaving him alone to deal with everything. To his utmost relief, she sighed and wiped sweat from her brow. She strode quickly to a basin and began washing her hands. Surreptitiously Bradford yanked a flask from his pocket and took a long, grateful gulp.

"Yes. I'm sure they will," Sandra said woodenly.

Bradford wiped his mouth and replaced the flask. Then he glanced around. "I haven't seen young Miss 'Becky' since the fighting started. I thought she was in your care."

"So did I," Sandra replied, "but she told me last night that she'd decided to stay with Mr. O'Casey at HQ. Said he's protected her quite sufficiently up till now, and she preferred to stay with him, where she might see more of the 'action.'" Sandra sounded worried, and maybe even a little disappointed. "It's just as well, I suppose. She should be perfectly safe, and"—she gestured at the wounded—"I doubt this is the best environment for a child."

"Perhaps . . ." said Bradford. He lowered his voice. "You do know she represents . . . considerably more than is apparent?"

Sandra nodded. "I suspected as much, but every time Matt seemed about to tell me what it was, there were always other people around. I gather it's a secret?"

"Of sorts," Bradford confirmed, "for now."

Sandra shrugged, gazing at the sea of wounded. "Well, whatever it is, right now I don't much care. I only hope she's safe."

A thundering rumble came from the dock, almost uninterrupted now. They'd grown accustomed to the sound of battle to the south, but this was closer, louder. She looked up worriedly.

"Don't fret, my dear. They'll stop the blighters," Bradford assured her. "It's all part of the plan, you see. Rest assured, I know everything that's going on, and it's all part of the plan." Sandra noticed that Bradford had picked up the rifle again, nervously fiddling with the rear sight.

"I haven't heard *Walker*'s guns for a while," she said, drying her hands and motioning the orderlies to bring another patient.

"Ah, well, of course not! She has limited ammunition, you know. Saving it for the Jappos! Besides, you wouldn't hear her, would you? Not over all that noise!" He waved vaguely westward. "Goodness me!" he said, tilting his head to one side, listening. "They're really going at it!"

On the waterfront, hundreds of firebombs arced through the night sky, leaving thin, wispy trails of smoke. Most fell behind the line, amid shops and storehouses, and erupted with a searing *whoosh!* of roiling flames. One fell directly atop a laboring gun crew, punctuated by a chorus of terrible screams. They were cut mercifully short when the ready ammunition placed nearby exploded. The rest of the guns never even slowed their firing, as the densely packed red-hulled ships drew closer and closer to the dock. Pivoting on her cable, *Big Sal* brought her augmented broadside of twenty heavy guns to bear on the enemy flank, and her well-aimed shots crashed remorselessly through the ships at point-blank range, demolishing those closest to her. But there were so many. With a tremendous shuddering crash, the first Grik ship smashed into the dock, splintering wood, and dropping both its remaining masts upon the anxious horde waiting in the bow. Many were crushed amid piteous shrieks. Regardless, the rest swarmed over the headrails and onto the dock. Another crash came, and another, as more ships followed the example of the first. The area between the dock and the seawall began to fill with Grik. Some appeared dazed in the face of the onslaught of fire and missiles raining upon them, so close on the heels of their rough landing. Most didn't even pause. They immediately swept into their instinctual, headlong assault. The slaughter was horrific. Mounds of bodies were heaped at the base of the wall as the big guns snapped out, hacking great swaths of carnage into the surging horde. The docks became slippery with blood and gore, but the furious, ululating, hissing shriek continued to grow as more ships grounded, or warriors leaped across to those that had, and found their way into the assault.

As promised, Adar had taken Selass ashore, but he hadn't gone much beyond it himself. Now he paced behind the wall with Chack's sister, Risa, at his side, calling encouragement to *Big Sal*'s warriors, who defended this section. They were heavily engaged. A single Grik warrior either vaulted or was launched entirely over the top of the wall and the warriors behind it. It landed nearby with a crunching thud, and, wild-eyed and slathering, it tried to rise to its feet. At least one of its legs was broken. Risa quickly dispatched it with a meaty *chunk* of her axe, and Adar looked at her appreciatively. "Well-done," he said. "You made that look quite simple."

"It was," she answered disdainfully. "It was crippled."

"Even so. I expect you've had much practice in war of late."

Risa shook her head. "Not much, really, since the fight for *Salissa*. I was on her during the battle before Aryaal. We were late to the fight."

Adar remembered. "Late perhaps, but instrumental. Both you and your brother have much honor due you."

Risa blinked, and with a wry grin she shook her head. "You knew, before this all began, that Chack did not even like to fight? He was afraid of injuring someone."

"I knew," Adar confirmed. "Your mother was perplexed, but proud of his restraint. She was always utterly without fear," he recalled fondly. "Where is she now?"

Risa gestured toward *Big Sal,* invisible through the choking clouds of smoke, except for the stabbing, orange flashes of her broadsides. "Home. She wouldn't leave. She only ever wanted to be a wing runner; now she is a warrior as well."

"We are all of us warriors now, I fear. Even your peaceful brother."

"Even you, Lord Priest?" Risa asked.

"Even I," he confirmed. "Even I have the battle lust upon me, if not the skill or training in war the smallest youngling has received. I yearn to do as you just did—slay the enemy that threatens my people, our way of life, our very existence as a species." He looked at his hands, held out before him. "I do not have the skill for that, and after what I saw . . .

once . . . it's frustrating. In a way I envy your brother. The skill I now crave came so easily to him, he never even knew it was there. I understand why the B'mbaadan queen thinks so highly of him. Hers have ever been a warlike people, and must recognize the talent"—he blinked dismay—"the *gift* for war when they see it."

He straightened. "I've learned much, however, about how battles are shaped. Major Shinya and the others have taught me that."

"How is this battle taking shape?" Risa asked, and Adar sighed.

"Very much as planned, I'm afraid."

Risa was confused. "But that is good, surely?"

Adar shook his head. "I believe the single greatest lesson in war we've learned from the Amer-i-caans is to hope for the best, but plan for the worst. Hope is necessary; without it you're defeated before you even begin. But you must plan for the worst, so if it happens you will be prepared." He blinked at her. "I fear this battle is going almost *exactly* as planned."

A roar came from beyond the wall, and a new flurry of bolts rained down beyond them. Warriors tumbled from their posts, and Risa hurried to fill a gap.

"I have no objection," she shouted over her shoulder, "as long as the plan was for victory!"

Perry Brister gulped water from an offered gourd. It soothed the pain in his throat a little, but he doubted it would restore his destroyed voice. Shinya and Rolak also drank as the gourd was passed to them. They gasped their thanks to the youngling who brought it. It had been dark for some hours, but with the fires burning in every direction they could see surprisingly well. Before them now, the coastal plain and the gap were almost deserted. A short while earlier Grik horns had sounded again, from the direction of the city, and as if it had been a dog whistle from hell, the Grik before the fort turned as one and practically fled in the direction of the sound. Across the gap and up through the road cut streamed the Grik as fast as they could, toward Baalkpan. None remained behind to even watch their trapped prey, except the wounded and the dead.

Thousands of Grik bodies lay heaped to the wall, and the

three thousand mixed troops occupying the fort had been reduced by nearly a third. Yet they'd held. Now they could begin to prepare for what Brister had been planning ever since he silenced the guns.

"How did you know they would leave?" Shinya finally asked.

"I didn't," Brister rasped. "I thought we'd have to fight through them. Those horn calls must have been a summons for all their reserves. They have to be gearing up for their final push."

They saw nothing of the city besides the flickering light of the fires, and the smoke was so dense they could hardly breathe. Cannon fire still thundered defiantly, however, and bright flashes lit the smoke-foggy sky to the north.

"I suggest we let the troops rest a couple hours, if we can," Brister gasped. "Then we'll form them up."

"I certainly hope you know what you're doing," said Lord Rolak.

Perry shrugged. "Hey, this stunt is mainly based on what you guys told me—and Bradford's cockeyed notions. I have no idea if it'll work. Maybe we'll at least create a diversion."

"It will be better than dying here," Shinya agreed, "trapped and cut off. You were right to silence the guns. There was nothing more they could contribute." He paused. "I apologize."

Brister waved it away. "Nothing to apologize for. I'm sorry I called you a Jap bastard."

Shinya chuckled. "I called you worse. In Japanese."

A runner approached. "Sirs," he said breathlessly, "the iron ship of the enemy is passing into the bay. More Grik ships are leading it in."

They looked to the west. Even in the darkness they saw the black, pagodalike superstructure of *Amagi* silhouetted against the sky. Smoke laced with sparks swirled from her stack, and small shapes moved behind the railings as she steamed relentlessly into the bay. It was a terrifyingly vulnerable moment. The ship was absolutely enormous, and in spite of her litany of imperfectly repaired wounds, she radiated an overwhelming, malevolent power. At this range her main guns were little threat to the fort, but the numerous secondaries and antiaircraft armaments certainly were. In the light of the many fires, the occupants of Fort Atkinson had to be visible. *Surely they see us,* Brister thought.

If they did, they made no sign, and the reason was obvious: the defenders in the fort were helpless. As far as the Japanese knew, the guns were knocked out, and even if they weren't, they'd have no effect against such a leviathan. She'd shelled the fort only to protect her allies, and whoever remained crouching behind its walls was no concern of hers. The Grik would take care of them at their convenience.

In spite of his relief, and his intent that she should, the *fact* that *Amagi* was ignoring them as harmless stoked the rising anger in Perry Brister's soul.

"We're going to make them wish they'd blown us to hell," he croaked.

"Why did we stop firing on the fort?" Kurokawa demanded, entering the bridge behind Sato. So far, the captain had spent the bulk of the "battle" on the flag bridge. Commander Okada spared him a nervous glance. He was shocked to see him wearing a pistol, of all things.

"The enemy there is helpless, sir. We have knocked out their guns."

"Precisely the best time to strike! Wipe them out while they cannot reply."

"Captain," Sato responded stiffly, "they could do little to reply *before* we silenced their guns. Against us, at any rate. Our ammunition is desperately low. I assumed you would wish to save what we have for the American ship. Besides, we don't know what surprises they may have awaiting us."

Kurokawa's face reddened, but he didn't attack as Sato expected. Eventually he even nodded. "Quite right, Commander. We can always pulverize the survivors in the fort at our convenience later. They are clearly cut off."

"Yes, Captain," Sato replied, with a sick feeling in his gut. He'd done everything in his power to avoid this moment, but there'd never been any real chance. He couldn't openly recruit supporters willing to defy the captain, and despite their hideous allies, they would, before this night was done, certainly battle the Americans—their legitimate enemies. To take their side even now would have lost him any support he had. He wondered if his and Kaufman's message got through. Not that it made any difference. His soul seethed with torment, and he knew *Amagi* had become a ship of the damned.

"Any sign of the American destroyer yet?"

"No, sir," he managed. "Signals indicate it has wreaked havoc with our 'allies,' though." Sato couldn't hide the bitter satisfaction in his voice when he made that report. To his surprise, Kurokawa chuckled.

"Excellent! The Americans will have depleted their ammunition as well, and besides, when we destroy them, it will show our barbaric friends who wields the *real* power here. The more Grik the Americans destroy, the more impressive our victory will seem! Let me know as soon as the enemy shows himself!" He paused, then added grimly, "This time, there is no place for him to run."

"The iron ship is entering the bay," General Esshk observed, standing on the quarterdeck of the great white command ship of the Invincible Swarm. So far, as was expected, they'd viewed the battle from a distance. They'd watched the annihilation of the cream of the Swarm as it forced its way past the troublesome fort guarding the mouth of the bay. The Uul that landed on the southern coast seemed to have fared somewhat better.

Tsalka nodded. "At last, perhaps we will gain some advantage for having tolerated those insufferable creatures," he said, meaning the Japanese.

"Kurokawa's plan seems to be working, Lord Regent," Esshk agreed. "His insistence on multiple attacks is contrary to doctrine, and at first glance seems to fly in the face of the very principle of the Swarm—yet never have we been able to utilize so much of our force at once. Many of our Uul have been slain—an unprecedented number, I fear—yet we have certainly 'softened up' the prey in preparation for his mighty ship to enter the bay. He did also put a stop to the slaughter of our ships by the guns in the fort. I am inclined to consider it a brilliant tactic."

"His 'tactics' are indeed effective. Wasteful of Uul, but effective," Tsalka agreed.

"The destruction of the fort of the prey was impressive, and accomplished at such a distance so ... effortlessly. ...

We would have to watch these new hunters, even if they were not so disagreeable."

"Their power is great"—Esshk nodded—"but so is the power of the prey." He hesitated, then mused aloud, "Worthy prey after all." He glanced at the regent-consort. "Perhaps we should have made the Offer? Never has any Swarm been mauled so. I fear, no matter how this battle turns, even this Invincible Swarm will remain but an empty shell."

"Perhaps," Tsalka agreed, and uttered a long, sad hiss. "But that is the lot of the Uul: to die in the battle of the hunt, doing what they love, what they were bred to do. But there is no way we could have made the Offer. We face the ancient Tree Prey, the ones that escaped! They were not worthy of the Offer before, and long have we hunted them. The prey may have grown since last we met, but it's still the same prey. The Offer cannot be made. Even so, I grieve for the Uul we will lose in this hunt. And I do envy them," he added wistfully.

"Of course. As do I."

Tsalka watched the massive iron ship drive deeper into the bay. "We should advance, I think," he said. "It's not the place of the Hij to gather the joy of the hunt to ourselves, but I would not have it said the New Hunters alone were responsible for success. I fear the Uul look to the iron ship too much as it is."

"I agree," General Esshk replied. "As may we all before this hunt is over."

"Lookout reports Jap battle cruiser, bearing two zero five degrees!" Reynolds shouted. He gulped. "She's coming in."

Walker had been steaming back and forth on the west side of the bay at the mouth of the inlet for over two hours now. To all appearances, she looked as if she were watching the distant battle with impotent frustration, her magazines empty at last. That wasn't far from the truth.

Matt tried to freeze the expression on his face so the searing apprehension he felt wouldn't show. All of *Walker*'s actions that day, and now into the night, had been building to this precise moment—when she'd deliberately put herself in *Amagi*'s sights. Now that the moment was finally at hand, doubt and fear warred with the certainty of necessity. So far everything had gone as they'd expected. In other words, nothing had broken their way. They'd slaughtered the enemy on a wholesale level beyond comprehension, beyond what any truly sentient species could endure, and reports from the city told of Grik piled as high as the walls. But still they came. It was up to *Walker* and *Mahan* now, just as they'd expected and dreaded. It was up to them to strike a blow that might shatter the enemy's single-minded, maniacal will. To replicate the panic they'd seen in front of Aryaal. Hopefully.

There was no guarantee the enemy would break, even if the plan succeeded. They had only marginal evidence to support Bradford's theory of "Grik Rout." They'd seen it once at Aryaal, and once aboard *Big Sal*. When things had turned suddenly and overwhelmingly against them, and the Grik found themselves on the defense, they'd fled in mindless terror. It was like a dog chasing a bear. The bear was fearless when attacking, but when attacked, its only thought was escape. They were banking everything that the Grik behaved much the same way. There was glaring evidence the reverse was also true, however. When they'd followed the Grik belowdecks on *Revenge*, the creatures had fought like cornered animals. Of course, that was what they'd been, after all. Just as the bear would finally turn on the dog if it were brought to bay, the Grik fought furiously in the hold of the ship. But there'd been no coordination, no discipline, and it had been every Grik for itself. Except the Grik captain. It hadn't fought at all, preferring suicide to capture—very much like what little Matt knew about the Japanese. He still wondered if that was significant.

Gray hadn't seen Grik Rout on Tarakan either. The enemy came ashore and charged and died and killed in the same old way. In the end they'd fought savagely, and the battle raged hand-to-hand—but they'd been cornered too, hadn't they? The sea was at their back, and there was nowhere for them to go. That had to be their weak spot; Lawrence, as safely as possible ensconced in Matt's own quarters, believed it might be so. Now all they could do was pray.

At long last the terrible day had dwindled into twilight,

and the twilight into an endless, terrible night. The sky was a muddy pall, shot through with flashes of light. Finally *Amagi* was coming—and *Walker* was the cornered beast.

Matt raised his binoculars. The dim shape of the battle cruiser was edging past Fort Atkinson into the bay. She was screened by at least a dozen Grik ships, probably there to soak up any remaining mines. One of the ships exploded and abruptly sank, even as the thought came to him. *Amagi* adjusted her course, carrying her farther into the cleared lane they'd left for her. Matt tensed. The "special" mine was their last chance to do it the easy way, their last chance to survive, more than likely. The minutes passed, and the dark apparition continued to grow, inexorably. Surely she must have passed over Mr. Sandison's mine by now! He sighed. He'd never really expected it to work. The MK-6 magnetic exploder had let them down so many times, he'd known in his heart it would fail. He was still surprised how let down he felt now that it had once again. That was one break that would have made all the difference.

Matt lowered the glasses and looked at the men around him. He sensed their fear, even in the gloom. They knew their chances were poor, but they also knew they had no choice. Even if they could still flee, they wouldn't choose to, despite the odds. This was the rematch. The game that was called on account of rain almost exactly a year ago would be played out here at last, and the opponent they faced wasn't only the hulking brute they associated with all their trials; it was the Japs. Somehow that seemed profoundly appropriate. The terrible battle raging around them on land and sea would be won or lost. Perhaps what they did here would influence that, but regardless, this was *Walker*'s fight, and *Mahan*'s. Nothing anyone else did could influence *that*. For a moment Matt was silent, remembering the long list of names stricken from the rolls since the last time these three ships met, and he could almost feel the ghosts gathering 'round, expecting him to exact revenge or join them in the attempt. He looked again at the men and 'Cats in the pilothouse, and forced a slight smile.

"Just a few good licks; then we run like hell." He rolled his shoulders and faced the front. Beneath his hand was the back of his chair, bolted to the front of the pilothouse. Part of the ship. Gently, almost lovingly, he patted it. "One more time, old girl," he whispered, then raised his voice. "All ahead full. Make your course zero one zero."

"Ahead full, zero one zero, aye," came the strained reply.

"Mr. Garrett may commence firing as soon as he has a solution. Armor-piercing."

"Aye, aye, Captain," Reynolds said, and repeated the order to the acting gunnery officer. "Sir, Mr. Garrett wants to know if he should withhold a reserve?"

Matt shook his head. "No. Give 'em all he's got."

Even as *Walker* accelerated, her tired sinews bunching for a final sprint, they saw winking flashes and blooms of fire erupt from the Japanese ship.

Kurokawa was just leaving to return to the more spacious flag bridge—a more comfortable vantage from which to view the battle—when he was stopped by the sighting of the American destroyer. He whirled and paced quickly to the windows.

"Where?!"

"Port bow, Captain," Sato said in a quiet, clipped voice. Kurokawa rubbed his hands together with glee.

"Commence firing, Commander Okada! I want that ship erased!"

"Yes, Captain." Sato prepared to relay the order with a heavy heart, but Kurokawa speared him with a cold stare. Sato's tone had finally penetrated the captain's euphoria.

"Commander Okada does not approve the destruction of His Majesty's enemies?" he mocked. Sato turned to him, expression hooded. But before he spoke, something deep inside him snapped and he stiffened to attention.

"On the contrary, Captain. But I remain unconvinced the American destroyer represents His Majesty's chief enemy in this world." He looked pointedly at Kurokawa. "We are about to waste ammunition, lives, and possibly an opportunity as well." Sato knew he'd said too much, and was fully aware of the consequences, but he couldn't stop himself. He no longer would, even if he could. Following his revenge-maddened captain's orders was one thing, but by doing so he was aiding the loathsome Grik. That made him feel loathsome too, and his honor was stained beyond any effort to cleanse it. "Sir, the emperor's greatest enemy in this world can only be the Grik, and you are their tool."

"You are relieved!" screeched Captain Kurokawa. "Place yourself under arrest and await punishment!" Sato only nodded. Suddenly the deck shuddered under his feet and there was a loud explosion from below, in the flag bridge. A sheet of fire enveloped the windows for an instant, and then it was gone.

"Commence firing!" the captain shrieked, then turned back to look at Sato. "Another blow to avenge, and all because of you! Your American friends are not restrained by *your* doubts, I see." Sato did not even challenge the ridiculous statement. He turned to leave the bridge.

"Wait! Fetch your American pet and bring him here! It might amuse him to watch the destruction of the last of his people on this world, and it's only fitting you should see it together—since you will share his fate!"

Kurokawa's sweaty, feverish face was illuminated by the flash from *Amagi*'s first salvo in response to the American fire.

"Looks like *Walker*'s starting her show," Alden gasped. Then he coughed and hacked for a moment before spitting. Bright flashes of fire and crisscrossing tracers seared the darkness of the bay. Based on positions, and the relative weight of fire, there was no question who was shooting at whom. *Amagi*'s forward searchlight winked on and, a mere instant later, died in a spray of sparks and a brief snap of yellow light. Other sharp flashes quickly followed in the same vicinity. *Walker* must be shooting for *Amagi*'s bridge, Pete guessed.

"I think the Grik are almost ready too," Chack warned. He pointed across the battlefield to the south. The ground in front of them was covered with dead Grik, and the moat before the wall was so packed with their bodies, the attackers could run straight across without even touching water. The sharpened stakes and other obstacles were so choked with corpses they'd lost most of their effectiveness. Small fires from burning brush and garments cast an eerie red glow upon the scene. A larger fire near the trees, where one of the big Grik bomb throwers was destroyed by a mortar, illuminated the seething mass of enemies beyond. It was impossible to guess how many there were, but it was apparent they'd been heavily reinforced.

"They've called up the last of their reserves," Chack speculated. His usually good English was difficult to understand because his lips were swollen and bloody. His fur was dark with sticky, half-dried blood, and he was limping from a slash on his leg. "After that last attack, they must believe one more heavy thrust must break our line."

"They've pulled out all the stops," Alden agreed. "And it might just work, because we have too. There's nothing left on the north and east walls. Everything's either here or down at the waterfront. The waterfront has bigger guns and more troops, but they're too spread out. It's tough going down there."

"Here as well."

Alden looked at him. "Listen. I don't know what those lizards use for brains, but if it were me, I'd pile as much as I could against a short section of wall, with just enough everywhere else to hold the defenders in place. If they do that, my guess is we'll crack wide-open. I want you to take personal command of the rifle company, and stand ready to hammer them back if they force a breach. Use the B'mbaadans too. Rifles are great for distance work, but up close you're going to need swords to back you up."

"My place is in the line with my Marines," Chack protested.

Alden suppressed a sad smile. "The rifles are your Marines too. I need someone I trust, who'll wait till they're needed, but won't wait too long." He paused. "I also need someone who'll keep his head, and knows when it *is* too late. If that occurs, pull back immediately. If they knock down the whole line, save what you can and fall back on the hospital. You'll be in command of the rear guard, as well as the effort to evacuate into the jungle. Is that understood?"

Chack blinked furiously. "You ask too much! To leave my Homes, my people . . ."

"I'm not asking shit!" Alden snarled. "I'm *telling* you what you *will* do! The only thing I'm *asking* is if you understand your duty."

Chack slowly nodded. In the distance the raucous horns began to blare. The terrible thrumming sound continued to build until it seemed like thousands of them this time. The thunderous rumble of the shields rivaled even the nearby guns. Across the field in the flickering light, the Grik began to move.

Then, from nearby, a low moan was heard that seemed to have nothing to do with the approaching horde. Pete quickly looked in the direction many heads had turned. On the bay, considerably farther to the north now, a rising ball of fiery black smoke roiled into the air, briefly illuminating the stricken destroyer beneath it.

"Oh, my God," Alden breathed. "*Walker* . . ."

"Damage report!" Matt bellowed, picking himself up off the deck. He already knew it was bad. He'd felt the heat of the blast, the ship physically yanked from under his feet. Already her speed was bleeding away. Throughout her sortie against the mammoth battle cruiser, *Walker* had seemed charmed. Salvo after salvo of her armor-piercing four-inch-fifties slammed home with telling effect, each shell blessed, kissed, or sent with a hateful curse. *Amagi*'s gunnery went wild, and Matt guessed they must've taken out her forward fire control. A few shell fragments from near misses, and some light antiaircraft fire was all the damage the destroyer received in return, in spite of the blizzard of five-and-a-half-inch shells thrashing the water all around her. Taking advantage of this, *Walker* continued to punish her adversary for several minutes longer than Matt originally intended; he just couldn't help himself. Reason finally clawed its way back into his consciousness, however, and finally, reluctantly, he gave the order to turn away. *Walker* raced up the bay toward the north inlet, making smoke.

By then, hidden in the darkness and her dense curtain of smoke, *Walker* had to have been invisible. The wind was still out of the south, and the man-made cloud spread, wafting around her. She'd ceased firing as soon as she turned, and all lights were out. Where she headed, there were no fires or lights to silhouette her, and overhead no moon betrayed her. It must have been just a lucky shot.

"All ahead flank!" Matt shouted as his ship slowed even further. A few shells continued falling, but the fire was desultory now. *They must think they got us*, he realized. Stepping around the chart house and looking aft, he could see why. *Walker* was afire from just behind the bridge to somewhere aft of the amidships deckhouse. The Japanese shell must have penetrated the fuel bunker they'd installed in place of the number one boiler, and blown burning oil all over the ship. Steam gushed from somewhere to rise and mix with the black, greasy smoke. Even as he watched, hoses began to play on the fires.

"Captain!" Reynolds called behind him. "Mr. McFarlane says the number two boiler took a direct hit, and the fuel bunker's been punctured! There's major flooding in the forward fire room—he says it's gone, Skipper—there's nothing he can do. There's also minor flooding in the aft fire room he thinks he can keep under control."

"We're losing steam!"

"Yes, sir. The valve's sprung. He can't cut number two out of the main line from below. He's going to have to do it topside, but the fire . . ."

"Right. Have the hoses concentrate on that area. We've got to have steam!"

Walker slowly drifted to a stop while her crew battled the inferno amidships, and Matt kept expecting another flurry of shells to finish them. For some reason the final salvo never came, even though his ship was an easy target now, burning like a beacon in the night. "Don't want to waste the shells," he mused aloud, watching the Japanese ship once more. "That, or they hope we can keep her afloat and they'll take her later at their leisure."

Chief Gray clambered up the ladder onto the bridge. He was covered with soot, his thinning hair and beard curled by the heat of the fire. "We got problems, Skipper," he said. Matt arched his eyebrows at the ridiculous statement. Gray realized what he'd said, and shrugged. "More problems. The fire main's losing pressure, because we gotta have steam to run the pumps—which Spanky says we ain't gonna get no steam till we can move the fire away from the topside cutoff—"

"Which we can't do without steam for the pumps. I know. Do the best you can. If you can't get to that valve, we can't move."

"Beggin' your pardon, Skipper, but I bet if we even twitch, the Japs'll pound hell out of us."

"That may be, but we can't just sit here like this." He

clenched his fists in frustration and paced. "How many did we lose?" he asked at last.

Gray shook his head. "I don't know yet, Skipper. Most of the guys got off the amidships gun platform. That damn Silva deserves a medal. He even saved the machine guns. Got burned some, too. Wasn't for him, a lot more woulda died. Other than that . . . we still have the comm, so we can talk, but the front of the ship's completely cut off from the back as long as that fire's burning. I just don't know."

"Captain . . . Mr. Garrett asks if he should resume firing. There are still a few AP shells left," Reynolds said.

Matt shook his head, looking at the distant enemy ship. "Not just yet." He cleared his throat. "Send a message to HQ. Tell them they'd better already be out of the Great Hall, because it's about to be remodeled."

Amagi had stopped her advance, and now lay reflecting the fires and the glow of battle right in the middle of the bay. Several Grik ships were still nearby. One looked a little larger than the others. Maybe it was one of the white ones like Mallory had seen, Matt thought, as he watched *Amagi*'s main gun turrets train out to starboard. They fired.

Amagi's bridge was a shambles. The American gunnery had been remarkably accurate, and several shells impacted uncomfortably close. Two of the bridge officers were dead, and even Kurokawa was lightly wounded when a shell fragment slashed his scalp and severed the brim of his hat. Even so, for the first time since the Strange Storm that brought them here, Captain Kurokawa felt an immense sense of satisfaction course through him. The puny American destroyer responsible for all his aggravation was afire and dead in the water. He'd contemplated finishing her, but she was clearly doomed. He'd let them see the destruction he wrought on the folk they'd tried to protect. That traitor Sato was right about one thing: *Amagi*'s ammunition was limited. Better to use it on the city. He was aware the "flagship" had followed them in, and he had an important audience to please.

Without a word, Sato Okada returned to the bridge, escorting the bedraggled, bearded American officer. Kurokawa regarded them both in silent triumph as Kaufman crept unsteadily to the windows and gazed into the darkness at the fiercely burning destroyer. His frail frame convulsed suddenly, as a most unmanly sob escaped him.

"You may use the radio now, Commander Okada," Kurokawa said in English. "Your American friends might appreciate an offer of unconditional surrender. The water will soon be rising, and without any boats . . ." He smiled. "A most unpleasant death, I should think."

"Go to *hell*!" Kaufman snarled.

Kurokawa paused, as if a thought just came to him. "Of course, you deserve my thanks, Captain Kaufman. If not for your capture, and all the important things you've told us, I would never have even known about that destroyer. At least, not before this campaign began. That knowledge was what ultimately made me decide to help the Grik." He looked keenly at the aviator. "Thank you."

Kaufman would have gone for him then. It was as though, for the first time since he'd stepped aboard *Walker* in Surabaya, his wits had finally completely returned. Only a battered, empty shell of the man he'd been remained, but regardless of what the Grik and the Japanese had done to him, he knew Kurokawa was right. They'd broken him, and it hadn't even been that hard. He was already broken when they got him. He *was* responsible. It *was* his fault. For an instant he stared at the Japanese captain, saw the mocking smile.

A hand like iron clasped his withered arm, restraining him before he could strike. It was Sato. Kaufman didn't know what he'd have done: torn out Kurokawa's throat with his teeth, he supposed. It didn't really matter.

"No," came a whispered voice in his ear. It was a voice of resignation, but it came from the only person who'd shown him any compassion at all. He stopped; then, realizing how easily he'd been restrained, he knew it was no use. He lowered his eyes in abject misery, and even above the sound of the crashing guns he heard Kurokawa's thin laugh rise within the confines of the bridge.

Alan Letts heard the incoming rounds. He, O'Casey, and Nakja-Mur, as well as members of the command staff who hadn't yet transferred to the secondary HQ, were preparing to descend the ladder from the lowest level of the Great Hall.

"Down!" Letts screamed, and for the next several moments there was nothing but the overwhelming sound and pressure of titanic detonations. The entire massive structure of the Great Hall sagged beneath them, and there was a terrific crash from above. Oil lamps fell from the walls and rolled away down the sloping floor. One came to rest beside a crumpled tapestry that once adorned the wall of the entrance chamber, and the beautifully woven fabric began to burn. In the eerie silence immediately following the salvo, a deep, rumbling groan could be heard.

Letts scrambled to his feet and looked quickly around. One of the runners had been crushed by a massive limb. It had fallen from the tree far above and crashed down through all three levels of the hall, driving him through the deck on which Alan stood with its jagged stump. The others rose shakily, but Nakja-Mur still lay sprawled. "Quickly!" he shouted at O'Casey. "We've got to get him out now! There may be only seconds before the next salvo!"

Between them and the staff members who'd gathered their wits, they managed to heave the High Chief through the opening and lower him quickly to the ground. By then Nakja-Mur was recovering his senses, and he looked around, blinking surprise. People were running in all directions, and the Great Hall no longer looked quite right. Flames leaped up from nearby structures, and over all there was a wailing, keening sound.

"Take his legs!" Alan yelled. O'Casey could only grab one, but there was plenty of help now. They ran as fast as they could toward the edge of the parade ground, while a sound like a roaring gale and tearing canvas descended upon them.

"Down!"

Even as they dropped, there came again the avalanche of deafening sound and mighty flashes of searing fire as the earth heaved into the sky.

Letts tried to stand, but fell to his knees, stunned by the proximity of the blast. He looked back. Somehow the Great Hall and Sacred Tree still stood, but the building was engulfed in flames. Any shells that actually struck it must have passed right through and detonated on the ground or against the tree itself. Flames licked up and across the huge sloping roof, clawing greedily at the branches above. Smol-

dering leaves and drifting ash descended all around. Up beyond the light of the fire where the tree disappeared into
darkness, they could only just hear Naga's plaintive, wailing
chant.

"So now I see war as you are accustomed to it," Nakja-
Mur rasped beside him.

Letts glanced down and saw that the High Chief had
risen to a sitting position. O'Casey just looked stunned. At
least he'd acted, though.

"Nobody ever gets accustomed to it," Alan said, managing to stand. "But yeah, this is the war we left behind when
we came here."

"You all tried to tell me, but I never . . ." Nakja-Mur's
eyes reflected an expression almost of wonder. He looked
back in the direction they'd come. "The Tree . . . !"

Letts motioned the others to grab him. "Never mind the
tree! We have to keep moving away from it, in case they
aren't satisfied with their handiwork yet."

"The Tree . . ."

The arrival of the wounded at the central hospital had
slowed to a trickle. Not that there was any shortage of them,
but with the sound of battle coming from everywhere now,
Sandra knew more should be arriving, not less. She saw
Courtney Bradford talking with one of the young runners,
and she quickly finished bandaging an Aryaalan's wounded
shoulder and jogged over to where he stood.

"What is it? What's happening?" she demanded. Bradford turned to her, and his face seemed pasty in the
torchlight.

"It's . . . it's all going according to plan," he repeated
once more.

She glared at him. "It's not!" she snarled. "It can't possibly be! There are no more wounded coming in. Have the
field hospitals been overrun?"

"No—no, that's not it at all. Most of the wounded are
returning to the fight, and those who cannot must remain
where they are for now. The ambulance corps have gone to
strengthen the walls."

"But . . . how . . ." She stopped. "We're losing then?"

"Not as you would say *losing*, precisely," Bradford
hedged.

"What were you and that messenger just talking about?"

"Um. Well, you see, I've been asked to send whoever can still wield a weapon up to the east wall. It's not engaged—and probably won't be," he quickly added, "but they've taken everyone off it to reinforce those areas that are." He stopped. "We've also been told to prepare to evacuate into the jungle if the word should come. If it does, we must move quickly."

Sandra felt numb. "Is there any word of *Walker*, or . . . or Captain Reddy?" she asked quietly.

Bradford's expression became even more strained, and he placed a hand on her shoulder. "*Walker* is afire, my dear," he said gently, "and dead in the water." He gestured vaguely. "She gave a lovely account of herself but . . ." He shook his head. "The Japs aren't even shooting at her anymore."

Sandra could only stand and stare at him as hot tears came to her eyes. "Mr. Bradford," she said very formally, voice brittle as glass, "would you be so kind as to cover for me here awhile?"

He gawked at her and then looked helplessly around. "Don't be ridiculous! I don't have the faintest idea—"

"Oh, but you do! You've been a tremendous help!" she pleaded.

"I am *not* a doctor!"

Sandra giggled hysterically. "Neither am I!"

Bradford's face became severe. "Listen to me, young lady! You *are* a doctor—the best in the world! There are hundreds of people here who need your help. If you leave now, many may die!" His voice softened slightly. "There's nothing you can do for him, my dear."

Suddenly she was in his arms, sobbing against his chest, and all he could do was stare straight ahead and pat her lightly on the back. A suspicious sensation caused his own eyes to blink.

"There, there. There, there," he said over and over. "All is not lost. I told you there was a plan. That young man of yours may surprise us yet."

A disturbance nearby alerted them to the arrival of several figures, carrying another. A few of the closest wounded recognized the burden, and a cry of alarm rose up.

"What is it?" Sandra demanded, wiping her face on her shirtsleeve. "Let me through!"

"Quick!" said Alan Letts. "It's Nakja-Mur! We got him out of the Great Hall when the Japs started shelling it. He was a little roughed up, but he seemed okay. He even walked a little. Then, all of a sudden, he just collapsed!"

"Get him on the table!" commanded Sandra. Letts, O'Casey, and a couple others set him down, and she shone a light into the High Chief's face. His mouth was slack and his eyes moved lazily from side to side. He seemed unable to focus. She plugged the stethoscope into her ears and listened to his chest. Lemurian hearts sounded different from humans', but she'd learned to recognize those differences. What she heard now wasn't just different; it was wrong. In the midst of all the turmoil and strife, Nakja-Mur's noble heart was fighting a battle of its own.

"Where is Rebecca?" O'Casey suddenly demanded, and Sandra, momentarily distracted, glared at him with wide eyes.

"I thought she was with you!"

Lawrence lay coiled on Captain Reddy's bunk, panting in the heat. He'd heard the sounds of battle and been curious, but then came the tremendous blast, seemingly just aft of where he lay, and he'd grown concerned—mainly that the ship of Rebecca's new friends might have been seriously damaged—and maybe a little that he might have been forgotten. But he wasn't afraid—not in the way Bradford and even, he suspected, the "Grik" might be afraid in a similar situation. He'd endured the Trial, after all. If this was where his existence would end, that was too bad, but so be it. It was getting very hot, though, and he'd have liked to leave the room he was in, but he'd been ordered not to. So there he stayed . . . and panted.

The green curtain parted suddenly, and he blinked in shock when Rebecca's small head poked inside.

"There you are, you silly thing! Come out of there this instant! You will be cooked alive!"

"'Ecky! Here?"

"Of course I'm here," she answered severely. "Where did you expect I'd be? Now come along!"

Without objection, Lawrence obeyed. He'd been given

an order, after all. As they passed down the short hallway, they heard the roaring flames and shouted commands nearby. "Do they know you're here?" he asked, already sure of the answer.

"Well, probably not, I suppose. Not everyone, anyway. Mr. Miller and a few of the wounded in the wardroom do— that's where I stowed away! Some of the cabinets are quite spacious. When I popped out and came looking for you, I'm sure he saw me, but he was somewhat busy." Her voice turned grim. "This battle has cost our friends severely, I'm afraid. We must discover some way to be of help."

"How?"

Rebecca chewed her lip. "That's the thing; I haven't the slightest idea. But we'll think of something; we must!"

Jim Ellis watched the battle from *Mahan*'s stark, rebuilt bridge, almost five miles from where *Amagi* loomed, out-lined against the burning city beyond. His ship had spent the battle carefully concealed along the shore in the west inlet, covered by foliage and low-hanging branches, in case an inquisitive Grik plane sneaked past *Walker* for a look, or the enemy spotting plane was a factor after all. Her topsides were blackened with tar and soot mixed with fat, so she'd be virtually invisible in the dark. Now, slowly, she made her way into the bay. The frustrating wait was over at last, and finally it was *Mahan*'s turn.

Amagi's attention had been firmly fixed on *Walker*, just as they'd hoped, but whatever catastrophic injury *Mahan*'s sister had suffered was definitely not part of the plan. The other four-stacker was supposed to be clear, "chased" into the dark, dead-end reaches of the north inlet. Jim watched her burn with a sick, wrenching sense of loss.

The effect was the same, however. With *Walker* afire and apparently no further threat, the last obstacle had been removed, and the Japanese diverted all their attention to reducing Baalkpan to rubble. With any luck, no one would even suspect *Mahan*'s approach. Bernard Sandison stood on the starboard bridge wing, running a final check on the sole surviving torpedo director. Everything had been care-fully examined over and over, but it never hurt to check again. They'd have only one chance, and all their hopes were riding on the single MK-10 torpedo in the number one mount. *Almost* all their hopes, Jim amended grimly to himself. If all else failed, he'd added one small addition to the plan.

Mahan had only a skeleton crew aboard, more than half of them Lemurians. All were volunteers. The crew was actually leaner than Jim had led Matt to believe it would be, and damage control might be a problem, but that couldn't be helped. There were full crews for the numbers one and two, four-inch-fifties, as well as the number one torpedo mount. Four people were in the boiler room and two at the throttle station. There was no one at all on the fire-control platform, since the equipment was destroyed. The bridge watch consisted of five, including Jim and Bernie, and all weapons except the torpedo mount were in local control. If all went well, *Mahan* would still have a larger crew than she needed for her task. If things didn't go well . . . *Mahan*'s only launch was towing far astern, beyond the worst of her wake. Just in case.

"Ahead two-thirds," Jim almost whispered. He sensed the ship respond with a growing vibration he felt through the soles of his shoes and the increased pitch of the blower. To him the ship was very much alive, with feelings and thoughts of her own. In spite of everything, he'd come to love her in a way he'd never expected when he first set foot on her shattered decks. Even more, he believed she somehow knew how he felt, and what, exactly, was expected of her that night. The two were of one mind, and each had become an extension of the other. *Mahan* was, after all, Jim Ellis's first command.

The closer they got, the larger and more formidable the enemy ship appeared. Blooms of fire erupted from her ten-inch guns as she continued pounding the city. At first *Amagi* had concentrated on the center of Baalkpan, where the Great Hall and Sacred Tree stood. They'd expected as much. It was an obvious target because of the excellent view it afforded of the battlefield. Now the great tree was enveloped in flames, burning with a surprising intensity like some great torch, illuminating everything for miles around. Satisfied with that achievement, the giant guns began hammering the harbor defenses. It was like taking a sledgehammer to an anthill. Doubtless far more Grik were being slaughtered by the dreadful salvos than defenders, but it was also clear they were having the desired effect. Already many guns along critical portions of the harbor wall had fallen silent, and fires raged out of control along the wharf and among the warehouses beyond.

Fires that beautifully backlit *Amagi*. She was a perfect target: stationary, unsuspecting, and highly visible. *Mahan*'s approach was from directly abeam of *Amagi*'s port side, and at over eight hundred feet in length, it was unthinkable they could miss her. Even so, the tension Jim felt was so intense, he couldn't stand in one place any longer. He began to pace.

"Mr. Sandison?" he asked, clutching nervous hands behind his back.

"Range to target is eleven thousand yards," Bernie replied, his voice strained.

"Very well."

Together they waited in silence with the others as the range wound down. Even as it did, the battle cruiser began raining destruction on *Big Sal*, but not a single shot was fired in *Mahan*'s direction.

"Eight thousand yards," Sandison announced.

Jim Ellis stopped his pacing and took a deep breath. "Come left, zero eight zero," he instructed the Lemurian helmsman.

"My course zero eight zero," announced the 'Cat after a few moments' pause.

"God be with us," whispered Jim, and then he spoke aloud: "You may fire your torpedo, Mr. Sandison."

With a shudder they felt through the ship itself, and a muffled *whump-chuff!*, the MK-10 torpedo leaped into the air, surrounded by a shroud of smoke and steam. The fires of the city cast an angry red glare on the burnished metal body, and an instant later the weapon was swallowed by the choppy sea flowing beside the ship. A gush of bubbles rose to the surface, barely visible in the gloom, as the torpedo accelerated toward its target. Just like that, they'd cast the final die. Now all they could do was wait until they rolled to a stop to see what the numbers were.

"Ahead full. Left full rudder! We'll wiggle around a little until we know whether they noticed the impulse charge." As the ship came about, Jim moved to the port wing and raised his glasses. First he looked aft, making sure the sharp turn wasn't too much for the launch to follow; then he looked to *Amagi* as she appeared aft, beyond the funnels.

"Rudder amidships!" he called. *Amagi* was still clearly outlined, still busy with her terrible work. She'd taken no notice of what transpired to port. Jim focused the glasses more carefully, then clenched them in his hands.

"No!" he moaned. A Grik ship was slowly creeping up alongside *Amagi*, the black outline of its masts and sails beginning to obscure the stern of the Japanese ship. "How deep is that fish?" he shouted across the pilothouse. Sandison looked up in alarm and raced to his side.

"Ten feet, more or less."

"*Shit!*" Everyone on the bridge was startled by Ellis's uncharacteristic profanity.

"What?" Bernie asked, then he saw it too. The Grik ship was almost directly abeam of *Amagi* now. "Maybe it'll pass under?" he said anxiously.

"Not a chance! *Revenge* drew thirteen feet, and they're all about the same!" Jim didn't stop to consider that, without her guns, the captured ship had drawn only slightly less than nine feet of water. The ship between *Amagi* and the torpedo was packed with hundreds of warriors, however. In the end, it didn't make any difference. A brightly luminescent column of water snapped the Grik vessel in half, lifting the stern high in the air. The bow section was already half-submerged when the shattered stern crashed down upon it. A loud, muffled *boom* reached them across the distance, almost drowned by *Amagi*'s next salvo. Jim turned to the helmsman and snarled: "Come about!"

Salissa was dying. All her tripod masts were down, and the pagodalike dwellings within them were a shambles. Fires raged unchecked in several portions of the ship, and only a few guns continued to belch defiance at the enemy. She'd been flooded heavily down so she might avoid major damage below the waterline, but she'd sunk much lower than intended now. Occasionally Keje felt her hull grinding against the bottom as the outgoing tide slowly dragged her across it. Before long she would truly rest on the bottom, one way or another, and the way things were going, there'd be no one left to pump her out.

Keje was sitting on his beloved wooden stool, which

someone had brought to him when an enormous splinter of wood slashed his leg. He was still on the rampart—what was left of it—and expected that he had only minutes to live. The Grik had made no real attempt to board *Big Sal* as yet; they were too preoccupied trying to break through the wall, and it even looked like they'd succeeded at a couple of points. *Amagi* had made that possible by knocking the wall flat. Somehow the Jaaps must have known they'd been successful and the ensuing salvos were only slaughtering their allies. That was when the mighty guns became devoted to demolishing Keje's Home.

Keje had never seen *Amagi* before this night, and he'd been simply incapable of imagining her power. He knew the Amer-i-caans were afraid of her, and that had given him pause. Because of that he'd known, intellectually, that the Japanese ship was a threat. But deep down, he realized now, he'd really had no idea. They'd been fools to stay and try to resist it! Fools. Cap-i-taan Reddy tried to warn them—to explain what they faced. But he'd been willing to stay and fight, and that had given them heart. Surely it couldn't be that bad? Keje now knew it was. He'd stayed out of pride and disbelieving ignorance. Friendship too, and a sense of duty to his people, but mostly because he hadn't truly known.

Alone, perhaps, among all the People now engaged in this apparently losing fight, Cap-i-taan Reddy and his Amer-i-caans had truly *known* what they faced. But instead of running, they'd elected to stay and defend their ignorant friends. Now, just as *Salissa* Home lay helpless under *Amagi*'s onslaught, *Walker* lay helpless and burning out in the bay. Keje had no idea what had happened to *Mahan*, but he suspected the explosion beyond *Amagi* was probably the result of the weapon she'd been sent to deploy. If that was the case, all was truly lost, and he felt a terrible grief for his friends and his people. Some might get away through the jungle to the east, and perhaps *Mahan* might yet escape. But for *Salissa* and her little sister *Walker*, who'd come to her aid so long ago, Keje was convinced this would be their final fight. Fire blossomed once more from end to end of the massive enemy ship, and he listened to the shells approach. A sudden calm overcame him. At least he'd die with his ship. He hoped the souls of the destroyermen would find their way to wherever it was they belonged, but he also hoped he'd be able to thank them first—and tell them farewell.

"Lookout reports ... some kind of explosion west of *Amagi*!" Reynolds cried. "He said something took out one of the Grik ships on that side. Maybe a loose mine," he speculated hopefully.

Matt closed his eyes and took a deep breath. He knew instinctively that the explosion had been no mine. It was too coincidental and the setup too perfect. He was convinced *Mahan* had made her attack and the Grik ship blundered into the torpedo's path.

"Any reaction from the Japs?"

"No, sir. A searchlight came on for a few seconds and scanned the water close aboard; then it went out. *They* must think it was a mine." Like all of them, Reynolds didn't want to admit their last chance was gone. Then he stiffened, listening to his headset. "We got steam!" he suddenly shouted excitedly. "Spanky—I mean Mr. McFarlane—just reported that they finally managed to make their way to the valve and shut it off! Steam pressure's coming up, and so's the water pressure in the mains!"

"What's the steam pressure?"

"Eighty-five, sir, but coming up fast."

"Very well. What's the status on the amidships guns?"

"Unknown, Skipper. It's still too hot to get up there. None of the ammunition's cooked off, though, so the damage may not be too bad."

"Very well. Ask Spanky to report when he's ready to move."

Thirty minutes later Reynolds announced: "Pressure's up to a hundred and ten. We can move, but just don't goose her ... Lieutenant McFarlane says."

"Right full rudder, starboard engine ahead slow, port slow astern," Matt commanded by way of response. "If the Japs are still looking at us, let's make 'em think we're just floating in circles," he explained.

Chief Gray reappeared on the bridge, looking even worse than before. This time his hands were bundled in rags, and he raised them up and shrugged when he caught the captain's glance. "Damn valve wheel was hot." *Walker* groaned beneath their feet as she began her turn. "You asked for a casualty report," he said, and Matt nodded. "Four men and nine 'Cats dead. Most of the 'Cats were in the forward fire room. There're also eleven more with major and minor burns. Some real minor, countin' me."

"The men?"

Gray let out a breath. "Mertz, Elden, Hobbs, and Yarbrough. Mertz was tryin' to make sandwiches for us." He snorted. "The galley's wrecked again and the refrigerator too, this time."

"Where was Lanier?"

"In the head. That must be his battle station."

Matt nodded sadly. The list was likely to get longer soon. He watched as the bow slowly came around. He could see *Amagi* now, dark and malignant. The flashes of her guns left bright red blobs across his vision. A new fire burned fiercely near the dock, and he could see the battle cruiser had turned her wrath on *Big Sal*. He felt a white-hot fist clutch his chest. "Left standard rudder. All ahead full! Gunners to the amidships platform, if they're able. Torpedo mount number one, prepare to fire impulse charges! Maybe that'll shake them up!"

Walker heaved against the unaccustomed weight of the flooded fire room, but sluggishly she gathered speed. The heat from aft began to ease, now that they were steering into the wind, and a refreshing breeze circulated inside the pilothouse, scouring away the acrid smoke. Matt looked at Chief Gray, standing beside him. Both knew this was the end, but there was nothing left for them.

Gray grinned. "It's been an honor, Skipper. A *strange* honor, but . . ." He shrugged. "I always knew we'd make an Asiatic Fleet destroyerman out of you, and we damn sure did."

"Thanks, Chief." Matt smiled. Then he raised his voice so the rest could hear. "Thank you all." He turned. "Reynolds, inform Mr. Garrett he may comm . . ." He stopped, looking out across the fo'c'sle. A blizzard of fire and tracers suddenly arced out into the night from *Amagi*'s portside secondary armament. The Japanese must have spotted *Mahan*. Maybe Jim had made the same decision he had. "Commence firing!"

The salvo buzzer rang, but there was only a single report,

and a lone tracer arced toward the enemy from the number one gun. They were almost bow-on to *Amagi*, and just like during their first meeting, if *Walker* could get close enough, there was little the Japanese could engage her with from that angle. Some of the heavy antiaircraft emplacements situated high on the superstructure could tear them apart, but so far they were silent. Perhaps they'd been hit during the earlier fight? The ten-inch guns were still trained to starboard, but for the moment they weren't firing. Just about everything on the port side was, however, and there were a series of explosions in the sea much closer to *Amagi* than they'd expected.

"Send a final signal to HQ. Tell them . . ." In his mind Matt saw an image of Sandra Tucker: her sad, pretty face looking up into his as he held her in his arms, tears reflecting the lights of the city that now lay in flaming ruin off the port bow. He shuddered at the thought of all the promise that was lost. He hoped Alan and Karen would survive, and somehow find happiness. "Tell our friends we love them all. God bless."

Walker's deck rumbled as she increased speed, and the buzzer rang again. *Amagi*'s foremost turret had begun to traverse in their direction. *Wham!* The number one gun was rewarded with an impact near the enemy's bridge. One of *Amagi*'s port-side searchlights flickered on again, and the beam stabbed down at the water. Matt was amazed to see *Mahan*'s riddled, smoking form illuminated less than four hundred yards from the Japanese ship. Incredibly, a tongue of fire spat from the gun on her exposed foredeck. An almost panicky fusillade churned the sea around the old four-stacker, but few shells were hitting her now. The unsuspected second destroyer had appeared so shockingly close, the gunners were taken completely by surprise. If she could make it just a little farther, she'd be beneath all but *Amagi*'s highest guns. If there was a single blessing in all this, powerful as she was, *Amagi* hadn't been designed for a knife fight.

Mahan was low by the bow, and smoke gushed from a hundred wounds. Her bridge was a gutted wreck, and yet some hand must still be guiding her, because she forged relentlessly ahead, unerringly aimed at *Amagi*'s side. Matt turned his attention back to the battle cruiser. In that instant the sky lit up in front of him, and *Walker* was tossed into the air like a dog would toss a stick. She came back down with a sickening lurch, and a towering column of water cascaded down upon the foredeck. There was another brilliant flash, and the next thing Matt knew he was facedown on the wooden strakes of the pilothouse, covered with broken glass.

His nose felt as if it had been pushed inside his face, and his lips were hot with the taste of blood. He struggled to his feet and shook his head. His hearing was totally gone except for a high-pitched, ringing buzz that sounded just like the salvo alarm. He couldn't focus his vision through the smoke filling the pilothouse and the tears in his eyes. For a moment he thought he was alone, because there was no movement whatsoever around him. Wiping desperately at his face with a suddenly dark and tattered sleeve, he finally saw Norman Kutas trying to rise and resume his post at the wheel. Kutas had blood running from his ears. Matt helped him up, and saw his mouth moving in the flickering light, but couldn't hear what he said. He glanced behind him and saw Reynolds was up, but dazed. Gray was sitting on the deck beside the unmoving form of a 'Cat. Two other men were still down as well. Matt looked through the window.

They were much closer to *Amagi* now. They'd made it under her main battery—which simply couldn't depress enough to fire at *Walker* anymore. They were still racing through a forest of smaller splashes from *Amagi*'s secondaries, however. Matt felt the staccato drumming as tracers probed for *Walker*'s bridge. He wondered why the number one gun was no longer firing and looked down at the fo'c'sle. A long, deep gouge began near the small anchor crane forward, and sprouted into a gaping, jagged hole just in front of the gun. One 'Cat was crawling around on her hands and knees, but the rest of the crew was just . . . gone. Then he saw Dennis Silva's unmistakable form, closely followed by another man and two 'Cats, dash through the sleeting tracers and duck behind the dubious protection of the gun's splinter shield. Each had a pair of shells under their arms.

A 5.5-inch shell exploded against the tall foremast behind and above their heads. With a tortured shriek of tearing steel and the high-pitched wail of the lookout, the whole thing crashed into the sea to starboard. Still secured by a twisted spiderweb of cables and stays, it began pounding against the hull. Two more heavy blows aft pitched Matt forward against his chair. Distractedly, he thought either his hearing was better or the explosions were very loud. Reynolds had recovered himself and was screaming into his microphone in frustration, apparently getting no response. The number one gun fired.

Gray was up now, pointing through the shattered windows. His mouth was moving in a shout, and Matt thought he heard the word "*Mahan.*"

"What is it?" Kurokawa demanded, when he heard the excited cries sweeping like a wave across the bridge from port to starboard.

"Enemy destroyer off the port beam, sir! Closing fast!" came the alarmed reply.

"But . . ." Beyond that, he couldn't speak. The American destroyer was in *front* of them! It was still burning—although it did seem to be moving now. . . .

Sato Okada seared him with an expression of utter contempt. "Surface action, *port!*" he shouted. "Commence firing, all guns, *commence firing!*"

Ahead of them, *Walker* had completed her turn. Her bow lit with the flash of her number one gun, and an instant later the forward part of the bridge near the helm exploded in upon them with a terrific blast and a searing ball of flame. From where he lay on the debris-strewn deck, Sato heard Kaufman's gleeful laugh.

Jim Ellis released the wheel and crouched on the splintered strakes just before *Mahan* crashed into *Amagi*'s side at almost fourteen knots. He slammed against the base of the wheel and fell back on the deck. Wincing from the pain of several cracked or broken ribs, he struggled to rise. Impossible. With a gasp, he sprawled backward. Strange, kaleidoscopic lights flashed through the hundreds of holes in the front of the bridge, and cables and shredded conduit dangled from the overhead. *Mahan*'s bridge had drawn a terrifying volume of fire during that final approach. Miraculously, Jim didn't think he'd been badly hit, but he was certain he was the last man alive in the forward part of the ship.

He clenched his teeth against the pain and tried to rise once more. To his surprise, he felt a pair of hands under his arms, helping him to his feet.

"You go!" came an urgent, heavily accented voice. "Go, go! Time ... small!" Jim shook his head, amazed by how quiet it suddenly seemed. The blower still roared behind him, but the shooting had all but stopped. There was a great rumbling, crunching sound forward, as *Mahan* still drove against the side of the Japanese ship.

"I can't go. I have a job to finish!"

The Lemurian fixed him with intense, desperate eyes, and Jim suddenly realized who it was. "I do!" said Saak-Fas. "I help make ready! I know, I ... do!" The Lemurian straightened to his full height. "I *need* do!"

Jim looked at him, but it was hard to see through the darkness and the blood running in his eyes. "It's my ship. My responsibility," he gasped. The 'Cat gestured to a form on deck. It moaned.

"'Spons-baal-tee?"

Torn, Jim could only stand rooted to the deck. He felt it beginning to settle. Suddenly the Lemurian blinked and began making his way to the ladder at the back of the pilothouse. "I *do*! No time!" With that, he disappeared down the ladder. Realizing he had no choice, Jim staggered to Bernard Sandison, lying in a pool of blood, and began dragging him toward the ladder.

Saak-Fas stepped lightly down the companionway stairs to the passage leading to the wardroom. The lights were dim and flickering, but that didn't matter; he could see as well in the dark as the Amer-i-caans could in daylight. Down yet another ladderlike stair, he entered the crew's forward berthing space. Water was half a tail deep on deck, and more gushed in through great rents in the side of the ship. Forward he sloshed through the rising water, until he came to the passageway leading to the chain locker. The collision damage was more evident here. The deck was buckled beneath his feet and the water was clammy and slick with oil leaking from ruptured fuel bunkers below.

He'd rarely been *in* the water before, except for baths of course. Other than surf, he'd never stood in seawater up to his waist. That just wasn't done. He felt a chill at the thought that some flasher fish might somehow have wriggled into the ship, but he knew it was unlikely. Most of the holes were probably too small, and besides, it was after dark. He stopped at the entrance to the passageway and looked inside with a sense of growing peace. The ordeal he'd suffered at the hands of the Grik still tortured him. He'd fought to suppress the terror, the agony of that experience, knowing that somehow, if he did, the Heavens would reward him with the opportunity now at hand.

It had been so hard at times, the added misery he heaped upon himself. The rejection of his beloved Selass, his self-imposed isolation from his people. But everything he did to torment himself further had helped create the buffer that now existed between his mind and the real pain and lingering terror that threatened to drive him mad. He'd passed the ultimate test, and now the reward was near. He looked fondly at the twelve half-submerged depth charges jumbled in the passageway by the collision. He smiled at the feeling of unaccustomed happiness that slowly filled his being. He'd savor the short additional time he'd give the Amer-i-caan, Ellis, to try to get clear. Then he'd strike a mighty blow against the hated Grik and finally end his agony in the same, glorious instant.

"Hold them back! *Hold* them!" Pete Alden bellowed. Even as he did, the volunteers from Manila broke. It was like a heavy cable supporting far too great a weight. The strands began to separate and fray, snapping and protesting as they did, but inexorably, as the cable began to thin, the strain on the surviving strands became ever greater. Finally, inevitably, it snapped. It wasn't really their fault. The small contingent of Maa-ni-lans had received the least amount of training of any of the defenders, and someone on the other side may have been savvy enough to notice that their short section of the line was a little softer than the others. They'd been hammered mercilessly ever since the start of the fight as well, and their numbers had dwindled by more than half.

With a wild, triumphant, hissing roar, like the sound of heavy surf pounding against the rocks, a densely packed mass of Grik sent them reeling back. A wedge was driven between the intermingled First and Fifth Baalkpan on the left, and Company B, First Marines, and the *Humfra-Dar*s on the right. What ensued was a wild melee like nothing Pete had yet seen since the long, long battle began.

Bellows of rage and screams of agony intermixed with the harsh clanging of weapon on weapon and shield on shield. The terrifying jaws and sickle-shaped Grik swords and claws slashed and tore and hacked their way through the line, while the defenders did their best to close the gap. Inexorably, the line peeled away from the break as the defenders tried, instinctively, to re-fuse their new flanks, and the Grik pressed even harder. Pete had a sick, sinking feeling in his gut, and he could almost see the entire line rolling up from within, and marauding, slaughtering Grik surging unopposed through the city pathways. The end of everything was as clear before him as if it had already happened.

Suddenly the ripping sound of a light machine gun, one of *Mahan*'s .30's most likely, chattered above the seething, shrieking mass. Then came the stutter of a Thompson, then two. Soon a steady crackle of rifle fire joined in. Chack must have committed his rifle company at last. Alden remembered his last conversation with the remarkable young Lemurian, and he only hoped he hadn't waited too long after all. For just an instant, the Grik penetration hesitated, confused.

With a wild, high-pitched squall like hundreds of maddened cats, and shouts of "B'mbaado! B'mbaado!" Queen Maraan's personal guard, with their silver sunbursts on jet-black shields, rose from behind the low secondary redoubt and slammed into the teetering Grik with a berserk frenzy. Without hesitation Pete joined the charge, emptying his automatic pistol almost as fast as he could slide magazines into it. His staff joined in, swinging their swords. The counterattacking force was far smaller than the enemy breakthrough, but the effect of the attack was all out of proportion to the numbers involved. The Grik staggered back, away from the devastating blow. Those directly at the point of contact turned to flee in wild-eyed panic. Finding their escape blocked by those behind them, they turned their weapons on their comrades—even as they were cut down from behind.

Pete watched in dumbfounded amazement as the catastrophic breakthrough degenerated into another kind of catastrophe—for the Grik. The battle to escape became a real battle, Grik on Grik, as those caught within the Baalkpan defenses fought against those still trying to get in. Because they were sandwiched between their own kind and the frenzied defenders, the breakthrough was quickly exterminated. And yet . . . something of what happened within the wall seemed to take hold beyond it. A small nucleus of panicked warriors had escaped destruction and continued fighting their way through the press. The entire attack ground to a halt while the situation in front of the breach sorted itself out.

Queen Maraan appeared beside him to his right, looking over the wall. She was panting heavily, bloody sword in hand. "It looked like we would break them for a moment, just as we did at Aryaal," she gasped. "It's like they cannot comprehend defense. If they are not attacking, they are losing." She shrugged. "But they are so many."

Pete stared at her, struck by sudden inspiration. He hadn't been at the Battle of Aryaal, and hadn't seen what she had. In the heat of battle, he'd completely forgotten Bradford's crackpot theory. Then, over her head, and far out in the bay where the flashes of *Amagi*'s guns had become so common, there was another mighty flash, much bigger than the others. A sheet of fire vomited into the sky, and *Amagi*'s stricken silhouette was at the very heart of the massive plume. Many others saw it too, on both sides, and the fighting became almost desultory as thousands of heads turned toward the bay. The noise of the explosion, when it came, was fantastic. Not so much in actual sound, though it was great, but in the sense of size and power it represented over such a great distance.

"My God!" shouted Pete. "It worked! That Goddamn, idiotic, torpedo stunt *worked*!" An enormous, rising, thunderous cheer built throughout the city. "*It worked!*" screamed Pete again as he turned back to look at the stunned sea of Grik. If there was any chance Bradford was right, now was the time to find out. "*Push them!*" he bellowed. "Push them back! Up and at 'em!" He holstered his pistol and unslung his Springfield. "The army will *advance!*"

Walker staggered under the force of the mighty blast, and the rest of the glass in the pilothouse streamed inward like shattered ice. Kutas cried out, reflexively raising his hands to his face. Matt lunged for the wheel. "Chief!" he shouted. "Get this man below!" He spun the wheel hard to port, preventing the completion of *Walker*'s suicidal dash to ram *Amagi* herself. The ship responded sluggishly, and once again it seemed like her speed was dropping off. He was grateful for the reprieve *Mahan* had given them, but horrified by her sacrifice as well. In a hidden corner of his soul, he might have even felt a little cheated. A wave of irrational anger swept over him, and he lashed out at Reynolds.

"I want a report from Spanky *now*!" he shouted.

"I'm *trying*, Skipper!" The young seaman looked close to tears. "I can't get through! I can't get *anything*!"

"I'll find out, Captain!" Gray shouted back, as he helped the blinded, moaning helmsman down the ladder. Matt looked back at *Amagi*. A giant towering mushroom of fire and smoke was still rising and expanding into the dark, hazy sky. At the base of that pyre would be *Mahan*'s shattered remains.

"My God."

He was thankful he couldn't see *Mahan*, as *Walker* ranged down *Amagi*'s opposite side. The battle cruiser was beginning to list heavily to port, and a wide strip of red bottom paint was rising into the light of the burning city. They'd make sure, Matt grimly determined, although he couldn't imagine anyone on *Mahan* having survived. A dreadful, heavy sadness descended upon him when he remembered *Mahan*'s farewell the night before. Jim must have been planning this all along, and never said a word. He continued *Walker*'s slow turn to port, and when Leo Davis appeared and relieved him at the wheel, Matt told him to steer around to the other side of the Japanese ship.

Amagi was engulfed in flames, from just aft of her funnel where *Mahan* struck, all the way to her number four turret. Japanese sailors scurried madly about her decks, dragging hoses and directing streams of water onto the conflagration. Some were removing covers from her lifeboats. Clearly her crew was concerned with more important matters than the battered, smoldering destroyer describing a wide, decrepit turn off her starboard side. It never even occurred to Matt that she wasn't finished yet.

Spanky himself staggered onto the bridge, looking even

worse than the chief. Most of his hair was gone, and his skin looked purple and angry. His clothes were a uniform dark gray from the soot and oil that stained them. He wiped his face with his hat.

"I didn't mean to take you from your work, Spanky," Matt told him. "Gray could've brought the word."

"Not this word, Skipper," he said, looking down at the deck. Then he raised his scorched face to Matt's and looked him in the eye. "We're gonna lose the ship." He spoke the words quietly, but they had the effect of a shouted curse. "The forward engine room's flooding, and we can't keep ahead of it in the aft fire room much longer." He sighed. "Hell, there's flooding everywhere. The pumps are overwhelmed. Those last two five-and-a-half's opened us up like a sardine can, aft. You don't even *want* to know what that ten-incher did to us belowdecks."

"How long does she have?" Matt asked him stiffly.

"Couple hours. Maybe three, if nobody shoots any more holes in her. Most of the leaks aren't too bad, but they're *everywhere*." He shook his head. "She's just had enough. We got maybe an hour and a half left for the engines, but after that she's gonna go fast."

Matt slowly nodded, and tried to keep his voice under control. "Thanks, Spanky. Stretch it out as long as you can. I'll try to get some shallow water under her before she goes down." He looked out through the bridge windows. Davis had glanced over his shoulder to listen to the conversation and saw the sudden surprise on the captain's face. He quickly turned back to the front. When they brought the ship about, she should have passed far ahead of the sinking battle cruiser. Now he could see they were headed almost directly at her, and her bow was now reaching for the west. Davis broke the stunned silence himself.

"Holy Toledo! The Japs are underway!" He pounded the wheel under his hands. "They can't *do* that!" As if in answer to his protest, a stream of tracers marched toward the ship. On the fo'c'sle, Silva opened fire without even waiting for orders.

"Grik Rout" was real, and it was happening everywhere. The weary defenders in the south charged up and over their wall with their curious but ferocious high-pitched yell. Alden imagined it was very much like what the old rebel yell of the Confederacy must have sounded like. Demoralized already by the evident destruction of their invincible iron ship, the Grik host recoiled from the onslaught. Once again, they fought viciously among themselves as those in the rear ranks battled to maintain the assault against those who'd already abandoned it. To them, the attack became one against those who would try to prevent their escape. And all the while, the former defenders waded behind them through the carnage, slaughtering them almost without resistance. The panicked Grik in front of them, fighting their own kind, added a substantial force multiplier to the charge.

Across the corpse-choked moat and onto the open plain beyond, the defenders-turned-attackers kept up the unrelenting pressure while somehow, miraculously, maintaining a semblance of shield-wall integrity. The discipline and careful training Alden had insisted on was paying off. Even so, the advance began to slow. The troops were exhausted after the long fight, and the exertion of just climbing over bodies so they could keep slaughtering Grik began to tell. The thousands who fled were being killed by both sides, and the unrouted mass behind them began to move forward bit by bit. The charge finally ground to a halt, and then it was like the field of Aryaal again in yet another way: both battle lines stood in the open without support or protection, and in that situation, the overwhelming numbers of the enemy began to swing the tide back.

Alden slashed with his rifle, butt-stroking and stabbing with the bayonet, as he'd demonstrated so many times on the drill field. His pistol was empty and he had no more ammunition. Before him was a scene from a nightmare hell. Gnashing teeth, slashing weapons, and high-pitched shrieks of pain punctuated the rumbling roar of shields grinding together. The damp earth at his feet had been churned into a bloody, viscous slurry, and the only traction afforded to those holding the shield wall were the mushy mounds of unrecognizable gore half-submerged in the ooze. The frothing, working mass of Grik beyond the shields were illuminated by a red, flickering light from the fires—adding to the unreal, otherworldly aspect of the battle. Chack almost stumbled past him, shouting his name, and Pete grabbed him by the arm. "Where's the rifle company?" he shouted.

"The machine guns are empty, and I ordered the others to stay on the wall. They're of little use in this type of fight. If all had bayonets it might be different. . . ."

"Never mind. You did right. Have them prepare to cover our withdrawal. I'm going to try to pull back to the wall."

"It will be risky. The enemy will sense victory and strike even harder."

"I know, but that's all there is. We can't move forward and we can't stay here. There're just too damn many." Chack blinked reluctant agreement. He turned to run back to the wall and prepare his troops. Then he stopped. Alden looked in the direction he faced and was stunned to see hundreds of Lemurians pouring over the wall and racing over the ground he'd been preparing to yield. More than hundreds, perhaps a few thousand in all, and he had no idea where they'd come from. There simply were no more reserves. Then he saw the proud regimental flags whipping in the breeze as their bearers crossed the wall in the wake of the charge. The Second Aryaal, the Second B'mbaado, and the Third Baalkpan were three he recognized. All were "veteran" units that had been deployed in defense of the shipyard and the north wall.

Screaming their rage, they streamed across the abattoir and surged directly into the faltering line. The weight of their unexpected charge carried the entire shield wall forward into the face of the enemy, and once again there was a distinct change in the Grik. Once again those facing the added spears turned on those behind them, slashing and screaming in panic, and slaying their unprepared comrades before they had a chance to even realize what had happened. The rout began to grow, and the air of terror was even greater this time. As the shield wall churned forward again, it became apparent that many Grik still fighting bore the same wild-eyed expressions as those trying to get away. Something was pushing them from behind, just as the reinforced attack was driving them back. Almost as if it shared a single collective awareness, the entire host suddenly shifted in the one direction it perceived safety might still be found: toward the sea.

What began as a steadily growing tendency to move west quickly built into a panicked rush. Soon the horde of Grik was flowing past the shield wall from left to right with the unstoppable chaotic urgency of a massive, flooding river. Spears continued to slay them as they hurried past, but there was no reaction from those around the victims except, perhaps, to quicken their pace. It was shocking and amazing and dreadful all at once, and a vague cheer began to build as Alden's troops realized that this time there'd be no stopping the rout. Whatever force enabled the Grik to operate with some semblance of cooperation, cunning, and courage had disappeared just as surely as if the strings of a marionette had been cut.

The cheering grew frenzied when the flag of the Second Marines resolved itself in the flickering gloom beyond the raging torrent of Grik.

"It's Shinya! Shinya!" came a gleeful shout at Alden's side. He turned and saw Alan Letts actually jumping up and down and waving his arms in the air. His hat was gone and his red hair was plastered to his scalp with blood and sweat. Mud spattered in all directions as he capered. Pete grinned happily at Letts's enthusiasm, and his unexpected presence. He was obviously right. Somehow the force in Fort Atkinson they'd feared was doomed had managed to break out and attack the enemy in the rear. Not only that, but they'd timed it just about perfectly as well. Now it looked like it would be only a matter of minutes before the forces were reunited, as what once had been the Grik right fled between them.

"Where the hell did you come from?" Alden asked the ecstatic Letts.

"After the Japs pounded the Great Hall, there was something wrong with Nakja-Mur, so we carried him to the hospital." He shook his head. "It looked like everything was falling apart. The lizards broke through on the waterfront, and some are even roaming through the city." He sobered. "*Big Sal* got pasted. I don't know if there's anybody left alive. Anyway, I sent runners to fetch every regiment not actually engaged. Stripped *everything*, and had them converge on the parade ground." He grinned. "Then when *Amagi* blew up, the lizard breakthrough just fell apart. We charged them, and most went scurrying back to their ships!" He laughed gleefully. "The ships're all hard aground, and the surviving gunners on the harbor wall are feedin' the fish with 'em right now! Anyway, we left them with it, and hurried here as fast as we could." He winked. "Good thing too."

"No foolin'!" Pete looked at Chack. "As soon as we link up with the 'lost garrison,' we'll continue to press the enemy! We'll sweep those bastards right into the sea!"

For a moment Chack just stood there, amazed. The Grik that fled before them still outnumbered them by a very large margin. And yet, somehow, they were no longer even warriors. They'd become more like the skuggiks they slightly resembled: dangerous individually, but no more capable of concerted action, and no longer a threat to the city. Many would still die destroying what was left when the army swept forward to finish them, but he agreed completely with Alden's intent to do it now while the panic was fresh. He didn't know if "Grik Rout" would ever fade from such an acute state; they'd never again seen any of the Grik that fled before Aryaal. Nevertheless, they couldn't take any chance it might, and besides, the combined defenders of Baalkpan deserved the slaughter that had been given them.

"It's hard to believe it's almost over," he said at last. Then he ran to detail a runner to make contact with Shinya.

"Almost over," Letts repeated happily; then his smile faded. Out on the water he could see the flames of the battle cruiser, but she wasn't where she'd been before. She was creeping toward the mouth of the bay. Behind her, moving just as slowly, was another, smaller ship, also burning. Tracers arced back and forth between them. Was that *Walker* or *Mahan*? He couldn't tell in the dark. Whichever it was, it wasn't over for her. With a hurried word to Alden, he raced back toward the city.

Amagi was listing hard to port, but somehow she remained afloat. Roaring flames leaped skyward, and black smoke coiled and billowed. Her tall, pagodalike superstructure shimmered in the heat and leaned to the left at a drunken angle. Two of the three aft turrets were still trained to starboard, guns slightly elevated at the angle from which they'd been battering the city and *Big Sal*. They were silent now. Their crews had either been cooked inside them, or abandoned them to the fire spreading swiftly aft. The third turret probably hadn't moved since that day so long ago when the dive-bomber crashed into it. She looked destroyed, yet still she floated. She was underway, and it looked more and more as if she might escape.

Walker had found a seemingly magical place directly astern of *Amagi*, where the battle cruiser could bring nothing heavier than light, fixed, or handheld machine guns to bear on the battered destroyer that dogged her. The problem was, that was all she needed. *Walker*'s bridge and foredeck were a bullet-riddled wreck. Only one of her machine guns still spoke from the fire-control platform, manned by Lieutenant Garrett alone. A steady stream of replacements ran to the number one gun, as those crewing it were killed or wounded. Only Dennis Silva remained of the original four who got it back in action, and he was wounded in a dozen places. Still he stood there, drenched in blood, directing the gun at the retreating ship. An occasional stream of yellow "tobacco" juice arced onto the deck. The shots he fired were few and far between, however. There couldn't be more than half a dozen AP shells left on the entire ship, and those were mainly scattered on the wrecked aft deckhouse, where the number four gun had been knocked out by that last 5.5-inch shell. They had to be found and carried forward the length of the ship.

On the bridge, Leo Davis was dead, hit above the left eye by a ricochet. The 'Cat who'd replaced him at the helm was also down. Matt now stood there alone, crouched low behind the thin bulwark and the upright compass housing. Communications were cut off throughout most of the ship, and Reynolds was effectively out of it, yet he stayed on the bridge, curled in a fetal position against the chart house bulkhead, still trying to raise the ship's various compartments. They'd heard only by word of mouth that the auxiliary conning station, aft, was destroyed. Its crew—including Larry Dowden—had never known what hit them. Matt mourned Larry, and all the others lost this night. If there was a later, he'd mourn them properly, but without the auxiliary conn, somebody had to steer from the pilothouse. And so it was there, on *Walker*'s bridge, that Matt played tag with the devil.

With the loss of the foremast, the radio was out, and Clancy had been ordered to remove it and place it in the whaleboat—the only boat left. The launch was a shattered wreck, and the other launch never returned from searching for survivors of the PBY. Of course, they'd been steaming at high speed ever since it left. Maybe it was still out there somewhere, vainly trying to catch them.

An intermittent pounding, metallic drumming, came from the front of the pilothouse where bullets struck, but the enemy fire had begun to slacken. Matt saw Spanky crawling across the strakes from the ladders. He was bleeding and seemed disoriented. Matt risked a peek out the window to make sure their position relative to *Amagi* was unchanged. His hat had been snatched off his head during a recent similar check. "Are you all right?" he shouted.

McFarlane shook his head. "I'm shot, Goddamn it. How're you?"

The captain almost laughed. "Nothing, would you believe it?" A throbbing pain resurfaced. "Busted nose, a few scratches," he amended. "How's she holding up?"

"The bow's a sieve, and she's down four feet by the head. I just came from there. A Jap bullet came through the goddamn hull and got me in the goddamn ass! Everybody's out of the aft fire room but the Mice, and they're in water up to their shins. If we don't head for shore right damn now, the fish'll get us all!"

Matt nodded, but at the same time he knew he couldn't give up. *Amagi* might be finished—*Walker* certainly was—but as long as the battle cruiser was afloat, she was a threat. He couldn't break off before the task was done—not as long as they had a single shell for the number one gun. It had to end here, now. If *Amagi* got away and somehow survived, Baalkpan would never survive her eventual return. Worse than that, the sacrifice of all those who'd died and suffered this long day and night would have been for nothing.

"Soon," Matt promised. "We'll break off soon."

"Goddamn it! Why won't that unholy bitch just sink?!" Silva raged into the night. He could barely see through the blood clouding his vision, and he suspected his left eye was ruined. A swarm of paint chips and bullet fragments were the cause. Even so, he could tell *Amagi* was listing twenty-five or thirty degrees—but that was where it stopped. Low in the water and creeping along at barely five knots, the Jap was still underway and entering the center of the channel. He'd thrown shell after shell into her stern, and there'd been no visible effect other than a growing, gaping hole in her fantail. Now, no matter how hard they searched, the runners who'd been bringing him shells couldn't find any more.

Machine-gun bullets still rattled off the splinter shield, but only a few. It was as if the Japanese sailors knew *Walker* had done her worst, and had nothing left to throw at them. They were going to get away.

"Mr. Silva!" came a cry behind him, and he whirled in shock. Through the warped, twisted hatch on the starboard front angle of the superstructure appeared a small girl and a striped lizard.

"What the *hell* are you *doing* here?" he choked. "God-damn, there's bullets and bombs . . . and we're fixin' to sink! Get your stupid asses under cover, for crissakes!"

Rebecca looked at her companion. "Well, Lawrence, clearly we're not wanted, and apparently they don't need *this* as badly as we thought—with everyone running around looking for them!" It was only then that Silva realized the small girl and large, but still sore lizard were struggling with a heavy, four-inch-fifty shell suspended between them.

Torn, he glanced at the retreating battle cruiser. For the moment the incoming fire had stopped completely. Maybe the enemy gunner was out of ammunition—or he'd simply given up. "Shit!" he groaned disgustedly. "Gimme that; then get the hell outta here!" He sprinted across the blood-slick deck to meet them. "Let me guess: Lieutenant Tucker still thinks you're with O'Casey and vicey-versey?"

"I tried to sto' her," Lawrence announced virtuously, but the girl only grinned.

"My safety is still primarily *your* responsibility, Mr. Silva. I have no control over assumptions others might make," Rebecca stated sternly. "Besides, whether they like it or not, or even know it, my people must be represented in this fight!"

"Skipper's gonna kill me," Silva muttered with absolute certainty, taking the shell in his massive hands. He noticed with a sinking feeling that it was high-explosive. "Here," he said, resignedly, handing it to the loader, "let's make it count!" He glared back at the girl. "I've pulled some stupid stunts, but this . . . at least get behind the splinter shield!"

Rebecca's grin faded. "Your eye!"

"Just a scratch." Silva turned to Pack Rat, the Lemurian pointer. "Well? Quit screwin' around, and let 'em have it!"

"You gonna aim for us?" Pack Rat cried sarcastically. His gunners were all Lemurians, too short to look through the sight and push the trigger pedal too. They could elevate and traverse if he guided them, though. He was positive just a few more rounds would finish *Amagi*, but they just didn't have them. A single HE shell wouldn't make much difference.

"Yeah, if somebody'll load the goddamn thing!" he growled disgustedly. It was then that he saw his trainer was down. "Hey . . . Lawrence! Get your stripey ass on the training wheel!"

Lawrence's jaw went slack. "Trainer? I?"

"Yeah, trainer, you! Step on it!"

The breech slammed shut, and Silva squinted with his good eye through the telescopic sight mounted on the left side of the gun. Only the smallest part of his consciousness even noticed when a tiny hand squirmed its way into his clenched, bloody fist.

"Port a little," he crooned, "port . . . port . . . Good! Up, up . . . Good. Shit! Stop when I say 'good,' damn you! Down . . . Good!" He stepped aside. "Fire!" Pack Rat stomped on the pedal. The gun barked and recoiled backward, but Silva was watching the tracer. It struck right in the middle of the gaping hole aft, and he thought he saw a brief flash deep inside the ship.

"A hit!" Rebecca cried excitedly.

"Woop-te-do. Might as well throw hand grenades at the bastard," Silva explained dejectedly. "Well, that's that," he said, squeezing Rebecca's hand before letting it go. Suddenly he hurt all over, and he was sick inside as well. "Beat feet back to the pilothouse. There's no sense standing around and getting shot if we ain't got no more bullets! I'll tell the captain we're dry." He started to turn.

"Silva, look!" Pack Rat shouted. Dennis did. *Amagi* was suddenly leaning a little farther to port and veering hard right.

"What the hell?" he murmured. "Maybe we hit her steering engine or something?" Whether that was the case, or *Amagi* had simply tired of the dog yapping at her heels and decided to present her remaining broadside of secondary guns and destroy the nuisance that tasked her, Silva had no idea. He knew the latter would be the result, however, and *Walker* heeled as the captain saw it too. Sluggishly, *Walker* turned hard a'port, but her grace and quickness were gone. The short delay was just enough to put her at a disadvantage, and there was nothing she could do. Silva clutched the girl to his side and braced himself for the final fusillade, while *Amagi* continued her sharp turn, out of the main channel, and into the prepared lane they'd left the day before. She was drawing considerably more water this time when she passed directly over the MK-6 magnetic exploder—and the cluster of depth charges it was anchored to.

The sea convulsed around her, just under the number two turret, and her entire bow heaved up upon the gigantic swelling of foam. Then a geyser of spray erupted forth and completely inundated the forward half of the ship. There was very little flash, but the sound of the blast was enormous. *Amagi* collapsed into the hole the charges left in the water, the sea closing over the bow before it shuddered back to the surface like a submarine. Only now, it was ... crooked ... somehow. The outline of the ship had visibly changed, and even as they watched, it contorted still more. Water surged near the base of the forward superstructure, but there was red paint visible beneath her pointed bow.

"*Broke her goddamn back!*" Silva bellowed. "I *knew* it would work!" Pack Rat looked at him incredulously, and Rebecca threw her arms around his waist.

Captain Kurokawa was thrown against the chart table by the force of the blast. His head struck the edge, and he lay stunned for several moments. He comprehended a great roaring, surging sensation, as well as screams and urgent shouts. *Amagi* heaved beneath him, and the deck began to cant.

"*Nooooo!*"

He didn't recognize the cry that escaped his lips. It was primordial. Staggering to his feet, he looked about. All the windows were smashed, and sparks fell like fiery rain from shorted conduits on the overhead. The flames that engulfed his ship aft boiled to unprecedented heights—then began to subside. The tilt of the deck was becoming more extreme. "No!" he shrieked again. The bridge seemed deserted of all but bodies. Those who'd left their posts would pay, he grimly swore. Then he saw movement on the blistered bridge wing. Still groggy, Kurokawa recognized the American, Kaufman, by his beard and skinny frame. The man was whooping with savage joy, even as the ship sank beneath him. Fumbling at his side, Kurokawa slipped the Nambu pistol from the leather holster and moved carefully across the sloping deck.

"This is the cost of your madness!" came a feeble shout from beneath the wreckage of the engine room telegraph. Without hesitation, Kurokawa snapped off a shot in the direction of the voice. He was rewarded by a moan of anguish. Looking closer, he peered into the sputtering darkness to see Sato Okada. Just as he thought. He leveled the pistol at the dark form and advanced.

"Your treachery has brought us to this, Commander." His voice was almost calm, but his eyes bulged with maniacal fury. "My strategy to subvert the Grik, and ultimately have them serve us, would have succeeded in the end." He straightened. "It will yet. They will win the battle and the ship will be saved. I will continue to serve the emperor in spite of you, wherever we are!" Carefully, he aimed the Nambu at an eye that seemed to glow in the darkness. "You won't live to see it, however." His finger tightened on the trigger.

More sparks seemed to pour from his eyes, and he crumpled under the force of a blow to the back of his head. He vaguely knew the pistol had fired again as he fell. Rolling over, he looked up in time to see his attacker. Skinny arms raised above his head, clutching a twisted piece of conduit, David Kaufman stood silhouetted against the burning night beyond the windows.

"Wait!" he cried, and to his amazement the man actually did. The final blow didn't fall, and Kaufman stood gasping, waiting expectantly. Kurokawa shot him. With a roar of rage, Kaufman raised the pipe to strike, but the Nambu barked again and again, until the conduit clattered feebly against the deck beside Kurokawa's head.

Kaufman was on his knees. "Goddamn sneaky Japs," he murmured, and pitched forward onto his face.

Amagi groaned in agony, and Kurokawa quickly pointed

the pistol at Okada, where he still lay trapped. "Where were we?" he asked.

"You were going to shoot me, but you can't anymore. The magazine is empty."

Kurokawa jerked the trigger, but nothing happened. Where did all the bullets go? "No matter!" he barked in frustration. "Your reprieve will be quite short, I assure you! As soon as the battle is over and the damage attended to, I'll have you executed in disgrace!" There was a shuddering rumble deep within the ship, and Sato Okada began to laugh. "Silence, you fool!" Kurokawa raged.

Okada stopped laughing and just looked at him for a moment. "You are the fool, Captain. There will be no repairs!"

Matt and Spanky were both standing now, staring in shock through the empty window frames. Less than four hundred yards away, *Amagi* quickly settled toward the silty bottom of Baalkpan Bay. Her bow broke away and capsized before it went down. The rest of her sank on a relatively even keel. Boats went over the side, and hundreds of white-clad forms scrambled into them, or as high in the superstructure as they could go. The water wasn't particularly deep, and chances were, much of the ship would remain above the surface. Many would survive. Chief Gray staggered onto the bridge without a word, and even Reynolds stood to see.

Great clouds of steam and smoke gushed skyward aft as the sea closed over the fires. A heavy detonation rumbled across the water, and soot and steam belched from the stack. Finally the savaged fantail disappeared from view with a tremendous, thundering gurgle of escaping air. Only then did a heartfelt cheer erupt from *Walker*'s survivors.

Finally! Matt thought. His entire body felt almost rubbery with relief. *My God ... Finally!* He closed his eyes briefly in thanks. A few Grik ships frantically tacked past the smoldering wreck, headed for the Makassar Strait. *Walker* had nothing left to shoot at them.

Matt looked at his watch. "Oh two five eight, Mr. Reynolds. Please record it in the log." He looked at Gray. "Now, if only things are going okay ashore," he said grimly, watching the fleeing ships. It was impossible to tell if they were going to reinforce the landing in the south, or just running away. He had no idea if they were winning or losing the battle on land, and all of Baalkpan seemed to burn.

"Survivors?" Gray asked with distaste, gesturing at the boats in the water and the protruding pagoda. Matt shook his head.

"They're fine for now," he said. "If we take time to bring them aboard, they'll just be in the water with us. How fast can we push her without putting too much stress on the forward bulkheads, Spanky?"

McFarlane seemed distracted, concentrating. "Six knots?" he hazarded. "Faster than that and you'll drive her under. Slower and she'll sink before we get there. I expect you'll try to make it to the shipyard?"

Matt nodded sadly. "That's my hope. I'll angle her toward shore, though, just in case she doesn't make it."

He looked back at *Amagi*'s wreck as he spun the wheel for home. "I wish Jim could've seen this," he said.

By some freakish miracle of buoyancy, *Mahan*'s stern still floated. The entire forward part of the ship had been obliterated by the blast, removing the flooded weight that would have quickly pulled the rest of her down. The explosion also heaved the shattered aft section backward against the continued thrust of her single screw. The watertight integrity was completely gone, however, and the stern was filling rapidly. Escaping air shrieked through the many rents, and the deck tilted ever downward.

Jim and two 'Cats had dragged Sandison into the meager protection of the battered aft deckhouse before the huge explosion drove them to the deck. One of the 'Cats was blown over the side, but the other had been there to revive him. Still lying on the deck, Jim watched with stunned bitterness, and a profound sense of betrayal and futility, as *Amagi* began to steam out of the harbor in spite of her massive wound. He'd killed his ship, and who knew how many of her crew, for nothing. Then, to his bleary-eyed astonishment, he saw *Walker* giving chase.

He knew it was a pointless gesture, as futile as his own had been. *Walker* could never finish the monster with only her lonely number one gun, and clearly that was all she had left to fight with. Even so, in spite of his despair, he felt a thrill of pride. In the flickering light he saw that *Walk-*

er's foremast was down, but someone had removed the big flag and run it up to the top of the shorter mast, aft. It was scorched and torn, but it streamed with a stately, defiant grace. The sight brought tears to his eyes.

He staggered painfully to his feet with the Lemurians' help, and stood unsteadily on the canted deck. The vibration of the engine had subsided at last, and the screw stopped thrashing at the water as it rose into the air. Far across the bay his friend pursued *Amagi*, an occasional flash from the four-inch gun amid the tracers proclaiming that, however hopeless, *Walker* was still in the fight.

The deck lurched beneath his feet. *Mahan* was going fast. He looked down at the unconscious torpedo officer and was grateful that Bernie wouldn't suffer what was to come. He hugged the 'Cat supporting him tightly against his side.

"Cap'n Ellis!" came a cry. Jim whirled and caught a glimpse of a dull white reflection in the water alongside. It was the launch! There was movement aboard, and it was full of men and 'Cats. He'd forgotten all about it—other than a brief suspicion that it had been sunk by the blast.

"Mr. Steele? Is that you?" he cried.

"Aye, sir. Sorry it took so long to come back for you, but with that screw churnin' up the water, we couldn't get close. Better hurry, sir; the old girl's goin'!"

"There's a wounded man up here. Can you give us a hand?"

At that moment his dying ship lurched again, but almost before it registered, he heard a momentous blast. He jerked his head back to the south. *Walker*'s now distant shape was outlined by *Amagi*'s flames, and an enormous cataract of luminous water engulfing the enemy ship.

Wild cheering erupted in the launch, but Frankie Steele's voice remained intent.

"Just slide him down the deck and we'll take him on the boat, Cap'n." He turned to the other occupants of the launch. "Shut up, you guys! I know it's a hell of a thing, but we gotta save the skipper!"

With a final magical image of the sinking battle cruiser etched on his mind, Jim and the Lemurian pushed Sandison down the sloping deck, toward the rising water and waiting hands.

*   *   *

Sandra Tucker and Sean O'Casey sprinted down the pathways of Baalkpan as the all-pervading, haze-gray world began to brighten almost imperceptibly. Fires still burned fiercely in many parts of the city, and soldiers and firefighters with buckets and skin bags of water raced to and fro. Even in the face of the ongoing disaster, however, the mood of those they met was jubilant. They'd won. In spite of everything, they'd won. Bradford ran with them, wheezing from exertion and the weight of the Krag he still carried. He'd come along ostensibly to protect them from marauding Grik—several hundred had broken into the inner city from the waterfront—but Sandra doubted they'd be much of a threat. Most had probably already been killed. She wouldn't have waited regardless. The casualties from the fight for the docks were proportionately greater than anywhere else. The Grik had attempted to land almost a hundred ships there, and *Amagi* had concentrated much of her fire in the area as well. Somewhere behind, the rest of the medical team she'd assembled followed as fast as they could, but she wouldn't wait. Her duty to the wounded would have drawn her anyway, but she'd heard *Walker* was coming in.

Across the cratered parade ground they ran, oblivious to the smoking ashes of the Great Hall and the blackened wreckage of the Sacred Tree, through throngs of celebrating people, and into the desolated trading sector. They finally emerged behind the battered seawall and stared in wonder and horror at the scene before them. It was like the very pit of hell. The colorful, cheerful ambience of the area was entirely gone. In its place was a gray, blood-washed ruin that must have resembled the Great War battlefields of France and Belgium. Bodies were everywhere, friend and foe, but the Grik corpses were beyond number. The earth behind the wall had been churned into a slush of gore, and the stench of death was overpowering. One of the huge cannons still poked through its embrasure, its exhausted crew leaning on it or lying nearby. They were covered in mud and blood, and their pelts were a uniform matted reddish brown. But their white teeth flashed incongruous grins as Sandra approached. They were alive, and they'd won.

She scrambled atop the wall, leaving the one-armed O'Casey struggling clumsily to join her. Beyond, the scene was even worse—if that was possible—except in this case almost all the dead were Grik. Forests of masts protruded from the water, and shattered hulks lay half-submerged against the docks. Fires burned out of control, and she saw some of the enemy still dying even now, writhing in the flames or cringing in parts of the ships not yet burning. Past the dock, and a little to the right, lay the massive sunken carcass of *Big Sal*, her pagodalike habitations blackened by fire, the foremost one still burning. All her masts were gone.

"Wait, my dear!" huffed Bradford behind her. "Please wait just a moment!"

She paid him no heed. Running along the top of the wall, she dashed down past the fitting-out pier and emerged among a large assembly of Lemurians gathered near the shipyard. There'd been no fighting there, almost as if the enemy had deliberately avoided damaging the facility. Probably they had. Because it was mostly clear of Grik, many of the wounded had been carried there, but not everyone present had been injured. Many had come just to see. They were staring seaward, and she looked in that direction.

Two motor launches, the whaleboat, numerous feluccas, and boats of every description strained to nudge or tow *Walker* into the large refit basin. With a rush of terror Sandra saw that the old destroyer had been savaged. Her bridge was riddled with holes, and empty windows gaped. An enormous hole in her foredeck was surrounded by jagged plates peeled back like flower petals. The weather deck was a scorched shambles, and the aft deckhouse had been demolished. The gun once perched atop it had collapsed into the debris and lay on its side, muzzle askew. Most of her length was blackened by fire, and the foremast trailed alongside, tangled in a jumble of cables. Smoke still wafted weakly from her aft funnel—the cantankerous number four boiler—but steam was escaping as well. Less than a foot separated the fo'c'sle from the debris-strewn water, as the bow slowly nudged through the flotsam. Her proud number, 163, was already lost to view. From the aft mast the giant flag still flew, almost shredded now, but stirring fitfully in the light morning breeze. Sandra choked back a sob.

The ship's blood-spattered decks were almost empty, and Sandra assumed most of her survivors had already been removed by the flotilla surrounding her. Several men and 'Cats stood on the fire-control platform, and there was movement on the bridge as well. If Matt still lived, that was where he'd be. She shouldered her way through the throng for a better look, and seeing who she was, most parted and made a lane for her to pass. She didn't notice them, but if she had, she'd have seen the deferential lowered ears and blinks of respect running through the crowd.

Walker edged into the basin and slowed to a stop less than fifty yards from the pier. The overtaxed launches tried to pull her closer, but it was clearly no use. The ship was going fast. As Sandra watched, the aft fire room access trunk opened with a clang, and a mist of steam gushed out. A short female 'Cat crawled onto the deck, then reached back inside the opening. With a mighty heave she pulled first one, then another pale, grimy form into the light. Coughing and leaning on one another, the three quickly shuffled under the amidships deckhouse toward the ladder at the back of the bridge. As if she'd been waiting for that very event, *Walker* finally surrendered herself to the sea. Water crept over the fo'c'sle and coursed into the jagged hole. The rasping blower went silent, but the sound was replaced with a massive, urgent *whoosh* as the bow dipped lower and lower. With a juddering, grinding thump, it struck the silty bottom. There was an almost dying groan as the rest of the ship quickly settled. All that remained above water was the top of the bridge and her four battered funnels resting at a slight angle to port. Most of the flag was still visible too, jostled by the rising, turbulent froth of escaping air.

There was an audible, mournful sigh from the crowd, replaced by a frenzied cheer when a large, bloodied man above the bridge—whom Sandra recognized as Dennis Silva—gave a jaunty wave with one hand, while the other supported a small girl sitting on his shoulders. Tabby and the Mice stiffly ascended the ladder to the crowded platform, and Sandra felt her heart leap into her throat when Matt climbed wearily up from the bridge to join them. She was yelling now too, waving her arms over her head, and tears streamed down her cheeks.

Wherever she came from, there was no doubt: USS *Walker*, DD-163, and her lost and lonely crew had found their way home at last.

EPILOGUE

*D*isaster," Tsalka hissed mournfully. "Utter and complete disaster." The rising sun presided over the beginnings of a bright, brisk morning in the Makassar Strait, and of the almost four hundred ships comprising the Invincible Swarm, less than seventy now accompanied the *Giorsh*, Esshk's flagship, as it sailed back toward Aryaal. To make matters even worse, most of those ships were empty of all but their crews, since they'd been the ones that launched the southern assault. Never in the millennia-long history of the Grik had there been such a catastrophe. Tsalka sighed. "I did not command here, but that will make little difference to the Celestial Mother. I am regent-consort of this territory now, and I am responsible. Would you care to join me, General Esshk, for a final repast? I intend to destroy myself at the midday, with all proper ceremony while it is still due me. You may join me in that as well, if you like."

Esshk leaned on the rail, his claws gouging the white-painted wood as he stared aft at the mighty plume of smoke still hovering over distant Baalkpan. He sighed as well. "I am honored, Lord Regent, but I shall not destroy myself today, nor, I believe, should you. To do so would be selfish, and possibly even a crime against our race."

"But, General," Tsalka hissed in shock, "you know I am no one's prey, and I fear nothing of this world, but surely a quick, clean, honorable death is preferable to what we can expect from the Celestial Mother amid such disgrace?"

"We are disgraced," Esshk agreed, "but not by our ac-

tions. We attacked our prey as we have always done, as
we have been raised and trained to do: with overwhelming numbers and even more overwhelming arrogance. We
are no more disgraced by our actions than the countless
Uul we sent to be slaughtered. Our disgrace lies in our arrogance and our stubborn, rote-dominated, unimaginative
ignorance! Don't you see? This prey is different from any
we have faced before. We thought they were the same as
those that escaped us long ago, but we were wrong. Perhaps it was the 'Americans' that changed them, but it really doesn't matter. The point is, they *have* changed, and
we have not. You accused me of being a philosopher, and
perhaps I am. I hope so, at any rate, because it will take
philosophers, not mindless Uul, to defeat this prey in the
end—and we must defeat them! Having beaten us, do you
think they will be content? Of course not! They will destroy
us all if we do not ready ourselves to meet them, and to
do that we will have to change." He paused. "And some of
those changes must be fundamental."

"But why must we be the ones to attempt this change?"
Tsalka almost wailed. "Better to destroy ourselves than
face such an impossible challenge!"

"It must be we," Esshk replied, "because we were here.
Only we know the truth. Perhaps bearing that truth, knowing the end we face, we will convince the Celestial Mother
it *is* truth. That, and something more." He snapped his
claws and his personal guards disappeared. They returned
escorting a haggard, stained, and bloodied Captain Hisashi
Kurokawa, who stood tensely before his "hosts."

"Captain Kurokawa," Esshk greeted him pleasantly, and
Kurokawa looked at him in surprise. "You failed to bring
the victory we relied on you to achieve, but you are not
entirely to blame. I pushed you when you were not ready,
I failed to heed what I now believe was your excellent advice, and I forced you to attack in a way not of your choosing. You did not, as you claimed, destroy the flying machine
of the prey, but again, that effort was poorly planned and
against your more ... experienced judgment. At any rate,
its contribution to their defense was negligible this time,
and numerous witnesses attest that it is now, in fact, destroyed. We will speak no more of that. As I said, we relied far too heavily upon your one ship—magnificent as

it was—and I have come to accept your radical argument that when the ground from which the hunter strikes disappears from under him, he is not necessarily made prey, or even to blame. I will therefore suffer your continued existence." Kurokawa stifled a gasp, but Esshk continued. "Only one in ten of your Uul shall go to the cook fires for your part in this terrible failure. Far more of our own will feed our remaining host, I assure you, since ours was the greatest failure of all. Choose the food yourself, and choose them wisely, because now we need your knowledge more than ever. We *must have* the wondrous things you promised: the smoking ships, the airplanes, the guns. . . . They are no longer mere trifles to amuse ourselves with; they are essential. You will make them for us."

Kurokawa cared nothing for the additional losses he'd sustain. Barely four hundred of his crew still survived, rescued by *Giorsh* and other ships as they retreated from the bay, but he could spare another forty if he must, if it meant he himself would live. He was just beginning to accept what he'd considered impossible: he would *live*! His fate was now tied inextricably to Esshk's and Tsalka's, and he doubted they were entirely safe themselves, but one thing was certain: he'd just been following orders. On second thought, maybe their fates weren't inextricable. He assumed now they would take him to meet this "Celestial Mother" of theirs, and if she was astute enough to recognize the wonders he could provide, and the threat that made them necessary, perhaps Esshk and Tsalka needed him more than he needed them. He smiled.

Five days after the terrible battle that would be added to the Sacred Scrolls, and ever after remembered as the Battle of Baalkpan, there was a gathering of friends at the shipyard. The air still smelled of smoke, not only from battle, but from the incessant pyres that had burned for the dead. Uncountable Grik bodies had simply been rolled into the sea, and the shoreline seethed with flasher fish as they did their grisly work. Even so, the scent of death lingered, and the mood of those who gathered near the sunken destroyer was already somber.

The great Nakja-Mur, U-Amaki ay Baalkpan, had been carried to the sky along with an unimaginable eleven thousand others. Sandra said his heart failed in the stress and excitement, but most believed it simply broke. Never in the recorded history of the People had there been such traumatic loss of life. The only consolation was that he'd died knowing his people were safe and the victory he'd given everything for was at hand. Along with him, the flames had carried Naga and Ramic-Sa-Ar to the Heavens. Ramic died in the final fighting, knowing at least part of his vengeance was complete. Young Tassana was now High Chief of *Aracca.*

The destroyermen had lost dearly too, and there were graves in Baalkpan now. Thirteen just from *Walker*, including Larry Dowden, Dave Elden, and Leo Davis. They'd been laid beside Tony Scott's empty grave on the parade ground. Several others had gone down with *Mahan*, and their names would be added to a plaque listing all the destroyermen—human and Lemurian—who'd been lost from the start.

Adar wasn't with them. As long as the funeral pyres burned, he'd be very busy. He was High Sky Priest of Baalkpan now, as well as acting High Chief. He'd continue to perform those duties, by acclaim, at least until the rest of the city's people returned. Few doubted his elevation would be permanent. The views of the "runaways" weren't highly regarded, and Adar had made it clear he intended to press the Grik. The vengeance-minded People were more than happy to support that position. At least for now.

Chack and Queen Maraan were expected shortly. It was understood they were betrothed, and they were even more inseparable now than they'd been before the battle. The funeral pyre for *Big Sal*'s dead had already burned but today, B'mbaadan and Aryaalan souls flew together. Chack and Rolak were escorting Safir.

Sandison and Garrett were in the hospital suffering from serious wounds, but both were expected to recover. Others were still there as well: Kutas, Aubrey, Newman, Rodriguez.... Silva had lost his eye—and immediately gone AWOL. Only Risa and Pam Cross knew where he was, but no one really worried. It was clear the nurse was taking care of him herself, when she wasn't on duty, and sooner or later he'd turn back up.

Many others were present, however, for what felt like

it was shaping into a service for *Walker* and *Mahan* and their many dead. Saan-Kakja, U-Amaki ay Maa-ni-la, was there. She'd come herself, leading her personal Guard of a thousand warriors. It had been her timely arrival off the southern coast that bolstered Brister and Shinya's forces, tipping the balance in their desperate attack on the Grik rear. She'd apologized profusely for arriving so late, but Maa-ni-la was now a firm member of the Alliance, and she pledged that more troops and supplies were on the way.

Keje was using the same crutches Gray once hobbled on, shortened to fit his physique. Somehow he'd survived the almost total destruction of *Big Sal*'s upper levels, and was found by a rescue party the morning after the battle still sitting on his beloved stool. When Adar tried to suggest he should be High Chief of Baalkpan, he'd refused. *Big Sal* was his Home. With the sophisticated Lemurian pumps, coupled with the concept of hoses they'd learned from the Americans, he was sure she'd float again. For now he was content to recuperate, aided by the diligent attention of his daughter.

Shinya, Brister, Flynn, and Alden were there, as were Alan and Karen Letts. Letts's quick thinking in sending out rescue craft had undoubtedly saved most of *Walker*'s crew. Not only had they taken her people off, they'd helped get the ship into shallow water. The happy addition of *Mahan*'s and *Walker*'s launches—once the survivors were transferred—aided in that considerably, and Jim Ellis and Frankie Steele piloted the launch-turned-tugboats throughout.

To everyone's surprise, *Walker*'s launch had actually rescued most of the PBY's crew. Ben Mallory, Jis-Tikkar, and one of the gunners were found clinging precariously on one of the leaking wing floats. Somehow they'd survived the crash and escaped the sinking wreckage. Most of the flashies had been drawn to other parts of the bay. Tikker was in the hospital, but Mallory was, miraculously, uninjured. Sometimes it was like that. A pilot might break his neck when his parachute opened, or crawl out of a catastrophic crash.

Her Highness Rebecca Anne McDonald, princess of the Empire of the New Britain Isles, still wore battered dungarees, fuming at Silva's behavior and the fact she was now virtually a prisoner of Sandra Tucker and Sean O'Casey. Lawrence and Silva had recounted her exploits during the battle, and if she and her strange Grik-like friend were now heroes of Baalkpan (and represented a possible end to the dame famine to the Americans), they were also never allowed to go anywhere without a particularly attentive escort. Most knew of her status now—such a secret was impossible to keep for long—and it was considered just a matter of time before Jenks and his squadron arrived. Jenks would be disappointed. She intended that her people and her new friends should become allies against the Grik, and though she wanted to go home, she'd already proclaimed that she'd do so only if Captain Reddy took her himself.

Now the gathering stood, silent for the most part, staring at the sad remains of the proud old ship. The flag still flew from the aft mast, and Matt couldn't bear to see it taken down. Not yet. He remembered the first time he'd seen her, riding at anchor in Manila Bay, in another time—another world. He never would have thought back then that he'd mourn her loss like he did. After what they'd been through and all they'd achieved—and lost—it was like a huge piece of his soul had gone to the bottom with her. Sandra stood beside him holding his hand, a concerned expression on her face. All the pretense of professional distance they'd worked so hard to maintain had gone down with the ship. He needed her now, just as badly as one of her patients might who'd lost a leg.

"Do you think they'll come back?" Karen Letts quietly broke the silence.

"Sure," said Gray.

Unconsciously, Karen's hand went protectively to her lower abdomen, and Sandra smiled wistfully. Karen hadn't said anything, but Sandra had suspected. She'd seen the signs.

"We're all on the same footing now, technologically speaking," Gray continued. "All the modern warships are gone, but they know about cannons, and they've still got the Japs to help 'em—if they don't eat 'em."

Before they could go out and claim the Japanese survivors, several Grik ships, including one of the white ones, had taken them off. All they found was a single wounded officer who'd decided to defect to the Americans. He was waiting patiently when they finally arrived, having hidden from the Grik, as well as his own people. For now he was under guard, but he'd told them a great deal—not least of which was how Captain Kaufman met his end. The sad aviator's body had been buried with full honors alongside the others in the little cemetery.

"Not to mention," mentioned Courtney Bradford dryly, "there are still far more of them than there are of us."

"It doesn't matter," Matt said tiredly. "Even if they don't, we have to keep after them. Adar's right; we have to wipe them out." He paused. "They're even worse than we thought, and that's saying a lot. They don't know how to surrender, and they're not going to leave us alone. If we don't chase them now, keep the pressure up, they'll be back eventually, and all this"—he gestured at the destruction all around, but his eyes never left his ship—"will have been for nothing."

"How long do you think we have?" Sandra asked. Matt shrugged and looked at Bradford.

"Difficult to say, of course," the Australian opined. "According to our 'new' Jappo—a Commander Okada, if I'm not mistaken—we did hurt them rather badly. It may take as many as three years to make good their losses in ships and warriors. Five at the absolute most. You do understand I'm only guessing?"

"My God. That fast?" Jim Ellis interjected.

"Most likely." Bradford nodded.

"That means we've only about half that time to strike before they're fully prepared," Keje said thoughtfully.

"How?" whispered Matt. Beyond his earlier statement of fact, he didn't really want to talk long-term strategy just then. His heart wasn't in it. He just wanted to mourn his ship.

"Easy, Skipper." Spanky grinned. "We'll build battle-wagons!"

Matt blinked. "What the hell are you talking about?"

"Ever see a walking-beam steam engine? Put one—a *big* one—on something the size of *Big Sal*, stick on some paddle wheels, and pack her full of guns . . . 'Cat battlewagons!"

Keje was intrigued. "Steam engines . . . in a *Home*! Remarkable! You must tell me more, Mr. Maac-Faar-Laan." Then he shook his head. "First we must consider, however, that we still need more help." He bowed to Saan-Kakja. "Less now, of course, but Princess Re-beccaa's people will surely appreciate the necessity of our cause. We must send a delegation across the Eastern Ocean. Take her home, Cap-i-taan Reddy; let her speak for us." He glanced at Chief Gray. "In light of our victory, they may be ... easier to convince than before."

"Not much time for that," Matt murmured dolefully, still looking at *Walker*'s grave. The destroyer's speed would have made communications across such a distance much simpler. He sighed. No point in wishing for the impossible. Unintentionally, Matt was sure, Keje rubbed salt into the wound.

"Why not raise *Waa-kur*?" Keje asked, genuinely curious.

Matt snorted bitter laughter, then blinked apology in the Lemurian way. "I'm sorry. I sure wish we could, but it's impossible."

Keje blinked perplexity. "Why? She is not heavier than *Salissa*, yet I know my Home can be raised."

"Look," said Spanky, "I know you guys have great pumps; I've seen 'em work. But no matter how much air we put in her, it'll just come out faster. We can't dive and weld, so we can't plug the holes. There's no way."

Keje looked at him and blinked surprise. "Have you never wondered how we build something the size of *Salissa* and then float it?"

"Well ..." Spanky looked flustered. "I just thought you built 'em on land and launched them down a ways, like we did the frigates."

Keje shook his head. "I understand your ... misunderstanding ... now. We build smaller ships, like feluccas, like that. But I assure you, we do not build the great Homes on land."

Spanky's eyes widened. "A dry dock?!"

Keje now had everyone's attention. "You have spoken at some length about what you call a 'proper' dry dock," he said with a touch of irritation, "but we make do with a simpler expedient. We build a wall in the sea and pump out the water behind it. That is what we use this very basin for. I thought you knew? Why else put your ship into it? Here it is very simple. We flood down two Homes across the mouth of the basin, and build the walls only between them. It takes many days to pump the water out, but then you may freely work."

"A cofferdam!" Matt shouted triumphantly, and grinned. It was as though the weight of the world had fallen from his shoulders. Dared he hope? "We *didn't* know! By the time we got here, I was just following the boats pulling us in!"

"And I was following the pilot's directions on the felucca!" Jim said. "I bet Frankie was too!"

"At least somebody knew what they were doing!" growled Gray. Everyone laughed.

Rolak, Chack, and Queen Maraan appeared, joining a happier group than they'd expected.

"What have we missed?" Safir asked pleasantly. She was still sad from the funeral, but uplifted as well.

"We're going to raise the ship!" Sandra announced triumphantly, squeezing her captain's hand.

Spanky's brow knitted into a frown. "Still won't work," he said. "I'm sorry. The damage is just too severe. If we had some steel it might be different, but her structural integrity's shot. We can't keep patchin' her with copper plates and rivets."

Faces fell, but Chack only grinned.

"Steel is like iron, is it not? I've heard the term used interchangeably at times."

"Yeah . . . sorta," Spanky replied.

"Then what are you worried about?" He barked a laugh. "Sometimes you Amer-i-caans are so clever I almost think you are gods. But often you miss the painfully obvious." He gestured vaguely over his shoulder toward where *Amagi* lay on the bottom of Baalkpan Bay, broken and gutted by flames, her warped and dreary superstructure still protruding above the water as a constant, grim reminder. "Out there is all the iron in the world!"

What had been a gloomy gathering became almost a celebration of sorts. Voices rose with excited, animated suggestions, punctuated by occasional laughter. Finally, the great victory they'd achieved actually began to *feel* like a victory instead of yet another ordeal they'd somehow managed to survive. Eventually, as the afternoon waned, the friends began to disperse.

Finally alone, as the sun touched the dense jungle horizon, Sandra wrapped her arms around Matt's neck, pulling him down for a joyful, passionate kiss.

"Gotta go," she whispered at last, tears streaking her face. "Work to do."

"I'll be along."

"You'll be all right?"

Matt smiled at her and nodded. "I think I *am*. Right now, finally, I think we all will be." She hugged him tight, and as she disengaged herself, her fingers trailing away from his, her smile turned impish.

"Karen's pregnant," she announced.

Matt was stunned, as all men are by such sudden, momentous statements. "She didn't look any different to me."

Sandra giggled and shook her head. "See you later, sailor," she said, and stepped away into the gathering twilight.

"Huh," Matt said, turning to walk along the dock. Eventually he grinned.

A short distance away he was surprised to encounter the Mice sitting on coiled cables and leaning against a fallen piling. All three had their elbows on their knees and their chins in their hands as they stared glumly at their sunken Home.

"Evening, uh . . . men," he said, inwardly amused by his own confusion regarding how to address them. The trio began to stand and he waved them back. "Why the long faces?" They looked at him as if he were nuts.

Gilbert hopped up anyway, whipping his hat from his head. No matter how crazy he thought he was, there was no way he could answer the skipper sitting down. "Well, sir, beggin' yer pardon, but our ship's, well . . . sunk."

"So? We'll raise her. What's that compared to everything else we've done?" Isak and Tabby both jumped up.

"But . . . beggin' yer pardon too, how we gonna patch her?" Isak demanded.

Tabby suddenly blinked inspiration. "We gonna use iron from that Jap ship, ain't we!" she exclaimed in a passable copy of her companion's lazy drawl.

Isak stiffened. In a voice both excited and scandalized at the same time, he spoke. "Hally-looya, we're gonna get our boilers back . . . but goddamn! Jap iron? It ain't decent!" Catching himself, he yanked his own hat off his head and mumbled, "Sir."

Matt laughed. "Settle down! Steel is steel. Besides, remember all that scrap we sold the Japs before the war? Maybe *Amagi* used to be a Packard!"

He was still laughing when he left them talking excitedly among themselves. Slowly he walked around the basin, inspecting the remains of his ship with a critical eye. Inevitably, looking at her, he became more somber. No question about it: raising and refitting the old destroyer would be a daunting task. But they *had* performed miracles; they could do it again. The mere fact that any of them were still alive was a miracle in itself.

He stopped when he reached the other side of the basin. The ship was farther from him now, and the exposed damage didn't look so bad. An errant ray of the setting sun managed to blink through the jungle on the far side of the bay and cast his long shadow upon the distant pilothouse. That was where he'd been standing when they fought *Amagi* the first time, he reflected, and when they came through the Squall. It was from there that he'd first seen the Lemurians, and directed the first action in their aid. It was probably where he'd first realized he was in love with Sandra Tucker. He'd fought the Battle of Aryaal/B'mbaado Bay and tried to save *Nerracca* from within its confines. And that was where he'd been standing just the other night. . . .

It suddenly occurred to him that *Walker*'s pilothouse, her *bridge*, was where he had become the man he was. More properly, that . . . living . . . ship, and—he couldn't find the words for her crew—had taken the man he'd been and molded, *refined* him into the man he had become. Hot tears stung his cheeks, and, impatiently, he wiped them away. No time for that, and *she* wouldn't want it. As his shadow disappeared and *Walker*'s bridge grew dark, he knew someday, somehow, he'd stand there again. When he did, it would be at the head of a *fleet* that would scour the Grik from existence and secure the safety of his people—regardless of race—and the memory of all those who'd died to make it happen.

Matt Reddy and the crew of *Walker* return in

DISTANT THUNDERS

on sale in June 2010 from Roc.
For a preview on what happens next,
read an excerpt from Reddy's log,
written especially for this edition
of *Maelstrom*.

LOG BOOK
OF THE
U.S.S. WALKER (DD-163)
DD Rate, COMMANDED BY:
M. P. REDDY, LIEUTENANT COMMANDER, USNR
DESTROYER SQUADRON 29
Attached to: **ABDAFLOAT**

Commencing: 0000, **July 1**   1943
at: Baalkpan—formerly Balikpapan
and ending: _____   1943

LIST OF OFFICERS

Attached to and on board of the U.S.S. WALKER (DD-163), commanded
by *M.P. REDDY, Captain, USNR*, during the period covered by this Log
Book, with date of reporting for duty, detachment, transfer, or death, from
1 July 1943 to 31 July 1943

NAME:	RANK:	DATE OF DUTY	DETACHED
M.P. REDDY	Lt. Cmdr/Capt.	5 Sept. 1941	Commanding*

*TDY Commanding 2nd Allied Expeditionary Force.

J.G. ELLIS	Lt./Capt.	6 Sept. 1941	XO*

*TDY Commanding USS Mahan 1 Mar, 1942. Commanding USS Dowden 23 June, 1943.

B. McFARLANE	Lt./Cmdr.	18 Oct. 1938	Engineering*

*TDY "Minister of Naval Engineering," Baalkpan. Commanding salvage/refit operation USS Walker.

B.L. SANDISON	Lt./Cmdr.	1 Nov. 1941	Torpedo*

*TDY "Minister of Ordnance," Baalkpan.

G.C. GARRETT	Lt./Cmdr.	8 Oct. 1941	Gunnery*

*TDY Commanding USS Donaghey.

S.B. CAMPETI	2CPO/Lt.Cmdr.	9 May 1940	Ordnance*

*TDY B.L. SANDISON

NAME:	RANK:	DATE OF DUTY	DETACHED

P.J. BRISTER Lt./Cmdr 6 Sept. 1942 Asst. Engineering*
*TDY "Minister of Defensive and Industrial Works," Baalkpan.

S.H. RIGGS 1CPO/Cmdr 12 Aug. 1940 Comm&Navigation*
*TDY "Minister of Communications and Electrical Contrivances," Baalkpan.

A.G. LETTS Lt./Cmdr 15 May, 1941 Commisary&Supply*
*TDY "Minister of Industry and Chief of Staff 'President' of Baalkpan."

S.M. TUCKER Lt. 28 Feb, 1942 Medical Officer*
*TDY "Minister of Medicine," Baalkpan.

J.R. MILLER Lt. 22 June, 1941 Medical Officer*
*TDY 2nd Allied Expeditionary Force.

(This page to be sent to Bureau of Navigation monthly with Log sheets)

UNITED STATES SHIP WALKER (DD-163)   Tuesday, Sept. 2, 1943

00-04 As before. No problems to report. Woke up pumping detail and inspection party so they could begin final preparations.

Sonny Campeti, Lt. Cmdr., USN

04-08 As before. Pump boilers at full steam pressure despite leaks. Detail reports all in readiness. Inspection party discovered and repaired a faulty joint in the #4 main pipe. Split ends were the cause—like we have seen before. Inspection parties will continue to observe all joints throughout the operation.

Bernard L. Sandison, Lt. Cmdr., USNR

08-12 As before. Weather clear. Water smooth on the bay. Slight easterly wind. Conditions optimum. 0800 mustered all hands and fed them at their stations. No absentees. Final visual inspection of all lines and seals. Heard reports from divisions. Lemurian Homes *Humfra-Dar* and *Woor-Naa* standing by to assist with shipboard pumps. Engaged primary pumps 0920. Observed first streams of water being expelled from dry dock basin. Engaged in brief verbal celebration.

Brad McFarlane, Cmdr., USN

12-16 NOT as before. 1350 observed slight reduction of water level around exposed superstructure of ship. Having difficulty controlling exuberance of all divisions. Self included. Large numbers of civilians have come down to the dock to observe. Detached Marines from other duties to make sure they did not interfere. No question of deliberate interference, just do not want them underfoot and causing distractions. Water flow is difficult to estimate but best guess is 6000 g.p.m.

Brad McFarlane, Cmdr., USN

16-20 Pumps steaming as before. (Great relief to use that phrase again.) Two minor casualties in the water pipes repaired. Pump engine running well and within Mr. McFarlane's expectations. Humfra-Dar has added her pumps to the operation. Water level dropping slowly still, but noticeably. His Excellency, Adar, High Chief of Baalkpan, appeared briefly at the dock to inspect the proceedings. Informed Cmdr McFarlane that a celebration of thanksgiving and appreciation would commence at 1900. Celebration seems general already at 1700. Chief Laney took a banca boat out to the protruding aft mast of the ship and ran a new ensign up. Tattered remnants of the old ensign (there since the Battle of Baalkpan) were removed and carefully brought ashore. Letts took them in his charge.

PERRY BRISTER, CMDR., USN

20-24 Lights rigged. Water flow uninterrupted. No stoppages. Cmdr McFarlane has allowed the hands to join the celebration by divisions. Inspection details to remain in place by rotation. A damn good day.

Steven P. Riggs, Cmdr., USN

Approved: Examined:

Riggs held a lighted Zippo so he could see, and Spanky signed his name by "Approved" at the bottom of the page. Then he handed the log to Letts, who signed beside "Examined." Before he closed the log on the previous day, Letts glanced up at the date and shook his head.

"Five days late of the 'year and a third,' but close enough I guess."

"That's one of the reasons I pushed so hard to pull the

plug yesterday. Give the guys something to celebrate so they wouldn't dwell on what we left behind. What we lost," Spanky replied.

Letts returned the log to Spanky, who handed it to Campeti, who had the watch again. They were all tired, but *nobody* was going to oversee this operation but *Walker*s. Sandra Tucker had arrived, looking disheveled, but as anxious as they were for her first glimpse of the ship. Now she stood beside them, peering intently into the predawn gloom of the drydock basin at the still only vaguely defined shape.

They stood on what had once been the old fitting-out pier, but was now merely a walkway between new, massive wooden cranes and equipment sheds. The skeletons of still more new warships rose on the other side of the basin, silhouetted against the new dawn. Until recently, when the drydock neared completion, the new ships had remained the priority projects. Now, for just a few days, work on them would slow while a large percentage of the laborers concentrated on another task. Steam and smoke jetted from crude, noisy engines while 'Cat "snipes in training" crawled all over them, oiling every conceivable point of friction. Some spun the huge, amazingly efficient Lemurian-designed pumps and others powered generators that ran electric pumps of human design. The jury was still out on which were better, but Spanky was pretty sure the 'Cat machines would last longer. Hoses pulsed and brown water coursed into the sea beyond the drydock wall.

Together, Sandra, Spanky, Alan, Campeti, Bernie, a growing crowd of human and Lemurian sailors and Marines, sleepy civilian revelers, and finally, to no one's real surprise, Adar himself, watched the dawn gradually reveal what the ravages of seawater and battle had done to USS *Walker*. Throughout the night, while most of her crew and the people of the city celebrated her raising, the water level in the drydock had steadily dropped. Now she lay, with a slight list to port, where she'd settled after her fight with *Amagi*. Almost half of her upper hull was now exposed and every heart sank as they looked upon her.

A clear demarcation showed how much of the ship had remained above the surface when she sank. It was plain to see, about three-fourths of the way up her four slender funnels and about halfway up her aft mast. The forward mast was gone. Automatic weapons had riddled her bridge, but the line glared dark and glistening below her empty pilothouse windows like an angry, oily slash. Above it, the paint was blackened by fire and dark with rust. Below the line she looked . . . even worse.

An entirely new color had been created. Dark brown mixed with tan, with malignant yellow streaks for contrast. A fair amount of blackened green dangled here and there, where rotting vegetation festooned her. Angry red globs and smears were everywhere and of every different hue, as the rust that caused them dried. Slimy gray-black tar pooled and oozed, and covering all was a translucent rainbow slick of oil that had leaked from her ruptured bunkers. Hatches stood agape, revealing dank interiors. Tangled cables drooped down her side and brackish water gushed from countless holes as the water level in the basin receded below that still inside the ship. Eel-like chopper fish squirmed like maggots on her deck, their vicious jaws gaping and snapping as their gills labored in the morning air. As primitive as they were, it might take them hours to die.

Walker was a corpse, Sandra thought, and they'd been nothing more than ghoulish grave robbers to expose her to the sun. Hot tears ran down her cheeks. Thank God Matthew wasn't there to see it.

"Lord," Sandison murmured, "what are we going to do?"

Spanky patted his arm and sighed. "We're gonna fix her, Bernie."

The way *Walker* rested looked almost normal by the time the first boats went across; listing slightly and a little low by the stern, but the water wasn't much higher than the greasy black boot topping. She was still full of water however, and jets of varying intensity coursed from her many wounds. As a result, the volume of water the pumps displaced was reduced as the day wore on. If they emptied the basin more quickly than the ship could drain, they ran the risk of causing even more damage. But her crew was restless to get to work and by early that afternoon, the first repair parties clamored up her slippery side and stood once more on her leaning deck.

Spanky McFarlane put his hands on his skinny hips and stared hard in all directions, his lips grimly set. A short while before, he'd been "Minister of Naval Engineering" for an infant nation. Right now, for a time, he was *Walker*'s engineering officer again and nothing else. "Alright ladies," he said at last, as men and Lemurians squelched through the ooze, "we got work to do. Mister Riggs? Take your party to the bridge. Charts, manuals, anything like that we might've missed before are the first priority. Easy does it. If there's anything left of that stuff, it'll go to pieces if you're not careful." He looked quickly around. "Campeti! Where's Mister Sandison?" Campeti gestured over his shoulder.

"Went tearing-ass up to the bridge. We removed the gun director a long time ago 'cause we could get to the platform, but he wanted to see the torpedo directors. He was like a cat havin' kittens!" Campeti caught himself and looked quickly around. Some of the Lemurians were looking at him strangely. "Uh, no offense. Different kinda cats . . . Little buggers . . ." He held his hands close together, but then his face clouded with embarrassment. "Oh, just get to work, damn it."

Spanky shook his head. "Well, until he gets back, or sends for you to help him, I want you to check the four inch-fifties and see if there's anything left of that one machine gun Silva had to leave on the amidships deckhouse. When you get through with that, put together a detail to salvage as many fire hoses as you can. We'll start rinsing the old girl off." He couldn't stop a grin. "Just think what the Bosun would say if he saw his decks in such a state."

Campeti almost giggled. In spite of the Herculean task ahead of them, the spirits of those who'd come aboard were rising. Finally, after the long months of anticipation and helplessness, of toil and labor on other projects, they could get to work on what mattered most to *them*. It almost seemed as if they could sense something within the ship itself begin to stir as well. A renewed sense of purpose. A new lease on life.

"We wanna go down," grouched a reedy voice behind Spanky and he turned to look at the pair standing there. It was Gilbert Yager and the silken, gray-furred 'Cat named

Tabby. He had to concentrate for an instant because without Isak Reuben, the scene just didn't add up. Then he remembered Isak was the one they'd decided would accompany the AEF. Understanding complete, Spanky glared at Tabby when he saw she'd stripped almost completely, in the Lemurian way, to the point that all she wore was what looked like a skimpy little skirt. Despite her fine fur, her breasts appeared very human. It was distracting and annoying and she knew it. Sometimes Spanky harbored a secret, superstitious sense that the presence of women (the nurses first) aboard his ship was what had caused all their problems to start with. He'd finally allowed Tabby to stay in the fire rooms at the Captain's orders and because she was a damn fine snipe. He'd broken one of his own cardinal rules however: if something someone is doing bugs you, either make them stop, or pretend it doesn't bug you. In Tabby's case, he'd failed miserably in both respects. He couldn't—wouldn't now— make her "go away," and there was no way he could pretend she didn't bug him.

"You're out of uniform, sailor!" he said harshly, almost plaintively. "Again!"

"Dirty work ahead, Chief," she replied with a creditable drawl. "We ain't got enough new uniforms yet to get 'em all scruffed up."

She even sounds like them now, Spanky thought uncomfortably. She was also the only creature alive that the Mice were actually nice to, in their way. As a result of their association, she'd begun to take on many of their less agreeable attributes. But she *looked* like a pinup in a cat suit.

"I don't give a good Goddamn! You *will* put on some clothes or I'll have you on report!" he bellowed. "We'll see if you can remember to . . ." He stopped and watched her slowly unroll a T-shirt she'd been holding behind her back.

"Aye, aye, *Mister McFaar-lane*. I'll throw somethin' on if it'll make you happy."

"You . . !" He stopped. She'd done it to him *again*! He whirled and pointed at the very deck access she'd pulled her companions from, months before. "Down there. Let me know if the water's draining out of the aft fire room! I want you to describe every single piece of equipment as it becomes visible!" He ignored them then, and began delegating other tasks to different details. The "Mice" shuffled away and ducked down the hatch. Once inside, out of earshot, Gilbert began to chuckle.

"I swear Tabby, you keep waggin' yer boobs at Spanky like that, one o' these days he's gonna bust a vessel—or grab hold of 'em! You know it drives him nuts. Just havin' wimmin aboard ship is enough to cause him fits—then you keep doin' that!"

"He still needs to laugh," Tabby replied. "I like to make him laugh and he will, later. He always does." Her eyes grew unfocused and she continued softly: "And maybe someday he *will* 'grab' 'em." She looked away, but Gilbert could tell she was blinking embarrassment.

Jeez! Gilbert thought, stunned. *Tabby's sweet on Spanky!* "Yeah, well," he said, his chuckle now gone as he peered into the darkness below. The stench was unbearable and the water was still over the top of his beloved boilers, "Ain't much to laugh about right now. Look at this mess!"

The oily water receded slowly and brown, purplish foam swirled and clung to everything as its support drained away. At some point, one of *Walker*'s own hoses snaked down through the trunk with a bellowed "Slide it in!" and moments later, it began to pulse and throb. The drainage picked up. Another hose, new made, joined the first and was soon jolting and juddering alongside it. Gilbert no longer noticed the smell and as the water went down, he carefully descended to the upper catwalk, creeping slowly so he wouldn't slip in the oily slurry. His beloved fire room was a dreary sight in the gloom. He didn't dare make a light.

He suddenly remembered finding a dead, bloated cow out in a pasture when he was a kid. It was one of his maw's, and he'd been curious why it died. While he stood there staring at it, its hind legs started to move. At first, he thought he'd met a ghost cow, because there was no question it was dead. He started to run, but something stopped him. He'd never been scared of a live cow. What could a dead one do to him? With that certain mixture of horror and fascination only kids can conjure, he'd watched a medium-sized possum come crawling out of the cow's ass!

He'd pondered that occasionally over the years; that possum squirming around up in there. No matter how hungry he got after that—and there'd been some starving times during the Depression—he'd never eaten possum again.

Now, looking at the inside of his fire room he suddenly imagined he knew what the inside of that old cow had looked like to that possum so long ago.

"Go get another hose, Tabby. A water hose!" he shouted. "Might as well rinse some of this shit down while they're suckin' it out!"

The water came from the basin and wasn't by any means clean, but at least the pressure let him blow the worst of the goo away. Also, it didn't hurt that he'd exposed at least a little of the lighter paint and it grew brighter in the compartment as the sun moved overhead. Soon, he and Tabby were standing on the slimy deck plates. While he aimed the hose, she held it for him. A couple of times, they raised a plate and stuffed one of the drain hoses in the bilge.

"Gonna need some kind of detergent!" he shouted.

"We use wood ashes, make lye soap?"

"I dunno. Lye does goofy stuff. Not much aluminum down here, but there's zinc in brass and galvanize. Shoot lye on that and we get hydrogen gas! I doubt wood ashes'd be pure enough, but it might corrode the hell out of stuff." Gilbert paused and wiped his face with his shirt. It was stiflingly hot. "I wish somebody'd raise those goddamn vents!" he roared. Almost as if they'd heard him—and maybe someone had—the grungy, opaque skylight vents started going up. Soon, the fire room was relatively bathed in the mid-afternoon light and at least a little air was getting in. A few more 'Cats soon came to join them. Gilbert felt mildly guilty. He knew everyone was busy, but hell. He and Tabby turned the hose over to their relief and started to go topside for a much-needed drink. He paused.

"You know?" he shouted over the gushing water, "speakin' of corrosion, there ain't much here. Not new, anyway. Maybe all this oily, slimy shit did us a favor." He moved to one of the big Yarrow boilers, kicked the latch and opened the door. A flood of black water gushed out all over him, knocking him down. Tabby picked him up and together, they peered inside.

"Ook," Gilbert said. He couldn't see much, but the firebricks were gone. Probably disintegrated when the cool water hit them. The lines looked okay though, and even if a few had popped, he could fix that. New firebrick had been stockpiled long ago during their previous refits. He gently patted the old boiler. "Hey! We can hose her out! No need to get all black and sooty cleanin' her!"

Tabby looked at him. He was covered from head to foot with black, slimy ooze. She laughed aloud. Gilbert grinned too, realizing how ridiculous the statement was under the circumstances.

"Well we can," he said. "Mainly though"—he patted the boiler again—"we can fix this."

It was nearly dusk and it had been a long, eventful, and mostly happy day in spite of their early misgivings. Faces grew somber a few times when the occasional bone was discovered and reverently removed. There weren't very many and those they found were deeply gnawed. There was no way to identify whose they were and it didn't really matter anyway. Courtney Bradford might have told them if the bones were human or Lemurian, but it ultimately made no difference. Lemurians traditionally preferred to be burned, so their spirits might rise with the smoke and join those in the heavens who'd gone before. But regardless of how distasteful most Lemurians considered the human practice of burying their remains, many Lemurian "destroyermen" had requested burial, like and beside their shipmates. Their clan.

All the bones were sent to join those of destroyermen already buried in the little cemetery at the Parade Ground in the center of the city. The cemetery that lay in the returning shade of the Great Tree of Baalkpan. The tree, and the new leaves sprouting from it, was a symbol of hope, that all might be made right in the end—not least because of the graves it sheltered with its mighty boughs.

After the grisly chore of removing the dead was complete, spirits rose again. Not because anyone had discovered the task before them would be easier than they thought; if anything they were beginning to cope with the fact that it would be much harder. Absolutely everything would have to be painstakingly repaired, including all the little things they hadn't even thought of before. But now at least the wondering was over. They knew what they had to do. It would be hard, but they could do it. *Walker* would live again.

Alan leaned across a table erected under a colorful awning on the pier. A tired but upbeat Spanky was using a blueprint he'd hand-drawn from memory to describe some of the belowdecks damage he'd seen.

"I was really surprised by how little silt there was in the turbines and boilers. The lube oil in the port reduction gear looks like peanut butter, though. Worn-out seals must have leaked." He shrugged. "Everything'll have to be taken apart, piece by piece and cleaned, and the seals and gaskets will all have to be replaced—thank God we have plenty of gasket material! You really came through with that weird corklike stuff!"

Alan nodded self-consciously. "Yeah well, like I said, Bradford discovered it. Some sort of tree in the northwestern marshes—where all those tar pits are. The trees draw the stuff up in their roots and deposit it in the lower outer layers of their trunks. Bradford says it protects them from insects."

"Whatever. It's good stuff. Mallory swears by it. He ran his little airplane motor for twenty hours straight the other day and never got a leak. He says it's kind of hard to take stuff *apart* after it's been heated up, though. It sort of glues things together. He's calling it the 'Letts gasket' and says you ought to take out a patent since you're the one who figured out the application."

"I'll be sure to share my wealth with Courtney."

Adar had joined them and when the laughter subsided, he addressed Alan. "What is a 'patent'?"

Alan looked at him and his expression turned serious. "Well, it's sort of a reward, I guess. It's a way people are rewarded for coming up with good ideas. Where we come from, laws protect those ideas from being used by other people. For example, if I invented a new gizmo—say the 'Letts gasket'—and got a patent on it, nobody else could swipe my idea and make the same thing without my permission. Usually, people would pay . . . or, ah, trade for permission."

Adar blinked concern. "Among our people there are clans or guilds that possess 'secret skills' only they may pass. That has caused many of my problems with the shipwrights. Is that much the same? Are you telling me you want permission to use your 'gaas-kets'?"

"No, Adar. It was a joke. 'My' gasket material is at everyone's disposal! I'm afraid we do need to have a long talk about that sort of thing when we get a chance, though."

Alan knew he was going to have to sit down with Adar one of these days and figure out some sort of financial system. Right now, everyone was highly motivated by the war effort and there was little grumbling about long hours, depletion of resources and a somewhat lopsided distribution of labor and wealth. Before the war, Lemurian finance was based on an age-old, carefully refined and fairly sophisticated barter system. Everything was worth exactly so much of something else. Even labor was valued in such a way. Some types of labor were "worth" more than others, but "wages" were still calculated by time-honored equivalent values. So much time in the shipyard, for example, was worth so many measures of gri-kakka oil, or grain or seep. One length of fabric was worth so many weights of copper or fish, and so on. Obviously, people didn't carry their "wealth" around with them, or always even have possession of it, but everyone kept careful tabulations of who owed whom what. To Alan, it was all profoundly confusing and inefficient, but he could see how it had worked for so long, and admittedly, well.

The problem was, right now, there was an awful lot of activity and production underway and nobody was being "paid" anything. The situation struck a lot of the destroyermen as downright Stalinist, or at least mildly "Red." With so much time ashore to think about such things, there'd been increased grumbling over how many barrels of gri-kakka oil a month being in the U.S. Navy was worth. The guys were fed and their booze at the Busted Screw was free, but the time was approaching when they might want to *buy* something. Going back to the old barter system was almost impossible too, since no one had been keeping tabs for a long time now. They'd have to start all over from scratch and Alan knew from experience how hard it was to "clear the books" when it came to trades and favors.

He'd been reluctant to approach Adar about the problem because the guy already had so much on his plate. There was the war of course, and the question of what to do about Jenks. Sister Audry and the presence of the descendents of the "ancient tailless ones" had him all stirred up about religious matters and he was walking a tightrope while he tried to figure that out. All were serious matters, but the financial cloud beginning to loom had the potential to eclipse all those other concerns. Somehow, Alan and Adar had to make time for this talk. Soon.

Adar sighed. "Very well. I think I know what you mean and you are right. If we had been keeping track, the people's surplus—guarded by Nakja-Mur and now myself—would have been gone long ago. With everything else . . . I do not look forward to that 'talk,' but I welcome your suggestions." He motioned to the ship in the deepening gloom. "What have you discovered . . . besides bones?" His tone was suddenly urgent. "Can you fix her? You do understand she has become something of a . . . talisman to my people. Younglings carve images—icons of her, almost like Sister Audry's saints. The good Sister speaks of your Lux Mundi, ah, Jesu Christo, and I must give that issue much thought." He paused. "Perhaps very much was lost in translation long ago. In any event, right now *Walker* is seen as the 'savior' of my people—the People of Baalkpan and many others. Can you comprehend how important she has become to all of us?"

"Yeah," said Spanky, uncharacteristically quiet. "I wouldn't go runnin' around calling her a 'savior' or anything if I was you"—he glanced at Letts—"but we can damn sure comprehend how important she is. Trust me."

TAYLOR ANDERSON

INTO THE STORM

Destroyermen, Book I

Pressed into service when World War II breaks out in the Pacific, the USS *Walker*—a Great War-era destroyer—finds itself retreating from pursuing Japanese battleships. Its captain, Lieutenant Commander Matthew Patrick Reddy, desperately leads the *Walker* into a squall, hoping it will give them cover—only to emerge into an alternate world. A world where two species have evolved: the cat-like Lemurians and the reptilian Griks—and they are at war.

With its power and weaponry, the Walker's very existence could alter the balance of power. And for Reddy and his crew, who have the means to turn a primitive war into a genocidal Armageddon, one thing becomes clear. They must determine whose side they're on. Because whichever species they choose is the winner.

Learn more at
taylorandersonauthor.com

**Available wherever books are sold or at
penguin.com**

TAYLOR ANDERSON

CRUSADE

Destroyermen, Book II

Lieutenant Commander Matthew Reddy, along with the men and women of the USS *Walker*, have chosen sides in a war not of their making. Swept from the World War II Pacific into an alternate world, they have allied with the Lemurians—a mammalian race threatened by the warlike reptilian Grik.

The Lemurians are vastly outnumbered and ignorant of warfare, and even the guns and technology of *Walker* cannot turn the tide of battle. Luckily they are not alone—Reddy finally finds Mahan, the other destroyer that passed through the rift. Together, the two American ships will teach the Lemurians to take a stand.

Or so they think—for the massive Japanese battleship *Amagi*, the very ship that *Walker* was fleeing from when the rift took them, has followed them through. And now the *Amagi* is in the hands of the Grik.

Available wherever books are sold or at
penguin.com

R0017